The Legacy

Of

Sleepy Hollow

by

Morgan Leshay

www.lbfbooks.com

Published Internationally by LBF Books,
1787 Cartier Court, RR 1,
Kingston, Nova Scotia, B0P 1R0, Canada

A catalogue record for the print format of this title is available from the
National Library of Canada
ISBN 1-897370-95-4

A catalogue record for the Ebook is available from the
National Library of Canada
multiple ebook formats are available from
www.lbfbooks.com
ISBN 1-897370-96-2

Credit: Michelle Devon, editor

This is a work of fiction. Names, characters, places and incidents are either the product of the author's imagination or are used fictitiously, and any resemblance to any person or persons, living or dead, events or locales is entirely coincidental.

Teaser

Icharus spied her immediately. He caught hold of one of the beams and swung himself out of the framework, hanging for a moment before he dropped to the floor beneath.

He walked over to where she stood with Dirck, and dusted his hands against his thighs.

"Dirck, go up and help your father with that beam," he said before turning his attention to Katherine. He smiled. "Behold your inn, Mistress Van Brunt."

She grinned. "Well, almost," she said, and he laughed.

Taking hold of her arm, he led her away from the worksite. "We'll be safer over here."

She followed him, but when he would have stopped, she gestured toward the tall tree near the brook.

"Actually, I thought we might sit over there," she said. "Are you hungry, Master Crane?"

His gaze practically devoured her on the spot. "Starving."

She held out the basket Edda had prepared. "Since today is such a beautiful day, I thought we might sit beneath the shade and share what I have in this basket."

Her voice was so playful, and yet so timid. Icharus arched a brow. "A picnic?"

She nodded, her smile teasing him, and he noticed the bright sparkle in her gaze. Almost regretfully, he looked back toward the inn where the others were still hard at work, and sighed.

Katherine stepped in front of him, peering up at him with those wonderful eyes of hers, and said, "Please. You've been working so hard. You deserve a rest."

Icharus started to protest, to remind her that he hadn't been the only one working, but the happy twinkle in her gaze stopped him. For the life of him, he couldn't allow himself to be the one who made that joyful shine disappear from her gaze.

"A picnic you say? Why, I remember as a child, Mum would pack a veritable bounty of pies and puddings and sweetmeats into a basket just like that one. We'd all go off to the meadow and spend the afternoon enjoying the warm sunshine and a meal made more delicious for having eaten it outdoors. Father especially enjoyed such times. He had rather peculiar fondness for eating."

Katherine smiled. "See? Your father knew that everyone must take time away from toiling to enjoy a good meal. Now, take this basket, if you please, and follow me."

His lips twitched, but he nodded and took the basket, hefting it onto his shoulder.

"Indeed, Mistress Van Brunt. It seems you are correct. Let us away, my dear." He gestured toward the brook. "After you."

Icharus found it a bit humorous that she chose a spot beneath the very tree his father had often spoken of...the very place Ichabod had wiled away many an hour spinning fantasies of himself and Katrina Van Tassel. He grinned. "You know, my father used to come here of an evening," he told her.

Katherine had busied herself with spreading a colorful quilt over the ground and laying out the scrumptious smelling repast Mrs. Porter had packed into the basket for them. She sat down on a corner of the quilt now, and cast him a glance. "Indeed?"

Icharus nodded. "He told me so himself, many a time. He said he would come here to this exact spot and spend hours with his imagination, casting lurid images of himself and your mother round in his mind. Many a time, he said, his mind would produce an image of the two of them sharing a kiss so vividly he almost thought the deed done in reality."

She chuckled. "And what of *you*, Master Crane? Will you spend this hour allowing some lovely female to enchant your thoughts? With whom shall you share a vivid but imaginary kiss?"

Icharus joined her on the blanket and leaned close. "I only indulge in real kisses, dear lady," he said, his voice
husky.

She laughed and he reached out, cradling her cheek in his palm. "Flights of imagination are for dreamers. I prefer to feel the warmth of real lips beneath mine, to watch as they part just the tiniest bit in breathless anticipation, to taste the sweetness offered … in broad daylight."

His thumb teased her lower lip, and her eyelids drifted downward.

"I prefer real lips, Katherine. Like yours. Now," he said, leaning ever closer as he spoke.

"Now?" she whispered.

He gave the barest of nods an instant before his lips brushed hers. He teased her lips with his own, brushing them against hers in a featherlike caress. Once. Again.

She sighed against his mouth, and he shifted on the quilt, pulling her against him, his fingers sifting through her soft curls.

"Katherine. I want to taste you." He breathed the words against her parted lips. He slid his tongue over her lower lip, and then his mouth closed over hers, his tongue sliding inside to taste the nectar of her kiss.

The feel of her own tongue timidly sliding against his near destroyed what bit of sanity he had left to claim.

Desire, hot and ready, slammed through him. He

groaned and pulled her closer, deepening the kiss.

He devoured her mouth with his own, his tongue plunging again and again to taste of her sweetness, but he wanted more. His hand slid down, along the gentle curve of her side to her hip, and he cupped her bottom, pulling her as close as he dared.

A moan slid from her throat, and he broke away from her lips to kiss her there, and again at the tender area beneath her ear before he reached up to nibble at her earlobe.

Her hands seemed to have taken on a life of their own, one moment sliding through his hair while she held him close, and then gliding across his shoulders and lower before coming back up again to tangle in his hair.

He delighted in the soft sounds coming from her in response to his kiss. How he wanted this woman, he thought, in every possible way. He shifted again. She wiggled closer… and then froze.

"Icharus?" she whispered.

"Yes?"

She shifted away from him, and leaned up on an elbow. "I think we're lying in the potato salad."

Other Works from this author:

Redemption

Dedication

For my daughter Brittany who said it couldn't be done, and for believing if anyone COULD do it, it would be me... And for my own Katherine, our little 'spring chicken'. :-) I love you both!

Acknowledgements

God...for giving me such a wonderful story to write.

To my family, who always seem to have more faith in me and my abilities than I ever have in myself.

To the musical group Within Temptation (www.within-temptation.com) for the continual inspiration provided by the song *Say My Name*. I must have listened to it a million and one times while writing this book.

Also to Gary Halbert and Kathleen Woodiwiss. I miss you both.

And finally, for my son, Trevor: *"...and he put his horse in reverse!..."*

The Legacy

Of

Sleepy Hollow

Chapter 1

Brom Bones was dead.

Down in the village, a short distance from the Old Dutch Church, a small group of people huddled in a tight circle around an open grave, seemingly unaware of the unnatural silence and bitter, biting cold.

At the head of the small gathering of folks who had come to pay their final respects, Katherine Van Brunt felt isolated and alone, quite apart from the rest of the group gathered together on the miserably cold November day, a day made doubly wretched by the nature of events taking place.

Katherine glanced around, taking in the heavy laden and ominous gunmetal gray of the late autumn skies over the small village of Sleepy Hollow that held the promise of coming rain – the only forward-looking vow of which the tiny, desolate parish could boast.

From early morn, an uncanny silence had settled across the land, huddled in watchful wait against the dark, thick trunks of barren trees. No fowl called from a high perch within the stark branches and not a single insect or rodent scurried beneath the damp fallen leaves at their base.

1

The quiet spread itself insidiously atop unkempt, overgrown fields that had lain fallow for a thrice of years, mingling with the thick fog of smoke from the chimneys of the few remaining homes in Sleepy Hollow.

The billowy clouds of puffy white smoke, much like the hunkering silence which preferred to hug close and lie still, refused to climb high into the thickening gloom of clouds, preferring instead to cower in wait near the ground and no breeze forced it upward to meet the coming squall.

Not even the low of nearby cattle or the irate cackle of a militant guinea hen dared disrupt the almost reverent quiet of the day.

Indeed, the day was one marked with soul-deep sadness for Katherine. It would forever after be observed as the day of burial for her father, Abraham Van Brunt, or Brom, as the townspeople were wont to call him.

Though she staunchly held herself upright, maintaining a tight rein on turbulent emotions whirling inside her while the people of Sleepy Hollow bid a final farewell to the redoubtable Brom, her spirits were deeply troubled.

A jagged thread of lightning raced across the sky, and a thunderous boom drowned out Reverend Von Groot's words. Katherine's gaze rose skyward.

'Tis a poor day to lay yourself down, Father.

A heartsick sigh slipped from her, and Brau tightened his hold around her waist, giving her a gentle squeeze for comfort.

Her heart ached to think of the loneliness she knew would come, just as it had when her grandfather, Baltus Van Tassel, had gone to his final rest – exactly as it had when, a mere four years ago, her mother and the child she'd been carrying passed into the ever after.

Her attention on the proceedings once more, the words of the honorable Reverend Bartholomew Von

Groot registered upon her thoughts as though from a distance.

"May God's peace find you, Brom. Ashes to ashes. Dust to dust. Amen."

Such finality, not only for the dead, but for the living also.

A chorus of melancholy amens followed the reverend's own, and Katherine released another tremulous sigh before she stepped forward to toss the first handful of Sleepy Hollow soil into the open grave. Each of the town's few residents did the same and, one by one, they moved away toward the church.

"Come, Katherine," Braughton said. "We'll join the others briefly and see the Von Groots off. Then it's home and a nice hot toddy for you."

His concerned gaze skimmed her. "It has been a trying day for us all, but most especially for you, my dear. I wish I could have spared you this."

Katherine tried to smile. "He's with Mother now, Brau. He always was happiest when she was at his side."

A tear, one of many she had shed since her father had drawn his last breath, slid down her cheek.

Brau lifted his handkerchief to catch it. "It will be over soon, Katherine. Just a bit more and we'll see you home. You've borne the day remarkably well … especially for one so fragile." His fingers brushed a comforting caress against her cheek.

Katherine turned away to hide the sudden rush of tears, unwilling to further burden him with her sorrowful thoughts. "I'm sorry, Brau. I can't seem to hold them in."

Gently, he guided her forward, a bit apart from the rest of the small group. "Let the tears fall, Katherine. Heaven knows you've had more than your share of hardships in life these past years. You've earned the right to them."

3

He offered his handkerchief and she took it. Wiping away the wetness on her cheeks, she managed a small nod, and the two moved on in silence.

Lifting her gaze when they drew near the church, Katherine studied the downcast faces of those gathered about. John and Clara Tanner and their two children, Anne and Dehann, had lived in the Hollow for as long as she could remember.

Anne and Dehann have grown up while Father lay ill.

Next to the Tanners stood Heinrick and Mary Vandercleef. Master Heinrick was Sleepy Hollow's notary – had been for at least ten years. It was Heinrick, or Heins, as most of the residents of the Hollow called him, who handled the legalities of her father's many business transactions in the Hollow and in the city.

There was the schoolmaster, Everett Bleecker; his wife, Nell; and their son, Eustace. Alma Von Groot stood next, and then there was Callum.

Dear, sweet Callum.

It was providence, really, that Callum Mather was here in the Hollow.

Katherine remembered her father's story about how he had been about his business in the city and, as he had told it the day he had brought Callum to live with them in the Hollow, a young boy had been arguing with the gentleman he'd gone to meet. The man had called out, "Away with you, boy! Your brains are addled. What good could come of your being here? None!"

To which young Callum had replied, "You're about to conduct a business transaction with a headless man. What good could come of that, sir?"

Her father had laughed at the boy's comment, clapped his associate on the shoulder, and chortled about the fancies of young men. Katherine knew he had been intrigued by the youth's cryptic words. He had called the lad over, slipped him a coin, and told him to wait outside the gentleman's office.

Callum had waited, her father had said, and after a warm meal and a long conversation, her father had invited Callum to come to Sleepy Hollow to live.

Katherine paused in her reverie, sighing wistfully. *That was the summer before Mother died.*

Thoughts of her mother brought her attention back to the gentleman at her side – Brau Van Ripper.

As a young man, Brau had thought the sun rose and set on Katrina Van Brunt, and Katherine feared he might never find a woman to live up to his vision of her mother. Still, Brau had become a fine man since Katrina's passing.

Katherine had been told Brau had come to the Hollow shortly after her birth. He'd taken quite a shine to Master Van Brunt and spent each day dogging Brom's every footstep.

She knew many of the residents of Sleepy Hollow at that time had thought Brom was grooming young Van Ripper to follow in his own footsteps.

While Katherine grew from a bright, happy child to a more serious adult saddled with the responsibility of tending to her ailing father, Brau's attention had become increasingly centered on her. Most of Sleepy Hollow's current residents believed an announcement would soon be forthcoming from the two.

The sound of a carriage drawing up before the church drew her attention. Mr. Rawlins, the Van Brunt butler-cum-coachman, waited in front, his coat buttoned high against the chill autumn wind and the ominous threat of a downpour.

The Von Groots were leaving Sleepy Hollow.

Katherine waited while Mr. Rawlins and the reverend loaded the last of the Von Groots' belongings into the coach. Alma stepped to her side and embraced her.

"Be strong, child. Perhaps some day there shall be happiness in Sleepy Hollow once more," the elderly woman said.

Katherine offered a watery smile. "Yes, someday. I hope for it very dearly, Mistress Von Groot."

The reverend came to stand at his wife's side. "Dearest Katherine, my heart is with you today, my dear. I hope you will be well. So much heartache for you."

"Thank you, Reverend. My thoughts go with you as well. Are you certain you will not reconsider?"

He sighed. "Alas, I cannot, my dear. My old eyes have seen enough of sorrow in this hollow. I fear my poor heart cannot take more."

Katherine swallowed back tears and uttered a somewhat choked laugh. "Then have a thought for the rest of us, sir, as you begin your new life outside the Hollow."

He gave her a kindly smile. "You will never be far from our thoughts, Katherine Van Brunt. This I promise you."

The reverend turned to his wife and took her hand. "Let us be away, my dear, or we'll never get to shelter before the rain comes."

Alma Von Groot offered another half smile, and let her husband hand her up into the coach. He followed and Mr. Rawlins whistled and shouted to the team.

The coach started off with a jerk, and Katherine moved to stand beside Braughton and the rest of Sleepy Hollow's residents. She waved until the coach had drawn out of sight, a brittle farewell smile frozen in place on her lips.

Brau gently patted her on the shoulder. "Will you be all right for a moment, Katherine? There is a matter about which I need to speak with Master Vandercleef."

Katherine nodded, and he walked away, leaving her

to stare bleakly about at the Sleepy Hollow countryside and the desolate little town that had once been teeming with laughter and abundance at every turn.

Fields were laid to waste – the orchards had become little more than a tumble of overgrown weeds and life-draining suckers. The charred remains of several houses, once filled with proud, happy families, rose up from the near barren countryside, a scorched, blackened mockery of the prosperous homes they once had been.

Everywhere she turned lay desolation, and it was more than she could bear.

She heard footsteps approaching from behind. "It's too quiet, Brau. Too quiet, too cold, and too … empty," she said.

Brau took her hands into his own. "You're distraught, my dear. Today has been a long and trying day. You should rest."

Katherine looked away, shaking her head, her saddened gaze gliding over the barren countryside once more. "No. No, I'm not distraught, Brau. Yes, I am saddened to have lost my father, but, Brau, Father was ill for a very long time. Today is not the first that I noticed Sleepy Hollow slipping into ruin."

He looked away, letting her fingers slip from his. "What would you have me do, Katherine? What is it you wish to see?"

"Prosperity! Abundance." She turned to face him, gesturing toward the fields, the pond, the barn, and the orchards. "I want to see freshly turned soil, Brau. Green growing things. I desire to see life in Sleepy Hollow once more.

"There should be waterfowl resting upon the pond, mounds and mounds of hay bursting forth from every single crack in that barn. And piglets … there should be piglets running about underfoot when we make our way toward home."

7

She shook her head, a deep vee of confusion furrowing her brow. "Did the trees bear not a single fruit this season, Brau? Look about you and tell me you do not see misery and desolation at every turn!"

He looked disgruntled. "Yes, I see it, Katherine, but there is nothing I can do—"

She whirled toward him. "Nothing, Brau? Look there."

She pointed toward the remaining homes, where thick plumes of smoke curled from the chimneys, and then to the churchyard where the families were still gathered, chatting amongst themselves.

"Look to the people, Brau. Each of them remembers how the Hollow was before. Every man, woman, and child look back with remembered fondness, dreaming of life as it was before the fever. Look to them. They will help us restore the Hollow, Brau. I know they will."

Brau gave her a look of impatience. "Three men and some children, Katherine? Surely you haven't forgotten how few citizens of Sleepy Hollow remain? Even the good reverend departed for better climes!"

"More will come—" she began.

Brau cut her off. "No one will come, Katherine. They fear the Horseman and the Witch's curse. People shun Sleepy Hollow for fear of losing what little they have left in this life. Now come, my sweet. Let us get you home."

Taking her arm, he turned her about and added, "Besides, you should be looking forward, Katherine, not backward. Time does not reverse its course … for anyone. We'll move to the city—"

She shook her head, fighting tears once more. "I have no wish to live in the city, Brau. Sleepy Hollow is my home. My grandfather worked here his entire life, and my father after him, to leave a grand legacy for future generations. I'll not forsake it in its hour of need."

He laughed, a harsh bark of censure and amazement. "You speak of the town as if it were a living, breathing entity, Katherine. Such is the way of nonsense."

Katherine lowered her head, fighting her need to protest more lest Brau find it necessary to remind her such thoughts did not belong in the head of a young lady.

Though she tried not to, Katherine realized she oft found herself contemplating the world from what Brau believed a point of view reserved only for men, and Brau was never wont to hesitate to remind her that proper young ladies minded only things of a gentler nature, such as her mother had, and never did they attempt to intrude upon matters best left to a man – in thought or in deed.

"I'm sorry, Brau. I know you have done all you can, and I have no right to expect more. You've been a dear friend of the family, and you've always been here when we needed you most. But it's—"

She glanced away, her attention suddenly focused upon the gathering at the front of the church, and she frowned. Everyone had moved to stand apart from the lone figure at the center of the throng, looks of fearful caution haunting their faces.

"Oh dear," she whispered.

With one glance at Callum, she immediately recognized the dazed, faraway look in his eyes. It was the same he wore whenever his gift of prophecy came upon him.

"The crane flies."

His words were spoken low, almost at a whisper, but still she heard. A terrible chill of foreboding chased its way through her.

Katherine shook free of Brau's hold, and started forward. "Callum? Callum dear, we're going home now."

"The crane flies," he said again. "Fear flushes the raven … and the Horseman rides once again."

At the word "Horseman," a murmurous clamor broke out amongst the townspeople. Gaining momentum born of fear, the noise of fervent whispers rose so quickly Katherine almost did not recognize the low sound coming from behind her.

Turning, her curious stare focused on the covered bridge that acted as a gateway of sorts to the town and she wondered what brave soul dared to come into the Hollow on this the most morose of days, for the sound she heard was that of a horse slowly making its way up the lane toward the bridge.

After a moment the steady clip-clop of hooves rang against the thick oaken boards that stretched across the brook. The wooden covering over the bridge magnified the sound, and within seconds every eye was frozen on the opening that would soon reveal the traveler's identity.

Katherine gasped.

If she lived to be one hundred and three, she knew she would never forget the first time she laid eyes on the man.

Mounted on his midnight steed, he sat regally erect, his leisurely but measured gaze moving from man to man over the crowd assembled before the church.

From the top of his blond head to his black leather-clad feet, Katherine saw only pure, unadulterated powerful masculinity. Her heart picked up a beat, and she pressed her palm to her chest, forgetting the hapless psychic at her back.

His hair is too long. She watched it blow from his face in roguish disarray in the chill breeze. It fell too far below his collar for decency, yet she could not imagine it at a more respectable length.

Nay, she mused, *it suits him.*

Given his countenance, it did suit him. Just as the midnight stallion beneath him that shared the same stately arrogance his master exuded also suited him.

Forcing her gaze upward once more, she noted his shoulders – arrogantly squared and impressively broad beneath the heavy black coat he wore. That same coat had been left open to reveal his snowy white shirt of finest lawn beneath.

Scandalously, he wore no cravat. His shirt had been left open, baring a shocking amount of bronzed male chest to her hungry gaze.

Her breath caught and she felt heat flood her cheeks. Pressing closer to the man at her side, she whispered, "Brau? Who is that man?"

* * * *

The closer he had ridden toward town, the more convinced Icharus had become that some horrible tragedy must have befallen Sleepy Hollow, for even the few broken-down scarecrows he had passed along the road wore a look of stricken melancholy.

His thoughts were as much a jumble of confusion as the fields to his left and right, all tangled with brambles. The meadows were in dire need of a herd of skinny sheep, he thought, for they too showed signs of severe neglect and non-use.

A frown furrowed his brow. *This is Sleepy Hollow, the almost mystical place that was entirely responsible for changing my father's life?*

Taking in the unkempt, completely dilapidated farmhouses, broken-down fences, and unturned, weed-tangled fields, he found it hard to believe.

Where are the fatted pigs of Father's stories? Where are the strutting gobblers, the proudly ferocious guinea hens and smug, rounded cattle? Why is there no sign of freshly hewn fields of wheat, rye, and Indian corn?

Not a single speck of pumpkin orange did he witness for as far as his eye could see, yet many times over the years his father had lauded the plump beauty and orange glow of a Van Tassel pumpkin over his own.

Surely a catastrophe of dire proportions had overtaken the Hollow, he surmised, but he would not let that deter him from his goal. Nay, Abraham Van Brunt had made a promise to his father, and he intended to see that promise kept ... at any cost.

Van Brunt's promise was the only thing that had kept his father going long after most men would have simply given up, encouraging him with dreamy visions of the wealth, riches, and security of Sleepy Hollow, which had all but forced him to strive harder each day to carve out such a fanciful place for his own.

Throughout his last years, his father had constantly urged Icharus to do his best and more. "For the prize is close at hand," he would say.

Knowing just how much the reward he had been promised had meant to his father, Icharus vowed he would not rest until he had acquired all that had been pledged to his father on that dark, midnight ride out of Sleepy Hollow so many years ago.

At last, the bridge that led into the once quaint town came into sight.

So this is the infamous bridge, eh, Father? It's not so frightening in the light, you know.

Though he knew it unlikely he should see such a thing, Icharus could not prevent his gaze from seeking out the remains of a shattered pumpkin on the covered oaken boards that crossed over the brook.

With a little chuckle over his reminiscence of the tale his father often told regarding his last ride across this very bridge, Icharus straightened his shoulders and with a click of his tongue to urge his mount onward, he made his way onto the bridge.

Just on the other side, he could see a small gathering of people before the church. At the center of attention was a braw young man with hair the color of wet sand. Icharus wondered what the fellow was saying, for he certainly had the full, apparently horrified concentration of the assemblage.

He rode ever nearer, the sound of Defiance's footsteps ringing loudly in his ears. After a moment, he let his gaze roam over the others.

Five men, three children – two who were definitely approaching adulthood – and five women. One of those was a servant.

All of them were garbed in dreary black or somber gray. None were smiling. Icharus felt the sudden need to turn and ride away as fast as Defiance could carry him. A shiver crawled his spine, and he felt the urge to retreat, to shake the gloom of this place from him before he became possessed by it.

He forced himself to continue.

On the other side of the bridge, his attention was caught and held by one woman in particular – a brunette with eyes so blue he could make out their color from where he sat. She had turned at the sound of his approach and was openly staring at him even now.

A thin black veil covered her hair for the most part, but at her waist and temples, he could see chocolate colored ringlets stealing forth to play in the light breeze that blew through the Hollow.

He judged her height to come just beneath his chin.

Yes, she'd fit snugly against my chest, he thought, then chided himself. *You have business here, nothing more. Just speak with Van Brunt, collect the papers, and leave.*

Still, the lady's warm blue gaze was so direct he could not help but return it with an intent look of his own.

She moved closer to the tall gentleman who'd stepped to her side, and he saw her press her hand to her chest.

Did the lady think him someone to fear by chance? He wondered.

Drawing Defiance to a halt before the assembly, his gaze sought out and then rested upon who he presumed to be the eldest male in the group.

"I am seeking Abraham Van Brunt. We have business to discuss," he said.

The somewhat younger man standing beside the lady whose gaze had all but devoured him on the way in spoke up. "Master Van Brunt sadly was laid to his final rest just this morning."

The news hit Icharus like a blow to the gut. "He's dead?"

Dead? A feeling of panicked dread stole through him. *How am I to acquire what I came here for if the man who held it is no longer alive?*

A fierce determination rose up within him.

I will not give up! Nay, he had come with a purpose, and he would not leave without accomplishing what he sought to achieve.

"Quite," the man rejoined. "Van Brunt was a brilliant fellow and a shrewd businessman before he took ill. A tragedy, that. We shall all miss him."

Icharus pinned the man with his gaze, curious as to how well-versed the man was with the late Van Brunt's business affairs. If Abraham Van Brunt, or *Brom,* as his father had called him, was gone, perhaps he could conclude his business with this man in his stead.

"You speak as if you are familiar with his business."

The man nodded. "If Master Van Brunt had business with you, I would know of it. What is your name, sir?"

Icharus glanced at the crowd, then back at the man with hair as black as a raven's wing and a voice as chill as the heart of winter itself. His tone had hinted that Icharus lied, that there was no true business between his father and the now deceased Van Brunt. Icharus pinned the man with what he felt was a chilling glare.

"Icharus Crane," he said. "Eldest son of Ichabod Crane. My father was once schoolmaster here."

A murmur of whispers ran through the crowd.

Icharus saw shock and even panic on the faces of the townspeople though he did not readily recognize the cause ... until he heard the whispered words *Witch's curse* and *Headless Horseman*.

He was very careful to show no outward sign he had noticed the alarm aroused by the mere stating of his name. Instead, he said, "Abraham Van Brunt made a promise to my father when he left Sleepy Hollow twenty-five years ago. I have come to collect what is due."

A rather large man stepped forward, a look of pained disgust mingled with curiosity on his face. "Our mistress has just today laid her father to rest, young man. Surely it would not be too much to ask that you show some respect for the deceased!"

He spat upon the ground, his irritation with Icharus's unknowing insolence winning out over his curiosity.

Icharus frowned.

"Your business will hold until next week. Come back then," the man said.

"No!"

The word practically shouted, bursting forth from the lady with the eager gaze. Icharus turned to her, curious as to the reason for her outburst.

She stepped forward, an awkward smile twisting her lips. When the man who had derided him for his lack of respect looked about to protest once more, she shook her head in denial. "No, John, really. It's fine. I should like to hear more about this promise between my father and Ichabod Crane."

She turned her full gaze back to Icharus, and he imagined he saw a bit of apology in her eyes for her would-be protector's vigilance. *Is it a conjuring of my mind, or do I also see a bit of desperation mingled with hesitant interest there in her lovely gaze?*

"Would you care to join me for supper, Master Crane?" she asked.

In light of the circumstances, Icharus's first thought was to regretfully decline. He considered the words of the man she had called John, and felt a bit of remorse for his appalling lack of manners. "I would not have you think I've no respect for the recently deceased. Perhaps later would be best, as your John here suggests, Mistress …?"

The lady smiled, a real smile this time that brought a glow to her face and a merry twinkle to her eyes. Icharus was taken aback.

She is quite lovely.

"Katherine Van Brunt, sir," she said, "and I'll hear no more of waiting. Supper is at eight. I shall expect you to sit down with us."

Icharus was still wont to decline, despite how her soft voice played merrily upon his ear, pleading gently with him to agree. His notice had not missed the slight stiffening of the man by her side, and he acknowledged it now.

"I think perhaps your young man here feels you're not quite prepared to entertain guests this eve, Mistress Van Brunt. Later in the week perhaps?" he offered.

The man at her side nodded. "Indeed, Katherine, I think that would be for the best, considering …."

Did no one else notice the brilliant light extinguish from her gaze at those words? It is odd that she should have such a reaction to them.

It seemed to him that her fiancé – for surely the man hovering protectively at her side was at least that – meant only to see to her welfare.

Still, she attempted a polite smile. "Nonsense, Brau. Master Crane will not test my endurance any further than you yourself might."

She turned again to Icharus. "I shall have Mrs. Porter lay a place at the table for you."

Icharus sensed the tense undercurrents between Mistress Van Brunt and her fellow, but apparently he was the only one who did. Not wanting to upset the lovely Miss Van Brunt or the townsfolk any further, Icharus nodded.

"Until evening, then, Mistress Van Brunt. It shall be my pleasure."

* * * *

Brau waited until Icharus had ridden out of sight before he turned to Katherine. "You are clearly overwrought, my dear. Inviting a stranger to your table mere hours after laying your father to rest? Katherine, what were you thinking?"

Katherine ignored the somewhat parental censure in his voice. "He's not a stranger, Brau. He is one of my father's business associates, as he said. As such, he is welcome in my father's home and at our dinner table, is he not?"

Brau stood silent for a moment, as though giving their audience time to agree with his reprimand or give protest of her clearly inaccurate observation. When no one spoke, he sighed. "In that case, I suppose I shall join you for dinner as well. You forget your father is no longer here to look after you, Katherine. In all kindness, I suppose I must be delighted to have the responsibility fall to me." He turned to the others, giving her no time to object to his words. "If you'll excuse us now, I will see Miss Van Brunt to her home. Thank you, all of you, for being here for Katherine and myself in our hour of grief."

"But what about Crane, sir?" Dehann Tanner called. "Do you think his arrival will stir up the Hessian's wrath, as his father's did? Should we fear a visit from the Horseman?"

Brau offered an amused quirk of a smile. "Dear boy, of course you should not. I shall settle things with Master Crane, if indeed there is aught to be settled."

The cynical tone of his voice suggested Brau did not believe Master Crane's claims one small whit.

"As for the Hessian," Brau continued, "there is nothing to fear. The Headless Horseman is nothing more than a figment of imagination, and you'd do well to remember that."

He pinned John Tanner with a speaking glare, as if to reprimand that one as well for allowing his son to believe and carry tales of such outlandish nonsense.

Anne Tanner leaned near to her brother. "Aye, but what about the Witch?" she whispered loudly.

Brau had turned and placed Katherine's hand upon his arm, but now he paused. Facing the small assembly once more, he held both Tanner youngsters within his glacial gaze.

"Enough. There will be no more talk of horsemen gallivanting wildly about, sporting pumpkins for heads, nor of witches, ravens, curses, nor aught else which may further upset Mistress Van Brunt. She's been distressed quite enough with the events of the day as it is."

With an encompassing look that included the entire

assemblage, he said, "We'll speak no more of it."

No one seemed wont to argue, so with a brief, curt nod in acceptance of their unspoken understanding, he said, "Good day to you all."

Katherine kept her gaze steadily forward. She knew it would do little good to attempt to speak with Brau regarding Master Crane's visit that night. It was clear to her he thought the matter none of her concern.

She might well agree but for a vague memory at the back of her thoughts. She knew from his words and his tone that Brau disbelieved Master Crane's claims, but Katherine had a feeling deep in her heart that he had been sincere.

All that remained was to discover precisely what that promise had entailed.

Chapter 2

"You shouldn't fill your head with such nonsense, you know. You'll be as spooked and suspicious as the rest of the folks in the Hollow."

Katherine smiled and laid aside the well-worn copy of Cotton Mather's *History of New England Witchcraft* that had once belonged to Ichabod Crane. "Come now, Callum. Master Mather is your ancestor. Do not presume to tell me you disbelieve his words?"

"Not one syllable do I believe," Callum replied. He sat in his favorite chair near the fire, legs crossed at the ankles.

Katherine chuckled. "Then I should admit to a bit of skepticism as well, but it does make for fine entertainment."

He smiled in agreement. "Entertainment, certainly, but truth? Not a whit."

He studied her carefully for a moment. "Should you be in here, Katherine? Brau seemed to think you in need of rest."

Katherine's smile disappeared. "Brau often thinks he knows my mind better than I. Betimes I believe he sees me as incapable of making the smallest of decisions for myself, as if it were impossible for a mere female to know her own mind."

"I believe he thinks you're going to marry him. Will you, Katherine?"

She sighed. "I wish I could say aye or nay, Callum, but I cannot. Brau is a good friend, a dear friend who has always been here for us anytime there was a need. Do I feel some affection for him? Of course I do. Yet I'm not sure the strength of my regard is enough to base a more permanent relationship upon."

Callum studied her for a moment, and then nodded. "You do care for him, then?"

A small laugh escaped her lips. "Of course I care for him. As I said, he is a dear friend … just as you are."

A tiny smile twisted Callum's lips. "Aye, but you've no intention of pledging yourself to me."

Katherine arched a brow. "I've no intention of pledging myself to anyone, Callum."

He nodded. "Fair enough. I suppose I should go into the kitchen. Mrs. Porter could probably use a hand with those hares."

He stood to leave, but Katherine halted him. "Callum?"

He paused. "Yes?"

Remembering Callum's prophecy of her mother's death, she hesitated. He'd not wished to speak of it at the time, but her father had insisted, though speaking of it had changed nothing. "Today, at the church … when you spoke of the crane and the raven … what did you see? Can you tell me?"

He stiffened. "Katherine, perhaps we should speak of this later. Your father—"

"It was Master Crane, wasn't it?"

He sighed. "Yes, it was Master Crane. And Master Van Ripper."

She bit her lip. "And the Hessian?"

22

He flushed and looked a bit uncomfortable. "Yes, and the Hessian, Katherine. Is that what you wished to hear? You would hear me say that I, one of the Hollow's staunchest skeptics against the whispers of a headless horseman galloping about the roads and wood, doing some unseen mischief under cover of night, have now to admit there may be some truth to those preposterous tales?"

Katherine blinked at the scorn she heard in his voice. "I'm sorry …"

He scoffed. "Don't be. Instead hope that I see more clearly, for I say to you now *this* Headless Horseman is naught but a man bent upon devilry and injustice."

Without explanation of those words, he left her alone with her thoughts.

It seemed only a few moments had passed when he rejoined her in the parlor. "Your guest has arrived. I thought you might want to prepare yourself."

Katherine stood. "I am as ready as need be. Will you be joining us for supper?"

He nodded, gesturing to his hands. "I've but to wash up and put on a fresh shirt. I'll be down before you can miss me."

The sound of booted feet rang against the floorboards outside, and Katherine hurriedly smoothed her hair. After a moment, Mrs. Porter appeared in the parlor doorway. "Master Crane has arrived, Miss Katherine."

"Show him in here, please," she said. Her breathing changed, and her heart was filled with an unfamiliar sense of anticipation.

Katherine thought it rather odd, but then he came across the hall, and she forgot the somewhat strange sensation. A smile lifted her lips. She'd thought him quite handsome when she'd seen him at the church earlier today, but now he seemed even more so.

23

"Master Crane, you're early. Dare I hope you were eager to better our acquaintance?"

Stunned by her own words, Katherine felt the heat of a blush steal across her cheeks. She'd sounded almost like her mother. Not that her mother had been a bad person. It was quite the opposite, actually. Yet, no one would have been swifter to tell that Katrina Van Brunt had been a bit of a coquette than Katrina herself.

Katherine had no wish to be seen as an enchantress. Indeed, she'd rather be known for her quick mind and clear thoughts.

Icharus offered a stiff smile. "Indeed, Mistress Van Brunt. I vow I could detect the delicious aroma of rabbit stew or dumplings and apple pie from the bridge."

Katherine's smile widened. "Mrs. Porter has prepared a fine supper for us, Master Crane, and everyone in the Hollow says she makes the best green apple pies. I'm glad you could join us."

She gestured inside the room. "Come and sit. Callum will be down shortly, and Master Van Ripper will be joining us as well."

Icharus followed her into the parlor. "If the rain doesn't detain him. It was a fair drizzle, and I feared I might get drenched before I could reach the cover of the piazza."

Katherine nodded. "The day has been a gloomy one. You must be chilled. Here, sit by the fire and warm yourself," she said, sweeping her gold shawl from the chair where Callum had sat earlier.

She took a seat opposite him on the sofa. Picking up the volume she had been reading earlier, she said, "I have something for you … something of your father's."

Icharus had taken off his gloves and had been warming his hands before the fire. At her words, he swung round to face her. "You have them, then? The papers?"

24

Katherine's brow furrowed, and she gave an uncertain laugh. "Papers? Nay, no papers. 'Tis but a book, a favorite of your father's, as I understand it. My father said yours quoted from the volume so often he must have known each verse and line by heart."

Icharus took the book from her and studied the title—*History of New England Witchcraft.*

Katherine nodded. " 'Tis said your father was a highly superstitious man."

Icharus's brow rose. "Indeed he was … and easily spooked in his youth, but just so. He was a genuinely ordinary man … most days."

"He is no longer with you, then?"

Icharus shook his head. "Not since winter last. He'd developed a congestion in his lung, you see."

Katherine nodded. "I'm sorry."

Icharus had been thumbing through the pages of the volume she'd given him. He closed it with a quiet thump and tucked it beneath his arm. "Thank you. I am sorry to have learned of your own father's death as well."

Katherine leaned her head against the sofa. "Father has … had been ill for quite some time. After mother died, he seemed to lose his usual zest for life. He simply had no desire to go on without her." She looked at Icharus. "I believe his heart was broken."

When he said nothing, she continued. "He loved my mother very much, you see."

"Everyone loved Katrina Van Brunt," Callum said, entering the room with a dramatic flourish. "How could they not? She was the envy of every female for miles, and the dream of every male," he said, souring his face in imitation of jealous ladies one second, and pretending to be a panting fellow the next.

Katherine grinned at his antics. "Icharus Crane, meet Callum Mather … a somewhat silly scoundrel, occasional prophet, and a direct descendant of the author

25

of the book you hold."

Icharus smiled. "A pleasure to make your acquaintance, Master Mather."

Callum nodded, and took a seat next to Katherine. "Likewise, Master Crane. Likewise. So tell us again about this business that brings you to Sleepy Hollow. Tell us of this promise between Master Brom and your father."

An ominous jag of lightning flashed across the window, and a loud crack of thunder filled the momentary silence. Katherine jumped. Tense now, she managed a tenuous smile. "Yes, please do. I would love to know more about it."

* * * *

Heinrick Vandercleef was just locking up his office.

Holding the lantern high, he fumbled with the key and heavy lock for a moment, his movements unwieldy in the darkness. Finally satisfied he'd secured the shop against intruders, he turned and peered out into the eerie stillness of the night. A fine mist of rain created a dense, near impenetrable fog, making it difficult for him to see the soft lights from the manor high upon the hill across the way.

A fierce blue streak of lightning crept out of nowhere and zipped swiftly across the sky. Close on its heels, the heavy crack of thunder rolled through the air, shattering the silence of the night. Immediately following the violent sound, the skies seemed to open, for a deluge was released upon the land.

Heinrick turned toward the back, intent upon seeking his supper just as another jag of lightning flashed, illuminating the large shape of a man standing near. He gasped, clutching his aged hand to his heart.

The man had a rather spookish ability to suddenly

appear where one was certain there had been no one but a moment before, Heinrick thought. It was uncanny.

"Master Brau, you startled me. I didn't expect to see you there."

Brau's lips twitched, though he did not smile. "I came round from the back, Heins. Quite frightening, was it?"

Heinrick gave a hesitant laugh. "Quite."

Brau dipped his chin. "My apologies."

Placing the keys to the notary office in his coat, Heinrick patted his pocket, as if to assure himself they were safely tucked away. "You're joining the young mistress for supper, I presume?"

Brau nodded. "In a bit, yes. First, however, I need to speak with you concerning Brom's will …"

Heinrick frowned. "It is as I told you this morning, sir. Master Brom left everything to Mistress Katherine, as was proper and fitting, considering …"

Brau lifted his cane to study the gleaming silver head. "Yes, so it was."

He turned to face Heinrick. "You heard young Master Crane this morning, Heins?"

Heinrick nodded. "Of course. Everyone heard him."

Brau sighed. "And?"

Heinrick's brow furrowed in confusion. "And, sir?"

Brau let his cane thump menacingly against the porch and sighed. "*And* … if Master Van Brunt had any dealings with the elder Crane, as young Icharus alleged, I felt you would know of it, Heins."

Heinrick shook his head. "I've told you everything I know about Master Van Brunt's will."

Brau's eyes narrowed and Heinrick felt his heart thumping hard against his chest. Brau Van Ripper was a man oftentimes possessed of a chilling gaze, such as now.

"So you have," Brau said, after a long moment of

27

silence. He nodded. "Very well, Heins. I shall leave you to Mary and to your supper."

Heins swallowed. "Thank you, sir. Give my best to Mistress Katherine."

Brau turned. "I shall, thank you. And Heins?"

Heins looked up in query. "Yes, sir?"

Brau studied him for a moment before he spoke. "If you should *remember* anything …."

Hesitantly, Heinrick nodded.

Turning up the collar of his coat against the slashing rain, Brau stepped out into the downpour.

* * * *

From the moment he'd ridden away from Sleepy Hollow this morning, Icharus had thought of little more than the conversation at hand. He'd planned to simply state the story exactly the way his father had told it to him. But this was Brom's daughter he was speaking to, the daughter of a man who had been buried just this morning, and now he wasn't so sure that would be the best way to go about it.

He feared her emotions would be unstable, and he needed her to trust in his words. He cleared his throat.

"It's no secret your mother was highly sought after in her youth. Tales of her beauty continue to be spread to this day, and it is said no man was immune. Not even my father," he began. "But Brom, my father said, seemed to see straight through my father's infatuation to the true love of his heart. It was the richness of the land he wanted, and not the fair Katrina, as Brom had first thought. He'd seen nothing more than a rival for his love's affection initially, but it did not take long for him to realize what lay at the heart of my father's desire."

Katherine was frowning, and Icharus questioned the soundness of his words.

28

Have I gone about this all wrong after all?

"And what of you, sir?" Katherine asked. "Are you after the richness of Sleepy Hollow as well? If so, I find I must disbelieve you, for as you can see, the Hollow is little more than a shadow of what it once was …"

Icharus shook his head. "Nay, allow me to finish, please."

Callum smiled. "Yes, do let him finish, Katherine. I find myself intrigued over any man who might desire the Hollow over our fair Katrina."

Katherine rolled her eyes. "You begin to sound like Brau, Callum. Perhaps you've spent a bit too much of these past days in his company. You've become a mimic."

Callum's face became a closed mask. "Not enough time, I fear."

Katherine found his words a bit cryptic, but rather than question him, she gestured to her guest. "Please continue, Master Crane."

Icharus nodded. "As I have said, your father recognized a hunger in mine – a yearning for land and place of his own. That is why he made the agreement with my father … that, and to aptly remove what many thought a possible rival for the affections of your mother – as a precautionary measure, mind you."

Katherine laughed.

"Of course," she said. "But if my father was so eager to see yours gone, I'm sure he would simply have asked him to leave the Hollow. Do you not agree, Callum?"

Icharus grinned. "Oh, he did, in his own way. I'm sure you know the tale of how my father disappeared that fateful night so long ago, leaving nothing behind but a few personal effects and the shattered remains of a pumpkin?"

Callum nodded. "We've heard the story many,

many times. Deep in the heart of the darkest midnight, the Headless Horseman leapt onto his demon steed and chased him away, of course."

Icharus laughed. "Precisely. Only the horseman who chased my father away wasn't headless. Not really. Your father was well known for his sense of revelry and mischief-making in his day, Mistress, and this occasion is one in which he played it well. He had intended only to frighten my father, to spook him a bit, if you will."

Icharus shook his head in remembered amazement. "But my father, superstitious and easily led as he was at the time, took what should have been nothing more than a harmless prank a bit harder than Master Brom intended. He fell from the mighty Gunpowder, his fearless mount for the evening, climbed to his knees and began to sob in despair, repenting every sin and begging for mercy from the ghostly specter who had run him aground."

He saw Katherine bite her lip to keep from laughing, but he could see merriment in her eyes.

"Some might have called him a spineless half-wit to have seen him at that moment, but not your father." Icharus swallowed hard against the emotions rising up within him. He missed his father terribly.

"Nay," he continued. "Instead, your father doffed the pillowed contraption that made him appear to be riding about the night without a head, pulled my father to his feet, brushed him off, and offered to buy him a drink at the tavern up the way in TarryTown to help settle his wayward nerves."

Callum looked pointedly at Katherine. "That sounds like your father, Katherine, if ever I heard a tale that did."

Icharus agreed. "Indeed. In any case, those few hours in that tavern changed my father's life forever."

He turned to Katherine, hoping she could read the

sincerity in his gaze. "My father always said thanks to Our Heavenly Father for yours, for it was Abraham Van Brunt alone who made way for him to set his life aright."

Katherine looked down at her hands, and he could see the sheen of tears in her eyes.

"I'm sorry. I do not wish to upset you …"

She shook her head. "Nay, it is only memories coming to plague me at the moment. Continue, please. How did my father change the life of Ichabod Crane?"

The moment of truth was upon him now, and Icharus could see no way to state it but forthright. "Baltus Van Tassel knew his daughter's heart like no other, it is said. It was the same with her affection for Abraham Van Brunt … your father. Baltus knew the true bend of Katrina's heart, and so knowing, had granted your father tithe and title to a parcel of land adjoining his."

Icharus drew a breath. "The night my father left Sleepy Hollow, it was because Abraham Van Brunt promised that land to him, if only he would apply himself to making it as rich and prosperous as the land he craved to have through marriage to your mother – as prosperous as Sleepy Hollow."

"And where is this adjoining land located, might I ask?" Katherine queried.

Icharus looked into her eyes. "Just across the Western Wood."

"Miss Katherine, Master Brau has arrived," the servant who had led him to the parlor on his arrival called from the doorway.

Katherine rose from the sofa. "Shall we go in to supper, gentlemen?"

* * * *

Leading the way through the foyer to the dining room,

Katherine pondered on all that Icharus had said, and again, some long-forgotten memory tugged at her thoughts. She brushed it aside, and went to greet Brau.

She raised her cheek for the habitual peck he always gave her, and reached for his coat. "You're soaked through. Would you like to dry off a bit?"

The ornate clock in the foyer chimed the hour.

"Eight o'clock precisely," Callum noted. "You've arrived just in time."

Brau removed his coat and shook it lightly before handing it over to Katherine. "Punctuality is a virtue, Mather. A man is known for it."

He turned a disdainful gaze on Icharus. "You're a bit early, I see. Have I missed anything?"

Katherine's laugh sounded nervous to her own ears. "Only the tale of what really happened when Ichabod Crane left the Hollow all those years ago."

Brau's smile was brittle. "Well then, I must hear it. Come, let us adjourn to the dining room, and you can catch me up on all I've missed."

Some time later, Brau lay his napkin beside his plate and sat back, his dark brows rising.

"Well, the evening has certainly been entertaining to say the least," he said, "but our lady must have her rest. Today has been a most grueling one, as you might expect under the circumstances, so ..." He paused for a moment, as though to let his words sink in, and then continued. "If you would be so kind as to see Katherine upstairs, Callum, Master Crane and I shall remove ourselves to Master Brom's study."

Katherine protested. "I should like to join you."

Brau smiled. "Another time perhaps, my dear. I'm sure anything we have to say will be nothing if not boring. Dull, dreary business matters, such as they are, are best left to those of us with sterner minds."

Katherine bit her lip and lowered her gaze, but not

before she saw Icharus's brows rise.

"Mistress Van Brunt is already aware of my reason for being here, Master Van Ripper. I have no objection to her accompanying us."

Brau waved away his words. "Nonsense. Katherine is quite used to her father or myself attending to such matters on her behalf." She saw him hesitate, as if considering another rebuttal, but then he simply nodded. "Let us get to it then."

Katherine gave a little smile. "In that case, I shall say goodbye Master Crane. Your company has been quite delightful, and I do hope you'll visit us again soon."

Icharus held up his hand. "It has been my pleasure, Mistress Van Brunt."

She stood, and Icharus looked to first Callum and then Brau.

"If I may, I should like to have a private word with Mistress Van Brunt?"

Brau's eyes narrowed, but he nodded. "As you wish. Katherine, if you will see Master Crane to the study when you're quite finished?"

"Of course," she said, wondering what reason Master Crane would have for requesting a private audience with her.

He stood by her chair while she folded her napkin, and then followed her through to the parlor where he retrieved the book she'd given him earlier. "Thank you for the gift, Mistress—"

"Katherine, please," she said.

He nodded. "Katherine. Thank you, Mistress Katherine. It means a lot to me to have something once treasured by my father."

She smiled. "I thought as much."

He thumbed through the pages. "But what of you? If I take it, with what questionable literature will you then amuse yourself?"

It took only a moment for her to realize he was teasing her. She grinned. "Oh, you need not worry over it, Master Crane, for you see, I've made an exact copy for myself and hidden it in my chambers."

He chuckled. "Very well. Then I shall treasure it."

She nodded, waiting, for he seemed wont yet to speak further.

"Mistress Katherine, did your father have an attorney, or solicitor, who handled his business affairs?" he finally asked.

Katherine's brow furrowed. "Master Vandercleef is Sleepy Hollow's notary. He took care of Father's legal documents and the like. Why do you ask?"

He fingered the volume in his hands for a moment. "It may be to both our best interests that you seek him out at your earliest convenience regarding the matter of your father's promise to mine. Perhaps he knows something of your father's affairs that your ... that is to say ... Master Van Ripper does not."

Katherine was a bit surprised he'd asked her to look into a matter of business, whether on his behalf or hers. That he'd trusted her to understand when Brau never had ...

Then again, this isn't Brau standing here, speaking to me.

She nodded. "Of course. I shall do so as soon as it is light."

He smiled. "In that case, I bid you goodnight, fair Katherine. Perhaps we'll meet again soon."

She returned the smile. "I think I should like that very much."

He held out his arm, and she placed her hand in the bend, letting him lead her from the room. She gestured toward her father's study. "I'll leave you gentlemen to your business."

From inside her father's study, she saw Brau nod.

"Goodnight, Katherine," he said, his voice cool, as always. "Pleasant dreams."

* * * *

Brau motioned to a chair in front of Van Brunt's desk, taking the position behind it for himself.

Icharus declined. "I prefer to stand. Our business will not take long."

Brau inclined his head. "Very well."

He raised his hand to stroke his chin thoughtfully. "I've spoken with the local notary, Master Crane, and he denies any knowledge of an agreement existing between Van Brunt and your father."

Icharus's gaze drilled into Brau's. "And I say there was an agreement. Abraham Van Brunt promised my father tithe and title to the parcel of land bordering Sleepy Hollow beyond the Western Woods, provided Father saw to its vigilant increase, and he has done so.

"I have records for the past twenty-five years," Icharus stated, "record of every measure of seed, of each head of cattle, every sheep, every tree and vine planted in or removed from Wake Grove during that time. I have record also of every harvest, of all coin earned and of Master Van Brunt's percentage of it, marked received and duly noted by Van Brunt himself."

A brittle smile curved Brau's lips but did not reach the iciness of his eyes. "Be that as it may, Master Crane, there is still no formal proof, no documentation other than that of these records of which you speak anywhere to give truth to your claims of an agreement between Abraham and your father Ichabod regarding an exchange of the land."

His eyes glittered darkly. "It is your word against that of a dead man who cannot speak out on his own

35

behalf."

Icharus glared. "Are you calling me a liar, Master Van Ripper?"

At last, the smile twisting Brau's lips reached his eyes, but swiftly disappeared. "I am saying nothing of the sort, Master Crane. Rather, I am saying there is no legal proof of your claim. Therefore, sadly, you have no claim at all."

Chapter 3

The following morning Katherine was up early, even for her. Sleep had been fitful, her dreams plagued by nightmares of a raven plucking out the eyes of a crane, and though she'd placed a cool cloth over her eyelids, she knew her rather sleepless night was evident still.

Her intention had been to go right away to speak with Master Vandercleef regarding the possibility of an agreement between her father and Ichabod Crane, but she was forced, by her own disinclination to give Brau any reason to linger at the Van Brunt manor this morning, to wait in her chamber a good half hour for the gentlemen to leave before making her way downstairs.

From the window of her second story bedchamber, she saw Callum ride away from the house and start for the wooded glen not far away. He carried a rifle, so she assumed he was going hunting. Minutes later, Mr. Rawlins appeared, leading two horses – Brau's chestnut steed and Master Crane's sable-coated mount. Then both Brau and Master Crane appeared in the yard below.

Katherine wondered about the discussion between the two of them the night before, but knew Brau would relate nothing of it to her, should she inquire as to what was said.

She could see the two gentlemen speaking, and it appeared to her Master Crane was angry about something. Brau only nodded after his apparently heated exchange, and Icharus turned his mount and headed off. Moments later, Brau followed.

When she was certain both men had had time aplenty to be well along on their way to their separate destinations, Katherine hurried down the stairs, pausing only long enough to call through to the kitchen for Mrs. Porter not to worry about breakfast for her. She was going for a ride.

The morning air carried a bite, and she was glad for the thick velvet cloak she wore. Pulling it closer against the chill, she thought ahead to her meeting with Heinrick Vandercleef. She worried he might well be as unwilling to discuss the matter as Brau would be, but she was determined to try. If there had been an arrangement between her father and Ichabod Crane, justice would only be served by seeing it put to rights.

Katherine rode straight to the Vandercleef house, but once there, Heinrick's wife, Mary, told her Heins had already gone off to his office. Leaving her mount tied in front of the Vandercleef's home, she walked the short distance to the office of the notary.

"Good morning, Mistress Katherine. You fared well through the night, I see," Heinrick called in greeting.

A nice fire crackled in the hearth at the back of the room. Katherine removed her cloak and folded it over her arm. "The storm was quite noisesome and the winds fierce, but it passed quickly enough."

Heinrick was busy with some paperwork, but bobbed his head in distracted agreement. "I feared for the shingles at one point. 'Twas like a banshee wailing through the trees. I was pleasantly surprised to find the morning such a lovely one, and the night without coincidence."

Katherine lifted a book from one of the tables near the front windows. "Master Heinrick, there is a matter of some importance about which I should like to speak with you, concerning an agreement made many years ago between my father and Ichabod Crane …"

The pen with which he'd been writing scraped sidewise across the parchment, leaving a nasty blue scrawl in its wake. He laid it aside, his brows pulled downward in a frown. "Master Van Ripper had a similar inquiry just yesterday. I've told him there is nothing more in Master Van Brunt's will than what was read the morning of his death. He spoke nothing of it to you, my dear?"

"I have read Father's will several times," she said, and it was truth. Late into the night, after the gentlemen had slept, she'd crept down to her father's study and sat for hours, poring over the papers, looking for any clue or mention of the land Icharus declared as belonging to the Cranes.

"Master Van Ripper does not discuss his business with me. He believes such matters best left to a man, a sentiment I pray you do not share for henceforth you will look to me concerning any matter related to Sleepy Hollow." She paused, awaiting his consent. Finally, he nodded, and she turned to face him directly, their gazes meeting. "But this matter of which I now speak has nothing to do with my father's will, Master Vandercleef."

Heinrick looked quickly away from her gaze. "Does anyone know you're here, child? Where is your mount?"

Katherine shook her head. "Nay. Callum is off hunting. Mrs. Porter is busy in the kitchen, and I left word only that I was going for a ride. Isolde waits for me at your door. Mary, she said you were here—"

He looked away from her, his expression that of a

man considering some weighty matter of import. Finally, he nodded.

"They will think you visiting with Mary." Heinrick now met her gaze directly, clearly having come to a decision. "You're right, my dear. This has naught to do with Master Van Brunt's last will and testament. Close the shutters, if you please, Katherine. There is something I must show you."

While Katherine busied herself at the windows, Heinrick placed a notice outside the door indicating he was unavailable for business, and then slid the bolt, locking the two of them inside. Katherine frowned at that, but Heinrick merely placed a finger to his lips in a silent request. He retrieved a lamp from near his desk, and then motioned her toward a small room off the back of the notary office – his private chamber, she presumed. She followed him inside, and he again locked the door.

There was a smaller desk there, turned cornerwise in the back of the room. Heinrick went to it, having retrieved a key from his coat, and leaned down to fumble with the lock on a side drawer. He slid the drawer open slowly, with great care. Katherine noted that his hands had begun to shake but said nothing of her observation.

He withdrew a thick sheaf of parchment and held it close to his heart. Head tilted, his eyes closed briefly, as though in private supplication to the heavens. After a moment, he waved her into a seat across from the desk. He, too, sat, his worried gaze studying her intently. Another long moment of contemplative silence passed.

Finally, he laid the folded parchments carefully on the desktop, his fingers tracing the squared edges of the mysterious packet. On the front was the Van Brunt seal. It had never been broken.

"Your father gave these into my care not long after your mother's passing," Heinrick began. "He did so with dire instruction that I should never open them, but should pass them to you only in the event of his death. I was bade to speak nothing of it to no one, and as God is my witness, I have not done so before this very moment."

Katherine leaned forward, excited. "Are these the papers of which Master Crane spoke?"

Heinrick Vandercleef covered the papers with his hand and shook his head. "As I have said, your father bade me never to speak of what lies inside. I have honored his request."

She noticed a bright stain of red creep across the high bones of his cheeks. "The people of Sleepy Hollow saw your father as a stern leader, my dear, but a fair one. He was oftentimes a hard taskmaster, as was your grandfather, Baltus. But the reward was well worth any hardship suffered, as any of the people of the Hollow would tell you. Brom was a good man, Katherine, and one of keen instincts regarding others. Never forget that."

Her thoughts turned wistful. "Indeed he was. I remember when he brought Callum to the Hollow …"

With a shake of her head, she broke off. Now was no time to succumb to memories.

After a moment, she asked, "Why would my father occasion such momentous importance to these documents, Master Vandercleef?"

"Your father felt there were some in the Hollow who might not agree with whatever he's written within these pages. Some who might even be angry, or become spiteful and mean should they learn of it." His gaze took on a faraway look and he paled. "Or murderous."

With shaking hands, he lifted the packet and handed it to her. He stood. "Go home, child. Go home, study whatever is inside, and then, for your own safety, say nothing of them to no one … especially Master Van Ripper. Burn them if you must, but do not allow anyone other than yourself to gain sure knowledge of what lays inside."

Katherine's gaze snapped to his. "Brau?"

Heinrick nodded.

"But if the documents Master Crane seeks lay inside—"

Heins gave a negative shake of his head. "You will know what to do, child. Remember, you must say nothing of it. Your safety, indeed your life, may well depend upon it."

He peered at her. "Do you understand me, girl?"

Katherine nodded. "Yes, I—"

He shushed her with a motion of his hand. "I must get back to work. Come, I'll see you out."

* * * *

Locked inside her father's study, Katherine carefully studied the packet Heinrick had given her. Her hands shook as she did so, her fingers sliding tenderly over the letters of her name flourished across the front, penned by her father's own hand. This would be the last communication she would ever have of him, she thought, and tears pricked her eyelids. What would she find written inside? She wondered.

She closed her eyes to ease the sting and drew in a calming breath, and then another. Composed once more, she opened her eyes and carefully broke the seal.

There was a single, thickly folded sheet inside, also addressed to her. Katherine opened it a bit hesitantly. Fastened in the upper left corner was a small key attached to a thin leather cord. Folded in the center was a second, smaller page. Katherine touched the key, wondering what it belonged to, what secret treasures it might unlock. Curious now, she laid the folded page inside the letter her father had written aside and began to read.

My dearest Katherine ...

Moments later, she dropped the letter onto the desk and looked around her father's study, her eyes peering at the shelves of books she was so fond of reading. Having found what she sought, she carefully removed the key from the page, and went to the shelves for a closer look. Her eyes widened, and her heart thumped wildly against her chest.

There in the space where the book she had given to Icharus just the night before had been, were the edges of a small, unadorned door in the back of the shelving. Hurriedly, she removed several other volumes and laid them hastily aside. Using the tips of her fingers, she pried at the edges of the small entrance, noiselessly opening the tiny door. Hands shaking, she reached inside to lift out a small wooden box.

Some time later, a knock sounded on the door, and Katherine jumped in fright. "Yes? Who's there?"

" 'Tis Callum. Is anything amiss, Katherine? Mrs. Porter said you've been in there since you returned from your ride this morning."

Quickly folding away the paper she'd had spread in front of her, she called, "I'm fine, Callum. Was there something more you needed?"

"Mrs. Porter thought you might be hungry since you missed breakfast. She says to tell you that she's laid a plate for you in the dining room."

Katherine slowly released her breath. "Thank you, Callum. I'll be right there."

She heard his footsteps retreat, yet still she waited. When she was certain no one else would disturb her, she refolded the letter her father had written, but the second page that had been inside it, the page that had pointed the way to the secret door in the bookcase, she tossed into the fire.

With shaking hands, she opened the small wooden strongbox her father had directed her to retrieve from its hiding place, and lifted the false bottom out so she could replace what she had found inside.

The box had contained more documents, thickly folded pieces of parchment that might have been considered insignificant as a treasure to be locked away, but not to her.

Though remarkably similar to the one given her by Master Vandercleef just this morning, the outside of the packet she'd found inside the locked box her father had obviously taken great care to conceal bore a label of significant importance.

It was marked simply "CRANE."

Carefully, she placed the documents back inside, and then replaced the false bottom. With a quick twist of the key, she secured the lock before she carried the box back to the concealed door in the shelving where it had been hidden.

Making sure she covered the location of the little door behind several thick volumes, Katherine sent a quick glance around the study to assure herself she'd not forgotten to put away anything that might give away her secret. The letter her father had written to her she hid inside her bodice to be put away later once she reached the privacy of her chamber.

Satisfied nothing was left to reveal her, she unlocked the door and headed to the dining room with one thought uppermost in her mind. She must get word to Icharus.

* * * *

Callum was already seated at the table. Offering a shaky smile of greeting, she joined him there. "How was the hunt?"

"A prosperous one. We'll have venison for supper tonight." He drew his napkin across his mouth. "You look tired. Were you unable to sleep?"

Katherine picked at the food on her plate, her appetite nonexistent in light of her recent discovery.

"A bit," she murmured.

More than a bit, actually. She wouldn't tell him she'd spent a goodly portion of the night poring over her father's will, looking for any mention of the name *Crane.*

Her thoughts turned to Icharus, and excitement bubbled up inside her. *Will he be as delighted as I am to learn he is right, that there is an agreement between my father and his?*

Callum tossed his napkin onto the table. "Something is troubling you. Out with it, Katherine. Was it my prophecy that kept you up into the wee hours?"

Katherine denied his words with a shake of her head but kept her gaze focused on the plate in front of her. "Nay, I barely gave it a thought. Truly."

She'd uttered no falsehood, for indeed she had not given his ominous words much thought while reading and rereading her father's last will and testament. Rather, her thoughts had been almost wholly centered on Icharus Crane.

She found him to be a very handsome man. Indeed, each time his name crossed her mind, she became heated and a bit giddy. Perhaps it was his eyes that intrigued her, she thought, remembering how they'd glittered with excitement when he'd told the tale of his father's last night in Sleepy Hollow, and then they had become clouded with some unnamable emotion when Brau had refused her company in her father's study.

From the corner of her eye, she saw Callum frown. "I'm sorry, Callum. Did you say something? I'm afraid my thoughts were far away."

"I saw you, you know. Leaving Vandercleefs'."

Katherine's heart skipped a beat and her gaze snapped up to meet his. "And?"

His brows arched upward. "And since the reading of your father's will took place the morning of his passing, I merely wondered what business you could possibly have with him that would send you tearing back to the manor as one possessed." His lips quirked upward. "Or did you hear something in the wood that gave you a fright? The Witch, perhaps? Or the demonic snort of the Hessian's steed?"

Katherine frowned, her thoughts scattered. Had he been near enough to Master Vandercleefs to overhear their conversation? "I heard nothing of the sort."

Callum merely stared at her for a moment before returning his attention to his meal.

After a moment, her fear resided, and her thoughts turned once more to Icharus Crane. If her father's letter was accurate, and she had no reason to believe otherwise, Icharus Crane was quite knowledgeable regarding matters of planting and the clearing of timber. Fleetingly, Katherine wondered if she might somehow be able to entice him to help her with the restoration of Sleepy Hollow.

She brushed the thought away, but it refused to be ignored. It was perfect. She needed Icharus and she had something he desperately wanted.

Yes, she mused, he could most definitely be persuaded to lend his aid to her cause. The question was whether or not she would be able to withhold from him the one thing that was sure to bring him back to Sleepy Hollow. At that moment, she almost believed she could.

Decision made, her gaze bore into his. "Callum? I need you to do something for me."

He glanced up at her words. "Anything. You have

only to ask."

"Fetch Icharus Crane back to Sleepy Hollow … with all haste."

Callum leaned back in his chair, a teasing smile playing about on his lips. "So you've taken a shine to the younger Crane, have you?" he teased.

Katherine frowned for a moment and then, as though she had only just realized what he had said and that he had been teasing her, she returned his smile. "Perhaps I have."

Callum laughed. "I can't say I'd be disappointed. The fellow's a full sight chattier than your Master Van Ripper, and much more handsome."

Katherine tossed her napkin at him. "Stop fishing and behave yourself, Callum. And Brau is not *my* Master Van Ripper."

Callum nodded in agreement. "Indeed. He merely thinks he is."

* * * *

In the late afternoon, Brau arrived just as Callum was leaving on his mission to find Icharus Crane and bring him back to the Hollow. Mr. Rawlins took the reins of Brau's mount and led the steed toward the stables at the back of the house while Brau came forward to greet Katherine with a fatherly kiss. "Where is he off to now? Not up to mischief, I hope?"

Katherine's stomach clenched. She hated lying, and although she had no intention of revealing to Brau precisely where she had sent Callum, or why, she knew she must tell him something.

"I've asked him to ride into town and let it be known we have a vacant home here in Sleepy Hollow. He should be back later tonight … no later than morning."

She smiled, feeling much better with that out of the way. What she'd said was truth. It was the other, the part she hadn't said that had her nerves all a-jitter.

Brau's brows rose, and he put a hand to Katherine's back to lead her toward the house, his gaze on Callum as he rode away.

"Well, I hope he meets with more enthusiasm in the telling than I. Earlier this morning, I spoke with several prospective tenants, and it took only a mention of Sleepy Hollow to send them all scurrying back to their rooms."

Katherine kept her gaze on the door, fearful to look into his eyes lest she give herself away. "Yes, let us hope, for we shall need all the help we can get to set things to rights here in the Hollow over the coming months."

"You may need more than hope, Katherine, to get anyone to venture here. In fact, you may need a great deal more than hope," he said, holding the door for her.

With Callum gone, Katherine had instructed Mrs. Porter to prepare a light meal for the two of them.

Mrs. Porter was something of a romantic, and she'd taken advantage of the opportunity of Callum's absence to create an informal but cozy atmosphere in the parlor. Mr. Rawlins had lit a fire there, and then Mrs. Porter had laid out their dinner on a small mahogany table between two stuffed high-backed wingchairs.

Katherine did not miss the fact that her mother's silver candelabra had been placed in the center of the table, atop a fine Belgian lace cloth, and that Mrs. Porter had used Katrina's best china and silver to serve.

Katherine let him assist her to her chair, and waited until he was seated before she spoke again. "I presume you spoke of money. Is that correct? You believe I shall need a great deal of money with which to entice people into the Hollow?"

He frowned at the feminine napkin of pristine

white, edged with delicate lace, before placing it across his lap. He glanced up. "I think there is a very good possibility, yes. Shall we dine?"

Katherine unfolded her own napkin and took a forkful of tasty venison stew into her mouth. After a moment, she said, "My father was not destitute, Brau, so there should be no problem there. I should like to go into town soon myself and post a notice of inquiry for workers to help with the clearing of the fields."

Brau did not even deign to look up from his meal. "You shall do no such thing. The areas where one would need to place such notices are not fit for a woman to enter. Nor is the company of most who might respond to your inquiry, for that matter."

Katherine laid her fork aside and folded her hands in her lap. "I intend to see the fields turned and planted. All of them. We will need men to help us."

Brau leaned back in his chair, chewing thoughtfully while pinning her with an upbraiding stare. "Have you given a thought to what your dear, sweet mother might think of you, her only daughter, flitting into the ale houses and taverns along the docks? She would turn in her grave."

Katherine felt tears of anger rising up, and swallowed hard. She wondered if he would ever see her for herself or ever forget the shining example of virtue that was her mother, and just for once, look at her ... Katherine?

"Mother isn't here, Brau! Mother has been gone for ... for four years. She's not coming back, and ... and I'm not Katrina Van Brunt."

He arched a brow. "Indeed. But that is no reason for you to show such blatant disrespect for her memory and everything she taught you by forgetting your place in this world."

Katherine fought to control her rising temper. "I do

not forget my place. I am daughter and heir to Abraham Van Brunt, granddaughter to Baltus Van Tassel. Both my father and my grandfather sought to create a place of peace and prosperity in Sleepy Hollow, and I can do no less."

Brau retrieved his fork. "Yes, Katherine, but note, if you please, what you have said and what your words reveal. Both Brom and Baltus were *men*. Males fully grown and fully capable of attending to the hard work and mental effort of attending to such a goal. Tell me, Katherine, in all the time your mother was alive, did you ever see her attempt to meddle in your father's affairs?"

His words were quite belittling. In all Katherine's life, she'd never once seen or heard her mother speak of or turn a hand to anything outside what was considered proper work for a female. Still, her father and grandfather were no longer here, and as the last living Van Brunt, the responsibility of the welfare and wellbeing of Sleepy Hollow fell to her and her alone.

"Being a woman does not make me any less capable of thinking or engaging in manual labor."

Brau shook his head, refusing to listen to reason. "I do not wish to argue with you, Katherine. As I have said, such activities are best left to a man."

Katherine ground her teeth to keep from screaming in frustration, wondering why he couldn't see that she was no less capable of seeing to the needs and wants of the people of Sleepy Hollow than he. No matter how often she brought the subject to his attention, he remained stubbornly immovable on it. She sighed.

"Perhaps you are right, Brau," she conceded, knowing any effort to the contrary would be useless this night.

His eyes glinted with victory, and the corners of his lips turned up in a tiny but overly stiff smile. "Thank you, my dear."

"You may take the notices into TarryTown on my behalf," she said.

His smile vanished. "Merely distributing a few inquiries would not be the end of it, Katherine. One would need to conduct an interview with each man who showed an interest, provided anyone did show interest, considering the history of this place …"

Katherine leaned forward. "You may handle the interviews as well, Brau."

Brau sighed, and pushed back from the table. "And who then would you appoint to oversee the workmanship? To take care of discipline to ensure there were no slaggards who sought to cheat you of your father's coin?"

"I shall be happy to do so," she volunteered with a smile, but he was hearing none of it.

Pushing the heavy wingback chair away from the small table, he stood. "We'll speak no more of this, Katherine. I have said I shall do what I can for you in the Hollow, and that will be an end of it."

He came up beside her chair and held out his hand for her. "You've quite ruined your complexion with your anger. Run upstairs and put a cool cloth on your cheeks, and I shall have Mrs. Porter clear the meal away."

Katherine took his hand, and he helped her to her feet. With a hand to her lower back, he guided her toward the door. "When you return, we shall speak of more pleasant things."

He must have seen the sheen of tears in her eyes, for he turned her to face him, his expression now apologetic. "Come now, Katherine, none of that, please. You know I cannot bear to see you weep."

Katherine sniffed and nodded. "I'm sorry, I—"

"I only wish to help you do that which is expected of you, my dear. You are correct to realize the people of the Hollow will look to you now that your father is gone."

She gave him a suspicious glance, and he nodded. "Yes, Katherine. I do know that you are your father's heir, and you must know I would never think of asking you to relinquish that responsibility."

He sighed and lifted his hand to caress a loose tendril at her temple. "Katherine, dearest Katherine. My only desire is to see you aptly portray that exalted role which is your rightful duty, as your mother's daughter and your father's heir – that of a serenely dignified lady who knows her status and place. Surely you, of all people, can see that?"

Katherine sniffled again and nodded. "Yes, I ... I understand. Thank you."

He offered a tender smile. "Good. You're quite welcome. Now, do go and refresh yourself, my dear. I shall be waiting here when you come down."

* * * *

Riding away from the Van Brunt manor some time later, Brau kicked his mount to a furious pace, hoping the ride would chase away some of his anger and frustration with Katherine and her ridiculous notion to try to rebuild Sleepy Hollow to the prosperity it had known in her grandfather's day.

He knew her interest in restoring the tiny, near-deserted village had become a kind of passion within her now that her father was gone, and he dearly hoped that passion would recede quickly for he had no intention of staying in Sleepy Hollow after they were wed. He intended to live in the city, enjoying the lifestyle of a gentleman of great wealth and leisure, and he would not let her feminine whims sway him from the course he'd mapped out of his future long ago – the day he had discovered the Witch of the Western Wood.

Racing at breakneck speed through the woods along the eerie, darkened roads of Sleepy Hollow, Brau cursed the man who had died before properly making him his heir, as Katherine's soon-to-be husband. He cursed the bewitchingly beautiful girl who dared attempt to change the things he'd carefully but cautiously set into motion several years ago, and finally, he cursed his own neglect, for he had all but forgotten the tenderness of Katherine's youth would practically demand he carry out a careful and diligent courtship if he ever hoped to win her heart and hand ... and win it he would, for now there was no alternate course.

With Brom dead, the only avenue left to him to gain control of Sleepy Hollow was through marriage to Katherine Van Brunt.

Or murder.

Knowing as he did that Katherine would never relinquish hold of the Hollow as long as she yet lived, Brau knew he would do whatever it took to see the two of them wed.

Failing that—

No, he would *not* fail. He could not.

There was simply too much at stake.

Chapter 4

Katherine struggled to push away the burned timber, a heavy beam that had fallen across the chimney and destroyed what might have been salvaged of the fireplace, but it would not budge. She wiped her hand across her cheek, pushing the tendrils of hair that had escaped their moorings away from her eyes, and walked around the beam to attempt to pry it loose from a different angle.

"Stop that at once!"

With a jerk, Katherine turned at Brau's brusque command. He sat astride his chestnut mount, his gaze one of absolute authority. "Remove yourself from that rubble before it comes crashing down around you. Have you no sense at all, Katherine? What if you had managed to move the beam and were crushed beneath it?"

His flawless dismount gave testament to his horsemanship. The swiftness with which he vaulted himself onto the ruined and broken bits of burned and splintered oak that had once been a floor gave Katherine a bit of a fright. A tiny squeak of surprise burst from her lips, but she did not abandon her goal despite the unpleasant look he gave her.

"It must be moved, Brau. There is no way to clear the rest of these fallen timbers and stone until this one," she said as she gave it a hardy shove, "has been displaced."

Without a word, he crossed to her side and turned her. "Look at your gown, Katherine. It is surely ruined from the smut and grime you've been crawling about in. Go home. I will dislodge the beam and join you shortly."

She frowned. "But I would like to help. There is much to be removed, and—"

He slid his hands beneath her arms and settled her on the ground beside the ruined farmhouse. "Absolutely not. You will do as I've said, Katherine, and without another word, if you please."

Brau had turned and was removing his gloves in preparation for the odious task of repositioning the fallen beam, when Callum came galloping into sight. He came to a stop near the burned hull and looked askance at Katherine.

"Well, the messenger returns," Brau drawled. "Were you successful?"

Callum's gaze slid quickly to Katherine, who hurried to Isolde's side. She pulled her cloak from its resting place across Isolde's saddle, where she'd lain it before scrambling onto the burned out structure earlier and shook it out.

"I mentioned that you'd ridden into town to spread word of the availability now that the Von Groot place is no longer occupied," she hastened to explain, letting him know with raised brow and a nod he should not mention anything beyond that. The soft material of her cape swirled before settling across her shoulders.

Callum dipped his head, giving the barest of nods. "Aye. There was a family just come into town when I arrived. They appeared to be a bit down on their luck, and I felt perhaps they'd be interested in the Von Groot place. The gentleman, goes by the name of Carter Wesley, says he's somewhat lacking in skills, but a swift learner."

Katherine nodded and turned her attention back to Brau, who had shifted the beam she couldn't budge at all. He gave it a shove, and it toppled onto the floorboards, unsettling both loose stone and charred timber when it fell. It came to rest with a resounding crash.

Katherine jumped, causing Isolde to stamp her feet and whicker nervously. Katherine stroked the animal's nose and whispered consolingly. "Shhh. It's okay, girl. Just a fright."

Her gaze went back to Callum. "So, this gentleman and his family, they will be coming to the Hollow?"

Callum nodded. "When last I spoke to them, both Master Wesley and his missus indicated that to be their intent."

He paused and Katherine looked at him hard. With a little half smile twisting his lips, he offered an almost imperceptible nod in answer to her unspoken question. "I believe you should expect someone within the week."

Swept with a sense of hope and a feeling of excitement, Katherine smiled. Icharus Crane would soon return to Sleepy Hollow, and she suddenly wished he were there already. Indeed, she'd thought of little else these past days but his return.

From his vantage point above the couple on the ground, Brau seemed to notice the secretive looks and nods between Callum and Katherine, but chose to say nothing of it. Instead, his brows rose.

"In that case, it appears I was wrong. Perhaps there are still a few brave souls willing to overlook the Witch's curse and the ominous threat of the Hessian's midnight cadavers to come into Sleepy Hollow after all."

His words cut right through the joy of the moment

for Katherine, bringing back her frustrations from years upon years of hearing every harsh deed or action that occurred within the Hollow blamed on either the Hessian or the elusive 'Witch of the Western Wood,' who had supposedly laid a curse upon Sleepy Hollow many, many years ago.

She turned on him now with a scowl and a disgusted, heartfelt sigh and pinned him with her narrowed gaze. "Braughton Van Ripper, you are well aware there is no curse on Sleepy Hollow."

He merely arched a brow, his expression dubious.

His apparent skepticism set Katherine's temper to boiling. He jumped the short distance from the ruins of the farmhouse to the ground and she rounded on him, hands curled into fists. She propped one on each hip and her chin came up defiantly.

"You know it was not the working of a curse that called in my grandfather, Baltus Van Tassel's, life. And it was simply the working of nature that my mother, God rest her, wasn't strong enough to carry her first child."

It frustrated her to no end that her beloved home was thought some evil place to be avoided. The endless whispers bandied about to and fro, between both foe and friend alike – indeed by anyone who merely rode through the area! – of the Witch and the Headless Horseman sorely tried her temper. For Brau, whom she believed to be a dear friend, to perpetrate and give credence to such nonsense cut her to the marrow of her bones.

She tossed her head, flinging away the riotous curls with which the early breeze was wont to cover her vision and raised her hand to scold, her finger slicing in angry strokes across the air like the Hessian's devilish blade.

"Four summers ago 'twas a fever that came to the Hollow and took my mother and her unborn child – as well as most of the townsfolk who resided here at the time. You were here, Brau. You yourself are a survivor of that dreadful outbreak, so henceforth I'll not hear you speak otherwise," she demanded.

Callum had straightened in his seat and was watching her vent in tirade, his expression one of silent awe.

Katherine had paid neither man but little heed in her need to vent her turmoil. She continued. "And certainly there was no curse at work when the Lord decided just days ago, in his infinite wisdom, to free my father from his grief and bring him to my mother's side in eternal sleep!"

She glared at Brau, but he avoided her gaze, ignoring her vexation.

"So you say," he said, and silently offered his hand to help her mount Isolde for the ride home.

Later that afternoon, Brau left her to her sewing to speak with John Tanner about some matter of which he divulged no detail. It was during his absence Katherine heard heavy footsteps at the front entrance.

Icharus Crane had returned.

* * * *

Icharus climbed the front steps of the Van Brunt manor and raised a gloved fist to knock upon the heavy oak door. It immediately opened, and he stared, fascinated. A woman stared back at him – a woman fully grown.

Katherine Van Brunt.

His mind drifted to the many times he had thought of her over the past few days, remembering the fall of her hair, the sparkle in her eyes and how it had seemed to dim whenever Master Van Ripper addressed her directly. There were too many of those moments for his peace of mind, he thought. She'd invaded his thoughts far too frequently for his liking.

59

Standing before her now, he noted how her dark hair had been pulled back at the sides and twisted into an intricate knot, leaving the back to fall in a charmingly disarrayed spill of tiny curls to her hips.

Beneath his attentive gaze her eyes, each crowned by a delicate slash of brow the color of warm chocolate and fringed by softly curled lashes of the same hue, sparkled. Her cheekbones, high and smooth, were flushed. Her neck, slender and graceful in its own right, was made to look more so by the strand of tiny pearls resting demurely against the creamy skin of her throat, and he wondered how that skin would taste should he lean forward and press a kiss there.

His gaze drifted downward, noting how her gown, an elegant, feminine creation the color of a summer sky, brought out the deep midnight blue of her eyes and also gave perfect complement to her breasts. The sleeves, long and full, ended in a delicate fall of lace-edged ruffles, revealing small wrists and delicately formed hands. From there, the gown fitted snugly, its heavy skirts disclosing the slimness of her waist before falling in graceful folds to the floor.

Icharus imagined she'd have long, slender legs beneath those skirts, and wondered how they would feel entwined with his own. He envisioned himself running his hands from the top of her hips, down across her thighs in pure male appreciation, pictured his hands curling gently around her trim calves and delicate ankles before travelling upward once more.

"Master Crane, you've arrived!"

Her voice, equally breathless and excited, was a combination he found quite sensual, and Icharus felt the tug of desire low in his gut.

There was simply no denying Katherine Van Brunt was a very lovely woman.

Fighting the sudden heat thrumming through his

body, Icharus forced his gaze to meet hers. "Your man said you wished to discuss a matter most urgent."

A fact he'd do well to remember, he thought, rather than allowing his mind to be carried away with lustful thoughts of his host ensconced in his bed, naked and writhing beneath him. He chastened his own lack of control and cleared his throat a bit gruffly. "Shall I come inside, Mistress Van Brunt?"

Katherine stepped aside. "Yes, of course. We'll talk in my father's study."

Icharus waited for her just inside the door, and then followed behind her to the room she'd indicated, his lurid gaze admiring the swing of her skirts all the while. His thoughts otherwise occupied, he was more than a little surprised when she closed the door and turned the key in the lock. His brow arched high.

"That's a little daring, don't you think? Locking the two of us in here, alone?"

Katherine looked confused. "Privacy is necessary in this instance, Master Crane, and please lower your voice. I shouldn't want anyone to overhear our conversation."

She flitted about the study, struggling to draw the heavy, brocade drapes across the wide windows overlooking the valley. Icharus took advantage of the opportunity her actions afforded, admiring how the fabric of her dress stretched taut across her breasts and against the curve of her side each time she did so.

"As you wish, Mistress," he said, his voice lower now. "I am at your disposal."

Katherine flicked a glance in his direction before continuing her mission to seal them from view of the outside world. When the last of the large windows was covered, Katherine hurried to her father's desk and opened a drawer there. From it, she withdrew a sheaf of papers and held them clutched tightly between her fingers. "I paid a visit to Notary Vandercleef the morning you left Sleepy Hollow, as you suggested. You were right, Master Crane."

Icharus's heartbeat slowed to a heavy thump, and all thoughts of a lustful nature evaporated immediately. His gaze flew to hers. "Dare I hope you're speaking of the promise between your father and mine, Mistress Van Brunt?"

She nodded. Gesturing with the packet she held, she said, "Everything is in order, duly assigned and notarized. Your father ... no, as his heir that means you, Icharus Crane, are indeed the sole owner of the parcel of land bordering the Hollow beyond the Western Wood."

Icharus could not contain his feelings of relief and triumph. He gave vent to the emotions and a full-throated, joyously victorious laugh escaped. He almost reached for her, his intention to swing her about the room in a dance of elation until he realized she had made no move to relinquish the documents she held. Instead, she all but crushed the packet in her grip.

He frowned. "And the papers you now hold, the legal certificates I require as proof – you have no intention of surrendering them into my care, do you, Mistress Van Brunt?"

She shook her head. "No. Yes, I ... that is, yes, it is my full intention to surrender to you all that is rightfully yours, but ..."

Katherine crossed to the fire, still holding the packet of documents close. She closed her eyes, debating the merit of what she was about to do. Coming to a decision, she turned to stare at him, her pleading gaze imploring him to understand.

"Master Crane, I find that I cannot, in all conscience, withhold that which rightfully belongs to you, and the documents I now hold absolutely do belong in your care," she said, her voice low, husky with emotion. He could see the sheen of unshed tears in her eyes as she continued. "But I also cannot deny my responsibility to my father and grandfather's memory to do what I can to restore the Van Tassel legacy ... to restore and maintain something worthy of passing on to future generations."

Icharus stiffened, anger stealing over him.

"How dare you. How dare you sit there, staring at me with a look of innocent pleading in your gaze while you seek to deprive me of that which—"

"No!" The word was a harsh whisper. "No, I have no wish to keep anything from you, Master Crane. What I desire ..." Icharus pinned her with a glare, and she drew in a deep, steadying breath. "What I desire is your promise, Master Crane, and nothing more. I should like you to promise that you will help me."

"And if I should help you, Mistress Van Brunt, you will relinquish the documents to me once I have completed whatever task you should deem worthy?"

Katherine stood and crossed the room to face him. She stood so close he could to feel the very heat of her. "No. I will give you all that you have come for the instant you give your word you will assist me in my quest to restore Sleepy Hollow to its former dignity."

When he said nothing more, she continued.

"This parchment in my hand gives you everything you've worked to have, and your father before you," she reminded him. "But what of me? The legacy borne of my grandfather and nurtured by my father until the sickness overcame him and he could do no more ... it all but lies in ruin. Please, Icharus. Help me."

Still fighting the anger that filled him moments before, Icharus said, "What of Master Van Ripper, your benevolent protector? Let him help you."

"Brau will not help me." Katherine left him and went to sit on the sofa, her head lowered in defeat.

She placed the packet of certificates and letters on

the seat beside her. "Here is what you came for, Master Crane. Take them. Take them and leave me be."

Though his first thought had been to take the papers and walk away, Icharus's conscious prodded him. Had it not been for the Van Brunts, he and his family might be in much poorer circumstances today. Indeed, had it not been for Brom, his own father might have gone off to become a complete wastrel, letting his irrational fears conquer his spirit of survival for the rest of his life.

Besides, if you help her, you'll have the satisfaction of seeing Braughton Van Ripper proved wrong.

Just now, seeing Katherine as she was with her head bent while tears of defeat ran in slow rivulets, he knew any triumph over that man's gloating superiority would feel magnificent.

"I promise."

Katherine's head snapped up. "What did you say?"

Icharus sighed. "I said I promise to help you in every way I can to restore Sleepy Hollow, Katherine Van Brunt. Is that not what you wished to hear?"

The smile that spread across her face was breathtaking.

"Thank you," she whispered. She crossed the room, took both his hands in her own, and gave them a tight squeeze of gratitude before she raised herself up on her tiptoes and placed a happy little kiss on his cheek. "Thank you so much, Master Crane. I shall endeavor to make your sacrifice worthwhile."

Icharus was enchanted by the joyous sparkle in her eyes, by the jubilant smile on her lips, and a bit thoughtless due to the mash of his own emotions vying for place within.

"Icharus. Call me Icharus," he said, an instant before his lips touched hers. His arms had already closed around her, pulling her close while his head dipped low, his only thought that of how badly he'd yearned to know the taste of her these past days.

* * * *

Surprised to find herself suddenly wrapped in his embrace, Katherine pulled back the tiniest bit, her gaze searching his, confused, questioning.

Never had she been held thusly by a man. Brau often offered a familial kiss on the cheek or brow, but he never took her into his arms as Icharus had.

And he was touching her, holding her.

Kissing her.

An odd sensation unfurled within her stomach, and Katherine slowly relaxed in his embrace. His arms tightened in response and his lips touched hers once more, softly, gliding over her own with the barest of pressure.

Her pulse skittered.

He is so warm, and his embrace so comforting and yet ...

Unsure how to describe the riot of unusual sensations rapidly spreading through her entire body, Katherine let her eyelids drift downward and edged closer, enjoying the feelings he roused within her just by holding her.

So this *is a lover's embrace.* She realized she was enjoying it very much.

Cautiously, curiously, she kissed him back, mimicking the movements his lips had made against hers.

He groaned, a low, masculine sound from deep in his throat, and Katherine jerked from his embrace, certain she'd hurt him somehow, for he'd sounded as if he were in pain.

"I'm sorry, I ..." He'd closed his eyes, and she noticed his hands were now clenched at his sides. Her gaze flew upward. "I've hurt you …"

His eyes opened, and Katherine noticed there was no dull glint of pain there. Rather, he looked a bit drowsy. Confusion swept through her.

He shook his head, and his lips turned up in a sardonic grin. "Nay, do not be sorry. I am unhurt. You kiss so sweetly, Mistress Katherine, but I wonder …"

Katherine peered up at him. "You wonder … what … Master Crane?"

Icharus grinned. "When you were pleading your cause so passionately moments ago, you called me *Icharus*, yet when the discussion turns to you, to your very womanly and very intriguing inner passions and my suspicion that they've long laid dormant and un-awakened inside you, you revert to the formal *Master Crane*. Why is that?"

Her eyes widened. "*Master Crane*, I think we should not speak of such things—"

Icharus's brows rose. "We should feel them, think them, but not speak of them? Why ever not, *Mistress Van Brunt?*"

Her brow furrowed, and she made to turn away. " 'Tis … indecent."

Icharus reached out and ran his hand along her arm, halting her with his touch. His palm caressed her from shoulder to wrist. Heat followed, and an unfamiliar yearning coursed through her.

"Mistress Van Brunt, *Katherine*, I must disagree. There is nothing indecent about a man who is otherwise unengaged sharing a kiss with a desirable woman."

Katherine's gaze met his, and then skittered uncomfortably away. A prick of hurt stabbed her. She knew he was lying. If she were in any way attractive to men, she'd have suitors vying for her hand, would she not? There were none.

"I am not a desirable woman."

He touched her once more, and she could not keep her gaze from straying back to his when he pulled her close once more.

"But you are, Katherine," he said, and he leaned down to kiss her again, and again, each of his words punctuated by another kiss. "Most ... definitely ... desirable."

She pulled away.

"Master Crane, we should return to the subject at hand ... there ..." She paused.

His kisses had quite unsettled her, and she found merely drawing an even breath difficult at this moment. Pulling air into her lungs, she moved to the desk once more, putting a bit of space between them. "There are matters we must yet discuss."

When he seemed about to continue, Katherine shook her head. She could feel the hot stain of a blush on her cheeks and was almost certain she would burst into flames if he dared kiss her again. "Please. I am ... unused to such conversation. Let us forget it."

* * * *

Icharus would have heartily loved to ignore her protests, and at the moment his body demanded he simply pull her close and show her just how desirable he found her to be. But there was something in her voice, some indecipherable hurt in her gaze that stopped him. He sighed. "Very well. What are these other matters we need to discuss, Mistress Van Brunt?"

She gestured to the papers on the sofa where she'd left them. "My father went to great lengths to preserve those documents ... secreting them away with the command they never be revealed until his death."

Icharus frowned. "Why?"

Katherine turned to face him. "Because you aren't

the only one who desires to possess them. There are others, some who my father fears may even resort to committing heinous crimes in order to lay hands upon them."

Icharus shrugged. "And again I ask, why?"

Katherine peered at him questioningly. "Something lies within the boundaries of your property that someone desperately desires to have, I suppose. Do you know what that could be?"

* * * *

It was decided that Icharus would stay at the Van Brunt manor for the night. At supper, Katherine would inform Brau she had sent Callum to plead her case with Icharus concerning her desire to build the Hollow up once more, and had convinced Icharus to join her, to aid her in the restoration of Sleepy Hollow. He would act as her advisor and would also oversee the workmen who came into the Hollow, thus relieving Brau of the responsibility.

Katherine and Icharus had agreed to keep quiet about the documents she'd given him. Her father's fears might well be something or just as easily nothing and quite unfounded, but Icharus and Katherine both agreed there was no need asking for trouble if it could be avoided.

Still, she could not hide her nervousness when they all sat together at the table later that evening.

"I've asked Master Crane to join us for supper because I have an announcement to make," she said, her fingers busily twisting her napkin in her lap all the while.

Brau's virulent gaze narrowed on her, and she drew herself up. Her chin rose defensively. "I've asked Icharus to stay in Sleepy Hollow for a while, to act as my advisor and oversee the work to be done here over the coming months, and he has agreed."

She watched his gaze flicker to Icharus, and then come to rest almost nonchalantly on the meal before him. "Indeed? And may I ask what was offered to secure his agreement? Surely it must have been something of immense value or importance, for anyone with eyes to see knows the restoration of Sleepy Hollow to the state in which our Katherine hopes to see it rise will be tantamount to performing a bloody miracle."

Katherine's gaze flew to Icharus.

He smiled, and then turned his attention to slicing the roasted venison on his plate. He considered the question for a moment, and then he nodded, a mischievous smile curving his lips. "Immense value. Yes, I quite think Mistress Van Brunt's offer was just that. One of … immense value."

Callum began to cough, and Katherine turned to him with a frown. "Are you quite all right, Callum?"

He nodded, but continued to cough for a moment. When he'd gained control and was able to breathe a bit normally once more, he croaked, "It was the water."

She thought she heard Icharus chuckle, but couldn't be sure. Brau had turned the full chill of his glare on him, and Katherine feared he might be moved to violence, such was the fury she saw there.

Then he smiled.

It was a forced smile, and offered upon tightly drawn lips, but a smile nonetheless. She released a pent-up breath.

"In that case, I should be glad to aid you in whatever manner I may," he said, but Katherine could clearly sense his displeasure. Not only that, his offer of assistance was unmistakably lacking in sincerity.

Katherine watched the cloud come over Brau's face. She could tell he was trying to contain his anger, but he barely managed.

* * * *

He knew, somewhere, somehow, Katherine had found the proof Icharus so desperately needed. Only the promise of title to the land he coveted would have brought him back here, Brau was certain. That meant the documents were here in Van Brunt manor.

... but where?

Keeping his attention focused on his meal in order to hide his anger, it barely registered in Brau's thoughts that Icharus had begun to speak of his plans to aid Katherine in her endeavor.

"Katherine has said she would like to begin by removing the rabble of several old farmhouses that were burned to rid the Hollow of the dread disease that swept through some years ago. I must return to Wake Grove and set things in order there, but the clearing of those burned-out hulls will be my first order of business upon my return."

Katherine's eyes misted. "Father had planned to do much the same before he too fell ill."

Brau turned a sympathetic gaze her way. "I would not want these doings to upset you, my dear."

She shook her head. "No. Quite the contrary actually. I am happy beyond measure to see his intentions met, at last."

Brau's brow raised. "Those intentions have yet to be met, still, but it gladdens my heart to know you are not disturbed by the thought of another stepping in where your father hoped to be."

A frown marred her brow. "I do not think Father would mind in the least, do you? He was always pleased to see a good man step up to any worthy task, and even you yourself have said the saving of Sleepy Hollow is nigh beyond mortal intervention."

He offered a thin smile. "So I have. Well, if you've finished your meal, Katherine, I would like to speak with you in the parlor ... privately, if you please."

He watched her gaze slide to Icharus before she tipped her head in a hesitant nod.

Chapter 5

In the parlor, Katherine elected to stand near the windows. She'd always enjoyed looking out over the moonlit fields, and this evening was no different. Only a few stars peeked from the dark curtain of the sky, but those that did sparkled brightly. "It is so lovely, is it not?"

"Indeed," he replied, but when she glanced his way, she found him looking at her rather than the night sky beyond the thick-paned glass.

His intense gaze unnerved her. She felt a chill, and brought her hands up to chafe some warmth into her arms.

"You wished to speak with me, Brau? I know you offered to help where you could in the Hollow, and that you aren't thrilled with me for requesting Master Crane's assistance, though I must confess I thought you'd be happy. The responsibilities you belabored a few nights past now will not fall upon your shoulders."

Brau peered at her. "What did you promise him, Katherine? And please tell me it was not an offer of your charms, for I find I shall be quite fearsome to learn of it."

Katherine's eyes widened. "Braughton Van Ripper! How dare you even think such vulgarities! I—"

He stepped forward and caught her by the arms. "Then he did not take liberties with you?"

She scowled. "Of course not! Why would he?"

His gaze darkened. "You are a very beautiful woman, Katherine mine. I must confess that, upon further consideration, I should think it quite odd if he did not at least try."

His fingers loosened their grip on her upper arms, and he slid them downward in a caress. "Forgive me, my dear. With your father's death, and then all this nonsense about a long-lost agreement with the elder Crane and your hopes of restoring Sleepy Hollow while I can own up to but slim resources …"

Katherine nodded and pulled away from his touch. "I understand, Brau. You have done what you could for the Van Brunts over the years, and I do appreciate the sacrifices you have made on our behalf—"

Brau shushed her. "On your behalf, Katherine. It has only ever been my desire for you to have all that is best for you."

He lifted his hand and made a show of examining his nails a bit peevishly.

Like a petulant child.

"I do admit to being a bit peaked by your blatant disregard for my wishes in this matter, but I can understand your need to continue carrying the torch your father carried."

Carry the torch? He made her sound like some zealot in search of impossibility. He stepped close once more, and his hand came out to brush against her cheek. It was all she could do to keep from flinching away from his touch. He lifted her chin to better gaze into her eyes.

"If the young Master Crane thinks he is able to do that which I have not been, I shall endeavor to further his

– and your – cause as much as I can, if that is what makes you happy."

She nodded. "It does, Brau."

He dipped his head in acknowledgement. "Very well. I shall see myself out then. Pleasant dreams, Katherine."

He bent to give her the customary kiss on the cheek before taking his leave, or so she thought. When his lips, cool and hard, pressed against hers, she pulled quickly away. "Brau, please!"

Lifting his head, he peered at her. "My apologies. I had hoped you were now ready to move our relationship further, but perhaps you need a bit of time. With the recentness of your father's passing ... I should have better control of my desires. Good night, my dear." He turned to leave.

He made his way to the door where Mr. Rawlins was waiting to show him out.

Inside the parlor, Katherine stayed where she was, somewhat stunned. A deep frown puckered her brow.

Our relationship? There was none of which to speak.

She remembered Callum's words to her a few days past, that Brau thought to marry her, and shook her head. For a man harboring thoughts of matrimony, Brau had been especially distant and cool with the supposed object of his affection these past years.

In a bit of wonder, she lifted her hand and pressed her fingers against her lips, recounting the events of the day. Two men, both insisting they each found her beautiful, two kisses, and both in the same day. Katherine found it exceedingly odd, considering not one male aside of her father had ever said as much to her before. Indeed, she found such declarations quite impossible to believe.

Now that Brau had gone, Katherine couldn't help

but compare his kiss with the one Icharus had given her this morning … and she discovered there simply was no comparison.

Brau's touch had chilled her, while Icharus's had filled her with heat. Brau's kiss left her cold and unmoved, but such had definitely not been the case while she had stood in the circle of Icharus Crane's arms in her father's study. No, for she had practically melted in his embrace, much to her confusion and embarrassment.

What came over me that I had behaved so brazenly with a man I barely know?

Having met Icharus Crane barely a week previously, she could not confess to knowing him at all. Indeed, he was a complete stranger.

Did Father's death imbalance me so I've become a wanton?

Heat filled her cheeks, and she pressed her fingers to her forehead.

"Does your head pain you, Katherine?" Callum entered the room. He crossed to prod at the fire while Icharus, waiting in the doorway, looked quite discomfited.

Katherine snatched her fingers away. "No, my head is fine, thank you. Shall we sit, gentlemen?" She turned to Icharus, motioned for him to join her on the settee. "Perhaps you'd like to discuss some of your plans for Sleepy Hollow with Callum."

Callum had turned from the fire, and he was now glancing between her and Icharus. "Master Van Brunt had intended to clear away those burned bits of rabble only weeks after he gave the order for the houses to be torched. Then the sickness took him, and …" He broke off.

At her urging, Icharus made his way into the room and he, too, crossed to the fire, joining Callum there before saying, "Life has ways of stopping a man from doing that what he feels he must, to be sure. As I have said, I agree with Brom. The ruins must be taken down. Once they are cleared, we can build anew, but first, however, there are fences to be mended and repairs to be made elsewhere in the Hollow."

He looked at Katherine, his gaze both open and questioning. "Katherine will ride with me tomorrow so I may assess all that needs be done, and when I return … I hope you are prepared for a lean but busy winter, my friend."

Callum's gaze sought Katherine's, surprise evident in the curve of his brow. "Van Ripper will perish on the spot does he learn of it." He turned to Icharus. "Sir, I can well understand how difficult it often is to refuse the pleas of a lovely lady, and I can certainly imagine how Katherine might have cajoled and pestered you until you agreed to allow her to come along. I have no doubt that she even refused to allow you take a step through the Hollow were she not at your side, but—"

Icharus shook his head. "She did no such thing. I invited her to ride with me, the same as I now invite you to join us, Master Mather. Sleepy Hollow is your home. Who better to point out those things requiring utmost urgency and those which may be left for a later date?"

Glancing her way, Icharus tipped his head, acknowledging her obvious pleasure in his decision.

Callum's brows rose high in wonder for a moment, after which he turned to Icharus and offered his hand. "Call me Callum, sir, and I'd be delighted to join you. When do we leave?"

Katherine spoke up. "At first light, of course. Will you be fit to rise at such an early hour, or should I send Mrs. Porter down with Isha's bell again?" she teased.

* * * *

"We're going to need a great deal of timber."

With morning and most of the afternoon gone, Icharus, Katherine, and Callum sat upon their horses high on a ridge overlooking the slumberous village. Though Icharus had spent much of the day with his attention on the lovely Mistress Van Brunt rather than the many tasks both she and Callum pointed out, there was no denying the magnitude of work to be done.

Of the old farmhouses that had not been burned on Brom's orders, two were in desperate need of repairs while the third, he had ordered unfit for even that. It would need to be pulled down and rebuilt along with the charred remains of the others. Having been informed of the new family coming in soon, Icharus declared those homes that were repairable should first be seen to.

The homes which had been burned due to the fever that had stricken so many of Sleepy Hollow's residents in its passing would have to be rebuilt, and swiftly. The barn needed repairs. A large section of shingles was missing from the roof, and inside, there was damage from the many rains that had swept through over the past few years.

Many of the livestock pens had fallen to disrepair and were deemed unfit for use until they had been mended. Then there were the fields, which were in dire need of clearing and turning, and the orchards also were in need of clearing and pruning. Seed and livestock would need to be purchased. Equipment would require repairs.

Icharus looked about, feeling the exhilarating rush of challenge sweep through him.

Not one able body will be allowed to sit laggard this winter.

Everyone who could work would do so, even if he had to go into town to bring in others. Surely there would be some who were willing to work for a decent wage.

His gaze drifting over the Hollow below him, Icharus determined that with the coming of spring, Sleepy Hollow would show definite signs of growth and rebirth. He would accept nothing less.

Putting his heels to his horse's flanks, Icharus started forward, leaving Katherine and Callum to follow.

"I'll speak with John Tanner before I leave and have him begin to harvest timber from the forest there." He gestured with a nod toward the one place even Katherine feared to wander.

She stared at him, uncertain. "You mean to harvest the needed timber from the Western Woods?"

"Nay, we cannot. The Witch ..." Callum called from behind.

Icharus snorted. "Witch? You can't really expect me to believe there is truly a witch living in yon wood, can you, Master Mather?"

When no answer was forthcoming, Icharus shook his head, amazed by the tight grip of superstition that still seemed to hold the people of Sleepy Hollow in its grasp, even after all these years.

He pointed toward the forest. "For the past twenty-three years I have dwelt just on the other side, and in all that time there's been no sign of witchery in Wake Grove. Why? Because there is no such thing as a witch who dwells within those woods, practicing dark spells and mumbling curses upon the land. 'Tis but a childhood terror used by parents to frighten their children into staying out of the wood before they were old enough to find their way about."

Callum was quiet for a moment, obviously pondering the question and the apparent proof Icharus provided to rebut his belief in a being living deep in the heart of the Western Wood.

"Perhaps there is not," he answered after a time,

"but I must caution you ... the people of this village, few that there are who remain, certainly *do* believe it. They will most assuredly believe any attempt made by you to remove the trees from the Witch's lair will be met with disaster of some sort, mark my words."

Icharus nodded, taking heed of the young man's warning. "We shall deal with any such crisis only if and when it arrives. Until then, we harvest the timber. Agreed?"

Katherine urged her mount alongside Icharus's and gestured to the Bleeker's house just ahead. "There is John now. We may as well let him know our intention."

* * * *

Perched atop his wagon, having brought out a wagonload of wood for the Bleeker's hearth, John and his son Dehann were chatting with the schoolmaster and Brau.

After exchanging hellos, John peered at Icharus. "Braughton tells us you'll be staying in the Hollow for a bit?"

Icharus inclined his head. "Yes. At the request of Mistress Van Brunt, I will be overseeing quite a bit of restoration here. We plan to begin by harvesting timber from the forest there." He gestured toward the wood.

Katherine noticed a sudden pallor on the men's faces. The schoolmaster crossed himself and whispered a silent prayer.

John swung his gaze to her. "You have agreed to this?"

"Of course. We will need wood for construction and for repairs."

He shook his head in refusal. "Nay, we'll get the timber elsewhere. There," he said, pointing east to a stand of trees that could not be more than ten years old, if that.

Icharus spoke up. "The others are too young, too small. The trees in the Western Woods will provide the best timber for our needs. There is no reason to harvest the others before they are ready when there are so many ripe for the taking there."

In the instant before he looked away and swore beneath his breath, Katherine caught a glimpse of both fear and frustration in John's gaze. He shook his head in refusal. " 'Tis a full-out invitation to madness, and I'll have no part of it. No one dares venture into the Western Wood, Katherine. Not even you. I beg you recall the reason …"

Katherine flushed. He was right. She had never ventured too close for fear of the Witch. "You are right. I have avoided the Western Wood, the same as all of you, but no more. I refuse to live in unreasoned dread of some mythical witch or to believe in the possibility of her laying curses upon us for taking down a few trees. The village is dying, John! Even you can see that. Have you no wish to see it alive and flourishing once more?"

A smirk settled across Brau's features. "You see? I've told you she believes the place to be sentient. The madness begins …"

Katherine glared at him. "There is no madness in one's natural inclination to survive, Brau. I wish to see Sleepy Hollow become thriving and prosperous again – both the land and the people who live here. Those trees will be used to repair our homes and to further ensure our livelihood. We stand to gain much by laying aside our unsupported fears long enough to see reason."

She turned her attention back to John. "We need those trees, John," she implored.

"Katherine is right," Callum offered. "Don't be foolish, gentlemen. Harvesting the wood from the forest here is our best recourse, as doing so will not put a drain on Sleepy Hollow finances. We can begin immediately to make the much needed repairs."

"And to rebuild," Katherine added, and Icharus nodded his agreement.

"The sooner we get those homes in livable condition, the better," she said. Her mood, turned melancholy, revealed itself in her next words, spoken quietly but heard by all. "If we do not rebuild, soon there will be no Sleepy Hollow."

John sighed. "You're set on this? No matter the consequences?"

She nodded. "I know of no better alternative."

He looked away. "Very well. We shall begin harvesting on the morrow. Remember, however, that I have strong reservations against it."

Katherine nodded and smiled. "Fear not, John. Only good can come of this. You'll see."

His brows rose and he tilted his head, nodding in uncertain acknowledgement. "I hope you are right."

Assured of the man's compliance with both Katherine's and his wishes, Icharus bid the small group farewell, and set his course for home.

Brau had held his silence throughout their discussion for the most part, but now as the three of them rode toward Van Brunt manor, he warned Katherine of the insanity of her plan.

"Harvest the Western Wood, Katherine? Have you any idea of the possible repercussions of such an act? The people will think you've made a pact with the Devil, to be sure. Tell me this was not your inspiration …"

Katherine kept her gaze lowered. "No, it was not, but it is a practical plan. Where else are we to get the needed timber for reconstructing the homes and fences and …"

He slanted a searching, thoughtful look in her direction. He nodded. "Crane then. I thought as much."

Brau fell silent, lost in thought, his gaze speculative. After a moment, he said, "Perhaps you should caution Master Crane to have a care of those tasks he thinks to undertake here, Katherine. As you are well aware, Sleepy Hollow has a way of preserving what it holds dear ... no matter the cost."

* * * *

With Callum assisting John and Dehann with the cutting and culling of timber, and Brau away in the city, Katherine busied herself with the day-to-day tasks of running a household.

She spent a portion of each morning sewing quilts for the new family who were due to arrive at any time and her afternoons seeing to the ills and aches of the people in the village. If she was made aware of any need, Katherine put forth her best effort to see it met.

It was during one such afternoon she learned of the Vandercleef's happy news. After many years of thinking herself barren, Mary Vandercleef had recently conceived. Come summer, she and Heinrick would welcome their first child into the world, at last.

Delighted over their announcement, Katherine declared there should be a celebration to commemorate the coming addition to the Vandercleef family. It was decided that everyone would assemble at the church three nights hence to share in the happiness and give well-wishes all 'round to the newly blessed couple.

The days that followed her declaration were filled with preparations. Katherine and Mrs. Porter bustled about, making ready for the coming frolic.

Between assisting Mrs. Porter with the baking of sweets and cooking several dishes to bring to the church, and spending a portion of each day making the old Von Groot house ready for the new family, and keeping up with both Callum's and her own mending and laundry, Katherine had little time to fret over the people's superstitions regarding the harvesting of the Western Wood and their possible reactions to her and Icharus's somewhat reckless decision.

Busy though she was, Katherine was unable, however, to keep her thoughts from wandering to the intriguing enigma of Icarus Crane. During the daylight hours, she would ponder quite seriously how he'd never once shunned her thoughts and ideas regarding the restoration of Sleepy Hollow.

He didn't seem to mind at all that she was making decisions and offering suggestions as a woman, and each time she'd made a comment or inquiry, she'd been surprised because he'd honestly considered and answered every one. Not once did he say she should not be concerned with such details.

It wasn't just that he'd given consideration to what she'd said or desired. Nay, it was that he had been willing to do so apparently without thinking less of her for having those thoughts, ideas, and desires, quite unlike Brau, who forever chastised her and accused her of trying to usurp a role belonging solely to men.

The differences between the two men were nothing short of amazing to Katherine, and she pondered her awe suspiciously, for it led to thoughts and imaginings of what other differences there could be between the two.

In the darkest hour of night, however, Katherine's thoughts were not on matters concerning Sleepy Hollow at all. Nay, far from it. Instead, her fantasies centered solely upon the reenactment of the kisses she and Icharus had shared in her father's study and the curious yearning they had awakened within her.

Icharus had spoken of a mysterious, hidden passion inside her, and each time she thought of his kiss she was wont to agree that yes, something had definitely been stirred to wakefulness within her.

She was most curious to know what might happen should she dare to rouse it further.

* * * *

Finally, the day of the celebration arrived.

Mr. Rawlins assisted her and Mrs. Porter with loading the dishes they had prepared into the back of a wagon and then had gone ahead with Callum to help with preparations at the church.

The men folk had been enlisted to move aside the heavy wooden benches inside the church and to set up a long table along the center. Later, the women would fill the table with sumptuous dishes, pies, cakes, and cobblers fit to make even the most finicky of eaters beg for a tiny morsel.

At home, Katherine gathered together the blankets and swaddling and the two tiny outfits she'd made for Mary and Heinrick's babe, and after carefully tucking them into a satchel, she had Isolde brought around from the stables and set off for the church.

She had barely arrived when a carriage came across the bridge.

"Have I missed something of import?" Icharus asked from the carriage window.

Katherine suddenly felt warm and giddy. She smiled. "A celebration, Master Crane. The Vandercleefs are expecting a new babe come summer. 'Twill be their first. Won't you join us?"

He returned her smile. "I shall. If it will not be presumed rude of me, I should like to go up to the house to put away my things. I promise to return forthwith to join you in rejoicing the happy news."

Katherine laughed. "Mrs. Porter will show you your room. You should return with all haste, however, or you'll miss the dancing."

His eyes changed. "And will you dance with me, Mistress Katherine?"

Lowering her gaze in an attempt to hide the sudden rush of emotion spreading through her, Katherine inclined her head. "I will."

She looked at him again, a bit flustered from thoughts of him holding her close while they danced, and he grinned.

Rapping his knuckles against the top of the carriage, he called to his driver. "Let us make haste, Master Downes. I should not like to forfeit the chance to hold such a lovely lady close in the dance!"

From his seat at the front of the carriage, a large black man smiled down at Katherine, and then called. "Yes, sir, Master Crane!"

Katherine watched the carriage drive away, a smile playing about her lips. How strange that man made her feel. He had only just arrived and already her body flushed with warmth and the tingle of anticipation.

Shaking her head in wonder at her reaction, she went inside the church to join the others.

* * * *

Night had fallen and a slow drizzle of rain crept into the cloth of Icharus's coat, chilling his skin. He pulled a handkerchief from inside his coat to wipe away the misty droplets on his face.

Mounted on Defiance and in a bit of a rush now to reach Katherine's side and assure himself she was safe, Icharus prodded Defiance into a trot.

He would have come much sooner had it not been for the disturbing incident awaiting him inside the Van Brunt household when he had arrived.

Though he was most eager to reach the church and

claim the dance she had promised him, he first needed to speak with her about the intruder.

Mrs. Porter had been standing in the hallway outside the door of Brom's study when he'd arrived earlier this evening, clutching the glistening brass fire iron from the parlor to her chest.

The sound of the door opening had frightened her dreadfully, and she'd spun around, brandishing the iron like a weapon the instant before she recognized him.

"Oh, Master Crane, it's you!" she'd cried with relief when she realized who had entered.

"What has happened? Is everyone safe?" Icharus had moved toward the study, half-fearing to discover a gunman inside, or worse.

She'd nodded, tears glistening in her brown eyes. "Yes, sir. Everyone's down at the church by now ... everyone except myself and you. Master Crane, it appears someone stole inside while I was out helping Mistress Katherine with the loading of the wagon."

"Whoever it was has gone now, but they sure made a wreck of Master Brom's study," she had said. "Wonder what anyone thought to find in there?"

Icharus knew, but he said nothing. Instead, he'd moved Mrs. Porter aside and had a look at the room for himself. Books had been toppled from the shelves and strewn into the floor. Two of the three drawers on the desk were standing open with papers protruding from them at every angle. Even the rug that usually lay beneath the desk had been gathered into a wrinkled heap upon the floor. He frowned.

"Mrs. Porter, how long has Mistress Katherine been at the church?"

"Near to half an hour, sir."

Relieved she hadn't been in the house when whoever searched her father's study had, he nodded. "Mr. Rawlins should be back soon. Any minute now, in fact. He was just behind the carriage. When he arrives, the two of you clear this up as best you can. I'll speak with Mistress Katherine about it later."

Nearing the churchyard, his intention was to seek Katherine out immediately to let her know about the intrusion, but he never got the chance.

Just as he rode into the churchyard, several things seemed to happen at once, none of which managed to register clearly upon his thoughts until much later.

Overhead, a jagged streak of light flashed in the sky and a loud rumble of thunder pealed. The clouds parted, releasing the heavy droplets that had been gathering within them over the past hours, and the sudden rush of icy cold, stinging droplets near blinded him.

There seemed to be an explosion somewhere, for the very ground beneath him quivered and shook, and then he heard the thundering of hooves coming at him from behind.

Jerking back on Defiance's reins, he whirled the horse round to face whoever approached at such a maddening, dangerous pace, but saw no one racing toward him.

Instead, a vague blur of luminous midnight rushed past through the darkness, just outside the glow of lanterns that lit up the churchyard, and he heard the pounding of heavy hooves race across the bridge. He had seen no one, but Icharus could have sworn he heard the angry neighing of an ill-handled horse somewhere in the darkness across the way.

He frowned. *Was this the sort of thing Father had seen and heard while in the Hollow?* A shiver took him, and whether from the chill of the rain or a tremor caused from coming near face-to-face with some supernatural force, he could not have said.

The doors of the church swung wide and Heinrick rushed out into the churchyard, peering through the heavy downpour and into the darkness. Dehann and Eustace Bleeker followed soon after.

"Something's there, at the bridge! Just there, see!" Eustace called, pointing in that direction.

Icharus squinted to see through the pouring rain, and indeed there did appear to be something in the darkness. Touching his heels to Defiance's sides, he started forward. He could hear the others following behind as he made his way to the bridge.

What he found there was more chilling than the icy sheets of rain pelting now from every direction. At the end of the bridge lay a badly misshapen body. The head, though attached still, was cocked at an eerily odd angle and lying in a dark pool of blood that mingled with the rain, seeping into the ground beneath him.

Icharus pulled Defiance to a halt several paces from the body.

The woodsman.

He put up a hand to halt the others. He feared Katherine may have joined the group, and he did not wish for her to be subjected to the horror of seeing her friend in such a state.

"Come no closer," he called to the approaching group. " 'Tis John Tanner. He's dead."

He swung down from Defiance's back and bent to have a closer look, just to be sure he'd not mistaken the fellow's identity. The body was curled in an odd heap, lying face down in the road. The falling rain had already plastered the hair to his head, and was even now pounding strands of it into the mud.

With a tug, Icharus rolled the heavy body until it faced aright and immediately recoiled in shock. That the man had been murdered was no doubt and vile enough an act in itself, but gazing downward, Icharus noted with some alarm that the man's throat had been slit – from ear to ear.

" 'Tis John Tanner!" someone in the group shouted back to the others. "The Headless Horseman's murdered John Tanner!"

Chapter 6

Frozen in place, her eyes unfocused and dazed, Katherine didn't move – couldn't move – from her place just inside the doors of the church. From the instant the identity of the dead man near the bridge had been revealed, a single refrain repeating itself in her thoughts.

John cannot *be dead. No. He just can't!*

"No, not my John! No! For the love of God, no!"

From somewhere behind her, Clara Tanner's agonized scream snatched her out of the horrified stupor that had claimed her. Fighting against her own terror, Katherine hurried to the woman's side. Carefully, she laid a hand on the older woman's shoulder.

"Clara?"

Her gentle plea went unheard. Clara shrugged her hand away, pushing past in her rush to reach her husband's side. Katherine hurriedly stepped aside to keep from being trampled by the woman before her who succumbed to grief-stricken panic, racing out into the rainy night.

Heinrick, Dehann, Everett, and Eustace hurried forward at her scream. Halfway between the church and bridge they caught hold and held her back from the

91

gruesome sight awaiting her, her flight halted.

The poor woman furiously struggled furiously against them while they attempted to hold her upright. At the same time, they tried to prevent her from rushing to the side of her dead husband. Such was the violence of her thrashing, Katherine feared her vain struggles to free herself would surely cause her some hurt.

Retrieving her cloak from near the door, Katherine hastened to Clara's side. She tried to wrap the warm cloak around the other woman, but lost in a sea of pain and anguish and a desperate need to reach John's side, Clara would not cease her fight long enough to allow herself to be covered in its warmth.

"Clara, please, you must stop this!" Katherine called, hoping her words would reach inside the woman's terrified mind this time.

Katherine glanced back to the church. Mary and Nell approached, with a weeping Anne between them. She tried again. "The children, Clara. Think of the children."

Once more her words fell on deaf ears.

"Let me go!" Clara screamed. "Please, I have to help him! John! Oh, please let me go to him. John!"

Again and again she cried out into the night, her struggles never ceasing, but still the men held tight. Her voice had swiftly become ragged and hoarse with her pleas, but no matter how they tried, no one was able to reach her splintered mind to quiet her.

"Madam, *cease!*"

Icharus's voice rang out through the darkness, his tone full of command and authority. All eyes turned in his direction.

Clara's scuffling immediately stopped, but her eyes … Katherine could see the wildness, the terror and anguish within them.

Katherine squeezed her cloak in her hands, fighting

back her own tears. She felt helpless in the face of Clara's obvious grief, and she ached for the pain the woman must be feeling.

Knees shaking, Katherine held place, watching while fat tears poured down Clara's cheeks, mingling with rain and blood from several scratches across her forehead and jaw gained in her recent battle against the men who held her still.

Clara glared at Icharus in helpless agony. Sobs choked her and burst forth despite her attempts to hold them back. Her gaze changed to one filled with roiling fury.

Deep sobs tore through her, and she trembled violently. Her chest heaving with the effort to hold them back long enough to speak, Clara pointed her finger accusingly at Icharus.

"*You*! You are the cause of this, do you understand? I begged him to leave be, to stay away from those woods, but he would not. Because of *you!* And now he's gone. Gone!"

Katherine could hear the low whispers of the men as they tried in vain to soothe her, to ease her agony a bit, but Clara heard none of it.

Another high-pitched wail of anguish and torment rent the night, and again she screamed accusations at Icharus.

"Because of you, the Witch has taken my very heart, do you understand? She's taken my John from me and he's never coming back! Oh, John. John! Heaven save us, what shall we do? What shall we do?"

Clara's words went from the frenzied plea to the heavens for direction of a soul who has just realized it is lost to a pitifully aching, heartbroken whisper that ended in great, wracking sobs.

Surprised by the intensity of Clara's anger toward Icharus, the men had loosened their hold, and now she crumbled to the sodden ground, unable to bear her own weight in the face of her sorrow.

Dehann reached for her and pulled her up. In a moment, he had her on her feet, and almost unthinkingly, Katherine handed her now damp cloak to him. He laid it over his mother's shoulders and guided her back to the church, his jaw clenched tight.

Poor Dehann. He'd only just learned his father was dead and already the burden of responsibility for family fell onto his young shoulders.

Katherine felt the warmth of hot tears mingling with icy cold rain on her cheeks. Her hair was drenched and hung in sodden tendrils down her back, water dripping from the ends, soaking her skirts.

Shivering violently from a combination of cold and reaction to the horrifying events of the evening, she turned to go inside.

Her gaze met Icharus's and held; she flinched. Reflected within the depths of his beautiful green eyes was a look of abject misery such as she had never seen. Katherine knew he probably blamed himself for John's death as much as Clara had, but she hadn't realized how deeply Clara's accusations had affected him until just this moment. She ached for him.

While his eyes revealed a maelstrom of turmoil, he still managed to maintain control of the myriad emotions she could see writhing below the surface within his gaze. Her admiration for the strength of will he must possess – to feel so deeply and yet remain so in command – grew in that moment.

Some of the rioting emotions she felt must have shown on her face because Icharus motioned her to his side. Katherine stepped forward, more than willing to lean upon him for a moment, to let her chilled and shaking body draw upon his strength, absorb the warmth that radiated from him despite the cold and damp.

"Icharus, what Clara said—"

He shook his head. "Let us not discuss it now, Katherine."

He turned to the others. "Heinrick, Everett, get your ladies back inside before they catch their deaths. Once they're settled and warm, we'll attend to the body."

He doffed his coat, wrapped it around her, and led her back inside the church in silence. Inside, he waited until some of the shaking subsided and her fingers had regained a bit of warmth before he rose and headed for the door.

Katherine shrugged out of the coat he'd wrapped her in earlier. "Thank you."

He accepted the coat and acknowledged her thanks with a nod. "See to Clara as best you can. I'll be back soon."

At the door, he turned to her once more. "Do not leave this building until I return, Katherine. It may not be safe."

A frown of concern puckered her brow. "What of you?"

Icharus pulled on his coat. "I'll be fine."

She nodded. "I will wait for you."

Callum, who'd been curiously absent until now, stepped to her side. His hands twined behind his back, he leaned close to whisper for her ears alone. "Is it just me, or did that sound very much like a promise from the heart?"

Katherine studied him, confused. "Your meaning escapes me, Callum. Of course I will stay here until he returns. As he has said, to do otherwise could prove to be dangerous."

He straightened, a sardonic grin spread across his lips. "Of course."

Katherine scowled. "Your wit escapes me as well, I'm afraid. I must see to Clara. You would do well to assist Icharus and the others with …"

The mere thought of John's death caused her stomach to wrench. She cast her gaze downward, unable to speak the words. When she looked up a moment later, Callum was striding to the door.

* * * *

Outside the church, the others joined Icharus at the bridge to retrieve the body of John Tanner. When they reached the spot where he lay, Brau was waiting for them, squatted near the body. At Icharus's approach, he looked up, accusation clear in his gaze.

"You've awakened a demon."

Icharus did not wait for the others, but moved instead to lift the body from the cold, wet ground himself, heedless of the filth of mud and blood that smeared against his coat in the doing. Icharus hefted the body onto his shoulder and moved to settle it gently across his horse's saddle.

"John's murder was neither the workings of witchcraft, nor that of a Hessian demon, Brau. This heinous crime was committed by human hands."

Brau peered at him, his gaze cold. "Indeed? Then where will you cast the blame, Master Crane? John was well loved in Sleepy Hollow. He has … had no enemies of which to speak."

With a quick flick of his wrist, he motioned toward the body lying across the back of the horse. "Yet he lies dead before us."

Icharus's gaze remained focused on the task at hand, that of securing John's body onto the horse's back. "Indeed he does, Master Van Ripper, and so noting, it must be surmised that John had an enemy after all."

He turned his gaze on each man in turn. "All are suspect. With the exception of Master Vandercleef and

Masters Bleeker, none of us were inside the church when John was murdered. I was riding down from the house. Mrs. Porter can vouch for the time of my departure. I arrived just before the … the explosion sounded."

Brau arched a brow. "Explosion? Surely you are imagining things, Crane. I was just across the way there, and I heard no explosion. You were alone, were you not?"

Icharus's narrowed gaze focused on Brau. "Yes. And you, Van Ripper? Is there anyone who can vouch that you were, indeed, just across the way?"

Brau drew up. "No. It appears we are without alibi, yet I bear no burden of guilt. I was on my way to attend the festivities."

"As was I." Icharus turned to Callum. "And you, Master Mather? Have you a witness as to your whereabouts during the past hour?"

Callum drew up short. He shook his head.

Icharus nodded. "It is as I thought. Not one of us can prove beyond doubt we were where we say we were, and yet neither of us professes to be the guilty party. Therefore, one of us is a liar as well, for I tell you there is a murderer amongst us."

With that, he turned to lead Defiance away. "I will see to Master Tanner's body. Callum, you will fetch Mistress Katherine home immediately and do not leave her side for an instant. I will speak with you later."

He had led his mount but a few steps forward before he halted once more. "Gentlemen, we shall all meet at Master Vandercleef's office in the morning at sunup, to discuss the murder of John Tanner … and uncover just who had motive for his death."

"You are a fool, Master Crane. You intend that we should, all of us, simply continue as before? You have just said one of us is a murderer, and yet you would not immediately seek out the perpetrator of the crime! Why is that, I wonder? Ah. Perhaps it is because you already know the identity of the killer …"

Brau's words were cutting, casting doubt about Icharus's innocence in the minds of the other men where none might have been otherwise, or so Icharus believed.

Icharus halted and gazed at length at each man in turn. Finally he asked, "Which of you is prepared to hang this night?"

No one stepped forth, and Icharus nodded. "Neither am I. So there is your answer, Master Van Ripper. Rest assured that come morning there will be questions aplenty. Now, I, for one, have no wish to further spoil what was to have been a happy, celebratory evening for the Vandercleefs. I am sure each of you feels the same."

No one contested his words, and so he nodded yet again. "Then we are agreed … morning is soon enough."

The discussion ended, Icharus went back to the church, stopping just long enough to let Katherine know he had instructed Callum to fetch her home and warm up a bit before he began the long trek to the Tanner's home.

* * * *

The others had already left the church for home, leaving Katherine alone with Brau to wait for Callum, an arrangement that made her quite uncomfortable, though she could not fathom why.

She waited, her forehead pressed against the paned glass window near the front of the church, her thoughts troubled.

"Poor Clara. She was so very distraught, Brau, quite beside herself with grief. I fear she may take some time recovering from this trauma."

Brau joined her at the window. "Indeed she may. John's death was very much a shock to all, I think. Except for young Crane. He seemed to take it all rather calmly."

Katherine shook her head in denial. "No, he didn't. He was devastated. If you could have seen the look in his eyes, Brau ..."

He brought his hands up to rest on her shoulders, and she stiffened, finding no comfort in his touch. She moved to the fire.

"Clara raged at him, blaming him for John's death. She believes the Witch took him as punishment for his trespass into the Western Wood."

Brau turned to her. "You will remember I did warn you there would be consequences, Katherine. Though I hadn't imagined anything quite as ghastly as this, I—"

Her head snapped up, and her eyes widened in surprise. "You think John's death is a result of our decision to harvest the Western Wood, don't you?"

She shook her head in disbelief. "There is no witch, Brau."

He crossed the room and caught her to him. "You're very sure of that, Katherine? Have you ridden into the heart of the Western Woods to seek her out for yourself? Perhaps you've stumbled onto her lair, but she cast a forgetting spell upon you, to make you disremember?"

Katherine uttered a short bark of laughter. "Nay, I have not. Have you?"

He released her so suddenly she stumbled a bit before righting herself.

"Aye. I have, Katherine. I assure you there is cause to believe in the whispered tales bandied about this valley since before you were born."

His words were spoken with such sincerity.

Katherine frowned. "Braughton, please. You're frightening me."

He peered at her. "Would that I could have done so before John's death."

Fighting the anxiety his words brought, Katherine shook her head. "I do not believe you. There is no witch. John died at the hands of a man."

Brau arched a brow. "Believe what you will, Katherine. But I beg you, heed my warning. The Hollow will not let countenance interference where it is not wanted."

* * * *

Callum waited in the parlor with Katherine for Icharus to return from the Tanners'. The night drew long, but though the clock in the hall had already chimed two, he still had not arrived.

Katherine paced round the room, her hands going first to her skirts to mangle the material and then to her hair into which she plaited and removed braid after braid.

"A rut in the floor would look quite nice, I suppose. It had better, since you appear to be determined to walk one into it tonight," Callum said.

Katherine halted her pacing to pin him with her questioning gaze. "Where were you tonight, Callum? Everyone else was drenched. Not you. Why not?"

He turned away, avoiding her gaze. "Please don't ask me that, Katherine."

"I already have."

Callum sighed. "I cannot answer you."

Katherine crossed to stand in front of him. "You cannot? Or you will not?"

He left the chair to stand in front of the fire, his gaze focused on the flames. "Both. Neither. Please leave off, Katherine."

She went to him then, her hand coming out to catch him by the arm. He turned to face her. "I cannot, Callum. I have to know ... *please*. Tell me you had nothing to do with John's murder."

His eyes flared in surprise. "John's death? You think I murdered John?"

She denied his words with a shake of her head. "Nay, I do not. I think you're innocent, but Callum, I cannot say so without doubt because I do not know where you were, and you will not confess—"

He met her gaze full on now, a plea in his own. "Do not press me in this, Katherine, please. People might be hurt."

Her fear must have registered in her gaze, because he shook his head. "Not like that, Katherine. No one will be killed due to my absence at the church this eve – at least one can hope not."

A wry grin twisted his lips. "But there are other degrees of hurt that I would not wish for you or any other to suffer because of any confession I might make."

Katherine closed her eyes, and tears seeped between the tightly held edges. "I do not understand, Callum, but I trust you. Please, just tell me this much. Tell me you were not with John when he died. Can you promise me that?"

Callum drew her close. "Yes, I can promise you that, Katherine. I was not with John when he died. Does that help?"

A sob burst from her lips. "Aye, it does. Thank you."

The tears she'd been holding back all day spilled forth, and Callum pulled her closer into his embrace, her head resting against his chest. "There, there, Katherine. Shhh. Everything will be fine, you'll see. Shhh."

* * * *

His entrance unnoticed, Icharus doffed his sodden greatcoat and gloves in the front hall and moved into the parlor where a warm fire cracked and hissed in welcome, and for a second time he found Katherine wrapped in the arms of a man.

He'd entered just as Callum bent to press a kiss atop her burnished curls and an unreasonable annoyance filled him. He cleared his throat, alerting the oblivious couple to his presence.

Katherine turned and straightened a bit but she made no offer to leave the intimate circle of Callum's arms. "Icharus, you've returned! How is Clara? She was still quite distraught when we helped her into the wagon at the church."

Ignoring his disquieting irritation toward Callum, he crossed to the fire to warm himself. He was both drenched and frozen through, and the flames were quite appealing at the moment.

"She is quieter now. Braughton stopped by on his way back to town. He offered to stay the night, but Dehann insisted he and Anne could take care of their mother. They will also assist her with preparing John's body for his burial tomorrow."

"So Clara believes John's murder to be the work of the devil? Witchcraft?" Callum asked.

Icharus nodded in stiff greeting to Callum. "Yes, she does … and she believes it is my fault her John is dead. If I hadn't insisted John begin removing trees from the Western Wood, she says, he would still be alive."

With a last consoling pat to Katherine's shoulder, Callum moved away to sit in his usual place; the chair nearest the fire. "What of Anne and Dehann?"

Icharus closed his eyes and rubbed at the back of his neck. Tension radiated from him. "Neither of the Tanner siblings accused me of their father's murder, if that is what you are asking."

"That is good to know, but I was rather asking how the two were bearing up in the face of their father's death."

Icharus sighed. Trading his place at the hearth for a more comfortable seat on the sofa, he cocked his head to one side and peered at Callum, his gaze searching. "Both are doing well. The girl is holding up a sight better than her mother, though she too weeps. The boy, Dehann, stepped right into his role as the elder Tanner male. He grieves, of course, but I believe they will be well enough. In time."

Callum nodded. "Dehann always was one to take his responsibilities immediately to heart. Anne on the other hand ..." He paused and shook his head, momentarily lost in thought. After a moment, he slapped a hand against his thigh and nodded, as though coming to some decision. He stood. "It is good to hear they are doing well. I worried, what with their mother having taken it so hard, but as you say, time heals all wounds."

Icharus nodded. "Indeed it does. My thanks for seeing Katherine safely home."

With a nod, Callum accepted his thanks. He glanced in Katherine's direction. "I believe I shall seek my bed now. It has been a dreadful long night, and I should like to bury my grief in the sweet, forgetful bliss of sleep, if I may."

Katherine dipped her head. "Pleasant dreams, Cal," she whispered tiredly.

He smiled. "Yours as well, Katherine. If you should need me—"

Katherine shooed him away. "I will be fine. Seek your bed and rest now, Master Mather. We shall see you again come morning."

After a quick glance toward Icharus, and a somewhat hesitant nod to Katherine, he left the two of them alone.

* * * *

Katherine waited to hear the door to Callum's chamber open and then close behind him before she turned back to Icharus. He had closed his eyes and commenced to rub at the tension in his neck once more.

"I fear there may be some truth to Clara's words, Master Crane."

His hands immediately ceased their massaging motions and his eyes snapped open. He stared at her, his gaze questioning. She noticed the sudden coldness in their mossy green depths.

She hastened to explain. "I did not mean there was some truth to her belief in the Witch, of course, but rather I spoke in regard to there being some connection with John's death and the clearing of the Western Wood." Katherine frowned. "It does seem to have been the catalyst, does it not?"

Icharus studied her. "Perhaps, though I see no reason why it would. It is only trees, Katherine. And superstition, to which you should pay no heed."

Katherine looked away to hide her uncertainty. She brought her hands up to tangle nervously in her curls, her fingers busily forming a braid along its length. She could feel his gaze on her all the while. Intense. Watchful. But he held his silence.

When he did speak, she jumped in fright.

"Tell me what you know of the Tanners, Mistress Van Brunt. Is it possible that your John had an enemy outside of Sleepy Hollow?"

Katherine unbraided the plait she'd just braided and shook her head. "Not to my knowledge, no. John and Clara have lived here since before my birth and in all the time I've known him, he raised his voice in anger only once that I can recall."

Memories of that afternoon came flooding back. John had asked to speak with her father, and the two of them were closeted in Brom's study when the shouting began.

Her brow furrowed and she shook her head. A wistful smile curved her lips. "All the tenants looked up to John. To them, he was the village elder of sorts, second only to my father. Everyone loved him."

Icharus frowned. "Yet tonight, he was killed. Murdered. Why?"

Katherine went to stand in front of the fire. A shaky sigh escaped, and she closed her eyes. Letting her head drop back for a moment, she pondered his question. "I have spent these past hours asking myself the same question, Master Crane, and despite my efforts, I have yet to discover a logical solution."

She turned to look at him. "I will speak with Clara …"

At her mention of John's widow, Icharus's lips tightened. "That may be of little help. The lady appears to have gone quite mad, for the moment."

Katherine gave a sad little smile. "Aye, she does. I would likely do the same, had I lost the love of my life so unexpectedly. It must be near unbearable for her."

Her words were quiet, barely above a whisper. Icharus peered at her. "You've known such a love then, that you can identify with the depths of her loss?"

Katherine bent to stir the fire, her brow puckered in thought as she pondered his question and how best to answer it. "I have lost all those I held closest to my heart. Having lost first my grandfather, then mother, and more recently my father as well, yes. I believe I can say I fully comprehend the level and depths of her despair. Perhaps I, more so than anyone else in Sleepy Hollow, can do so. You see, Clara is blessed in that she has her children with her, to comfort her through her loss, but I …"

She slowly shook her head, loneliness and her own personal grief weighing heavily upon her heart. "I have no one."

Icharus had come up behind her and taken it upon himself to remove the fire iron from her limp fingers and place it back into its stand. He reached out to lay his hand against her cheek.

"I am truly sorry for your losses, Katherine. And today yet another is laid at your door, that of a dear friend. Would that I had known somehow, beforehand, of this possibility …"

Katherine turned her cheek against his palm, unconsciously inviting his caress. "John's death was not your fault, Icharus. No more than it could be mine. I was the one who demanded the timber be culled from that place while you merely made the suggestion. Let your thoughts be at ease."

Icharus's fingers swept upward into her hair and he pulled her closer, bringing her head to rest against his chest. His action appeared to be done without thought, and it seemed most natural to Katherine to comfort him in return by allowing him to hold her, to help her in this way.

He sighed, and hugged her closer still. "I should like to do nothing more, but regardless of whether or not our decision regarding the Western Wood has aught to do with it, John Tanner is dead. There is a killer running loose in Sleepy Hollow and none of us will be safe until he's been found out and brought to justice."

Katherine nodded, but her thoughts were distracted, slipping away from conjecture in regard to the possible identity of John's murderer to center more upon how peaceful it felt to be held so close in his embrace.

Drawing in a deep, calming breath, Katherine couldn't help but notice how delightful he smelled. Warm male and wood smoke rose up to tease her senses, and her eyes drifted shut. She inhaled deeply of his essence once more.

Were he her father, she would put her arms around his waist and cuddle close into his comforting embrace, as she'd done many times as a child when she'd become upset. But Icharus was not her father.

She pulled away.

"I know you are right, but I cannot imagine anyone wanting to end John's life. There is a madman on the loose, no doubt, and yet I cannot name a single man in the Hollow on whom I would turn the finger of guilt."

Icharus nodded in understanding. "When I arrived at the church the only men inside were Master Vandercleef, Eustace, and Everett Bleeker, and John's eldest, Dehann. Have you any idea where Callum had gone?"

Katherine pondered on that for a moment.

Where had *Callum been?*

"I don't think Callum had aught to do with John's murder. He respected John, looked up to him much like a son would defer to his father, if you will. Indeed, Callum has spent many an hour in the Tanner household, whiling away the hours with John and Clara right alongside Anne and Dehann."

She made a negative motion with her head. "He would not kill a man he admired so much. What reason would he have?"

Icharus sighed. "Aye, that is my question precisely. What reason?"

Katherine shook her head again, this time more vehemently. She leaned away from him, pulling away from the comfort of his arms. "No. Callum is not John's murderer. I know it."

Icharus's brow arched upward. "You cannot be certain … unless you were with him at the time of John's death?"

She pinned him with a look of warning. "I was not. Yet still I say Callum is innocent. He simply does not have it within him to kill in cold blood."

Icharus sighed. "I would not believe him capable either, Katherine, but we cannot be sure. Braughton was not in attendance, either, though he did arrive soon thereafter."

Katherine nodded, her thoughts going back to those moments she'd spent alone with Brau in the church before Callum returned. A chill came over her, and she moved further away from Icharus.

"Please ... can we discuss something else now? The subject wears thin, and I should like to forget about it, if only for a brief moment ..."

Icharus went to the chair where Callum usually preferred to sit and dropped into it wearily. "So also would I, Katherine, but time may well be against us. If the killer is not identified soon, who is to say he'll not strike again?"

She sighed, suddenly quite weary.

"Someone searched your father's study, Katherine."

Katherine spun about to look at him. "What? When? Why was I not informed?"

"When I arrived at the house this afternoon, Mrs. Porter was standing outside the door with a fire iron clutched to her chest, looking for all the world as if she expected to discover Satan himself inside that room."

He shifted in the chair. "No one was inside, but whoever was there before I arrived left the room a shambles. I directed Mrs. Porter to enlist Mr. Rawlin's aid and have the room put to rights before you returned from the gathering at the church."

Katherine felt a chill. "But there is nothing ..."

Her head snapped up and her gaze met his. "There is only one thing anyone might have searched Father's study for, Master Crane, and that is the certificates ..."

Icharus nodded. "Aye. The papers that belonged to my father, and so now, to me."

Katherine sat, her brow deeply furrowed. "But why? Those documents are worth nothing to anyone other than ... you."

Icharus held her gaze, his own steady. He nodded slowly. "No one is aware that the documents have been located, other than you and I ... are they?"

Her gaze drilled into his. "No, I have not spoken of them to anyone."

"Neither have I, which means someone has reason to believe you've discovered them, and meant to have them for themselves."

Katherine put her hands over her eyes and shook her head. So many things had happened these past weeks, and everything seemed to occur at such a rapid pace. It was simply too much for her to deal with at the moment.

"I don't understand what is happening here, Master Crane. My father is gone, and the one man to whom I might turn for advice has been murdered. Someone has come into my home to thieve and plunder my father's private study ..."

She lowered her hands, heedless of the glassy sheen of tears brightening her eyes. "There's so much suspicion and fear and grief inside me now, and I *hate* it. I wish I could just make it go away."

Icharus held his silence, letting her give vent to the emotions she'd held in check these many hours.

Katherine sniffed, fighting the tears that were wont to fall at the slightest provocation these days. She spread her hands wide, and with a voice cracked and broken from the riot of conflict inside her asked, "Who is left for me to trust?"

Chapter 7

Icarus studied her carefully. "Braughton …"

She groaned. "Before my father's death, I trusted him. I had no reason not to. But now …"

Icarus leaned forward. "Now? What do you mean? Do you think he could have something to do with Master Tanner's death?"

"No, I don't believe Brau would murder John. He had no reason. Besides, he knows how important the well being of the people of Sleepy Hollow is to me. I don't think he would do anything to jeopardize that … for my sake."

She walked to the window and stared out into the night. "He wants to marry me."

Her words, added almost as an afterthought, led Icarus to think she may have some reservations against his suit. His brows rose. "Yes, Brau's intentions are clear in that regard, but Katherine, do you not want to marry him as well?"

She shook her head and sighed. "I haven't given the matter much consideration, to tell the truth. So much has happened recently, and my thoughts have been centered mostly upon the Hollow and how best to turn things around, to make it better—"

"You've given little thought to your own wants and needs in the face of those who now depend upon you. I understand, and think it admirable of you, but Katherine, the question is going to come up, and unless I miss my guess, it will arise very soon."

He leaned forward in the chair. "In light of the recent events here, I think you should give careful consideration to how you feel about him. Is Braughton a man to which you are willing to entrust both your own future and that of the Hollow?"

She turned to face him. "There was a letter, you know. My father wrote to me about the papers you came here for. In that letter, he warned that I should be very careful in whom I put my trust."

"I don't understand what he felt was so important about keeping those documents secret, Katherine."

"Neither do I, but the fact remains he did. And I remembered …"

"You remembered what?"

"After my mother died, there was another death. A woman was found murdered. Brau discovered her, deep in the heart of the Western Wood, her body mangled and a knife wound across her throat. She'd bled to death, he said, before he found her there."

Icharus thought of John. "Who was she? Was there an inquiry made into her death?"

Katherine nodded. "Minerva lived alone in a tiny shack in those woods. She was an older woman and a bit … eccentric. Everyone in the Hollow avoided her. They thought her mad."

Icharus arched a brow. "A witch, maybe?"

Katherine nodded. "At least the younger folks in the village thought her to be. Her clothing had become ragged and threadbare, though many of the villagers would leave items for her near the edge of the forest."

Icharus listened, much enthralled by her tale.

Katherine looked at her hands. "William, her husband, was a master woodsman, but he'd been dead for a number of years, having fallen to his death while exploring a cave he discovered behind the waterfall within the Western Woods."

She shook her head. "Several of the elders tried to get her to come into the village proper, but Minerva refused, claiming she waited for her husband to return for her, to take her away from Sleepy Hollow. To Minerva, his death never occurred."

Icharus peered at her. "This waterfall, have you seen it?"

Katherine gave a negative shake of her head. "I've never been there myself, but there are those who profess to having seen it, my father included."

He nodded. "Go on."

Katherine sighed. "I remember my father questioning Brau about Minerva's death, about where he'd found her and how and whether or not anyone else had been in the area at the time."

She frowned. "They were in his study, and no one knew I'd come back inside. I … I don't really know why the memory decided to resurface, but I clearly remember hearing Father say he intended to speak with John about it later."

Icharus frowned, confused. "Your father suspected John of the woman's murder?"

Katherine looked sideways at him. "I'm not sure who he suspected. I only know what I heard."

"Could that be the reason John was so against cutting the trees in the Western Wood?"

Katherine ran her hand along the back of the sofa. "Who knows? And now, with John having fallen to much the same fate, we will likely never find out."

Icharus posed his next question a bit hesitantly. She

hadn't really revealed the extent of her feelings for Brau, and he feared she might become upset. Still, he asked, "Do you think it's possible your father suspected Braughton?"

She met his gaze full on, her own eyes cloudy with uncertainty. "He could have, I suppose. In his letter, he cautioned me against revealing the content of the documents you came here for to Brau."

Icharus looked away. "Your father did not trust him. Why?"

"I don't know. You asked if I felt I could trust him. I've told you about the letter from my father, and his warning. I never had any reason not to trust Brau before, but now … there is really no one I would feel safe enough to confide in."

He watched her. "But you have just revealed a number of confidences to me."

Katherine ran her fingers along the high back of the sofa once more. She nodded. "I have, yes. It occurs to me that you were not present at the church when … at the time of John's death either, Master Crane."

"Quite right, Mistress Van Brunt. I was not. As I told Master Van Ripper and the others earlier, I was on my way to the assemblage, and Mrs. Porter can vouch for the time of my leaving from here."

His eyes went cold. "But that is neither here or there, is it?"

He stood slowly, understanding the reason she'd seemed compelled to share her story at last. "You suspect me, don't you?"

A short bark of laughter echoed in the room. "I can't say that I blame you, really. I am no more than a stranger who came into your village demanding old debts that no one knew existed be paid. I've brought the secrets of the past to light, revealing the private arrangement your father made with mine, and that has made me worthy of suspicion and one not to be trusted. Is that it?"

Leaning close, he peered at her, his eyes blazing with some inner emotion that bore a startling resemblance to indignant, righteous anger.

"Is that what you really believe? Tell me, Katherine," he demanded. "Look into my eyes and tell me you think I murdered John Tanner."

Katherine glared at him. "I don't know what to believe! I don't know who to trust! It could have been you, just the same as it could have been Callum, or Brau, or ... or ..."

She spread her arms wide. "Or someone outside the Hollow."

She crossed to stand before him, a myriad of emotions warring inside her. "I am not accusing you. Do I believe you murdered John Tanner? No. No more than I believe Callum or Brau or anyone else in Sleepy Hollow capable of committing such a terrible crime. But I cannot be sure."

She looked away. "My uncertainty is disturbing, and though my intent was not to cast blame upon you, I have said no less than the others will when you speak to them come morning. What will you tell them?"

She raised her head to look at him once more. "One of our own is dead, Master Crane, and by cruel, vicious means. We've a right to be suspicious of an outsider. You would feel the same, would you not?"

Icharus sat back down, and sighed. "Like as not, yes."

After a moment of silence, he said, "I could tell you I am worthy of your trust, Katherine, but that would not make you believe in me."

She shook her head no.

"What would you have me do?"

Katherine closed her eyes, once again on the brink

of tears. "Give me something to believe in, Master Crane. Something I can count on no matter how mad the world around me appears to be."

Icharus struggled with his reply, with his reaction to her pain. "We seem to share a passion for survival, Katherine, and for progress … one that extends beyond mere getting by. Let us put our faith in that."

She opened her eyes and he leaned forward, appealing to her sense of loyalty to both the people and the land. "You wish to bring life back into this place, and I can help you do so. We can make it happen. You can believe in that, if nothing else."

* * * *

During the night, the rain had turned to snow. A soft, thick blanket of white covered the ground. The powdery stuff churned beneath Defiance's hooves with each step and a light breeze sent intermittent sprinkles pouring down upon horse and rider below from the branches overhead.

Icharus rode toward Heinrick Vandercleef's office, filled with determination to uncover the truth of John Tanner's murder this morning. His problem would be that no one in Sleepy Hollow knew him. Not really. As an outsider, a stranger, he would be the first to fall under the suspicious, accusatory stares of the villagers. Icharus knew somehow he must not only convince the people of his own innocence, but also rout the true villain.

He had no business delving into the matter. It was not his place to do so, and he would not, were it not for Katherine. She needed him.

Although the people of Sleepy Hollow loved her as one of their own, she was still a woman, and as he had seen, Braughton was determined to keep her firmly at home and 'in her place,' as he would likely say. Without him, Icharus thought she might never be allowed any greater part in the future of Sleepy Hollow other than that of the quietly timid wife of Braughton Van Ripper. That would destroy Katherine's spirit, and Icharus knew it. Perhaps *that* was why he felt so compelled to act on her behalf this morning. He could claim that with a killer so close to his own town, he was obliged to discover the identity, for the safety of his people as well as those in Sleepy Hollow, but he knew it wasn't true. He wanted to do this for Katherine, although he couldn't fathom why.

A sound alerted him to someone approaching from the rear, and he turned. Callum, mounted on a bay stallion, came up from behind at a slow trot. Icharus nodded in greeting.

"Good morning, Master Crane," Callum called back. "Since we're both for Vandercleefs', I thought there would be no harm in riding up together."

"Nay, no harm," Icharus agreed.

Callum drew up beside him and slowed his mount to match Defiance's stride. " 'Tis a grim meeting we're bound for, Crane. Think we'll uncover the identity of the killer this morn?"

Icharus shook his head. "We can hope, Mather."

Callum nodded. "Aye, we can."

He fell silent, but Icharus could sense that he was yet troubled. "Is there something on your mind, Mather? Something of import you'd like to tell me before we reach Vandercleefs'?"

Callum pulled his mount to a halt and Icharus did likewise. After a moment of indecisive quiet, he said, "I did not murder John Tanner. I am innocent, Master Crane."

Icharus nodded. "So you say, and duly noted. Which means you are prepared to reveal where you were last night at the time of John's death, and you have a witness who can vouch for the same, I presume?"

Callum frowned. "Can I trust you, Icharus Crane?"

The man studied him intently, and Icharus felt a misplaced urge to laugh at his question. He held back, but could not suppress the tiny upward quirk of his lips. "That seems to be the question of the day, Master Mather."

The younger man seemed distracted by his own thoughts. While Icharus watched, a number of conflicting expressions crossed the man's face. Finally he nodded. "Aye, it would be. You are a stranger here, Crane, an outsider, but Katherine ..."

Icharus sighed. "Ah, yes. Katherine."

Callum peered at him. "Katherine thinks you are a good man, Crane. Much like her grandfather, Baltus, you've an eye for the land, but also an ability to read people on a deeper level than might appear on the surface."

Icharus's eyes widened. "She said that of me?"

Callum nodded, distracted. "Aye, this morn before I rode out to meet you."

Curiously pleased to hear that, Icharus straightened in his seat. "Well then, will you cede to her opinion on the matter, or will you draw your own conclusion?"

Callum frowned. "I am my own man, Crane, not one led about by the flash and fascination of a frilly skirt. I meant only that I have a deep respect for Katherine's opinions in such matters, but my privy council is my own."

Icharus nodded. "As it should be. So, the question remains unanswered, Mather. Do you trust me?"

Callum's lips twitched. " 'Twas not a question of whether or not I trust you, Crane, but rather if you are a man in which one could and should trust."

Icharus smiled. "Quite right. Let us examine the matter then, shall we?" He nudged his horse into a slow walk, and Callum followed suit.

"First, you've questioned Mistress Katherine as to her opinion on the matter. It is clear to me by your admission of this that you would like to trust me. Am I right?"

Callum nodded. "Perhaps ..."

Icharus held up his hand for silence. "Then, you determined to ride out here alone, without an audience of friends to confirm our conversation and any conclusion you might draw from it. That says to me you consider your own judgment sufficient. As you have said, you are your own man."

Again Callum nodded, but this time he held his silence. Icharus frowned.

What next? Ah ...

"Next, you've come to me with no apparent fear for your own safety. If you thought me a cold-blooded murderer, Master Mather, I highly doubt you would seek to ride alone with me anywhere. Why, you could well be my next intended victim, could you not?"

Callum's brow furrowed, and Icharus wondered if he hadn't given thought to his own safety before riding out, a question whose obvious answer spoke much in regards to the question at hand. Somewhere deep inside, Icharus concluded, Callum Mather had already decided he was worthy of his trust.

"And finally, Mather, you've given me the opportunity to plead my case, to assure you of my cause when you could have simply drawn your conclusions from what you know of me to date."

He turned to face Callum. "What, then, is your verdict, sir?"

* * * *

When Icharus and Callum drew their mounts to a halt outside Heinrick Vandercleef's office, Brau and Everett had already arrived.

Brau nodded in greeting, and Everett did the same.

"Good morning, gentlemen," Brau offered. "Or it would have been, had it not seemed necessary to ride out here in the cold and snow to denounce the quite ridiculous charge of our having murdered a friend last eve."

He held the door, allowing the other men to precede him. He stepped inside the notary's office and closed the door, then removed his coat and gloves to place them aside before joining the others.

Notary Vandercleef waited near the fire. He'd turned when the door opened, and now he sighed. "The matter which has brought us here today is a sad one, gentlemen, but now that we're all assembled, I suppose we should begin."

Icharus held up his hand. "Not quite, Heins. But a moment more if you please."

The sound of a carriage drawing up outside drew their attention, and all but Icharus stared at the door in wait to learn the identity of their uninvited guest.

A moment later, the door opened and Katherine stepped inside. "Greetings, sirs."

She looked about the room, and after resting her gaze briefly upon each man in attendance, gave a quick nod. "Everyone has arrived. Good. Shall we start?"

Brau's brows flew upward, his eyes wide with shock. "What madness is this?"

He hurried to Katherine's side, and he reached out to her, took hold of her shoulders. "Katherine, darling, hurry back to the carriage and have Mr. Rawlins drive you straightway back to the house before you catch a chill. You should never have come out in the first place!"

Katherine stared at him, her gaze cold. "I believe we've gathered here this morning to discuss the murder of our own John Tanner—"

Brau cut her off. "Katherine, listen to me. The discussion in which we are about to partake, one of murder and extreme villainy, is sure to turn ugly. I believe the subject one much too distressing for your gentle nature. Please, go back to the house. You shouldn't be here, my dear."

His voice had dropped, his words low and intended for her ears alone, but everyone in the room had heard.

Katherine smiled. "Nonsense, Brau. John Tanner was one of my tenants, as well as a friend. As such, the matter of his death is as much my concern as anyone's. Besides, I was invited to listen in."

Brau's gaze went to Icharus and narrowed. "This is your idea, Crane?"

Icharus sat the figurine he'd been looking at onto the table. "It is as she said, Braughton. She has a perfect right to be here."

Brau made a sound, much like a hiss, before turning to Katherine once more. "Very well, but bear in mind not one of us gentlemen gathered here will be as likely to be completely candid about such a morbid subject with a lady in our presence … with the possible exception of yourself, Crane. As men, it is our God-given responsibility to protect the fairer sex from such garish details. How then, Master Crane, do you expect to uncover which of us may be John's murderer?"

Icharus's gaze shuttered. "You appear the most upset by her presence, Brau. It could be surmised there is something you might wish to keep hidden from her."

He turned to the others. "I think Katherine has a right and duty, as landholder, to witness what passes between us this day. What of you? Do either of you have argument against her presence?"

No one spoke. Icharus straightened. "Come, gentlemen. Perhaps you fear the lady will be overcome

121

by a few graphic details, such as our telling of the wound John suffered. Or mayhap she's seen as much before, and therefore will not be bothered by our mention of it."

Brau stiffened.

Callum frowned.

Everett Bleeker refused to meet his gaze.

Heins Vandercleef's eyes widened. "*Minerva.*"

Icharus nodded. "Aye, Katherine told me about the lady of the Western Woods just last night. Do none of you find it exceedingly odd that your Master Tanner appears to have been killed in the same fashion as this apparent madwoman ... both after some incident involving yon forest bordering your little village?"

Brau's eyes narrowed. "You were warned beforehand of the possible consequences of your plans, Master Crane."

Icharus shook his head. "I was met with fairytales regarding some mythical forest-dwelling witch, Van Ripper. No one in Sleepy Hollow spoke up with the truth. Nay, not one of you! All of you could have informed me of the fact you harbor a murderer amongst you, but each of you chose to remain silent."

His peering gaze moved to each of them in turn. "What I wish to know, gentlemen, is why? Why was Minerva murdered three summers ago? Why then was John Tanner murdered just last night? Further, what reason would the killer have for passing these deaths off as the vengeful act of a wretched creature more likely to be pitied than feared ..." he paused for a moment, recalling the story Katherine had told him, and then added, "who does not even exist?"

"What gives you the right to question us, Crane? You are an outsider here. Maybe it was *you* who slit John's throat and left him at the bridge!" Brau countered.

Icharus concurred. "You could be right, Master Van

Ripper. But what motive would I have? I barely knew John. I spoke to him only once, when I instructed him to begin clearing the Western Wood for timber. You were there, Braughton, and you, Bleeker. In fact, all of you but your good notary, Master Vandercleef, were there.

"Pray tell, gentlemen, what in the conversation that passed between us that day could have pressed me to murder John Tanner?"

Brau spoke up once more. "What motive could *any* of us have, Crane? We've lived in this hollow together for many years. We are like family. Why would any of us hold malice against a man we considered friend?" He snorted. "You might as well name young Mather there as his murderer, for he spent an inordinate amount of time with the man. Perhaps something passed between the two to enrage Callum enough to incite *him* to murder."

Icharus shook his head. "Mather is innocent. Vandercleef is innocent, and so also is Master Bleeker, for those two were with the women inside the church the entire time. That leaves myself, and you, Braughton."

Brau pinned him with a suspicious, narrow gaze. "And what information are you privy to, Crane, that you can absolve Mather here of the crime?"

Katherine's gaze flew to him as well, but Icharus merely shook his head. "That is none of your concern. Matters have come to light, matters that need not be discussed here, that clear young Mather of all guilt and suspicion."

He turned to Heinrick. "Please make a note of that, notary. By my word, Master Mather is innocent and heretofore not to be held accountable of the crime of the murder of John Tanner. I have heard his confession and declare proof sufficient of his innocence."

"By your word? By the word of a stranger who may or may not be worthy of our trust? Come now, Crane," Everett Bleeker spoke up. "We've no assurance you are not the killer yourself. Mather was not inside the church last night … we have ample reason to suspect him. Why should we believe you?"

Icharus turned to him. "Reason due to his absence, yes, but not motive. Not motive. Tell me, do you believe Callum guilty of the crime, Master Bleeker? You would be his accuser, then?"

Everett's face mottled. "Of course not. Callum looked to John like a son would a father. I no more think him capable of murdering John than I myself would be."

Icharus declined to comment on the last part, but turned to the others in turn. "Master Mather has no alibi to prove his innocence in this horrid crime, gentlemen, but I say he is not guilty. Master Bleeker concurs. What of the rest of you? Heinrick? Braughton? Katherine? Do any of you believe this man had sufficient motive to murder the friend he looked up to like a father?"

Heinrick shook his head. "I do not."

After a long moment, Brau gave a brief shake of his head. "Nay, I do not think Mather would have killed John. It was mere supposition, which is all any of us has to go on here," he reminded them.

Icharus looked to Katherine. She glanced at Callum and held his gaze for a moment. Finally, she turned back to Icharus. "I do not believe Callum is guilty of this crime."

Icharus nodded. "Let it be so noted that each of us has sufficient reason to believe Callum Mather is not guilty of the murder of John Tanner in Sleepy Hollow."

His gaze flickered to Brau. "That leaves myself and you, Braughton."

Brau shook his head. "This is preposterous. Mather has no evidence of his whereabouts, and yet each of us is willing to turn our backs to the possibility that he was perfectly capable of committing this crime."

Icharus's brows rose. "Yourself included,

Braughton, unless you'd like to rescind your earlier comments?"

He made a negative motion with his head.

"We are agreed then."

For the first time since the six of them had gathered in Vandercleef's office, Brau left his place slightly behind Katherine. He crossed to the fire.

"Let us now look to you, Crane, a stranger come into Sleepy Hollow demanding fulfillment of a promise to which no one other than your deceased father and Master Brom were privy. Or so you say."

He turned to the others. "Master Crane insists Brom promised his father tithe and title to the land adjoining the hollow to the West, gentlemen, a promise neither myself nor Master Vandercleef were aware of."

"I think each of you will agree that of all of us here, Heins and I knew Master Brom's business dealings better than anyone ... even John."

His gaze flitted about the room, taking in the nods of each of the gentlemen present and the slight tint of red that heated Icharus's face. A tiny smirk curved his lips.

"Therefore, as I have already explained to Crane here, there could have been no such promise made, for one of us would certainly have known of it."

He pinned Icharus with his gaze. "Armed with this knowledge, I have no alternative but to believe Icharus Crane is more than capable of lying to get what he wants."

He turned away. "However, I have no wish to make such a claim if it be unwarranted. Therefore I ask ... do either of you have knowledge of this supposed promise between Master Van Brunt and Ichabod Crane?"

Icharus glared at Brau. "It is fact, Van Ripper. I have knowledge of it, and that shall suffice."

Brau laughed. "Again we are asked to take you at your word, with naught a shred of evidence to support your claims. I say you are not to be trusted, Crane – neither in regard to this supposed promise, nor in the matter of John's murder."

Icharus speared him with a chilly look. "And what of you, Van Ripper? Twice there is a murder in Sleepy Hollow, both bodies broken, a wound to the throat. You found the first one. Who was with you at the time? Who is to say you did not kill the poor woman yourself? Who was with you, Braughton, to speak out of your innocence?"

Now Brau's face colored. "That is none of your concern, Crane. How dare you bring up matters from the past, matters I will remind all of you were settled long before this man came to Sleepy Hollow."

Icharus crossed to the fire and nonchalantly propped against the wall. "I dare, Van Ripper. Just as you dare to call me a liar with no evidence to the contrary. Who is not to say that you were Minerva's murderer rather than the man who just happened to find her body there near her cottage in the Western Woods? Who can say that you, having avoided suspicion in that first killing, did not decide to kill again?"

Heinrick Vandercleef rose from his place behind his desk. "Gentlemen, please. Let us not turn this into a mockery of an inquisition. Braughton, if you please, tell us where you were last night."

Brau kept his gaze on Icharus. "I was on my way to join you at the church for the festivities, of course. I'd had some business in town to attend to and was a bit late. The gentleman with whom I met left before I, so he is not available for questioning to give testimony, having departed on the Aleria, bound for England. He is not due back for some time, I'm afraid."

Heinrick nodded. "You met with this gentleman where, Braughton?"

His gaze moved to Katherine. "At the Cock and

Crow Tavern."

"And what time did this meeting end?"

"I left the tavern approximately three quarters of an hour before I arrived here, Heins. I would not have had sufficient time to reach the Hollow had I made any detours ... or paused to commit murder along the way," he said, his voice dripping with sarcasm.

He looked at Callum, and then at Everett Bleeker, his gaze a bit shuttered. "As occasional patrons of the tavern yourselves, gentlemen, I believe you will agree as regarding the time."

Blushes riding high on each of their faces, Callum, Everett, and even Heinrick nodded in agreement.

Brau tipped his head in acknowledgement. "I arrived just minutes before Crane came back to the bridge for John's body."

He turned to Katherine. "My apologies, my dear. I would not have you privy to such base information, but you did insist upon being present for this."

Heinrick straightened and drew in a deep breath. "In light of what we have heard here, gentlemen, I conclude it would have been impossible for Brau here to have murdered John. He simply would not have had time to do the deed."

Everett and Callum agreed.

Heinrick looked to Katherine and then to Icharus. "Master Crane? Mistress Katherine? What think you?"

Katherine released a breath. "As I have no knowledge of the time it would take to travel from the ... the Cock and Crow Tavern to Sleepy Hollow, I will take your word for it, Heins. I believe Brau is innocent as well."

Icharus kept his gaze on Brau for a long moment before he spoke. "So this is your alibi, Van Ripper? You were carousing at a local tavern?"

He shook his head. "No matter. As you have said,

you would not have had sufficient time, if you were indeed at the tavern as you have said ... to partake in John's murder. Be assured that I will investigate your claim. Unless I discover reason to believe otherwise, I will say that I too find you to be innocent in the matter of John Tanner's death."

Brau's gaze flickered to Katherine. She visibly relaxed before his eyes, and he tipped his head. "Thank you, Master Crane."

Heinrick turned to Icharus. "And you, Master Crane? Have you proof of your whereabouts last eve?"

Icharus nodded. "As much as Van Ripper, aye. I had gone to the Van Brunt place to change into more suitable attire for your celebration. Mrs. Porter can vouch for the time of my departure, and I arrived outside the church a mere minute before you, Everett here, and the two young men burst through the door."

Brau arched a brow. "You will not mind if we verify the hour of your departure with Mrs. Porter, I presume? Just as you have promised to check up on mine?"

Icharus shook his head. "Nay. In fact, I would expect nothing less."

Brau nodded to Heinrick. "That is that, then, eh, Heins? Innocent ... all of us. Which leads us precisely nowhere. If neither of us murdered John, and we are all agreed that none of us did, then the question remains. Who is John Tanner's murderer?"

Chapter 8

After an hour of debate, it was decided that an outsider was responsible for the murder of John Tanner. It was agreed that a watch would be set up in the village, with Icharus, Callum, Heinrick, and Icharus's man Jericho Downes rotating the position. Brau would not take part because, although he was a frequent visitor to the Van Brunt place, he maintained a residence outside the Hollow.

The schoolmaster declared his intention to leave the Hollow. He and his family would depart immediately after John's funeral on the morrow.

Katherine was saddened by the news. *Is everyone set to leave Sleepy Hollow?* Though she said nothing, she suddenly felt quite abandoned and alone.

Finally, the meeting drew to a close, and Katherine gathered her cloak close about her in preparation for the ride home. The temperature had not risen since she had journeyed forth this morning, and though the snow had stopped, a chill wind blew, and it found its way into every crook and crevice in her carriage.

"I'll ride up with you," Brau offered. He walked away without waiting for her consent to tie his horse's reins at the back of the vehicle.

Katherine looked in Icharus's direction, but he was deep in conversation with Heinrick and did not notice. She would much rather have spent the ride with him. Her congratulations on how he'd handled matters this morning would have to wait, she supposed.

Brau returned and extended a hand to assist her into the carriage. "Come, we'll get you home now. I still cannot believe you came out in this cold, Katherine. You'll have Mrs. Porter fix you a nice broth when we arrive. Promise me."

Katherine sighed. "A little cold is not going to harm me, Brau, nor a bit of coarse conversation," she said, pointedly referring to his admittance of being at a tavern before he'd joined them last eve.

He handed her into the carriage, and Mr. Rawlins hurried atop to take up the reins. Brau joined her, taking the opposite seat.

After giving a rap with his cane to the top of the box to signal the driver he should start their journey home, he said, "So my confession affected you not at all?"

She gave a little laugh. "Confession? Ah, that you'd been loitering in the tavern? Nay, not a whit. You forget, Brau, that my father often visited such places, along with many others of its like when we traveled. If I thought you'd never seen the inside of such a place, I might be at a loss as for what I should think of you."

He kept his gaze on her. "I often forget you are not like other females of my acquaintance, but I find your ability to understand and accept such behavior quite odd, Katherine. It did not disturb you in the least?"

"I would be disturbed if you arrived on my doorstep overwhelmed by strong spirits and acting the fool, Brau," she said wryly, "but thus far you have behaved quite as a gentleman should."

He watched her in silence for a long while. Katherine grew uncomfortable under his gaze, and turned to stare out the window.

"Why did you come to Heinrick's office this morning, Katherine? You have to have known I would object. Our business was not an appropriate topic for a female. Yet you came anyway, determined to intrude—"

Katherine met his gaze, her own hard. "There was no intrusion, Brau. Icharus asked if I should like to sit in on the proceedings, and I said yes. No one else seemed to be offended. Why were you?"

He scowled. "A murder inquiry is not proper conversation for a woman, as well you know."

Katherine's mocking laughter rang out. "A woman may commit murder, but she is not allowed to sit in on an examination? Come now, Brau. Isn't that a bit hypocritical?"

His scowl lessened to a frown. "It's just not done, Katherine. I shouldn't have wanted my bride to join us. It isn't seemly for a female to participate in such matters."

She looked away. "Then 'tis good we're not wed, is it not?"

He leaned forward, taking her hand in his. "Rather the contrary, Katherine. Had we been man and wife, I could have insisted you return home forthwith, and you would not have been subjected to the harsh conversations conducted these past hours."

She stared at him. "And I would forever have had the haunting fear one of you could be guilty of John's murder, Brau. I may never have trusted you again. How would that have benefited you? A wife who mistrusts her spouse?"

He maintained his careful regard. "You would have had no reason not to trust me."

"Because you willed it so?" She shook her head. "It

would not be enough for me, Brau."

He rubbed a gloved thumb against the top of her hand for a moment, caressing her through the doeskin. Finally, he released her fingers and leaned back in his seat. "You are quite an unusual woman, Katherine Van Brunt. Something I did not understand before."

He shook his head slowly. "An oddity, and yet ..."

She cocked her head to the side in question.

He nodded, as though coming to some conclusion within himself. "Perhaps I should give some consideration to this unique difference in you, Katherine. Mayhap it is not quite as unseemly as I have thought."

Her brow furrowed a bit, and then she gave a little nod. "Aye, perhaps you should, Brau. But truly, I am not so different from other women as you seem to think. It is just that I tend to speak my mind and follow my heart, where another woman might be more timid."

He shook his head and grinned. "A strong-minded woman who follows her heart. Heaven help us all."

She allowed the corners of her own mouth to turn up in an answering smile. "So it will, Brau. So it will."

* * * *

Several paces behind the Van Brunt carriage, Icharus and Callum rode in casual silence until Callum motioned to the conveyance. "He's probably berating her for joining us this morning."

Icharus smiled, remembering Katherine's surprise when he'd asked her to join them. "If so, he shall soon regret such foolishness."

Callum peered sideways at him. "Foolishness?"

Icharus nodded, and Callum's gaze rested curiously on the carriage once more. "And if you were inside with her? What would the two of you be discussing if not the wickedness of her intrusion into the affairs of men?"

Icharus laughed. "How soon construction could be started on the stables, no doubt. Or perhaps an accounting of the number of timbers needed for the new homes she wishes to see built."

Callum snorted. "Fools, the both of you."

Icharus's smile faded. "Oh? Then tell me, oh wise one, how should us slow-witted men spend our time, do we find a moment alone with the estimable Mistress Van Brunt?"

Callum frowned at him. "Minding your manners for one," he cautioned. Then he grinned.

"But should manners fail you, you might consider spending those moments uttering words of praise to her eyelashes or other nonsense ... if you wanted to gain her attention, that is."

Icharus shook his head. "It would never work, you know. Not with Katherine."

Callum pretended to be shocked by his revelation. "Why ever not, Crane? Are you telling me our lovely Kat is quite different from other females?"

Icharus fell silent for a moment, and then he said, "Aye, she is different. Most women would flutter about, rambling on about nothing more pressing than the chill turn of the weather, but Katherine ... her mind is possessed with a great wealth of substance, and so she is concerned least of all by whether the precipitation outside is rain or snow."

Callum nodded, and would have made an observation of his own, but Icharus continued.

"She's quite brilliant, and fully capable of making her own deductions ... or striking a difficult bargain," he said, his mouth tilting wryly.

He nodded his head toward the snow-covered landscape. "Further, she has a passion for this place – her home – a passion that shows itself in the radiance of her gaze when you allow her free rein to discuss it, which Braughton rarely does, apparently."

Once again, Callum would have added an observation, and once again, Icharus continued.

"Beyond that, I sense that she cares very deeply for those who hold a special place in her heart, and would fight to the death to protect anyone who was lucky enough to have won such a place."

Callum brows arched high. "Do I detect a bit of wistful yearning in your voice?" He snorted and shook his head, disbelieving. "I would have expected as much from your father over the fair Katrina, but you? For Katherine?"

Icharus turned to him then. "Why not Katherine? She has some weakness or flaw of which I'm not aware?"

Callum swallowed his laughter. "You certainly see a lot in a woman you've only just met a short time ago, Master Crane."

Ignoring the insinuation, Icharus shrugged. "I see what I see."

Callum nodded. "So do I, although occasionally I regret having seen anything at all."

Icharus cast him a curious glance. "You speak of your gift …?"

Callum laughed. "Gift. Curse. Sometimes it feels like both. It comes and goes on a whim. I have no control over it at all, and it can be quite frustrating."

"You saw something, a vision, the day I first came to Sleepy Hollow, did you not?"

"I did. A raven, a crane, and the Horseman."

Icharus frowned. "I would be the crane, of course, but what of the others?"

"Braughton. The raven." He shrugged. "Then the Hessian. John's death … it is all connected."

"You're saying that, according to your vision, John was killed by the Headless Horseman?" Icharus's brows rose in disbelief. "Master Mather, aren't you a bit old for subscribing to legend and folklore as truth?"

Callum scowled. "Would that I was, Crane. I alone have been the only person in the Hollow who refused to believe in the existence of either witch or horseman." He shrugged. "It is like you said, I see what I see."

"Have you seen anything recently?"

Callum looked away, a flush darkening his face. "Nothing I wish to discuss."

Icharus shifted in his saddle to peer at him. "If you have seen anything that may have bearing on—"

Callum was already shaking his head. "No. I've seen nothing that would reveal the identity of John's killer. My latest vision was … of a more romantic nature."

Icharus grinned. "Ah. A lady in your future?"

Callum snorted. "There is most definitely a lady in my future, but the vision was not one from my own life."

Icharus laughed out loud. "Voyeurism? What sort of spirit is this, to allow you to peek at another's love life?"

"An unusual one, no doubt," Callum mumbled. His gaze flicked to the carriage in front of them, and he shook his head.

Icharus caught his glance, and his brows rose. "Katherine?"

He nodded, and Icharus frowned. After a moment, his frown became a scowl. "Tell me of this vision you have seen of Katherine's … romantic … future."

Callum considered for a moment, and then shook his head. "Nay, I'll not speak of it."

His refusal irritated Icharus. "But your knowledge could have some bearing on the future of Sleepy Hollow."

Callum sighed. "Indeed it does, Crane, but I'll not rush it along by letting others know what I know. I prefer to wait and see. Things could change."

Icharus was scowling darkly now. "Do they often change, differ from whatever you have seen?"

Callum shook his head. "Sadly, no. At least they haven't thus far. But I continue to hope."

He continues to hope.

That could mean only one thing. He'd seen Katherine with Braughton Van Ripper, no doubt. That irritated him.

Drawing Defiance to a halt, he said, "You go on ahead, Mather. I'll be along later."

"Where are you heading?"

"Off to the cemetery. The gravediggers could probably use a hand, what with the ground being half frozen. After that, I'll check with Jericho to see how things are going in the forest."

Callum nodded. "I'll be ready after dinner. I want to ride out to the Tanner place, to make sure everything's okay. You're sure you won't join us? Katherine is likely looking forward to a more lively conversation by now," he chided.

Icharus placed a light kick against Defiance's side.

"You'll provide that aplenty, I'm sure. I'll see you tonight," he called, already headed off in the opposite direction.

* * * *

Callum caught up to the carriage just as it drew to a halt in front of the house. He dismounted, and after passing the reins of his mount to Mr. Rawlins, joined the couple on the steps. "I hope Mrs. Porter has dinner ready. I'm starved!"

Katherine smiled. "Nothing unusual there, Callum. You're always empty from the toes, it seems."

After a quick glance around, she asked, "Where is

Master Crane? I thought the two of you rode up together?"

"He said he'd be along later. There were some things he wanted to check on."

Her smile faded. "Should we hold dinner for him?"

Callum shook his head. "Nay, he won't be back for some time. He was going to lend a hand at the cemetery, then head over to the Western Wood to check progress there."

Disappointment settled over Katherine, and she turned away from the two men. The door opened before she could reach for it. Mrs. Porter wiped her hands on her apron. "You've guests in the parlor, mistress. I've laid a place for them at the table as well."

Katherine pulled her cloak from her shoulders and passed it to the elder woman. "Thank you, Mrs. Porter. Gentlemen, will you join me in greeting my guests before we dine?"

Brau was shrugging off his greatcoat, and Callum did likewise. "Of course we shall, Katherine."

She nodded and swept toward the parlor.

Inside the parlor, a young man scrambled hastily to his feet. Beside him, a woman Katherine thought to be near to her own age stood as well. It was quite obvious the lady was expecting, but before she could welcome them, or offer her well wishes for the child, the man extended his hand to her.

"Carter Wesley, mum, and this is me missus, Alaina. We spoke to your man some time back about the vacant house."

The men came into the parlor behind her. Brau shook the man's hand. "Braughton Van Ripper, Master Wesley. This charming lady before you is Katherine Van Brunt, daughter of the late Abraham Van Brunt."

The gentleman nodded in her direction, then put out a hand toward Callum.

Brau continued, "I believe you've already met Master Mather."

Carter nodded. "Yes, sir. In town we did. Mister Mather here tells me ye have plans for a bit of reconstruction, and well, mum, I may not be swift of mind, but I'm quite handy with a mallet."

Callum tilted his head in acknowledgement toward the young lady. "Mistress Wesley, Carter, welcome to Sleepy Hollow."

Katherine smiled. "Wonderful, Master Wesley. We'll have need of such a skill in the coming days."

She turned to the lady. "Mistress Wesley, I see you will be welcoming a new member into your family soon. Congratulations. You must be so happy!"

The lady, Alaina, offered a shy smile. "We are. Carter is hoping for a girl, but we both would be just as thrilled if 'tis a boy."

Katherine's smile widened. "Master and Mistress Vandercleef, the village notary and his wife, are also expecting their first child come summer. I am sure Mary and yourself will have much to discuss."

She turned to Brau. "Mrs. Porter has dinner prepared. Shall we go into the dining room? We can discuss where you'll be staying while we dine."

Brau nodded and with a hand at the small of Katherine's back, led the way to the dining room.

* * * *

At the cemetery, Icharus cast an irritated glower toward the Van Brunt house, and stabbed at the frozen ground with his spade. They were probably enjoying their dinner by now. Did she miss his presence at the table? Had she given him a thought since their meeting at Vandercleefs' this morning?

Hefting out a chunk of half-frozen dirt, he frowned.

Like as not, no. She really had no reason. He was just the man who'd agreed to help her achieve her dream, to bring life back into Sleepy Hollow. As such, he was nowhere near as important as the man with whom she would soon share the rest of her life.

He could imagine her sitting at the table, with Van Ripper stoically ignoring her from her left and Mather filling the awkward silence with his rakish wit on her right, and her smiling for the both of them.

Would she be content to do so for the rest of her days?

He tried to imagine her as Braughton's wife, and the image he conjured did not set well at all. He could see her some years into the future, quiet and withdrawn, her eyes having lost even the tiniest shred of light.

That was what life with Van Ripper would do to her.

But then again, what else is there for her?

Not him, certainly. He would be in Sleepy Hollow only long enough to set things into motion. After that, he'd go back to Wake Grove and his family there, just the way he had planned from the beginning.

Still, the thought of it disturbed him.

He cut into the ground once again, taking out his frustration on the wet earth at his feet. Tomorrow, they would bury John Tanner's body. The day after, he would start clearing away the burned ruins. His days would be full, to be sure, but he did not know how long he could ignore the dreams that came to him in the night, of Katherine, her eyes alight with passion, smiling only for him.

Beside Icharus, Thomas Gentry, Heinrick's manservant, lifted a heavy shovel full of frozen, wet earth from the grave they were digging, and straightened. Pulling a worn handkerchief from the cuff of his sleeve, he raised it to his brow, dabbing at the beads of perspiration there.

" 'Tis a shame about Master Tanner. 'Course we all knowed weren't no good to come of his meddlin' in those woods."

He shook his head in regret, and after tucking the handkerchief away, bent to remove another bit of dirt from the now waist-deep hole they were digging.

Icharus chopped into the earth. "The trees had nothing to do with John Tanner's death. He was murdered."

The man's brows drew together. "Of course he was murdered, sir. That witch woman, she sends out the Hessian to do her bidding. Me and the missus, we're always careful to stay clear of the forest when we're out."

He shrugged. "Not that we're out much, 'cept for diggin' holes. Dug a mighty lot of these lately."

Icharus swore and tossed the spade aside. "What is it with you people? What will it take to convince you there is no Headless Horseman, and there is no witch? A *man* killed John Tanner – a living, breathing, flesh and blood *man* – who could be anywhere, even as we speak! If you would have a care toward your safety, man, look to the people around you."

He heaved himself out of the pit, and dusted his hands together. A sigh of disgust escaped.

"I will send Mr. Rawlins 'round in a bit to help with the rest. Good day, Thomas. Give my regards to the Vandercleefs'."

He stalked to the tall stand of oaks where he'd tied Defiance's reins, and whipped them loose before vaulting onto the horse's back. With a swift nudge from his heels, he started forward with a jolt toward the forest.

Mayhap Jericho would prove better company.

* * * *

140

Callum waited for him on the piazza when he returned. It was late. He'd spent the remainder of the afternoon and most of the evening helping Jericho and Dehann in the forest. He had ridden to the Tanner house to look in on Anne and Clara before heading back to the Van Brunt manor, and he was tired and still irritable. He wanted nothing more than to go up to his room and collapse in his bed, to forget the events of the day and start afresh come morning, but Callum's presence meant he would have to wait.

"I wondered if you'd forgotten our agreement this morning. You're late."

Icharus frowned. "Late? Ah, for the watch. Yes. Sorry. I stopped off at the Tanners' and shared a late meal with the family."

Callum nodded. "Well, now that you're here, I'll head out."

He started down the steps and then halted. "Katherine waited up for you. She's in the study. Said she had something important to discuss."

Icharus inclined his head. "Thank you. I shall look in on her before I make my way to my room."

"Master Wesley and his wife arrived today. Katherine and I showed them out to the Von Groot place. Carter should put in an appearance 'round sunup."

"Braughton did not join you?"

Callum shook his head. "No. He departed shortly after dinner, but he'll be back in the afternoon tomorrow to speak with you about the stables and such."

Icharus arched a brow. "Really? I rather expected him to avoid all mention of it. Katherine said … well, that is neither here nor there, is it?"

Callum shrugged. "I'll be off now. I should return just before daybreak."

Icharus waved him off, and climbed the steps, his

thoughts already on Katherine, who awaited him in the study. He wondered what new matter of importance had arisen that she might possibly wish to speak with him about at this hour.

He paused outside the doorway of the study, and just stared, letting his gaze wander leisurely over her. Several lamps had been lit to ward off the darkness, and a fire cracked and hissed in the hearth, banishing even the hint of a chill from the room.

Bathed in the soft glow from the lamps, sitting behind the large mahogany desk in her father's chair, Katherine sat with her legs turned to the side rather than straight in front of her. She held a book in one hand while the other played with a dusky curl at her temple.

One elbow was propped against the shiny wooden surface, and several sable tendrils of her hair had twined themselves into the fall of pristine lace that spilled from the dark cuff of her gown.

Her expression was that of one completely absorbed, and he wondered at the nature of the text she was reading that so held her rapt attention.

Mather's ancestor's work, no doubt. The one she'd copied word for word.

Holding back the low chuckle that threatened, he leaned forward and knocked softly against the door facing. "Katherine? Callum said you wished to see me?"

A short yelp of surprise burst from her lips, and she leapt to her feet. The book she'd been holding dropped from her fingers and landed on the floor with a solid thud.

Her hands flew to her chest, and his gaze followed their flight, coming to rest on her firmly rounded, now heaving bosom.

"Master Crane! You gave me such a fright!"

He straightened and stepped into the room. "Icharus, please, and allow me to offer my most humble

142

apologies. I didn't mean to frighten you, Katherine."

Eyes wide, she lifted trembling fingers to her lips. She squeezed her eyes tightly shut for a moment, and he watched her draw in one calming breath, and then another. He let his gaze feast in silence upon her beauty while she fought to regain her composure. After a moment, she lowered her hands and offered a shaky smile.

"Icharus, yes. Perhaps I should choose reading material of a milder nature for late-night study. I was quite engrossed in the tale, and then you..." She broke off with a shake of her head, and waved toward a chair near the fire. "Please sit. You must be tired, so I shall only keep you for a moment."

He crossed to the seat she'd indicated and dropped into it with an exhausted sigh. "What is it you wished to speak with me about?"

She turned away, thoughtful now, her fingers pressed together, steepled at her waist.

When she faced him again, her eyes were alight with happiness, sparkling with excitement. She lowered her hands quickly to her sides, and though her feet never left their place on the floor, he would have sworn she was almost dancing with glee.

A bright smile parted her lips, and Icharus could feel his own mood lighten in the face of her exuberance.

"I should like to build an inn in Sleepy Hollow."

His brows flew upward. "An inn?"

She shook her head excitedly. "Yes. It's a wonderful idea, do you not agree? We need new people in Sleepy Hollow, and with the shortage of housing ... why, I think it's quite brilliant."

Icharus contemplated the idea, but as tired as he felt, he found he could not do so objectively. "An inn. Why? And where do you plan to build it? Have you given thought to that?"

She began to pace in front of him. "We could certainly use the extra coin for one thing, and it might prove helpful in bringing new people into the Hollow. And, in the beginning, an inn could provide the much needed room and board for those who come into Sleepy Hollow to labor on our behalf."

She stopped pacing and looked at him, her gaze suddenly soft and shy. "I thought we might build it where the old schoolhouse stood, Icharus, the one where your father once taught."

Icharus straightened in the chair and nodded, acknowledging her words. "While I thank you for thinking of my father, Katherine, I'm not sure … but then there isn't much of anything I am sure of at this moment."

He fell back against the back of the chair and closed his eyes. He raised a hand, pinching the bridge of his nose between finger and thumb. "An inn. In Sleepy Hollow."

He cracked one eye open and peered at her. She had turned away, but he could see the animation she'd shown but a moment before was gone and her shoulders slumped dejectedly.

And he was the sole cause of her rapid transformation.

Dash it!

He'd ruined her excitement, the thrill of the moment, and felt quite guilty for having done so. He sighed. "Katherine?"

She turned to look at him, and he motioned for her to come closer. When she would have halted a few paces from his chair, he waved her closer still, and then sat up and reached out for her hand.

He gave her fingers a little squeeze and brought them to his lips, where he placed a soft, lingering kiss just above her knuckles. "It's a good idea."

She watched him for a moment before her lips turned upward once more. "You really think so?"

He nodded. "I do. And shall likely have more to say about it in the morning, but after a day of digging, swinging Jericho's monstrous axe, and dragging treetops halfway across Sleepy Hollow, my mind's a little sluggish."

"And it's so late! I should have waited, I know, but—"

He forestalled her words with a shake of his head. "No, you were excited, and rightly so. I'm glad you waited to share your idea with me."

His fingers had begun to caress hers, his thumb moving in slow circles over the top of her hand. She pulled away, her teeth tugging at her lower lip.

"I … yes, thank you. I am glad too."

She lowered her gaze shyly and then walked to the door. She paused in the doorway, looking back at him. "Goodnight, Icharus."

Standing there, she looked so beautiful it was all he could to do remain seated, to not go to her and kiss her as he yearned to do.

"Goodnight, Katherine," he said, his voice husky. "Pleasant dreams."

He noticed a faint blush on her cheeks just before she quit the room. He could hear the rapid patter of her feet on the stairs as she rushed to her room, and he dropped back into the chair and closed his eyes. An illogical refrain whispered through his thoughts in the same staccato rhythm of her footsteps – *follow me, follow me, follow me.*

Chapter 9

The first day of winter dawned gray and cold. The heavy-laden clouds beginning to bank overhead promised to deliver more snow soon. The mourners gathered for John Tanner's burial, huddled about the gravesite in their thick cloaks and heavy coats. The ladies battled the icy morning breeze to keep their hats and veils in place for the ceremony.

The Honorable Reverend Jameson Weycliffe had come from TarryTown to perform the funeral services, and Everett Bleeker and his family left the Hollow soon after the ceremony. Nell had a sister upstate in New York City, and they would be staying with her through the holidays, maybe longer, Everett had said. Once he had found employment, they would look for a place of their own in the city.

A bit back from the crowd that had gathered at the church to see the Bleekers off, Icharus leaned against the trunk of a tall oak, idly noting how similar this day was to when he had first arrived in Sleepy Hollow – cold, drab, colorless.

It seemed the very life had been sucked out of both the people and the place, and he found it difficult to reconcile this Sleepy Hollow with the one of warmth and beauty and laughter revealed through his father's many stories.

Ichabod Crane had spoken of the day-to-day living in Sleepy Hollow as if it had been one long and joyous celebration of life, and that, he knew, was what Katherine sought to see restored here. She wanted almost desperately to bring back the heart and soul – nay, the very spirit – of the place.

And she'd asked him to help her.

He looked at her now, standing between Braughton and Callum while she reiterated her heartfelt condolences to Clara and the rest of the Tanner family.

So much had fallen on her slender shoulders of late. Looking around at the care-worn and sorrowful lot who were, for better or worse, the hope and future of Sleepy Hollow, Icharus found himself wondering, much like Braughton, if her dreams of renewal and rebirth were even possible.

Overhead, the clouds parted. Bright rays of sunlight spilled forth over the gently sloping hills and rolling valleys, bathing the lackluster village of Sleepy Hollow in soft, brilliant, golden hues.

The effect was breathtaking.

Off the tops and boughs of trees still sporting snow from the day before, the sunlight glinted off each crystal of ice like diamonds winking from the branches, setting the valley afire with a wash of light and color.

Where he had seen only fields laid to waste before, now he could see bejeweled blankets covering fertile treasures just waiting to be discovered, pockets of rich soil tucked hither and yon over the countryside, patiently awaiting the first kiss of spring and the births of many a bountiful harvest.

His gaze touched on the broken and twisted orchards, yet now he could almost feel the yearning, the inherent need within each limb and unborn leaf, to spread themselves in resplendent array and perfect obedience to nature. In wonder, he thought of the fruit that would grace each tree, the offspring of hope and diligent effort ripening to perfection on branch after branch.

Even the air around him seemed to sing in revelation, a joyous offering of good fortune for all, and for the first time since he'd ridden into this place, Icharus could see what his father before him had seen and all that Katherine held dear from her memories as well.

Hope.

And promise.

His gaze sought Katherine once more. She must have sensed it, because she looked up at him and smiled. The effect of her smile on him was much the same as that of the sunlight off the valley. He wanted to feel every ray of its brilliance, and in gratitude, offer equal value in return.

He smiled back.

* * * *

Seeing the exchange between the two, Brau slid his arm possessively around Katherine, letting his hand rest at the small of her back. With the other, he gestured for Icharus to join them near the church.

Katherine's glance flickered up to meet his, and he said, "I'd like to discuss a few things with Crane if you don't mind, and since I'll be leaving before dinner, I thought the four of us could ride up to the manor together."

From the corner of his eye, he could see the surprise in her gaze, but she didn't mention his unusual departure from the norm. Instead, she shook her head the tiniest bit and looked away, her lips twisting in effort to hide the slight smile that threatened to break forth.

"No, I don't mind at all."

Brau kept his gaze straightforward. "Good."

He turned at Icharus's approach. "Crane, join us, please. There are a few matters about which I'd like to speak with you, if you have time. Callum said you'd planned to begin working over at the Christoffel and Vandenberg places today—"

Icharus nodded. "Aye. The sooner those burnt hulls are pulled down the better. I'd like to see new homes there come spring."

Brau offered a slight nod. "Ride up to the house with us. We'll talk on the way."

Icharus glanced to Katherine and she shrugged. He inclined his head a bit. "I'll get Defiance."

He walked away, and Brau shook his head. "Defiance. What kind of name is that for a worthy mount?"

Katherine glanced sideways at him. "It's as good as any, I suppose. Certainly as fine as Thunder, don't you think?" she chided.

Brau arched a brow. "It reeks of rebellion and disorder."

Katherine's brows pulled downward. "Thunder? Nay, it rumbles across the sky in a storm, with lightning its harbinger, echoing into the silence long after voicing that first ominous roar."

Brau snorted. "I was speaking of Defiance, as well you know. Such silly games you play, Katherine."

"Such glorious displays of jealousy you offer, Braughton," she rejoined. "Over nothing more trivial than a name at that."

He scowled. "Cease, please. 'Tis nonsense."

Katherine pulled out of his embrace. "Aye, quite. You shouldn't want him to overhear. Whatever might he

150

think of you then?"

* * * *

Callum hurriedly disengaged himself from the group and moved off to the side of the church, hoping to escape everyone's notice as he did so. A repeat of the scene he'd last caused after Brom's burial was something he hoped to avoid.

He could feel the distracting haze of premonition surrounding him even now, like a thick cloud of cloistering smoke, enveloping him in its strange presence. This time he wanted no witnesses to whatever might be revealed.

Leaning against the side of the building, he drew in several deep, almost gasping breaths. His lungs burned, and he coughed. It was choking him.

His eyes burned. Hot. Unrelenting. His vision clouded, then cleared, and leaping flames licked at him from every direction, searing him.

Fire!

Everywhere he turned there was fire – hot, agonizing flames that destroyed everything in their wake.

He looked up, and overhead, a crane paced along a branch. A flash of silver drew his gaze, but was quickly overtaken by the flames.

"Silver. Fire. Crane," he gasped out, causing the burning in his throat to sear him even more. He doubled over, going down on his knees while the coughs wracked his body.

* * * *

That was how Icharus found him, gasping and heaving with violent coughs, whispering the same three words

151

between spasms.

"Silver. Fire. Crane."

Unsure how to proceed, Icharus remembered the day he'd come to Sleepy Hollow, and how Katherine had reached out to the man before, when he'd been in the clutches of a vision.

"Callum! Callum, Katherine is looking for you."

At first, he thought his words hadn't penetrated whatever fog held the fellow in its trance. He continued to cough, and slid down to sit upon the cold ground, his arms squeezing fiercely around his middle.

Icharus frowned. "Mather? Are you ill?"

He squeezed his eyes tightly shut, but the coughs seemed to be dissipating now. He shook his head, rolling it from side to side. "Go away, Crane."

Icharus started to leave him there, but he appeared to be unwell, and Icharus almost feared to leave him alone with whatever strange apoplexy had claimed him. He waited.

After a moment, Callum stopped coughing and sagged wearily against the side of the church, his head bent low. He'd released the tight grip he had held on his stomach, and his hands now lay limp against his thighs.

"Decided to stay and enjoy the show, did you? Gawk at the madman?" he accused Icharus.

Icharus ignored his sarcasm. "It was your gift, wasn't it? You saw something – silver, fire, and a crane. I heard you."

Callum sighed, and nodded. "Aye, I saw something. Felt it. Burning me. Choking me."

Icharus's eyes widened. "It's like you're there, isn't it? In the midst of whatever is happening?"

Callum drew his knees up and put his forehead against them. He linked his fingers across the back of his head, and nodded. "Yes, just like that."

Icharus peered at him. "What did it mean?"

Callum groaned. "Fire. I hate it. Last time—"

"Last time?"

Callum lifted his head and Icharus could see tears in his gaze. "The last time I saw fire in a vision, the village of Sleepy Hollow was all but decimated by a fever that burned through, leaving precious few in its wake. I didn't want to tell him, but he insisted—"

"Who insisted?"

"Brom."

Icharus straightened. "Explain."

Callum peered at him through reddened eyes. He stood and propped against the building behind him. "In my vision, I became Katrina, and I burned … from the inside. The fire was so hot it took my breath away, literally."

"So Brom insisted you tell him of his wife's coming death. Is that what you're saying?"

Callum nodded. "Aye, that and the death of the child she carried. It was a boy. No one ever knew that. You're the only one I've told."

He looked at Icharus again. "They had a name, you know, Brom and Katrina, for their unborn son. Brom told me the night Katrina died."

Icharus felt the gooseflesh rise along his arms. "What was the name?"

Callum narrowed his gaze for a moment, and then looked away.

"Icharus," he whispered. "They were going to call their son *Icharus*. But he died along with his mother. And then you showed up. Odd, isn't it?"

* * * *

Katherine sat beside Brau in the carriage, with Icharus and Callum sharing the seat across from them for the ride up to the Van Brunt house.

With her hands folded demurely in her lap, Katherine listened to their conversation with half an ear until it turned to Sleepy Hollow.

"I've a friend who lives just up north a bit who has offered to sell several head of cattle and sheep at a reasonable price, one I can't see anyone being willing to turn down," Brau said.

He shifted in his seat, propping one leg across the other and brushed at the cloth covering his knee. "I intend to make a purchase myself, and would like to make a gift of my acquisition, Katherine, to help restock Sleepy Hollow's pastures ... if you would not feel offended by the charitable gesture, of course."

Katherine was staring at him, eyes wide. "Offended? Nay, I would not be ... but I have coin—"

He offered a thin smile. "Aye, sweeting, but it would not be a gift if I allowed you to make the purchase, now would it?"

She frowned. "Brau, are you certain you wish to do this?"

Brau nodded. "Yes, quite certain. I want to do this for Sleepy Hollow, Katherine. For you ... and for your dream."

The smile that lit Katherine's face was brilliant to behold. "Thank you! Thank you so much, Brau."

She leaned over to press a kiss against his cheek, and Brau brought his hand up to her face letting his gloved fingers caress the line of her jaw. "It is my pleasure."

He turned his gaze to Icharus once more. "I wanted to discuss it with you gentlemen first, however ... will the fences be mended soon? I should hate to bring in livestock before you have secured the capacity to hold them."

Icharus leaned forward a bit. "We hope to have the repairs completed very soon. Jericho and I felled a number of trees yesterday, and he and young Tanner will bring them to the mill as early as tomorrow. It will take some time to bring the animals here. How far is your friend from Sleepy Hollow?"

Brau's gaze flickered to Katherine, and then came back to Icharus. "Several days on horseback. It'll take a fortnight at minimum to travel there and back with the beasts."

Icharus looked at Katherine. "We can have the repairs finished in that time. My younger brother, Balt, is versed in driving cattle. I'll have him ride with you to your friend's place. He can assist you on the return trip."

Katherine's gaze flew to his. "I wasn't aware you had a brother, Icharus."

Callum grinned. "Of course you weren't, Katherine. You were simply too busy imagining him as some singularly capable god of providence, fashioned by the hand of the Almighty with naught but the single purpose of coming here to aid you in your quest—"

"Mather, your insolence leaves much to be desired in the way of manners," Icharus reprimanded. He nodded to Katherine. "Two, actually. Balt is the elder, and Abram the younger. My father obviously felt he owed a great deal to yours, Katherine, as you can see. As a living legacy to the man who changed everything for him, my father named his sons after yours."

"Except for you," Callum said. "I wonder why?"

Icharus looked at him and frowned. "I'm sure he wished his firstborn to carry a name similar to his own."

Katherine was excited now. "I agree with Icharus, Callum." She looked at him now, her gaze curious. "Do you have sisters as well?"

Icharus chuckled. "Aye, two. Eliza and Kathleen. Liza was named for my mother, Elizabeth, and Kathleen … she was named for yours."

"Eliza and Kathleen." Katherine smiled. "I should

155

like to meet them someday."

"I don't doubt that you shall, Katherine, although you may regret it," he warned. "My family is a bit much to take on occasion, and it seems none of them learned an ounce of tact. The lot of them live to shame the life out of the other."

Brau shifted. "Yes, well, I'd like to leave three days hence, Crane. If you can reach your brother in that time, have him join me at the Cock and Crow. We will begin the journey northward from there."

Icharus nodded. "I will."

Callum sighed. "I suppose you'll want me to ride into Wake Grove tomorrow."

Icharus shook his head. "Nay. Master Wesley will go. You will go to TarryTown and bring back every free hand you can find who is willing to work for a daily wage, less room and board."

Katherine frowned. "Room and board? Icharus, I don't think I want ... that is to say, I wouldn't feel safe with so many strangers—"

He glanced at her and shook his head. "We'll put them up at the Bleeker place, for now. Later, when your inn is built, some of them may wish to bring in their families and stay there, at least until the new homes are completed."

"An inn? In Sleepy Hollow?" Brau interrupted.

Icharus nodded. "Where the old schoolhouse stood, I believe. In the meantime, however, Callum will stay at the Bleeker place as well, to keep an eye on things. Clara Tanner can see to meals. It will give her something to busy herself with and will help keep her thoughts occupied with something more constructive than those of John's death."

Brau pinned Icharus with a glare. "And you, Master Crane? Where will you be?"

Icharus shrugged. "For the most part, I'll be in the

forest or the fields. But I'll continue to sleep where I do now, unless you'd rather I stayed elsewhere, Katherine?"

"Nay, there's no need. I mean, you're already settled, and with Callum away, I'd feel safer—"

"I will be near, Katherine, so there's no need for you to worry over your safety. You know I'd never leave you here if I thought you might be harmed in any way," Brau said.

Icharus arched a brow. "You're so certain, Van Ripper? Strange, but I could vow there was a murder just three days past, right here in Sleepy Hollow. Unless you know something we're unaware of, I would say her safety is very much in question … the same as all of ours."

"Are you accusing me yet again, Crane? Katherine is as safe as can be expected, under the circumstances. Everyone in the Hollow will look after her in my absence, and she has Mr. Rawlins and Mrs. Porter—"

Icharus scoffed. "Servants. Old servants at that."

Brau held his gaze. "Loyal servants, Crane. Either of them would die for her."

Icharus's brows rose. "And well they could."

Callum cleared his throat. "Now, boys. Let's not fight. Remember your manners, if you please. We've a lady present."

"Perhaps he's right, Katherine. You should come with me to the city—"

Katherine was already shaking her head. "I am not leaving Sleepy Hollow, Brau. We've discussed this, and you know I feel my place is here."

His mocking gaze brought a blush to her cheeks. "So you do understand a woman has a definite place in life? Marvelous."

"Oh, look. We've arrived." Callum opened the carriage door without waiting for Mr. Rawlins and leapt to the ground. Holding a hand up for Katherine, he assisted her from the conveyance. "Ladies first! Come, Katherine, let us leave these gentlemen to their business. Such dull, dreary conversation."

The two of them started for the front door, and laughter sputtered from Katherine's lips. "Callum, someday that wit of yours is sure to cause you much trouble."

He smiled at her. "Not at all. I'm just thrilled someone appreciates the effort I go to."

Katherine lifted her skirts to ascend the steps, her thoughts distracted by Callum's banter. "Effort? I thought you were quite the natural."

Behind them, Brau and then Icharus left the carriage. Brau watched Katherine go inside, a thoughtful look on his face. He turned to Icharus. "If you're here because of her, Crane, you may as well head back to whatever stone you crawled from beneath. She is mine. Has been since the day her mother died."

Icharus straightened and cast a fleeting glance toward Brau before letting his gaze rest on Katherine.

"Feeling threatened, Van Ripper?" Icharus asked, and then he walked away, leaving Brau seething with impotent rage.

* * * *

Later that afternoon, Icharus returned to find Katherine happily ensconced in a now festooned and beribboned Hall, perched at the top of a rickety ladder, securing candles to the tips of several branches of a tall, scraggly pine.

"Enjoying yourself?"

She jerked around at the sound of his voice, causing the ladder to wobble threateningly. He reached out to steady it. "Careful …"

"Do you like it? I had almost forgotten, what with

everything that's happened recently. Dehann cut it. He said we simply must have a tree."

Icharus caught her around the waist and lifted her down. "I think I like it much better with you here, safely on the floor. Where is Callum? Send him up that poor excuse for a ladder."

She gathered more decorations in one hand and started back up. "With Master Wesley, out at the Christoffel's place. Pass me that bell, please?"

Icharus handed her the bauble, and she reached into the branches to fasten it to the tree. "Callum never dresses the tree. Says he's sensitive to the needles. They are prickly."

She glanced at him, and then climbed down for more decorations. "Mother said he was sensitive to height, and that was why he never assisted us with the garlands and streamers and the like at the holidays. But we weren't allowed to tease him about it, she'd say."

Icharus scoffed. "Of course not."

He handed her another bauble from those she'd scattered over the table near the tree. "What else did your mother say about our esteemed Master Mather?"

Katherine paused for a moment, thoughtful. Then she smiled. "That he was a dear, sweet boy who was largely misunderstood, due to the gift nature had chosen to bestow upon him. Mother said Callum was blessed, and as such, we should take special care to never ridicule him when a vision came upon him."

"Don't tease and don't ridicule. I see," Icharus said. He handed her another trinket.

"The Golden Rule, yes. Mother often reminded us children that we should do only that which we would have done to us in return."

Icharus looked up at her. "Us children? I thought you were an only child?"

Katherine nodded. "Of course I am. But there were

many others when Mother was alive. The Christoffels and Vandenbergs each had several children; and there were Clara and John's twins, Johann and Nathan; and Anne and Dehann; Eustace; and Leighton, the Von Groot's eldest. He'd moved away long before you came to the Hollow."

"So you weren't alone, as a child?"

Katherine laughed. "Never. It seemed there was never a moment of silence to be had."

"And then the fever came."

Her smile disappeared, and she nodded. "Yes. The fever. Father was so happy at the time. He and Mum were going to have another child, you know. Not that they weren't happy with me. They were simply ecstatic to have been blessed again after so many years."

"How old were you?"

"Fourteen."

She'd stopped twining baubles into the branches and leaned against the ladder, her mind turned to years past. Icharus could see sadness in her gaze where there had been laughter only moments before, and he bit back an oath.

You did it again, you dolt! Made her think of hurtful things when you'd rather see her smiling.

He held out his hand for her, to assist her descent. "Come down from there, and I'll put the ladder away. You're done here, aren't you?"

After a quick glance around the hall, she nodded. "I don't think there's room for anything else."

She took his hand and climbed down the steps. When she reached the floor, he didn't release her, but pulled her closer.

"I'm sorry, Katherine."

She shrugged. "Don't be sorry. It's life. There was nothing you or I or anyone could have done to prevent what happened."

160

He released her and looked away. "Nay, I meant I am sorry for reminding you of the sorrows you have suffered."

She cocked her head to the side, a little smile curving her lips as she stared at a spot above his head. "Master Crane, have you any idea what is hanging from that beam above you?"

Icharus was almost afraid to look. Still, he tilted his head upward. A small sprig of green met his leery gaze, and he cast her a questioning glance. "Mistletoe?"

She nodded, a sparkle of mischief in her gaze.

He peered at her. "And what of you? You're standing right in front of me, Mistress Van Brunt."

Katherine stepped closer and placed her hands against his chest. "I suppose that means I owe you a kiss, Master Crane."

He cocked a brow and waited while she leaned close.

A throaty laugh spilled from her lips just before they touched his. After nothing more than a quick meeting of mouths, she sprang away, out of his reach.

He chuckled and started after her. "Ah, and here I had hoped for a real kiss from a deliciously lovely lady, but found nothing more than the flirtatious teasing of a coquette."

Katherine froze. Clasping her hands in front of her, she said, "I am not a coquette."

Icharus halted; all humor fled. He could see his choice of words had disturbed her, but he didn't understand why. "You were serious when you kissed me?"

She started to walk away, but he caught her by the shoulders, his gaze locked with hers, refusing to let her escape. He shook his head.

* * * *

"Nay, I don't believe you were. Because if you had been, Katherine, if you really intended to give me a serious kiss, you would be in my arms even now, your mouth fused with mine."

He pulled her closer. "Your arms would have gone 'round my neck, here," he said, lifting them, settling them in place.

"Your body would have leaned in, and your lips would have met mine ... seeking, questing, savoring."

Katherine felt herself being drawn into the seductive spell he wove. Her gaze dropped to his lips, and her breathing changed, became slower, while her heartbeat raced.

She felt his arms come around her, felt him pull her closer to the warmth of his body, her chest nearly touching his. She looked up, into his eyes. They'd gone dark, intense.

"Kiss me now, Katherine. A serious kiss," he whispered.

"Ahem. I believe the mistletoe is over here, Kat."

Callum's voice broke in, and Katherine jerked out of Icharus's embrace, her face flaming. She noticed Icharus had turned away the instant she'd left his arms. He went to the ladder and lifted it from the wall where she'd had it propped.

"I'll just put this away now before someone gets hurt," he said, and reached to open the door.

Callum shrugged out of his coat. "Don't leave on my account. I only meant to let you know if you planned to blame a kiss on the mistletoe, your sense of direction was off a bit – quite a good bit, actually."

He grinned at Icharus.

Icharus glowered at him and hauled the ladder out the door.

Callum turned to Katherine. "I'll be among the first to admit you're lovely, Kat, but I don't think you were supposed to be decorating Master Crane, eh?"

Katherine narrowed her eyes. "Nay, and that's not what I was doing, Callum."

He eyed her speculatively. "Oh? Then allow me to attempt a guess at what happened. You ... fell off the ladder. Yes, that's it. You fell off the ladder, and he caught you."

He shook his head. "No, that couldn't be it. The ladder was over here with the mistletoe ..."

Katherine rolled her eyes. "For pity's sake, Callum. We were under the mistletoe. I kissed him. Not a real kiss, mind you. Just a tiny peck on the lips."

Callum arched a brow. "And somehow the two of you were magically transported from here to there?"

She groaned, feeling the color heighten on her cheeks. "Of course not. I ran away, and he followed me. It was silly of us, now that I think of it. A childish game ..."

His brows rose. "You looked pretty grown-up and serious when I came in."

Katherine huffed in exasperation.

Callum hung his coat on a peg near the door and crossed the hall to the parlor. "Perhaps Brau was right. Someone should be here with you while I'm looking after the workers over at the Bleeker place."

It was her turn to arch a brow. "Someone will be. You heard Icharus in the carriage. Mrs. Porter and Mr. Rawlins will be here. Besides, Icharus is no threat to my safety, Callum. If he were, he would have already shown himself to be a danger, don't you think?"

He frowned. "It's not your safety I'm worried about, Katherine. Rather, I fear for your virtue."

Katherine went about the room, straightening first the drapes and then the pillows on the sofa. "My virtue is quite safe, I assure you. There was nothing serious about that kiss."

163

Callum sat on the thick, rolled arm of the sofa and studied her, his gaze definitely serious, so serious Katherine wanted to shrink away from it – run and hide maybe.

"But he wanted it to be, didn't he? In fact, is that not exactly what I heard him ask for before I interrupted you? A serious kiss?"

Her mouth dropped open in surprise. "Just how long were you there, Callum, shamelessly eavesdropping on us? How could you?"

She picked up a pillow from the sofa and hit him with it.

"Ow!" He plucked the pillow from her fist. "Stop that, Katherine. It's not my fault you were so distracted you didn't hear me come in, now is it?"

He tossed the pillow at her. It glanced off her shoulder and bounced across the floor, coming to rest with one corner on the hot coals in the hearth. It burst into flame, and Katherine cried out.

"Now look what you've done, Callum. Mother worked for hours on that design, and …"

Callum's eyes dimmed.

He shook his head, and hurried to the hearth to retrieve the pillow and crush the flame beneath his boot. When he was certain he had doused even the smallest spark, he tossed the now singed pillow to her.

"There is a lesson here, for both of us. Don't play with fire, Katherine, or you may well be burned. Keep that in mind the next time you're playing at 'childish games' with Icharus Crane."

Chapter 10

Cold and wet seemed to be the pattern for the New Year. It had rained off and on for the past two weeks, since Christmas, Katherine recalled, which she and Icharus had shared with the Tanners.

Callum had suggested she invite Clara and the twins to share Christmas dinner with her and Icharus, and though she'd been a bit leery of Clara's feelings for Icharus since John's death, she had agreed. She was glad she had. The Tanners' presence had made the holiday a bit more bearable, and though there hadn't been an exchange of gifts, the shared company made the day passably joyful.

Icharus had brought them out in his carriage and later had taken them home. The rain had started then, before he returned, and it seemed it hadn't stopped since.

Today, now the third of January, Katherine stood at the parlor window, looking down toward the village, again watching sheets of rain sweep across the already sodden landscape.

Where is Icharus?

The rain had started almost an hour ago. She'd expected him to come riding up the lane at any moment, but no horse and rider had appeared under her watchful gaze.

She turned away and went to stand by the fire, rubbing away the chill that had settled across her shoulders.

Icharus must be freezing out there. Surely he was headed this way, and in that deluge, he would certainly be soaked to the bone.

She glanced at the window again, her brows pulled downward. It would be dark soon. Callum was staying at the old Bleeker place, which had been designated as a temporary public house for the workers who had come into Sleepy Hollow. Brau still had not returned from his trip north.

Mrs. Porter and Mr. Rawlins would be going below stairs soon, and she'd be alone.

Pulling her shawl tighter around her shoulders, she went to the sofa and took up the book she had been reading, although she couldn't remember much of what she had read.

She wasn't frightened to be there without the others. Rather, she was feeling a bit lonely.

With Callum gone and Brau away, and with Icharus spending every possible minute working on the fences, dismantling the burned houses, overseeing the workers who had begun to clear the fields and orchards, in addition to assisting Jericho in the Western Woods, or rebuilding the coops in the hen house – even the rain hadn't halted his efforts – there had been no one to talk to of late when her work for the day was done.

She missed Callum's wit and Brau's quiet companionship. She missed Icharus's ready smile, the way his warm gaze followed her about a room, the way his very presence made her feel relaxed and able to be herself.

On some of the days over the past few weeks, when

the weather had permitted, she had put on her warmest outfits and gone with Icharus to whichever worksite he planned to be at for the day. She had carried away bits of rubble from the burned hulls until her shoulders ached, while Icharus and Callum worked at dismantling the carcasses.

When it rained, like today, she had Mr. Rawlins drive her into the village where she assisted Clara and Mary with the cleaning, laundry, and cooking for the workers. In the evenings, Mr. Rawlins fetched her back so she could take care of her own household.

Anna Tanner had almost immediately taken up with Carter's young wife, Alaina, and she now spent a good deal of her time with her. Katherine, however, felt out of place with the younger ladies, and the older ladies seemed more the mothering sort rather than companions to share her thoughts with of late.

Callum would chide her if he knew how she felt, saying she set up walls where none existed and that the other women would love to chat with her about mending and sewing and working the churn or spinning wheel.

She smiled at the thought.

Callum had often stayed with the Tanners before her father took ill. She had missed him then, but he had always come home within a few days. When Brom was stricken by the fever, and his health had begun to deteriorate rather than improve, Callum had chosen to stay at the Van Brunt manor, in case she needed him, he had said.

And there had been times when she had needed his assistance, but more times than not, she had taken care of her father alone. Still, having him there, in the house, had been a great comfort to her. She had never felt alone … like she did now.

She sighed, shaking her head against the maudlin mood she'd fallen into.

"Edda? Could you bring more tea? Mine has gone cold."

Mrs. Porter bustled into the room a moment later, holding a steaming teapot, her apron folded beneath it so she wouldn't get burned. "This is the last of it, mum. Will Master Crane be joining you for dinner this evening, or will you eat alone again?"

Katherine waited while the elder woman refilled her cup, and then she lifted it to her lips. She blew gently across the steaming brew before taking a tiny sip.

"He's been working so hard, Edda. He has accomplished much in a short time, but I think he should rest at least a bit, don't you? Why, he could take ill out there in this weather, day after day—"

The sound of the front door opening and the scuffling of feet in the hall brought Katherine to her feet. She sat her cup aside and headed to the door.

"Icharus? Mrs. Porter wants to know if you'll be joining me for dinner ... oh."

Katherine stared at Mr. Rawlins and the young man in the entry, a wary frown drawing her brows downward. "I'm sorry. I thought you were ... can I help you?"

Mr. Rawlins shrugged and dismissed himself just before a large black man stepped inside, behind the younger man. He wore a big smile and seemed friendly enough. It took a moment before Katherine recognized him as Icharus's man, Jericho Downes.

"Master Downes."

He clapped the younger man on the shoulder. "This here's Balt, Mistress Katherine. He's looking for Icharus. Is Master Crane here?"

Katherine gave the younger man a polite smile. "It's a pleasure to meet you, Balt."

He returned her smile and nodded in her direction. "The pleasure's mine, Mistress. I hope you don't mind that I came up without Master Van Ripper. We parted back a ways. He said there were some matters he needed to see to at home and pointed me here. Said I'd find Icharus here in the big house at the end of the lane. He's not here?"

Katherine shook her head. "No, he's not. In fact, I thought you two were … he wasn't with you in the forest, Master Downes?"

Jericho shook his head. "No, ma'am. With the rain an' all, I thought he'd done come up here where it was a might warmer."

Katherine felt a frisson of alarm. She hugged herself, fighting off the shiver that chased through her. "Jericho, when did you last see Icharus?"

He shrugged. "Been a few hours, I guess. He left just before dark. Maybe he's 'round at the stables and you just didn't see him ride up?"

Katherine was reaching for her cloak. "No. I've been watching the road for hours. If Icharus had come that way, I would have seen him. Edda?"

Mrs. Porter came to the door of the parlor just as Katherine was pulling on her gloves.

"Fetch Mr. Rawlins and have him bring Isolde and the carriage around. He'll need to drive Master Crane here to Heinrick's."

She turned to Icharus's brother. "Icharus may have stopped there before Heins began his watch," she explained.

Balt frowned, but Katherine didn't elaborate. "Jericho, you'll ride with me … in case he didn't."

Mrs. Porter nodded and left them to do as Katherine had bid. A few minutes later, she returned with Mr. Rawlins in tow. He nodded a general greeting to the room, and then turned to Katherine.

"Mistress, you're thinking to go out in this weather to look for Master Crane?"

Katherine nodded. "Yes, Mr. Rawlins, I am. Please

169

ready Isolde and the carriage. I'll need you to drive young Master Crane to the Vandercleefs'. Icharus left the forest where he was working with Master Downes before dark, and unless he stopped to speak with Heins, I'm afraid …"

Mr. Rawlins nodded in understanding of her unspoken words, but he said, "Master Crane's carriage is not in the carriage house, Mistress Katherine. Perhaps he came 'round the back, having decided to go into town … or to go home for a stay?"

Katherine frowned, considering the possibility. She cast a worried glance to Jericho and saw a troubled frown gracing his features as well. Finally, she shook her head. "No, Mr. Rawlins. He would have had Jericho come to fetch the carriage had he thought to …. No. He's on Defiance, and he's out there alone. Something is wrong, I know it."

Katherine started for the door, but Balt reached out a hand to halt her. "What do you mean, 'something is wrong'? And what is this *watch* you mentioned earlier? If Icharus is in danger, I'd like to know why."

Katherine looked to the others, and then to Balt. "A man was murdered recently in Sleepy Hollow, Master Crane. The killer … the killer has yet to be found."

His gaze went to Jericho for confirmation. Jericho nodded. "Mistress Katherine is right. Master Crane wouldn't take the carriage out without me."

He turned to Katherine. "You'd best stay here with Mrs. Porter. If there's danger …"

She wore a mutinous expression. "I'll be right beside you, Master Downes. We're wasting time. Icharus could be hurt, or …"

Pounding footsteps sounded along the porch at the front of the house, and the door flew open. Callum burst inside, water dripping down his face, his chest heaving with every breath. "Where's Icharus?"

Katherine's heart was pounding in fright. "We're just about to go out to find him, Callum. What has happened?"

He squeezed his eyes shut, and shook his head. "Heaven help us. It may be too late …"

"No!" The word burst from her lips. "No, it is *not* too late. Icharus is fine, but he's out there somewhere, alone, cold and wet … and he may need our help."

Callum grabbed Katherine by the arm and pulled her into the parlor. He pointed out the window toward the village, to the leaping flames that, despite the steadily falling rain, devoured the storehouse even now.

"I was on my way here when it happened, Katherine. I saw Icharus's carriage go 'round the barn, saw him slip inside, and moments later the building went up in flames. I never saw him leave—"

* * * *

There was a quick scurry of footsteps, and then the bang of the front door being slammed. Callum could hear the men shouting as they raced for their horses.

Katherine turned to him, tears in her eyes. "Callum?"

Her voice was pleading, but he knew he could offer her no assurance. He shook his head. "I'm sorry, Katherine. I saw it … before. The flash of silver, the fire."

She shook her head frantically. "But not Icharus, Callum. Not Icharus. Think for a moment, please! You said you'd seen him go inside, but are you sure it was Icharus? Could it be possible you saw someone else? It is dark out, and …"

She took hold of his arms and gave him a firm shake, the look in her eyes a bit feral. "He can't be gone, Callum. He … he just can't!"

171

Katherine's obvious distress over the possibility of Icharus having been taken by the fire was quite out of character. She hadn't shown such depths of emotion when either of her parents had died, or more recently when John Tanner had been murdered.

It disturbed him, and Callum frowned, trying to remember the vision he'd had, the one Icharus had witnessed. After a moment, he whispered, "A crane … pacing along a branch."

Katherine's look of worried despair turned quickly to one of hope. "Pacing along? Then he's not … he can't be … quickly, Callum, please! We must hurry. He needs us!"

In the entry, Mr. Rawlins waited still, a look of uncertainty on his face. "Mistress?"

Katherine turned to him. "Yes, Mr. Rawlins? Is Isolde ready? We must make haste!"

He wrung his hands and shuffled his feet. "Ah, Mistress? Isolde was not in the stables either."

* * * *

Icharus raced through the darkness on foot, a string of muffled curses escaping his lips. His vision blinded by the downpour, he fought for purchase among the fallen limbs and brush littering the soggy ground beneath his feet, felt the lash and prick of numerous branches and spiked limbs as he ran through the bogs, paying little heed to anything other than his own determination not to lose sight of the cloaked man stealthily trying to elude him in the marshy swamp.

He could hear the occasional splash of the criminal's footsteps in the muck, and followed the direction of the sounds. *Whoever the brutish arson is, he'll wish he'd never set foot in Sleepy Hollow when I get my hands on him.*

He'd been coming across the field toward the center of the village when he'd seen a shadow detach itself from a nearby tree and race into the bog. Heinrick wouldn't begin his watch for at least another hour, he'd realized, so he'd spurred Defiance forward, certain whoever had been skulking about near the edge of the woods was up to no good. So he gave chase.

The swamp was no place for his mount, so he had dropped to the ground to follow the man. Giving Defiance a light slap on the rump, he sent the animal away and continued after his target on foot.

Although the darkness and rain hampered his flight, he'd gone a goodly distance before the acrid scent of smoke reached his nostrils. But he hadn't yet gone so deep into the fenland that he couldn't see the flickering flames, rising like pillars from the barn near the pond, when he looked back toward the village center.

He muttered a dark curse for the man who raced through the soggy wetland several paces ahead of him now. The filthy saboteur had sneaked through the swampland and set fire to the Van Brunt storehouse!

Livid, Icharus tore through the marsh after the culprit. Several minutes later, he paused. Darkness had settled fully, and no matter how intently he peered into it, he found no sign of the man he'd followed into the swamp only minutes before.

He listened intently for the villain's next move, hoping he could still hear the man's footsteps despite the subdued sounds of falling rain here in the bog.

Silence met his ears, and he frowned.

He turned about and cast a glance behind him, half expecting the man to leap from the darkness there to launch a cowardly attack at his back, but there was no sudden assault and still no sound to meet his ears other than that of his own labored breathing and the softly muted patter of falling rain.

Icharus tossed back his head in frustration, giving vent to a low growl of impotent fury.

The man can't have just disappeared from the middle of the swamp!

There was nowhere for him to have gone, yet somehow, the fellow had managed to elude Icharus after all.

With a disgusted sigh and a low whistle for Defiance, Icharus turned and loped back through the mire in the direction he had come, his thoughts on the villagers who surely had seen the flames by now.

The rain would surely douse the fire soon, but he knew there was no hope of saving anything inside the storehouse. The flames would have been far too hot.

He'd reached the edge of the marsh when he heard Defiance whicker low, and he headed for his mount. He would find Heinrick and let him know what he saw before heading up to the house to break the news to Katherine.

Then he saw a flash of white near the barn and heard a terrible high-pitched scream, one of pain and fear, much like an animal caught in a trap.

Isolde!

Katherine's mare was pacing agitatedly along the length of the building and back again but made no move away from the fiery structure despite the infernal heat of the flames that were surely searing her flesh.

Icharus frowned. He could see no reason for the mare not to move away from the raging inferno, and he wondered briefly why the animal did not flee to safety.

Katherine.

Isolde refused to move away from the danger of the fire because her mistress was trapped inside.

The mere thought made him go cold.

His gaze went back to the storehouse. Red-orange flames rolled toward the sky, dancing high and hot.

There wasn't a single square inch of the building that wasn't ablaze that he could see.

He all but choked from the sudden ferocity of emotion that rose up within him. In a brief, misplaced moment of reflection, he saw her – the day he'd first came to Sleepy Hollow, and the day she'd asked for his help, and then turned away in tears when she thought he would not give it.

He remembered how she had felt in his arms that first time he kissed her, and how she had melted against him after that second kiss, and then blushed when Callum found the two of them locked in an embrace just before Christmas nearly a fortnight past.

Gritting his teeth against the turmoil his thoughts stirred, and knowing there was absolutely no possible hope of saving her, Icharus broke out at a dead run for the barn, her name bursting from his lips like a prayer.

* * * *

From his vantage point on the other side of the bridge leading into Sleepy Hollow, Brau saw Icharus break from the woods and run toward the blazing storehouse.

He could hear the roar of the flames, feel the intense heat emanating from the inferno. The rain drove the thick, cloying smoke toward the ground, and it choked him. Its acrid scent was stifling, even though he had covered his mouth and nose with a handkerchief some moments before.

He had seen Isolde as well and knew Icharus was racing headlong into a trap. Katherine wasn't inside the burning building. That wasn't why the mare paced in agitated fear before the storehouse at all. Nay, it was because someone had her fettered to a line that only allowed her to move in two directions, and she could not free herself from it.

Brau knew the method. Stakes had been driven deep into the ground, and a lead had been fastened from Isolde's bridle to the thick cording strung between the stakes at her feet.

Poor Katherine. She'd be devastated by the mare's loss. Isolde had been a gift from her parents, and to lose the animal now would be painful.

A flash of movement in the lane beyond the storehouse drew his attention back to Icharus who had almost reached the barn. The debate within him was one purely of a moralistic bend. If he did nothing, Icharus would be gone, and he'd no longer need to worry that he might have a rival for Katherine's hand. However, if he raced forward to stop the man …

The choice was taken from him in the next instant. Crane's huge black stallion with the silly name practically flew out of the darkness, his mane flying, hooves churning up the mud beneath him, and barreled into his master's back from behind.

Crane was knocked forward from the impact. He flew into the air, and landed face down in the thick grass beside the pond.

With an angry whinny, the horse skidded to a halt some paces from his master, and then trotted over more slowly to stand guard over his now prostrate and unmoving form.

Brau closed his eyes for a moment, unsure what his decision would have been. It would have been so easy – but no, it was of no consequence now. He nudged his mount forward. Time to save Isolde … for Katherine.

The heat on the bridge was near unbearable. He knew he would have to make a run away from the barn, and then go around the back to free the mare. He kicked Thunder hard, forcing him into a gallop away from the fire as soon as they cleared the bridge. He rode in a broad half-circle around the burning structure and dove to the ground as soon as he was close enough to reach the mare.

At least he hoped he could reach her.

Crawling forward, he coughed from the smoke. Sweat mingled with rain ran along his brow and into his eyes, stinging them. He squeezed them shut and drew his knife, moving ever nearer the raging heat of the fire. By the time he reached the line Isolde's lead had been fettered to, the flames nigh scorched him. He lunged one last time, a growl of determination escaping his lips. With a swift arc, he sliced the line, and the mare reared onto her hind legs, pulling free of the line that had almost cost her life.

Brau watched her spin and race for the trees, her eyes rolling in terror and pain. Realizing he himself now lay in danger, he rolled sideways and then jumped to his feet, running away from the treacherous flames the moment he gained his balance.

He hadn't gone far when the building collapsed. Huge showers of sparks flew upward while thick, glowing beams tumbled haphazardly to the ground. Something struck him, and he fell. The darkness closed in before he touched the ground, and the last thing he remembered thinking was that he'd lost – everything.

* * * *

"Icharus?"

His world slowly came into focus. "Balt? You're back. Good. There was a fire …"

"I know. The storehouse burned. Can you sit up?"

Can I sit? What a silly question. Of course I …

"Agh!" he groaned and fell back against the pillows.

Pillows? Where am I? The last thing I remember was racing toward the barn to save … "Katherine!"

177

Icharus jerked upright and flung away the covers. His feet hit the floor a mere instant before his knees buckled. He sucked in a deep, gasping breath and immediately wished he hadn't. His throat felt as if it had been seared and his lungs ached. He started to cough.

"Balt ..." he managed between coughs. "Katherine was ... in that ... building ..."

His brother was already helping him back into the bed.

"The lady is unharmed. She was never in the storehouse and she's sleeping now, but she's been up to check on you three times already since we brought you back to the house, if knowing that will put your mind at ease."

Icharus curled onto his side in an effort to stop the burning in his lungs and throat, and the pain of a hundred stabbing knives along his spine. "Isolde ..."

"Jericho had to put the mare down. She ran into the woods and then up to the house after that Van Ripper fellow cut the line someone attached her to. When we found her, we knew there was no other choice. The poor girl, she was burned rather badly."

His coughing fit finally subdued, Icharus rolled to look toward his brother. "Braughton freed Isolde?"

Balt nodded. "He did. He said he'd seen the flames from the road and doubled back through the woods in case the lady needed assistance. It was quite heroic of him actually. Jericho and I watched him crawl toward that inferno on his hands and knees to free the mare." Balt shook his head.

Icharus frowned. "Through the woods? Brau said he came back through the woods. You're sure of it?"

"Aye. He's a lucky one, too. If Jericho and I hadn't reached the barn when we did, he'd have been burned alive. Jericho hit him. Knocked him out, I'm afraid, but the timbers were falling all 'round, and we had to get him out of there."

Icharus arched a brow. "You rescued Van Ripper, but left me to ... what? Where was I during these daring feats of which you speak?"

Balt grinned. "Napping."

Icharus glared at him.

He laughed. "Seriously. Defiance decided he'd had more than he could stomach of your heroism and charged full force into you, from behind. Saved your life, no doubt, even though he sent you flying across the field. Stood over you like some bestial guardian angel until we arrived."

Icharus grimaced. "That would explain the stabbing pains jolting up and down my spine, I suppose."

Balt nodded. "The storehouse was lost. The rain finally doused the flames a bit but there was nothing left to save. By morning I'd wager there will be nothing left but charred stone."

Icharus nodded. "The livestock. I had almost forgotten. Your trip was successful?"

"Until we arrived with the animals, yes. Jericho met me at the bridge and rode here with me to find you. When we arrived, your Katherine started handing out orders like a general. She seemed rather certain something was awry and was most determined to rescue your sorry hide." Balt grinned.

Icharus had a difficult time holding back his own smile, but somehow he managed. There was something nagging him, however, something straining to be acknowledged at the back of his mind. Something important ...

"Balt, you said Van Ripper came through the woods. Did he mention having seen anything unusual?"

Balt's brows rose. "You mean other than the fire, the somewhat clever trap someone had laid for you, and his falling asleep without any recognition of being tired?

No, I don't recall that he did. Why?"

"I saw … someone … in the woods."

Balt shrugged. "Could have been him, I suppose. I didn't see him cross the bridge, but he said he did so before he raced around to save the mare."

Icharus nodded. "It is possible, I suppose."

"But … you don't think so. Correct?"

Icharus shook his head.

Balt shifted and sighed. "Why do I get the feeling I'm not going to like the reason you think the person you saw in the woods tonight wasn't Van Ripper?"

Icharus stared at him for a moment, and then he blinked. "Because the man I chased through the swamp was lacking a very important appendage."

Balt became very attentive. "Am I to presume this appendage was one you removed in the chase?"

Icharus shook his head slowly from side to side.

Balt shrugged. "Ah, well. You were close enough to discover the lack. I'm sure that will make it easy for you to identify the man when you see him again, and I'm almost certain you will do so very soon. Did you get a look at his face? His hair? What shade was it?"

Icharus flinched. "I have no clue."

"You didn't get as close as I'd thought then."

Icharus shook his head again. "No, I almost had the fellow within my grasp before he … disappeared. But seeing his face or identifying his hair color would be an impossibility, Balt."

Again, Balt frowned. "Why so?"

Icharus stared at him. "Because the man did not have a head."

Chapter 11

Balt dropped into the chair near the bed. "A headless horseman? Well, a headless man in this instance. You didn't mention a horse …"

"There wasn't one. We were both on foot."

Balt snorted. "You're starting to sound like Father, Icharus, and we both know who his 'headless man' turned out to be."

Icharus sighed. "Aye, and I believe the man in the fens has a head as well … he only hid it as Brom did with our Da. But this fellow had intentions much darker than the carrying out of a harmless prank. I believe he is the one responsible for starting the fire."

Balt let out a low whistle. "You know he laid a trap for you, do you not? For both of you, actually."

"Both of us?"

"Aye, yourself and the lady, Mistress Van Brunt. I convinced the others to explain why she believed you to be in danger earlier, and after hearing the tales and then the fire tonight … someone wants you both out of Sleepy Hollow, it seems. Any idea why?"

Icharus rubbed his hands across his face. His whole body ached now, and his head was beginning to pound.

"I don't know, Balt, but I'm going to find out. I promise you." He sighed. "A trap. Yes, I can see that now, but I don't understand why you say it was meant for both Katherine and me. She would never have gone near those flames, even with Isolde in danger. Katherine's a smart woman, Balt."

He nodded. "I agree. But whoever laid this trap had much better bait than that of a mare in danger."

"What do you mean?"

Balt cocked his head to the side. "You recall the fancy carriage you had built despite Da's gentle suggestions to the contrary? The one you had Jericho drive you here in?"

Icharus snorted. "Da practically forbade me to commission the thing, and then he shamed me every time I thought to bring it out for a drive."

"You won't have to worry about that anymore. The villain who set fire to the barn rode down in your carriage. Master Mather thought he saw you go inside just before the building went up in flames. He said as much to Mistress Van Brunt. That's when Jericho and I lit out as if the devil himself were at our heels, of course. We were going to rescue you, and I think that's what whoever set the fire intended the lady to do."

Icharus considered the possibility that Katherine would have gone into the burning building if she thought he were inside. He didn't know for certain she would have, but he had a nagging suspicion she *might* have, and that scared him.

His head ached, and at the moment he cared only that Katherine was safe in her bed.

"You could be right, Balt. I'll speak with the others in the morning, but for now, I can't take this pounding in my head another minute. Will you be here when I wake?"

Balt nodded. "For a bit. I'll help with corralling the

animals, but I'm sure Abram is more than ready for me to return. He may be quick-minded for his age, but he's still just a boy."

Icharus nodded. "We'll talk again before you leave."

* * * *

Down the hall in her own chamber, Katherine listened to the low murmur of voices, and though she recognized who was speaking, she was unable to make out the words.

Wrapped in a warm cocoon of blankets, she turned onto her side to gaze into the glowing coals in the hearth, much relieved to know Icharus had finally awakened after his harrowing experience this evening.

Not knowing if he was alive or dead or injured earlier this evening had affected her on a level she had not known possible. She had felt her fear in the very depths of her soul and every time her memory replayed the moment she'd seen Icharus racing toward the barn, her insides went aquiver once more.

She'd been terrified.

Her fear had been so intense she had tried to scream at him to keep away, for him to stay well back from the fiery flames and be safe, but her throat refused to allow any sound to escape.

Her legs had almost refused to heed her bidding, but she had somehow managed to stand and open the carriage door. Callum caught her the instant her feet touched the ground.

She remembered struggling furiously against his hold, her only thoughts that Icharus planned to enter the burning storehouse, and if he succeeded in doing so, he would die.

Callum had caught both her hands and wrapped her

own arms around her to subdue her. Then he had pointed toward the lane and shouted for her to be still. With wide eyes, she'd watched Defiance leap from the darkness and rush to his master. With one hearty nudge of his head, Defiance had sent Icharus flying – and saved his life.

Katherine had begun to shake then, inside and out. Tears she hadn't been aware of shedding turned to wracking sobs, and she had turned in Callum's embrace, hiding her face against his chest to let the tears – tears of intense relief – fall.

The scene that met her gaze when she'd lifted her head some time later, her tears spent, was a ghastly one. The underlying structure of the storehouse had burned through, and with a whine and an ominous groan, the roof went crashing down, sending up huge showers of sparks and flinging burning chunks of wood and debris in all directions.

Katherine squeezed her eyes shut in an attempt to force the terrifying images away. Reliving those horrible moments made her feel sick inside because she had realized her greatest fear. Indeed, it had become a reality.

Everything had burned in that fire.

The people of Sleepy Hollow, the few who remained, were left with nothing. The meager stores they had managed to lay by for the winter, along with their hope for spring, were gone.

Katherine considered what losing the storehouse meant for the people – her people. But before, when she had seen Icharus racing out of the darkness toward that blazing inferno, everything else had dimmed in importance.

In her mind, Icharus was her last hope, her *only* hope, for saving Sleepy Hollow.

If anything should happen to him …

But her reaction at the time had not been about the

continued existence of Sleepy Hollow. It had been much more than that. Imagining him gone, she had felt defeated. Without him, she would have no reason to hope for a future herself, much less for the people of the Hollow. That confused her, frightened her even.

Icharus Crane had roused emotions inside her she'd never experienced before, emotions she didn't understand.

What exactly is it he makes me feel?

Katherine turned over to stare at the thick wooden beams crisscrossing the ceiling overhead, feeling quite bewildered. Her entire life seemed to have changed somehow, over the course of the few weeks since her father's death, and she attributed almost all of that change to Icharus Crane's arrival in Sleepy Hollow.

Indeed, her very first sight of him had been life-altering. From the first moment she had seen him, riding across the bridge into Sleepy Hollow looking so confident and determined, no other man seemed as handsome or capable – or as interesting.

He also made her feel other things, things she wasn't used to feeling. Icharus Crane made her feel important and capable. He made her feel beautiful and wanted, and yes, he gave her hope.

But he also caused her to have other, more confusing experiences too, she thought. Like the warm tingling feeling she felt whenever his gaze met hers, and the melting sensation she felt whenever he held her close that made her yearn to draw closer still.

Whatever name one might lay to the emotional upheaval he roused in the very heart of her being, Icharus Crane definitely made her feel more aware, more competent, and more alive than she had ever felt in her life.

With a smile, he took away her fear, her sense of insecurity as a woman. With a kiss he swept her inhibitions away, allowing the woman inside – the woman she never knew existed before he arrived – free rein. There were so many things he did that made a difference in her life.

Simple things.

Icharus listened to her, the same as he would a man. Unlike Brau, *he* made her feel her intelligence was appreciated rather than scandalous and to be abhorred.

A door closed and after a moment Katherine heard footsteps descending the stairs.

Balt? Or Icharus?

She rolled to face the door and sighed, snuggling deeper into the quilts. Moments later, the footsteps returned. A light rap sent her bolting upright in her bed. "Yes?"

"Mistress Van Brunt? It's Balt. You asked me to let you know when my brother awakened. He's up now but is nursing a bearish ache in his head."

Katherine swung her legs over the side of the bed. "I'll fetch something for the pain—"

"No, please, don't trouble yourself. A night of rest should put him to rights—"

"Katherine?" Icharus called from his chamber. "Balt, go away. If the lady wishes to help me, you should allow her to do so."

Katherine grinned and reached for her wrapper on the bed and then fetched tinder to light the candle on her bedside table. "It's no problem, Master Crane. I'll just go down to the kitchen. Will you keep him company until I return?"

She heard the shuffle of his feet, and then, "Of course."

Katherine belted her wrapper and took up the candle. She knew just the thing for his aching head, and it wouldn't take more than a few minutes to have it ready.

186

She opened the door to her chamber and noticed Balt had left Icharus's open as well. On her way to the stairs, she paused and peered inside. She saw only Balt, sitting with one leg crossed over the other in the chair she had had placed in the room for Icharus. He smiled at her and she flushed, embarrassed to have been caught peeking into Icharus's chamber.

"I'll just fetch the tea," she said, and hurried down the stairs to the kitchen.

Several minutes later, she returned with a steaming mug in her hand.

"Here we are, but it's hot. Be careful you don't scald yourself," she warned, passing the brew to Balt. "He wasn't burned anywhere, was he?"

"Come in and see for yourself, Katherine," Icharus called from the bed. "I'm dressed, in case you're worried. Balt doesn't believe in making a patient comfortable before dumping them into bed."

Hesitant, Katherine edged around the door. He was dressed, except for his boots. She noticed his bare feet, and smiled. "At least he removed your boots first."

Icharus dipped his head the smallest bit, and then winced in pain. "It was necessary. After my wild goose chase through the swamp, they were covered with muck and they reek with the foul odor of the bogs."

She hurried to the bedside and offered him the mug. "Be careful. It's hot."

Icharus sipped at the brew, and then took a long swallow. "*Ugh.* It tastes horrid."

Katherine grinned. "Aye, but its effect is wonderful."

He arched a brow and took another draught. "*Argh.* I'll take your word for it."

Katherine smoothed her hands down the side of her wrapper. "Yes, well …"

His gaze met hers and became serious. "Balt tells

me they had to put Isolde down because of the burns she suffered. I'm sorry, Katherine."

She looked away and nodded. "Thank you."

"He also tells me whoever set fire to the barn intended the two of us to become trapped inside. My carriage was brought in to make you think I was inside, or to make everyone think I was responsible for setting the fire at the very least."

She saw him look to Balt for confirmation. Balt nodded.

"Isolde was staked to a line behind the building as a lure for me. Apparently the arsonist wanted me to think you were already trapped inside in the fire."

Katherine shook her head. "I don't understand why. What is it they want? Is the person responsible for John's murder the same as the person who set fire to the storehouse?"

Icharus shrugged. "I believe they are the same, Katherine, and so does Balt. I'll speak with the others tomorrow, but I've a feeling they'll think as we do."

Katherine shook her head and raised her hands in a gesture of frustration and disbelief. "Why don't they simply come forward and say what they're after?"

Icharus finished the remedy she'd brought him, and then lowered the mug. He stared at her, his gaze somber. "Someone wants us gone, Katherine. Like with John, they're not above murdering the both of us to get us out of the way. I had thought it was the papers they wanted, but ..."

Katherine wrapped her arms around herself. "I'm not leaving Sleepy Hollow. This is my home, and if I have to fight for the rest of my life to keep it, I will do so."

Icharus smiled and looked past her to his brother. "She's a feisty one, eh, Balt?"

Balt returned his grin. "Indeed. She reminds me of

mother."

Katherine tapped her foot against the smooth boards of the floor. "Feisty? No. Determined rather. Sleepy Hollow was once a lovely place where everyone smiled. We were happy here and everything we touched seemed to prosper. I mean to see the Hollow peaceful and abundant again, and I can't do that if I'm not here."

Icharus placed the cup he had been holding onto the table near the bed and gingerly crossed his hands behind his head, cradling it · against the dull ache that still throbbed within, although the pain had already begun to lessen.

"What of Braughton? It's clear he wishes to take you to the city. In fact, I have heard him suggest just that. It would be safer for you—"

Katherine shook her head, her expression defiant. "Nay. I will not leave. Why should I flee to a safe haven when the others have no place to go? Do you think Clara wishes to leave, with her John at rest there in the grove across the way? Or Anne and Dehann? Sleepy Hollow is the only home they've ever known. Think of Mary and Heinrick ... their first child will be born this summer. They need a place to call home, a safe place to raise and nurture their firstborn. Callum has no place outside Sleepy Hollow. He's been here from his fourteenth year ... an orphan with no kin. I'm all the family he has, and I ..."

Tears pricked her eyelids, and she lowered her head to hide them. "There must be something we can do."

Silence held while each of them considered her words. After a moment, Icharus said, "There is."

Katherine raised her head to look at him, hope mingling with despair in her chest. "And that is?"

He looked first at Balt, and then at her. He crossed his arms over his chest. "Stay. We continue, just as you planned, to restore the village to its former prosperity.

As long as we're here and alive, we can rebuild. And protect."

* * * *

A cacophony of male voices greeted Katherine when she descended the stairs the following morning, some raised in frustration, others more calm and quiet.

"There is nothing left," Heinrick stated. "*Nothing.* Even with the livestock, there will be precious little to see us through until spring."

"It is nothing we haven't had to do before, Heins," Callum reminded him in a quiet voice. "We'll simply grow leaner and stronger for the work we have ahead of us."

Katherine came to a halt near the parlor door and held her silence. It seemed every male in the village had come to her door this morning with something to say about the burned storehouse, and Icharus, Callum, and Balt were trying to allay their fears.

Brau stood near the fire, and he turned to the others. "Your plight lay heavy on my mind through the night last night, gentlemen. As I lay sleepless in my bed, I recalled that Sleepy Hollow was much quieter before Master Crane arrived."

Heinrick lowered his gaze. "Yes, that's true. Since you came here, sir, we've had a man murdered ... a dear friend to all of us. And now *this* ..."

"You can't think to blame this on Icharus, Brau," Callum protested. "Katherine asked him to come to Sleepy Hollow to help us. Why would he murder John and destroy all that we had left of—"

Brau arched a brow. "Indeed, why? You yourself said you saw Icharus's carriage go into the barn and that you thought the man who went inside was he. Perhaps you were right after all."

190

Watching them from the doorway, Katherine felt the heat of anger boiling within her, especially when she saw the light of suspicion in the eyes of the men when they looked at Icharus. Her ire rising, she swept into the room. "That's quite enough, all of you. Master Crane is here at *my* behest. In the time he's been in the Hollow, he has done nothing save his best to see my wishes carried out."

She faced Brau, hands on hips. "Do you now accuse *me* of desiring the murder of John Tanner, or of having wanted the storehouse set ablaze when the only thing I've requested from any of you is for us to work together to bring peace and prosperity back into Sleepy Hollow?"

Brau sighed and shook his head. "That is entirely correct, my dear. It *was* you who asked him to come here. It was *you* who requested his aid, in spite of my advice to the contrary. You wish for us to simply follow him, a stranger. But I think we were doing just splendid without him."

Heinrick nodded. Callum frowned. Dehann scowled at Brau, and cast an odd look in Katherine's direction. "I think we've forgotten the topic at hand, gentlemen. If we could—"

Katherine shook her head, ignoring his words. "We weren't doing anything before Icharus came into Sleepy Hollow, Brau. We stood at stalemate, going neither back nor ahead. At least now we have some small hope of moving forward!"

Brau uttered a short bark of a laugh. "Hope? But wait … you are, once again, correct. We weren't being murdered. We weren't facing starvation. No, we were doing none of that. Yet now we are." He peered askance at her. "Tell me, why *is* he here, Katherine? Why would he even agree to come here, to take on the burden of Sleepy Hollow in the first place? There is no logical reason!"

He shook his head, a look of incredulity on his face. "By your command, each of us has striven to do as you asked us to, Katherine. We follow him at your behest … but I fear we may be following a madman, like sheep, directly to the slaughter."

He turned to Heinrick. "You know I speak the truth, Heins. In the short time Icharus Crane has been in Sleepy Hollow, he has already tweaked the ire of the Witch … and the provoked the wrath of the Horseman—"

The rhythmic sound of slow but steady clapping reached her through the haze of her anger, and Katherine turned to see Icharus standing with hands raised in applause.

"Nicely done, Van Ripper. You've managed to cast the seeds of suspicion and fear into the minds of every man present. If I did not know better, I would vow that to have been your aim from the start."

He turned to Katherine.

"I thank you, Mistress Van Brunt, for your spectacular defense. However," he said, and turned back to face the others. "I have no need of it in this instance. Last night I chased a man through the marsh across the brook. I believe that man to be responsible for firing the storehouse, and it is very possible he is the same who murdered your own Master Tanner some weeks past."

Brau looked surprised by Icharus's announcement, but Icharus was not finished. "My brother tells me you were in the woods last night, Braughton. Your story is that you saw the flames and doubled back in case Mistress Van Brunt required assistance, I believe."

He arched a brow in silent question, his eyes cold. He paused for a moment to let his words take root in the men's thoughts before continuing, and Katherine smiled, delighted by his clever turning of the tables.

"Clearly there is a madman at large, but the fellow's

identity remains undiscovered. Now we can stand about and cast accusations. We can argue the matter until the sun goes down and we've lost yet another day we could have spent working toward building a better future for the people of Sleepy Hollow ... or we can move forward, as Mistress Van Brunt has suggested. What say you, gentlemen?"

Balt had lowered his head, and he appeared to be fighting to keep the grin from his lips, but Callum showed no such restraint. With a wide smile on this face, he clapped Icharus on the shoulder. "Well said, Master Crane. I could not have done better myself. I say we go forward, and let the Horseman take the hindmost!"

Heinrick shrugged. "We have very little choice in the matter, Mather. Forward, of course."

Carter Wesley, who had held his silence throughout the conversation, nodded. "Forward."

Icharus turned to Dehann. "Master Tanner?"

Dehann gave Brau a quick look. When he turned back to Icharus, his gaze was one of confidence. "Forward, sir."

Icharus acknowledged his decision with a nod and then turned to Brau. "Of all these gathered here this morning, Van Ripper, you and I are the only ones who have lives outside Sleepy Hollow. It appears to me that we are both outsiders here, strangers if you will, but each with a common goal. Can we not set aside our differences, at least for the time being, and work together toward the better good of all?"

Katherine saw the seething beneath the surface in Brau's eyes though he pinned Icharus with a cold stare. She thought he might refuse Icharus's more than generous offer of peace, but after a moment, he gave a stiff nod of agreement.

Icharus acknowledged it with a nod of his own before he turned to address the others once more.

"In light of last night's travesty, haste is now of the essence. A new storehouse must be constructed, and soon. Callum, Balt, Jericho, and I have already seen to the livestock Master Van Ripper so kindly gifted us with, so Braughton, Callum, and I shall spend what is left of the day first putting together plans for both a new storehouse and an inn, and then we will begin to dismantle what remains of the barn."

He turned to Dehann. "You and Carter will go to the Bleeker place and have the men there join you and Master Downes in the forest."

"Heins," Icharus started, and then paused. The man seemed to be struggling with some dilemma. "Heinrick, I should like for you to sit in with Callum, Braughton, and I. You will need to make a record of our decisions as well as take an accounting of the livestock Master Van Ripper has brought in."

Heinrick agreed, and Icharus turned to his brother. "Balt." He sighed. "I apologize for the furor, and I thank you for your help with the animals. I may need your assistance again soon, but for now, Godspeed, brother. Give my love to Mum and the rest, will you?"

"Aye, I will," he said, and turned to leave. The other men followed him to the door where he paused. "Come home soon, Ichy. We miss you."

Icharus rolled his eyes at the ludicrous nickname. "Go on with you now. I'll be home soon enough. For now, however, there's work to be done."

Balt smiled, and nodded. "See you."

When everyone else had gone, Icharus turned to look at Katherine. His expression was carefully neutral, but she could see the glint of triumph in his gaze. She smiled.

He waggled his eyebrows in the manner she had only seen Callum use, and she turned hurriedly away before she lost control and gave in to the laughter she felt bubbling up inside.

"Gentlemen, if you will follow me to the study? I believe Mistress Van Brunt would like to enjoy her breakfast in peace, and then she will join us there. We've kept her long enough as it is."

* * * *

After breakfast, Katherine joined the men in her father's study to discuss plans for a new storehouse and the inn she wanted to build.

With a minimum of dissension, it was decided the new barn would be placed nearer to the Van Brunt mansion, along with the larger stable she and Icharus had already talked about soon after his arrival in the Hollow. The inn would be built where the old schoolhouse had once stood, just as she had wished.

With their discussion concluded, Icharus put the different drawings aside for later and after a quick bite to eat despite Katherine's protests that they should all sit down to a full dinner, he, Callum, and Heinrick headed into the village to start tearing down what remained of the storehouse.

Brau stayed at the house. He had volunteered to drive her down in the carriage, so she could help the other women at the Bleeker place while they worked on the barn, but he had been unusually quiet from the moment the others had gone.

Katherine had attempted to draw him into conversation several times, but he had held his silence, answering any questions she asked in monosyllables or with a shrug or nod.

Giving up on even idle chatter, Katherine busied herself with preparing to leave. She was pulling on her gloves when he stepped close to drape her cloak across her shoulders. She murmured her thanks. "I haven't had an opportunity to ask you about your trip, Brau. How were your friends?"

He retrieved his coat from the hallstand and shrugged into it. "Well enough, I suppose. The trip went better than I expected. Davrel is not as stingy with his stock as his father was."

She smiled, pleased to hear him finally speak more than a single word. "That is good news, then."

He nodded distractedly and pulled the door open for her before assisting her to the carriage, falling into silence once more.

Katherine frowned, guessing his current irritation and distraction was likely due to her heated words from this morning. Deciding the direct approach best, she said, "I'm sorry, Brau, for my display of temper earlier, but I couldn't simply stand by and let you stir up an animosity in those men for Icharus that is wholly undeserved. He—"

He pinned her with a heated stare, cutting off her words. "I have no wish to discuss Master Crane or whether or not he is deserving of our animosity, Katherine."

She held his gaze with her own. "Very well. What do you wish to discuss, Brau? You see, I do admit to having missed your presence these past weeks. I also must confess I cannot bear this tense silence you've wrapped the both of us in a moment longer." She waved her hands about in the space between them. "The air fairly cracks with it."

He studied her without speaking for a moment, his gaze filled with such intense disquiet, Katherine could only wonder at his thoughts.

Finally, he cocked his head to the side and sighed. "Us, Katherine. I would like to discuss the two of us … and our future. Together."

Katherine's cast him a questioning look. "Our

future, Brau?"

Brau nodded. "Yes. Please. Will you marry me, Katherine?"

Chapter 12

Katherine found she could not meet his gaze. "Brau, please. This is hardly the time to—"

"What could possibly be a more proper time, Katherine? With all that has happened lately, I hardly think waiting a few more days or weeks will matter. I need to know you are safe, Katherine."

She stared at him, feeling oddly hurt he had asked her to become his wife in order that his mind would be eased, but he hadn't mentioned his feelings for her at all, much less inquired as to hers for him.

"You do not mention love, Braughton. Surely such an emotion deserves a place in our future, does it not? In fact, I believe it needs be a prerequisite. But tell me, how could my being your wife make me any safer than I am at this moment?"

His breath hissed from between clenched teeth. "If you were my wife, I could take you away from this ... this calamity, Katherine."

She stiffened. "I have told you repeatedly that I will not leave Sleepy Hollow, Brau. If that is the only reason you wish to wed—"

"Do you think I enjoyed riding back here last night,

having seen the flames leaping into the sky from the road, Katherine? I had no reason to believe it was anything other than your house burning to the ground, and no assurances you were not inside it!"

Her brows drew together. "I can understand your fear, Brau, but—"

He shook his head. "You understand *nothing*, Katherine. You are so blinded by your dreams of the past that you cannot see the plain truth in front of you. There is nothing left for you here! Can you not see that?"

Katherine could feel her cheeks heating with the fire of her anger. "No, I cannot see what you see, Braughton, and I will not! You look about and see all that needs to be done and you think it is hopeless. A lost cause, you say, but rather it is a cause you refuse to take on. You would leave the problems you clearly see for others less able to cope, while you return to your comfortable home in the city and think only of yourself. *I* cannot do that. I will not."

He took hold of her hands. "You see it too, Katherine! Tell me you do not, and I shall call you on the lie. Everyone who lived here when your grandfather was alive has gone. Why did they leave? Because trying to make a life for themselves here was leeching the very heart and soul right out of them, that's why!"

Katherine shook her head in denial.

He pulled her closer. "Listen to me, Katherine. Do you want to know why the Von Groots and the Bleekers stayed here as long as they did? For Brom. They stayed here, knowing they were struggling for survival when there was none to be had because they felt they owed it to your father to at least try. But when your father died, they recognized it was an impossible task … and they moved on. Why can't *you* do the same?"

She stared at him, uncertain, her heart heavy.

Those things he said, they could not be true.

She refused to believe the very people she had worked so hard to find a way to make things better for cared so little about this place, this small slice of heaven that had nurtured her spirit for as long as she could remember.

After her mother died and her father had fallen ill, when she had felt she could not possibly go on, the very land itself had called to her, comforted her. Soothed her. *Is it not the same for them?*

"What has happened to you, Brau? You were never like this before—"

"I never had *reason* to be this way before, Katherine. But someone must force you to see what you refuse to see. The fire destroyed everything that was left, your last hope of making it through one more spring and summer to harvest. When the food runs out, what will you do, Katherine? What then?" he asked, his eyes cold.

The carriage wheel hit a dip in the lane, and Katherine pitched to the side. Brau reached out to steady her and then continued.

"If you'll not consider yourself, think of the others, as you so often instruct me to do. What of the Vandercleefs? Come summer, they will welcome a new child into the world. It is a blessing, yes, but Katherine, it is also another mouth to feed. Have you thought of that? And what of the new family, the Wesleys? Alaina will also bear a babe soon. Would you have those children, babes who did not ask to be brought into this struggle mind you, go without?"

Katherine frowned. "No, I—"

"Then cease this madness now. *Please!* Say you will marry me. Be my wife, Katherine, and let me take you *away* from this."

Katherine snatched her hands from his. "*Stop it!* Just stop it, Brau! There is hope for us, you will see.

201

Icharus—"

"Is nothing more than a man, Katherine, and even though you do not like to hear it, even though you like to think he's some champion come to save us all, things have become worse since he came here. Worse, not better!"

The carriage drew to a halt near the burned barn and Katherine stumbled forward, her hand struggling with the handle, her only thought to get as far away from Brau as possible as swiftly as she could manage. Tears blinding her, she gave it a twist and the door swung open. She tumbled out, barely gaining her feet rather than toppling headlong into the lane.

Brau hurried out after her and caught her barely in time to save her from a nasty spill into the slippery mud at their feet.

"Katherine, stop before you hurt yourself. You'll cause a scene—"

She turned on him, swatting at his hands. "I don't *care* if I cause a scene, Brau! If they want to stare at me, let them look. Let them hear me, and then they will know *exactly* how I feel. I *want* them to know how much I care about each and every one of them, and that I'm not about to just take up my things and leave without being certain they have the means to carry on, to survive."

He came up beside her, reached for her and drew her close, pressing her head against his shoulder. "Shhh. Katherine, please stop crying. I'm sorry. Truly. I never meant to upset you this way, and I ..."

Sobbing, she drew away, shrugging off his hands. "I'm sorry too, Brau. Sorry I believed you when you said you wished to help me ... to help us. I'm sorry I thought you cared as much for the people of Sleepy Hollow as I do, and most of all, I'm sorry I ever believed you cared about me!"

He reached for her again, and she was so distraught,

hurting so much inside at the moment she let him pull her back into his embrace.

He sighed. "Don't say that, please. I do care about you."

When she tried to pull away, he held her still. His hands framed her face, forcing her to meet his gaze. "I do care about you, Katherine. Very much."

He smoothed his hand along her hair, from her nape to her hips and back again, gentling her. Calming her. He leaned close to whisper soothing sounds against her ear.

She hiccoughed and sniffed against his shoulder. "If you truly care for me as you say you do, you will not ask me again to leave Sleepy Hollow, Brau."

He nodded. "I won't ever ask it of you again. I swear."

Katherine pulled back a little so she could look into his eyes and better gauge his sincerity. "Seriously?"

The look he gave her was somber in its solemnity.

"I vow it upon my very life," he said.

His answer disturbed her, and she frowned. "Your words are almost frightening when coupled with the intensity of the look you're giving me."

His hand swept her hair again before coming to rest against her jaw. "My words are not half as frightening as the thought of you refusing me out of hand, Katherine, and that is my fear as you have yet to give me an answer."

Taking her hands in his, he knelt in the lane before her. "Will you, Katherine Van Brunt, do me the honor of becoming my wife?"

Looking around, she saw that Callum and Icharus had stopped what they were doing and were watching the two of them. Callum's brows were arched high, and Icharus – she could not read his expression at all.

Her mouth gave a wry twist. "I've caused a scene

after all, haven't I?" She looked at Brau kneeling on the ground before her and sighed. "Oh, Brau. I cannot answer you. Not now. There are so many things to think about and so much to be done …"

He tugged at her fingers. "Just do not say no, Katherine. Say instead that you will think about my proposal. Please?"

After a moment, she nodded. "I will."

He smiled. "Thank you."

He came to his feet, and pulled her into his arms before she could move away.

"Thank you, Katherine," he said again before he lowered his mouth to hers.

Katherine tried to feel something – anything – in Brau's kiss, but she could not. His lips moved over hers, seeking, questing for a response, but she gave none.

After a moment, he moved away and his gaze moved from her to narrow suspiciously upon Icharus, who watched them still from the charred remains of the storehouse, his hands clenched round the wooden handle of the mallet he held.

Katherine put out a hand to him in supplication. "Be kind, Brau. He truly is trying to help us."

He was quiet for a moment, lost in thought, until the loud slamming of the Vandercleef's front door brought his mind out of the reverie he had slipped into, and he nodded. "We'll ride back together when you're done and I'm finished here."

His gaze swept her face. "Perhaps Mary will not mind if you go inside to tidy up a bit? Your eyes are red and swollen."

Katherine rolled her eyes. "Then I've no need to worry about the Witch or the Horseman coming after me this day. I would frighten them both away with my reddened eyes, no doubt," she teased.

He offered a quick smile before heading toward the

barn to help with clearing away the rubble. "One can always hope."

* * * *

Across the way, Icharus and Callum stood amid the burned timber and stone that had been the Van Brunt storehouse, watching the interaction between the couple in the middle of the lane.

"He's going to force me to kill him yet," Icharus said, his voice low.

Callum turned away from the couple and lifted a charred, splintered beam onto his shoulder. "For asking Katherine to marry him?"

Icharus shook his head. "Nay, for making her cry," he said and then turned, swinging the heavy mallet in a wide arc toward the wall.

* * * *

Later that evening at supper, Katherine avoided mentioning the scene he had witnessed between her and Brau that morning. Instead, conversation turned to plans for making it through what remained of winter, to harvest.

While Katherine and Brau spoke of purchasing some of what they would need from the neighboring farmers or in TarryTown, Icharus found his gaze wandering to her again and again throughout the meal, and each time her blue eyes met his, he became more agitated than he had the time before.

Why she would even consider spending the rest of her life with the man who had let her beloved Hollow fall to such ruin was beyond him. Brau had known the direction in which Sleepy Hollow had been headed long before Brom died, but he hadn't done a single thing to try to turn things around, a fact that irritated Icharus to no end.

Had *he* been here, known what was happening, he could have stopped the damage before it reached such a devastating level, would have stopped it. Or he would have at least tried.

Why hadn't Brau? If the man had intended all along to take Katherine for his wife, why hadn't he tried to make things better?

It was something that just didn't make sense, no matter which angle Icharus chose to look at it from.

Today, he'd heard Brau vow never to ask Katherine to leave the Hollow again, which meant that if the two of them married, Sleepy Hollow would become his home as well. Yet Icharus sensed no love for the place and no deep concern for the people who lived here at all in Braughton Van Ripper.

It seemed to him that Brau had no intention whatsoever of living in Sleepy Hollow once the two of them were wed. If he did, he would have done something, anything to ensure doing so would not pose so much of a hardship for him and his new wife. But as far as he could see, Brau had done nothing other than sit back and watch Sleepy Hollow grow more desolate. It was almost as though that was what Brau had been hoping for. Icharus frowned.

Brau would be largely responsible for the future of this place once Icharus left. He couldn't help but wonder what would become of Sleepy Hollow when he was gone.

A vision of everything slipping back into ruin filled his thoughts. Everything he had done thus far, everything he still planned to do before heading back to Wake Grove, would all be for naught.

Disgusted by what he saw in his thoughts, Icharus tossed his napkin onto the table beside his plate and pushed his chair back.

Katherine gaze snapped up to meet his. "The food was not to your liking?"

Icharus stood and pushed his chair up to the table before casting distracted look in her direction, a polite smile plastered on his lips. "What? Oh, no, the roasted hare was delicious. Mrs. Porter has quite outdone herself once again."

She studied him, her gaze uncertain. "You looked as if you were angry."

When he did not reply, she carefully folded her napkin and placed it onto the table. Brau did likewise before he slid his chair back and went to her side. Katherine stood and murmured her thanks to Brau before she started out of the dining room.

Icharus observed the little domestic ritual with something akin to disdain, and the polite smile he had worn but a moment before turned into a derisive smirk.

"Shall we sit in the parlor tonight?" Katherine asked. "I've some mending to do before I go upstairs and after spending so many days in quiet solitude, I would find the company most pleasant."

Brau shook his head. "I'm afraid I shall have to pass tonight, Katherine. I've a meeting to attend in the morning before I ride out to assist Master Crane here with carting off the rubble from the fire. Tomorrow evening, perhaps?"

Katherine smiled and nodded. "I'd like that. This house has been so quiet of late, I vow I thought I'd go mad before you returned."

Brau cast Icharus a questioning look. "Quiet? I would have thought the two of you would have plenty to discuss while I was away."

Icharus shrugged. "Not much time for talking, Van Ripper, or anything else for that matter, when you're as busy as we have been."

Brau turned back to Katherine. "Tomorrow then," he promised, offering a quick smile. He headed to the door to retrieve his coat and gloves.

Icharus propped against the doorframe of the dining room and watched while Katherine followed him.

She waited while he donned the garments and then opened the door before she tilted her head to receive his usual, familiar kiss on her upturned cheek.

"Goodnight, Katherine. Pleasant dreams," he said, and then pulled the door closed behind him.

Icharus shook his head at the obviously indifferent farewell, and when Katherine questioned the gesture, his brow went up in a cynical arch. "That was a bit formal for a goodnight kiss, don't you think? Especially from a man who proposed marriage earlier today."

Katherine crossed to the parlor, speaking over her shoulder as she went. "Brau is not a very demonstrative man, Icharus. If you haven't noticed, he's rarely given to indulging in displays of a passionate nature. In public at least," she added.

Icharus followed her. "So he saves all his most passionate displays for more private moments? Like this morning in the carriage?"

She went to the sofa and took up the shirt she'd been stitching before supper. "I wouldn't know."

"You were there with him, Katherine. What do you mean you wouldn't know? What did he do to you to make you so upset?"

Katherine concentrated on the stitches she was making, refusing to look at him. "He did nothing."

Icharus could feel his temper rising. "He did nothing? You were crying, Katherine. Nay, sobbing. You were bawling on his shoulder and you say there was no reason for your tears? Are you often given to fits of weeping hysteria?"

She glared at him then. "I did not say there was no

reason for me to be crying. I merely said Brau did nothing to cause my tears." She turned her attention to the garment in her hand once more. "It was something he said …"

Icharus leaned against the arm of the sofa. "And that was?"

"He asked me to marry him."

Icharus's brows rose, and after a moment, he started to laugh. "Well, I can certainly understand how that would send a woman into a bawling fit."

His laughter continued, and Katherine scowled at him. "Stop it, please. It wasn't his proposal that brought on my tears. Rather it was his reason for proposing."

Icharus's laughter quieted, though a half smile still curved his lips. "And his reason was?"

She didn't look up from her mending. "He fears for my safety. He asked me to become his wife so he could take me away from the unpleasantness here."

"Bollocks," Icharus blurted, and ignoring her light blush at his coarse language, he continued. "If he's so concerned about your safety, why did he leave?"

"What do you mean *why did he leave?* You heard him yourself. He has a meeting come morning, and—"

"And he could just as easily attend it whether he leaves from here or his home in the city. It doesn't wash, Katherine. Nor do a lot of other things."

Now it was her turn to arch a brow. "Such as?"

Icharus left the sofa in favor of the chair Callum usually sat in so he could see her expression when he spoke. "Such as his turning a blind eye to the turn of things while your father lay ill. Why did he do nothing to stop it, Katherine? From my point of view, Brau never even once tried to make life better for you … any of you. It's as though he wanted things to go awry."

Katherine shook her head. "You're being silly, Icharus. There was nothing he could have done. The fever—"

Icharus leaned forward. "I've heard about the fever, Katherine, and how it claimed most of the residents and nearly all of the servants who lived in Sleepy Hollow at the time, but that was more than three years ago, was it not?"

She nodded. "Yes, but—"

Icharus shook his head. "But nothing. Braughton could have gone into TarryTown and sought out others who needed work, just as I have done. He could have rebuilt the houses that burned, exactly as we plan to do now. He could have done so many things, Katherine, and yet he did not. What I would like to know is why didn't he?"

Katherine lay her mending aside and stared at him. "Braughton did not simply sit around doing nothing, as you're accusing. He was stricken by the fever as well, and his convalescence took several months. By the time he was able to return—"

"What? Your father had ordered the infected houses to be burned. Your mother had been buried, and your father had taken to his bed to nurse a broken heart. But the rest of it, Katherine, everything else was not gone. Not at that time."

Distracted and confused, Katherine reached for the shirt at her side and the needle pricked her skin.

"Ow!" she cried, and jerked her hand away from the material to survey the damage. A tiny drop of blood pooled at the edge of her hand, and she wiped it away with a finger. "I don't understand, Icharus. What is it you are trying to say?"

"I don't know what I'm trying to say." Icharus sighed and leaned his head back against the chair. "Yes, I do, actually. I am trying to caution you, Katherine, and to convince you to consider Van Ripper's past very carefully before you agree to accept his proposal of marriage."

He sat forward, his gaze boring into hers. "Think back over the past several years, and all that he has done, or rather, all that he could have done, but did not. Consider his reason for wanting to marry you in the first place. Katherine, the man is not overly concerned about your safety, I can promise you that."

Katherine frowned. "You can do no such thing, Icharus Crane. How could you possibly know what thoughts are in his mind? Nay, you cannot. He worries about me, being alone here with no one to look after me—"

"So much so that he leaves you here night after night with no one to see to your safety but two doddering old servants and a man neither of you know well enough to trust? A veritable stranger?"

He shook his head. "No, Katherine. You may trust me when I say your safety is not his most pressing concern. There must be some other reason he desires to make you his wife."

Katherine rolled her eyes. "Aye, there must. Perhaps he loves me, Icharus. Would that be so hard to believe?"

Icharus stared at her. "He said as much then?"

Katherine lowered her gaze, but not before he saw the prick of hurt there.

"Nay, he did not," she whispered.

"Which leads me to believe having you as his bride is not Brau's true goal, but rather a means to an end. But what end would that be? What does he want, Katherine?"

Katherine squeezed her eyes shut. Her fingers stopped their motions and lay still in her lap, the shirt she had been mending forgotten. "Go away, Icharus. You're as horrid with your suppositions as Brau was with his motives."

He left the chair and came to sit beside her and take the cloth from her hands. He took hold of her hands and squeezed them. "Look at me, Katherine, and listen. Please?"

She did as he asked, and when her pain-filled gaze met his, he felt it all the way to his heart. "Katherine, I'm not trying to hurt you. Believe me, that is the last thing I wish to do. But you have to see …"

Icharus knew this was not the sort of conversation she'd had in mind when she invited him and Brau into the parlor earlier, and he knew his words had hurt her. But he had to make her understand there was some other motive behind Brau's proposal, possibly a nefarious one.

"Katherine, your father trusted Brau, did he not? He trusted Brau with his business affairs, at least. Brau said so himself, the day I first came to Sleepy Hollow, remember?"

She nodded.

"Tell me, what happened with your father's various business dealings? There had to have been men who came here to speak with your father regarding those dealings. Where are they now?"

Katherine frowned. "I don't know. I just assumed that when both Father and Brau fell ill, the men took their business elsewhere."

Icharus shook his head. "What about the money, Katherine? The goods? Those men would have continued to come, to either give your father what was owed him, or to collect the goods for which they had already traded."

She looked down at their clasped hands. "Later, when Brau was better, I simply left such things to him, trusting he would take care of it."

He nodded. "Yes, you trusted him. Just as your father before you did. But was he worthy of that trust? Did he in fact carry out the tasks you assumed he was

212

taking care of? Are there receipts somewhere showing, like the papers your father kept for mine, that the conditions of trade your father engaged in with those men were duly met? Or, at the very least, that those dealings had come to an end?"

She frowned again. "I never thought of those things."

He shook his head. "You would not have because you didn't believe there was reason to be concerned."

He released her hands and turned to gaze unseeing through the doorway, deep in thought. "If it had been me, Katherine, I would have been in contact with those men. Had I been ill, as you've said Brau was, the moment I was able, I would have sought them out. Honor would have demanded I do so."

He turned back to her. "Had I a hope of having you as my bride, I would have done everything in my power to maintain life as you had known it until the day we were wed." She started to look away, but he continued. "Failing that, and I found myself faced with the very situation we are dealing with even now, I would never, ever leave you here in this house alone."

He refused to release her gaze. His hands reached for hers once more, and he gave her fingers a little squeeze. "I could not leave you, Katherine, knowing there was a murderer out there somewhere who could come in at any moment and snatch you away from me. Not knowing there was an arsonist lurking about who'd had every intention of letting you be burned alive in that barn."

He swallowed hard. "If I cared for you as Van Ripper should since he's asked you to marry him, I would be hard pressed to let you out of my arms for a single minute, Katherine, much less my sight." He uttered a short bark of laughter. "And *never* would I allow you to spend even a single night beneath the same roof with a man who was not related to you by blood or a servant. Van Ripper is a bloody fool."

Katherine stared at him, unsure how she should, or if she even could respond. He had spoken with such feeling, such conviction in his tone she felt his sincerity in the deepest part of her soul.

She realized everything he had said a moment ago, everything he had indicated *he* would have done if he were in Brau's place, he had done already, to some extent, or was at least working toward the doing of it.

Since the day he had come back to Sleepy Hollow he'd worked toward nothing else but what she had asked of him. *Her* wants were the ones he had taken into account – not Callum's, or Brau's, or even John Tanner's. Nay, he had listened to her and then allowed the others to make suggestions, but it had always been *her* wishes, *her* desires he sought to bring to fruition.

He had looked after her, letting her work alongside him every moment he possibly could. *Had he done so because he hadn't wished to leave me alone and unprotected?*

Every night these past weeks while Brau had been away and Callum had been at the Bleeker place, Icharus had been there, with her. Although he'd made sure he never dallied overly long below stairs, she'd known he was just right upstairs and she had felt safe knowing he was there to protect her should the need arise.

She realized he could have gone elsewhere. He could have chosen to stay at the Bleeker place and left Callum here with her, but he hadn't.

Why didn't he?

Her eyes rose to meet his, confusion and something else filling her, forcing the words from her lips. "But you don't care for me, Icharus Crane. Do you?"

Chapter 13

He didn't answer right away, but when he did, she almost wished he hadn't.

"Of course I care about you. You're Brom's daughter. Why wouldn't I?"

Katherine lowered her gaze, embarrassed now by her thoughts. "I see. You only care about me because I am my father's daughter."

Icharus leaned his head back, and looked at her, his gaze shuttered. "It isn't like that, Katherine. When I first came here, perhaps that was the only reason. Your father could well have been responsible for my very existence. If he hadn't stepped in where my father was concerned, I might never have been born."

She retrieved Callum's shirt from the back of the sofa where Icharus had placed it earlier and shook it out. "You don't have to explain, Icharus."

He turned away. "I want to explain. The day you asked me to come here, to help you restore the livelihood of the people of Sleepy Hollow, I felt a sense of duty to you, as Brom's daughter. Think on it, Katherine. Your father made it possible for me and my family to know and enjoy the very lifestyle you now seek to see restored to Sleepy Hollow. It's only natural, don't you think, that I would feel obligated to look after you and help out in every way that I could."

She shrugged. "I suppose it could be."

He nodded. "It most definitely could be. It is. But the longer I stayed here, Katherine, the more time I spent with you, that sense of duty faded and … something else took its place."

Katherine peered at him from beneath her lashes, wanting to ask about that 'something else' but resisting the urge.

She had no desire to feel the pain of hearing him say he cared about her as he might a sister or dear friend, although she really didn't know why what he felt for her mattered so much to her in the first place.

"There. All finished," she said, and tied off the last stitch in the tear she had been mending. She held up the shirt to inspect her work. "Much like our conversation, I believe. Thank you for keeping me company, Master Crane, but I realize suddenly that I am quite tired."

Icharus arched a brow. "Master Crane? I thought we'd long since dispensed with such formalities?"

"And I thought you'd agreed to help me out of the goodness of your heart, not some misplaced sense of loyalty to my father."

He studied her in silence for a few moments, his jaw rigid. "I agreed to help you because of your eyes, Katherine. When you talk about Sleepy Hollow, about your home and your people and how things were before, your eyes light up with an inner glow that affects me in ways I find difficult to explain."

He leaned toward her, brought his hand up to caress her brow. "Your face changes, becomes more alive, so full of joy and happiness, and all I can think is that I want to keep that expression on your face forever."

His words made her feel strange inside. The gentle

216

caresses of his fingers made her want more of the same. She closed her eyes and turned her head, seeking his touch.

* * * *

Icharus wanted to groan at the situation in which he found himself. He wanted so badly to lean forward and kiss her, to pull her close and explore every sweet inch of her lips with his own, but he knew if he did so he would never want to stop.

His desire for her intensified with every second he spent in her presence, but he would not give in to it, not when she had yet to make a decision about Brau's proposal. When he made love with Katherine Van Brunt, there would be no possibility of another man entering her life sometime in the future looming between them.

There was no way he could kiss her now and make himself leave her there later … but he could hold her. He shifted on the sofa so he could bring her into his arms.

Icharus had no idea how long he sat there with Katherine cuddled close against his side, her head resting on his shoulder while he stroked her arm and hair. All he knew was that he didn't want the moment to end.

She had stretched her other arm across his middle, letting her fingers rest against his ribs, and lurid imaginings of her delicate hand sweeping along his bare skin near sent him over the brink.

Insanity.

His perverse desire to sit here with her in the near dark while his mind tortured him with images of the two of them sharing long kisses and scorching caresses could be nothing less than insanity.

The fire had burned low, the candles had guttered out, and the lamps had long since dimmed to a soft glow before he brushed a light, lingering kiss against her brow.

"Katherine?" he whispered against her hair.

"Hmmm?" she mumbled sleepily.

"The fire will be out soon. You should go on up to your chamber now."

She shook her head, and mumbled against his shoulder. "… 's warm enough here."

He smiled, wondering what she would do if he simply rested his head against hers and slept with her there, in the parlor, where anyone might come in and find them come morning. Like as not, she wouldn't be too happy about it. With a sigh, he shifted until he could slide his free hand beneath her knees and carefully lifted her onto his lap, biting back a groan at the sensation doing so caused in his groin. He slid to the edge of the sofa and stood with her fully in his arms.

He only hoped he could manage to get her up to her room and into bed without waking her or climbing in beside her once he did so.

She was so light, weighed barely more than Kathleen and just a bit less than Eliza, he judged as he moved toward the stairs. And she smelled delicious.

Stop it right now, Crane. The last thing she needs is for you to turn dishonorable in her moment of vulnerability.

He took each tread of the stairs carefully lest he wake her from her slumber before they reached their destination, but it turned out he had worried for naught. She shifted only once, and that had been to lock her arms more securely about his neck and snuggle her face closer, her lips resting just below his ear. The heat of her warm breath blowing out in a gentle caress against the sensitive skin of his neck was almost more than he could stand, but he clenched his teeth and carried on.

At the top of the stairs, he shifted her in his arms a

218

bit and made for the door at the farthest end of the hall. Then, balancing on one foot, he let her hip rest atop one knee while he used the hand beneath her knees to open the door to her chamber.

Inside, he quickly carried her across the room and deposited her gently onto her bed, alone, and then hurried across to the fire under the pretense of needing to put more logs on it, lest he give in to the urgings of his body and join her.

Satisfied the wood he had added to the fire would burn until morning, he turned back to the bed, letting his gaze linger regretfully on her sleeping form. Finally, he eased over to the side of the bed and leaned down to place a soft kiss on her parted lips.

She gave a sleepy hum of pleasure, and he smiled.

"Goodnight, Katherine. Sleep well," he whispered, and then quit the room, making his way back to his own chamber down the hall.

* * * *

Katherine woke feeling disoriented, her toes aching inside her shoes, and her legs tangled in the skirts of the gown she hadn't removed the night before. She thought it odd she hadn't undressed before getting into bed, but then, she didn't remember a thing past sitting on the sofa with Icharus last night, her cheek resting against his shoulder ….

Icharus!

She could feel the heat rising in her cheeks.

Did he bring me here, to my room? He must have, she thought, because she obviously hadn't made her way there on her own. She would have remembered. At least she believed she would have.

She thought she would prefer to have remembered being carried up in Icharus's arms. Shoving the thought aside, she said, "Stop that, Katherine. He's here because of Father, remember?"

Disentangling her legs from the heavy skirts of her badly rumpled dress, she stood and hurried from the bed to pull off her slept-in gown, and then searched through her wardrobe for one more suited to her plans for the day.

Icharus and the others would be moving the rubble they had collected from the burned buildings into the empty rye field, and she intended to help, but if she didn't hurry, he would be gone.

She was dressed and halfway down the stairs before she remembered she had no mount. Her steps faltered and slowed until she stood unmoving on the stairs, just a few steps from the bottom.

Isolde.

The beautiful white mare her father had bought especially for her was gone. She had been badly burned, she remembered, and they had put her down rather than see her suffer and die later from infection or some other complication. Disheartened, she sank onto the step, her energetic mood depleted.

What will I do without Isolde?

Icharus came out of the dining room where he'd been nursing a hot cup of coffee, and spied her sitting dejectedly on the stairs. "Katherine? I didn't hear you come down. You slept well, I trust?"

She gave a distracted nod, and he frowned.

"Is something wrong?"

"Isolde. She's gone, Icharus. I wanted to ride into the village with you this morning, to help, but Isolde …" She broke off, shaking her head. After a moment, she continued, "I suppose I can ask Mr. Rawlins to ready the carriage. Will you wait for me?"

Icharus reached for her, and taking her hand, pulled her the rest of the way down the stairs. He placed her hand on his arm and led her into the dining room where Mrs. Porter had laid a plate for her. "You can ride with me. That is, if you aren't afraid of Defiance?"

She shook her head, still lost in thought. "No, I'm not frightened. Thank you, Icharus."

"You should eat first," he said, his gaze gliding appreciatively over her figure. "You're as light as down."

His reference to her weight confirmed her suspicion that he had carried her up to her room the night before. She blushed. "I'm sorry about last night. I fell asleep …"

"Don't give it a thought. You were tired. I carried you up, but I'm sorry to say I didn't think about removing your shoes until this morning."

She wriggled her aching toes in her shoes and made a face. "My feet were positively aching when I woke. Serves me right for nodding off during our conversation."

He pulled out a chair for her and held it while she seated herself, then took the one beside her. He sipped his coffee in silence while she ate.

When she laid her napkin aside, he stood and offered his hand. "Ready?"

She took it, nodding, and after slipping her cloak around her shoulders and pulling on her gloves, he led her outside to where Defiance waited near the steps.

With a quick motion, he mounted the tall, black steed, and then held out a hand for her. "You can ride here, in front. That way, I can make sure you don't fall and get trampled beneath this old rogue's feet."

Katherine placed both her hands in his, and he pulled her up to sit in front of him. He waited while she adjusted her knee around the pommel and situated her skirts, and then took up the reins, his arms holding her on either side.

Almost hesitantly, she placed a hand on each of his

forearms and looked back at him for approval.

He nodded.

"Let's get to work," he said, and with a click of his tongue to the beast, they started forward.

* * * *

After giving Katherine several smaller tasks, enough to keep her busy but nothing that might allow her to be injured, he set to work himself, lifting the heavier bits and loading them into the wagon.

By the time the two of them had the first wagon loaded, three of the men who usually helped Jericho and Dehann in the forest had arrived.

Icharus nodded a greeting. "Good morning, gentlemen. You've arrived just in the nick of time. Walter, if you and Phillip will drive this lot over to the field there and unload it, the three of us will get the other wagon ready."

"Yes, sir, Master Crane," the man he had called Walter said, and he and Phillip climbed up onto the wagon.

The men had gone only a short distance when Icharus came to stand in front of her and nodded. "How may I help you gentlemen?" he said, his gaze fixed on some point behind her.

Surprised, Katherine turned. Three men on horseback had ridden up, and she had been so distracted by her work she hadn't even heard them approach.

She must look a fright, she thought, and smoothed her palms down her skirts. She hoped they weren't covered with soot, but knew they likely were.

"We're looking for Icharus Crane. Can you tell us where we might find him, sir?"

Icharus stepped in front of her, gesturing for her to continue with the loading. "I am Icharus Crane. What business finds you in Sleepy Hollow this chilly morn?"

The elder of the three leaned forward. "We're looking for work, sir. A gentleman in town said we could find it here."

Katherine started forward, and Icharus caught her back, putting her safely behind him.

"Stay here until Braughton crosses the bridge," he murmured, and then nodded to the man who had spoken. "There is plenty to be done here. You three have a place to stay?"

Katherine saw something flicker in the man's gaze. "For now."

Icharus hesitated for a moment. Katherine thought he might be about to send them away, and would have come forward, but again, he put her behind him.

"We've fallen on hard times here, gentlemen. While the offer of a daily wage still stands if that's what you're seeking, Mistress Van Brunt would much prefer to bring in tenants who are interested in putting down roots."

The spokesman for the group frowned. "If you don't mind my asking, sir, why would your mistress want to bring in others if you're already having difficulties?"

Icharus crossed his arms over his chest. "To rebuild. Mistress Van Brunt intends to see this fertile valley prosper, as it did in the days of her grandfather, Baltus Van Tassel."

Icharus stared at each man in turn. "For now, times are tight. But the land holds promise of great return for those who are willing to work hard for it."

The fellow in the middle nodded and leaned back with a sigh. "We're no strangers to hard times, sir, and we're all willing to work hard in exchange for a fair return. My name's Van Kersten, Nicolaas Van Kersten, and these gentlemen here are my sons, Dirck and Gregor."

Icharus nodded in greeting. "You have families, I presume?"

Nicolaas nodded. "Gregor here's newly wed, and Dirck and his missus have a small brood. We're staying with relatives for now, but the missus and I would be happy to change that. So would the boys, I believe."

Both Gregor and Dirck quickly nodded their agreement, and Icharus smiled.

"While I can't promise to have a place for your families to join you here immediately, we hope to raise framework on several new cottages soon." He peered upward. "If the snows hold off, we'll have them up in a se'ennight or so, but I don't think they will."

Katherine, who had been watching for Brau and finally saw him riding toward them across the bridge, stepped to Icharus's side. "Come spring, there will be place for your families. Until then, you're welcome to stay with the others at the Bleeker place. You'll receive a fair wage for a day's work, plus room and board when the weather makes traveling back and forth too difficult."

The elder gentleman nodded. "We'd appreciate that, Missus Crane," he said.

Katherine's eyes widened at his mistake. "Oh, I'm not—"

Icharus turned to her then. "I'm sorry, Katherine. I thought you'd gone back to assist Wilhelm. Gentlemen, allow me to present Katherine Van Brunt, daughter of Abraham Van Brunt, or perhaps you may have heard him called Brom."

He looked back toward the men. "Katherine, this is Nicolaas Van Kersten and his sons, Dirck and Gregor."

She smiled. "It's a pleasure to make your acquaintance, sirs."

Brau reined his mount to a halt beside Icharus and dismounted. His gaze went to Katherine and her disheveled appearance, and his disapproval was clear in his eyes.

"My meeting took longer than expected, but I see you've already started here."

The elder Master Van Kersten grinned at Katherine. "Brom Bones is your father? I've heard many a tale about him since we arrived in New York," he said.

"Was, I am sad to say," Brau answered for her. "Master Van Brunt passed away late in the fall of this year. You say you've heard of him?"

The younger Van Kersten, Dirck, smiled. "Aye, we have, and of your father as well, Master Crane."

Brau cocked his head to the side a bit, and nodded. "In that case, I shall assume you've also heard the rest?"

Nicolaas's gaze became shuttered. "Our families have told many a colorful tale, sir, most of which I'd put down to superstition and wives' tales."

Brau turned to Icharus. "You didn't tell them about John?"

Icharus frowned and shook his head. "I've not had time, Van Ripper."

"A few weeks back, a murder took place here in Sleepy Hollow," Brau told them. "I wouldn't presume to say we all feel the same about John's death, but there are some here who will tell you our Master Tanner was killed because the Witch's ire had been stirred and she called upon the Horseman to mete out her justice."

One of the younger men released a low whistle, and a look of shared uncertainty passed between the three of them. "The Headless Horseman of Sleepy Hollow?" Gregor asked.

It was clear to Katherine each of them had heard the local folklore, and judging by the young man's sudden pallor, she had a feeling he believed most of what he'd heard.

Icharus shook his head, and clapped Brau on the

shoulder in a gesture of camaraderie Katherine knew did not exist between the two of them. She frowned, but Icharus smiled. "As you can likely tell, our Van Ripper here loves to share a good tale, though much like Brom, he usually prefers to do the telling of it before a warm fire surrounded by a rapt audience."

He gestured to the charred remains of the barn behind him. "In addition to having to deal with a murdering madman who has yet to be apprehended, we were also visited recently by an arsonist who set fire to our storehouse. Everything was destroyed, and we were left to face what remains of winter with only those provisions laid away in the cellars of each household."

"It's true then?" Gregor asked. "The Hessian has come back from the dead and rides once again in Sleepy Hollow?"

Katherine shook her head and turned a brittle smile upon Brau. "Of course not, gentlemen. Tell them, Brau. Tell them as you told Anne and Dehann the day we buried my father."

Brau gave her a chilling look, and she turned back to the others and snapped her gloved fingers. "Wait, I remember now. You said, 'the Headless Horseman is nothing more than a figment of imagination, and you'd do well to remember that!' "

She offered a bright smile. "So you see, gentlemen, there is nothing to fear. At least not from the Hessian."

Gregor shook his head. "No offense, Mistress Van Brunt, but my Lina won't believe it safe to come here, especially should she learn of the murder and the fire."

He took up the reins and made a clicking sound. "I'm afraid I'll have to go elsewhere," he said, and after a nod to his father and brother, he turned his mount and headed out of Sleepy Hollow.

Nicolaas shook his head. "My apologies for that one. He's just recently wed, and still letting that filly of

226

his lead him around by the forelocks, I'm afraid."

Icharus cast a quick glance to Katherine before he looked back at Nicolaas. "Some ladies are not quite as fearless as others, Master Van Kersten. It takes a woman of fine mettle to stand tall in the face of the recent trials here in the Hollow."

Nicolaas nodded. "True. True. So ... when do we start?"

Icharus looked around at the burned timbers and stone behind him, and then back to the two men. "No time like the present, I suppose. We're hauling this mass to that empty field to be burned, and we'll spread the ashes over it when it's all consumed. The stone will go down there a ways, to divert the water ..."

Brau went to Katherine's side and, taking her by the arm, led her away from Icharus. "What are you doing down here, Katherine? Your gown is ruined, my dear, and you must be frozen through."

He lifted her hand, and shook his head at the black soot covering her gloved palms. "Just as I suspected. Your mother would never believe what a hoyden you've become. Nor would she tolerate it."

Katherine ignored his comment about her mother. "I came down to help Icharus and the others move this lot, but I suppose I won't be needed now."

"You should go back to the house before you catch your death out here. You'll have time to tidy up before lunch." He looked around. "Where are Mr. Rawlins and the carriage?"

A blush spread across her cheeks. "I rode down with Icharus."

His gaze flickered to Icharus and back to her, and after a moment he nodded. "I'll take you up. Come with me," he said, leading her toward the tall chestnut steed he called Thunder.

"Katherine, can I speak with you for a moment?"

Icharus called.

Relief swept through her. Although she was feeling the cold a bit more now that she was standing about doing nothing instead of working, she wasn't ready to go back to the house.

Remembering what Icharus had said last night, that if he were the man who had asked her to marry him, *he* wouldn't let her out of his sight, even for a moment, she wondered if he, too, was about to suggest she return home with Mrs. Porter and Mr. Rawlins where she'd be relatively safe and warm … but alone.

Offering Brau a hesitant smile, she said, "Excuse me, please."

She hurried to Icharus's side.

He stood near the wagon he and the new arrivals had filled while she'd been speaking with Brau. "Cold?"

She nodded, and her teeth chattered, giving evidence she'd spoken the truth. "Aye, but only because I'm just standing here, doing nothing. If I were working still …"

He nodded and reached up to pull the hood of her cloak close about her neck. "Come on. You can help me unload these stones and you'll be warm again in no time."

* * * *

Brau watched Icharus hand Katherine up into the wagon before he climbed onto the high seat and shook out the reins. The wagon gave a jerk and rolled away toward the brook, and Brau squeezed his hands into tight fists at his sides.

He could hear the other wagon returning from the field, and heard Walter, Phillip, and the other gentlemen when they began to heft the burned timbers into it, but still he stared after the wagon bearing Icharus and

Katherine toward the stream.

"Enjoy it while you can, Crane," he whispered darkly. "Your time is running out."

* * * *

The next morning, Katherine woke to an almost eerie silence with overly bright sunlight streaming through her window. Without looking, she knew the snow Icharus had mentioned the day before had come in the night, blanketing the Hollow in a thick layer of white.

She stretched beneath the covers and groaned, her muscles protesting the movement after all the lifting and tugging she had done the day before. Gingerly, she removed the covers and tiptoed across the floor to stir up the coals in the hearth and add a few small slithers and logs to it to chase the chill from the room while she dressed.

Below stairs, she found Icharus standing in the open doorway watching the snowflakes continue to fall. He must have heard her coming down the stairs because he said, "Much more of this and we'll have to dig ourselves out."

Katherine smiled. "You'd think you haven't lived in the area, just across the way, all your life. It will stop soon, but more will come before this is gone. It'll be good for the ground, for crops."

He turned around and his gaze drifted over her from head to feet, and his eyes darkened. "Good for the ground, yes. For my sanity? No."

Katherine chuckled. "You sound like Father. He never was one for staying inside very long." She wrapped her arms about herself and shivered. "Close the door, Master Crane. It's freezing in here!"

He stepped back to do as she had bid, and she went into the dining room where Mrs. Porter had just set a plate and a mug of fresh milk onto the table for her.

"Good morning, Edda." She lifted the mug and took a long drink. "Mmm, that is delicious. Remind me to thank Brau again for his generosity."

"I don't think you'll have the opportunity anytime soon. Even Braughton wouldn't brave this weather for a simple word of thanks," Icharus said, joining her at the table.

Katherine shrugged. "I am just happy we were able to clear away the remains of those burned buildings before Mother Nature decided to enshroud the land in white."

The sound of horses outside drew their attention. Icharus went to the door, and shook his head. "Van Kersten. Hasn't a sensible brain in his head."

Katherine had followed him from the dining room to identify their morning visitor as well, and she shook her head. "As if you weren't already planning to head over to help Jericho and the others this morning."

His brows rose. "You're right. We're still going to need those timbers and it'll do us little good to try to wait for a spring thaw."

Katherine stepped back from the door. "Icharus, I think we should suggest Nicolaas and Dirck bring their families here as soon as the weather allows."

He looked at her. "To the Bleeker place? Katherine, there are already several men there, men without families who—"

"No, I meant here." She gestured to the room in general. "There are empty chambers upstairs, and I think I should enjoy the company."

He studied her for a moment, considering her suggestion. Finally he nodded. "I will mention it to Nicolaas."

* * * *

Nicolaas Van Kersten had approved wholeheartedly of the idea, and just over a week later, the Van Kerstens arrived en masse at the Van Brunt manor.

Katherine greeted them at the door, taking an immediate liking to Nicolaas's wife, Gwendolyn. She was the quiet sort, and short in stature, but she and her two oldest daughters, the twins Isobel and Eleanor, managed the youngest of the Van Kersten brood with quiet looks and gestures that were instantly obeyed as if a whip had been cracked overhead.

Katherine watched how the two older girls aided their mother with the younger children, moving on nothing more than a flicker of their mother's eye or a slight gesture of her hands to remove one or the other of the children from whatever mischief they'd decided to engage in at the moment. She felt a momentary prick of sadness that she'd never had the chance to do as much with her own mother.

At barely a year younger than Katherine, Isobel and Eleanor were very lovely and, though they were twins, they were as different as night and day. Isobel was dark, with sable hair and warm chocolate eyes where Eleanor was light. Her blonde curls and blue eyes were quite striking to behold, and Katherine immediately thought of Callum when she looked at Eleanor. The two would make a lovely pair, she thought.

After a bit, Gorge and Hans, also twins and Nicolaas and Gwen's youngest at the grand age of eight, seemed content to stare out the wide windows in the parlor, looking down over the village below.

Olivia, Dirck's wife, was more reserved. She seemed nervous and shy, and a bit unsure of herself in her mother-in-law's presence, though Katherine could not fathom why. She did her best to make the lady feel comfortable and welcome, but sensed it might be quite some time before she would get a reaction other than a hesitant nod or timid smile from her.

Dirck and Olivia's three children, more boys than girls ranging in age from two to five years, were wonderful and Katherine chuckled at their antics while they ran about from parlor to the main hall and back again, pleading with their mothers to let them out to play in the melting snow.

Their pleas reminded Katherine much of herself and the other children who had lived in the Hollow during her youth, and put a reminiscent smile on her face.

* * * *

It hadn't taken long to get everyone settled. Katherine had readied the rooms upstairs before they'd arrived, with the elder Van Kerstens in the chamber that had belonged to her parents and the younger in the room nearest the top of the stairs, across from Callum's chamber.

She had put the two older Van Kersten girls in the chamber beside her own, and the younger children would share a chamber across the hall, next door to Icharus.

With Isobel and Eleanor occupying the children upstairs for a time, Gwen and Olivia joined Katherine and Mrs. Porter in the kitchen to help with the cooking.

For Katherine, having the other ladies in the house was a welcome change, and she was quite enjoying herself … until the men returned from the forest and everyone was called in to sit down for supper, and she noticed how Isobel's dark eyes seemed wont to follow Icharus everywhere he went.

Chapter 14

Brau had joined them for supper, as he often did, and now he placed his hand at the small of Katherine's back and led her to her seat at the table. He held out her chair and waited for her to be seated before seeking out his own place.

"We are all delighted you've decided to join us," he said, taking it upon himself to act as host, and with her thoughts otherwise occupied, Katherine allowed it.

With a less than genuine smile now curving her lips, Katherine agreed. "It has been too quiet in this house for far too long."

Conversation turned to all that had been accomplished thus far in the forest and at the sawmill. Katherine listened with half an ear, her attention distracted by the smiling Isobel who made no secret of the fact she liked what she saw each time her gaze rested upon Icharus ... as it did throughout most of the meal.

Icharus did nothing to discourage the girl, Katherine thought, by returning her smiles with his own and the occasional nod of acknowledgment in her direction. His easy acceptance of the girl's obvious interest irritated Katherine.

233

"From the estimate Jericho and I made earlier today, I believe we should have enough timber for both a new storehouse and stable by the time spring arrives in earnest, in addition to the inn," she heard Icharus answer in reply to Brau's question regarding how things were progressing in the Western Wood.

"With all the noise we made out there today, you'd think if there were indeed a witch in residence, she would have come out of hiding to curse us all," he teased.

Both Van Kersten gentlemen laughed at Icharus's quip, but Brau held his silence, exchanging a meaningful glance with Katherine, reminding her of their conversation in the church after John's murder.

Katherine tensed, her gaze flitting from Icharus, who she offered a warning frown, to Brau. Her gaze returned to Icharus. "Let us have no talk of witches and curses today, please," she asked, her eyes pleading with him to change the subject.

His nod was almost imperceptible. "Callum and I were discussing the housing situation, and that, once the inn is built to accommodate the workers we will still employ for tilling and planting, the Bleeker residence will be available once again. I spoke with Dirck earlier, and he agrees the house will be most suitable for himself and his family."

Dirck nodded, confirming his agreement, and Katherine relaxed a bit. "A fine idea, Icharus. I hadn't thought of it, but Olivia, Nell had a small flower garden in the back where the sun falls in the afternoon ... a perfect spot to spend your leisure hours before nightfall. I think you'll enjoy living there."

"Provided we have any leisure hours. Not likely with those three," Dirck chided, gesturing to their youngsters seated at a low table Olivia had helped Katherine to set up across from the main table earlier.

Another smile from Isobel, and Icharus tipped his glass in her direction in a silent but unmistakable response to her coy flirtation.

Katherine's brows drew downward and she forced herself to ignore their interactions. *What do I care if he acknowledges a few feminine smiles?* The answer to that question refused to make itself known, and though she did her best to ignore it, the unusual feeling of uneasy agitation within her grew.

"Yes, well, we still must find a place for Nicolaas and Gwendolyn, Icharus," Brau reminded. "Have you any thoughts in that direction?"

Icharus nodded. "Dehann had a suggestion, actually. It seems John's widow is quite content with helping out at the Bleeker place. The work there keeps her busy and her mind occupied, Dehann says. Apparently, she has expressed an interest in your inn, Katherine."

Katherine was both surprised and delighted. Isobel and her overtures to Icharus forgotten for the moment, she said, "Why, that's a wonderful idea! If Clara and the twins were to oversee the running of the inn, Nicolaas and Gwendolyn could stay at their place. There would be no need to hurry the construction of new housing … we will do so later, of course, but with everyone settled, we could concentrate on the planting and …"

Her sudden animation and obvious delight brought smiles to all their faces. Icharus chuckled. "I believe that was the idea."

Only Brau maintained a somber composure. "It seems you have everything well in hand, Crane. My congratulations to you," he offered sardonically.

"It seems you are industrious and capable as well as handsome, Master Crane," Isobel rejoined. "All of which are qualities I much admire in a man."

She offered a bright smile, and Katherine's gaze

flew to Icharus. She saw the questioning arch of his brow, but his reply did nothing to pacify the gnawing feeling of uncertainty within her.

"Just as beauty and a keen wit are qualities I admire in a woman, Mistress Isobel," he said.

Katherine folded her hands in her lap and lowered her gaze, demure once more. She had almost forgotten the others at the table until Brau's somewhat cutting tone had put an immediate damper on her momentarily cheerful mood, and now she felt unwelcome and somehow out of place at her own table.

* * * *

After she and the other ladies cleared away the dishes from supper, Brau had invited the men into her father's study for a drink or smoke, and the ladies had elected to take the children upstairs to settle them for the night.

Finding herself alone in a houseful of people, Katherine took her cloak from the peg near the door and went out into the chilly night to stroll along the porch. Her grandmother's spinning wheel still sat in the corner, and she went to it now, her hand sliding over the wooden frame, her thoughts a tangle of confusion.

She wondered dejectedly why she had ever thought it a good idea to invite the Van Kerstens into her home. She had thought their company would be uplifting and maybe the companionship of other ladies would make her feel less alone somehow, but now …

She peered out over the snow-covered yard, a heavy sigh escaping her lips. Now all she wanted to do was send them back to wherever they had come from, and she knew the petty desire had arisen because of Isobel and her obvious attraction to Icharus.

Watching the girl ogle him throughout the entire meal had been bad enough, Katherine thought, but for him to acknowledge and encourage her was even worse.

She shook her head.

It doesn't matter, Katherine. If Master Crane wishes to dally with the daughter of your guest, what business is it of yours?

None.

But somehow, sometime during the days and weeks Icharus had been in Sleepy Hollow, Katherine realized, she had come to feel as though she did have some rights in his life. For some reason she didn't even comprehend, much less understand, she'd begun to think of Icharus as *hers.*

Her hero.

There was no denying it. She had come to see Icharus as the only man in the world she believed could turn things around in Sleepy Hollow, at last, and bring joy and happiness back into her life.

While her goals had been centered on creating a new and better life for the people of Sleepy Hollow, and her thoughts had settled on Icharus as the only man she felt complete confidence in as far as his ability to help her achieve that goal, her emotions had somehow become entangled.

Watching him tonight, witnessing firsthand his responses to Isobel with her come-hither looks and seductive, promising smiles, Katherine became conscious of the fact that, although having Icharus Crane in her life had somehow become a requirement for her own sense of security and future happiness, Icharus's future obviously was not dependent on her.

"Katherine? Are you out here?" Icharus called quietly from the door, and she felt the prick of tears behind her eyelids. Squeezing her eyes closed to ward off the self-pitying sniffles she so wanted to indulge in at the moment, she released a halting sigh.

"I'm here, Icharus. I ... just needed a moment to

myself."

He closed the door and followed the sound of her voice to the end of the piazza. "You really shouldn't be out here alone. You should have told me if you wished to take some air." He propped his hip casually against the railing along the edge of the porch. "The Van Kerstens can be a bit overpowering when you bring them all together, can't they?"

Avoiding his gaze, Katherine looked away and shrugged. "A bit."

"Katherine, are you feeling all right? You sound … sad."

She straightened and walked away from the spinning wheel, preferring to look across the snow-covered fields rather than chance him seeing the despondency she was feeling in her gaze. She gave a little laugh. "Actually, I am feeling a little unsettled. Gwen and Olivia and the others have been so nice, and I think they're good people, Icharus, but they also make me feel so …"

"Unsettled," he said with a nod. He shrugged. "I thought you'd be glad to have them here, to have other females to talk to about … female things, I suppose."

Katherine's brows arched high. "As did I."

"And now?"

She heaved a sigh and let her head fall back, her eyes closed. "Now I'm not sure having them come here was a good idea … but what is done is done, as my grandmother was fond of saying." She shook her head. "It's nothing, really. It'll be spring soon, and …"

She could see her current mood confused him. It bewildered her as well. This past week she had been so eager, looking forward to the Van Kersten's arrival with more excitement than a three-year-old on Christmas Eve.

"You aren't going to be like this until spring, I hope?" he asked.

She looked at him then, a question in her eyes. "This?"

He made a gesture with his hands. "Maudlin. Depressed. Sad. Katherine, Nicolaas told me his family lost everything other than what they could fit into the wagon they brought with them. Up until today they were living with Nicolaas's sister and her family in a house the size of the Bleeker place ... a large family. Can you imagine how 'unsettled' they must have felt?"

She looked away, feeling ashamed of herself for her selfishness.

"Nicolaas and Gwen are looking to start over, just as you are," he continued. "Dirck and Olivia too, and they can help you, Katherine. They will help you."

She slanted a glance in his direction. "Isobel and Eleanor too? How will they help me, Icharus?"

He frowned. "Somehow. I don't know exactly, but I'm sure—"

She uttered a brittle laugh. "You're sure. That's amusing, Master Crane, because I suddenly feel quite uncertain about everything."

He fell silent, and she did her best to ignore him, but no matter how she tried, she could feel his presence, smell the warm, male scent of him. Her thoughts filled with memories of him holding her close on the sofa, of his gentle, soothing caresses lulling her.

She shivered.

The chill night air had finally found its way beneath the folds of her cloak, and she hurried to the door. "I think I'll go back inside now. Brau will be ready to leave soon, and I should see him out."

* * * *

Icharus watched her go, completely baffled by her sudden turn of mood. He wondered what had happened

239

to the high-spirited, cheerful lady she had been every day since she had suggested the Van Kerstens come here to stay a se'ennight ago.

With two sisters in his household, he thought he well knew the workings of the female mind, but Katherine Van Brunt remained an elusive mystery. *What drastic event had occurred to cause such a complete turnabout?*

He hadn't seen her like this since the day her father was buried.

Van Ripper. He'd been the one to drain the light from Katherine's eyes then, and Icharus reasoned he was likely the one responsible for her current despondent mood.

Irritation replaced his puzzlement, and he stood, ready to confront the man this minute, guests or no guests. He wanted nothing more than to force Brau to go to Katherine and make amends for whatever he'd done to send her off into the depths of despair again … to make things right again for her though he refused to acknowledge the cause of his sudden annoyance.

As much as he wished to deny it, to blame his fury on the seeming unfairness of it all, he did not think Katherine deserved to suffer in such sadness. The truth was he simply couldn't bear seeing her this way. He wanted her to smile, and he wanted to see her smile reflected in the depths of those gorgeous blue eyes of hers, reflected in her soul.

Her happiness had become very important to him over these past weeks, and he despised his current feeling of helplessness, his inability to immediately bring a moment of joy into her life.

But she could see that, couldn't she?

Surely she recognized how badly he wanted to help her. She had to know he wanted nothing more than for her to be happy. But his hands were pretty much tied if she wouldn't let him know what was bothering her, what had upset her so badly. He didn't know how he could fix whatever had gone wrong if he did not know what it was.

Questions continued to plague him while he sat there in the darkness, ignoring the cold and the occasional snowflake that blew beneath the shelter of the roof to lay unseen on his coat for a moment before it melted in the wake of his heat. He was still sitting there, pondering the bend of Katherine's mind, when the door opened once more.

Brau did not see him, hidden in the shadows as he was, and Icharus watched in peeved silence while Brau pulled the high collar of his coat close before hurriedly descending the steps to the yard. He watched him swing onto the back of his mount and head down the lane leading out of Sleepy Hollow, and he saw him change direction before he reached the bridge, riding out across the fields instead of out of the village, heading for the Tanner's place. He frowned.

Why would Brau be paying such a late visit to the Tanners? He stood and almost called for Mr. Rawlins to bring Defiance around so he could follow the man, but he remembered Katherine had said she felt unsettled with the Van Kerstens here, and he didn't want to leave her alone with them if it could be avoided.

In the end, he decided to stay. He would ask Dehann about Brau's visit tomorrow. His dilemma satisfied, he went into the house to find Katherine, but she'd already retired to her chamber.

* * * *

For Katherine, the next several weeks were the longest of her life, or so it seemed. Her days were filled with a myriad of tasks, each one oriented toward simply getting

241

through another day and making ready for spring. Every night she sought her bed feeling more than ready for sleep, but more and more she found herself unable to rest until the bright fingers of dawn began to light the eastern sky in the wee hours of early morning.

Even then, her time for sleep was cut short because she had begun to force herself to rise before anyone else in the household in hope of snatching a few moments alone with Icharus before he left the house.

It wasn't as bad once the snow had finally melted and she could spend a part of each day with Clara, Mary, and Alaina at the Bleeker place.

Before, though, when it had been unsafe to leave the house, she'd thought she would quietly go mad if she had to watch Isobel's continuing quest to win Icharus's undivided attention for even a single second more.

As soon as it had been safe to do so, she'd had Mr. Rawlins ready the carriage immediately after breakfast, and she'd joined the three women to do laundry, mending, cleaning, and cooking for the workers who were staying at the Bleeker house.

She would return in the afternoon, her mood much improved, but the moment Icharus returned in the evening, it would turn sour once more, just as it did this afternoon.

During the past few weeks, Isobel had somehow managed to maneuver seating arrangements at the table so that she sat at Icharus's left, and Eleanor at his right. Katherine maintained her usual place, but doing so was no better because she had a perfect, unobstructed view of Icharus, and was forced to observe his being fawned over by two of the loveliest ladies in the county throughout the entire meal.

Brau didn't help matters when he was in attendance, encouraging the girls with improper tales regarding Icharus's eligibility. She knew it made Icharus uncomfortable, and had even mentioned it to Brau, but he had responded with, "Nonsense. Why would Crane care if I make it easier for him to win the young woman over?"

* * * *

Having worked late into the evening the past couple of weeks, the men had agreed to an early supper so they might spend more time with their families.

Callum, who had spent most of his nights these many weeks at the Bleeker place with the hired workers, agreed to join them. It had been too long since he'd last looked in on Katherine, and he had missed her these past weeks.

Although she hadn't said a word about her feelings of resentment toward the younger Van Kersten ladies, or heaven forbid, given the slightest clue why she felt such bitterness, Callum noticed it and her withdrawal the moment Icarus entered the dining room. Callum frowned, wondering if something untoward happened between the two of them.

Whatever it was, he figured it must have been quite dire to cause such a noticeable affect in Katherine. He said nothing, however, choosing to simply observe rather than make uneducated guesses into the matter.

When they adjourned to the table, Callum did not miss the fact that Katherine had seated him directly to Icarus's right, with Eleanor Van Kersten on his other side. He recognized her not-so-subtle attempt for what it was, but didn't have the heart to tell her he wasn't the slightest bit interested in the lovely blonde she had placed at his side.

Time and again throughout the meal he saw Katherine's gaze drawn to his end of the table, and each time her face fell and her spirits seemed to become more diminished. He frowned.

Is she really that eager to pair me with the young woman? She was so obviously overwrought, he considered asking Eleanor to play along with him for the duration of the meal, just to make Katherine feel better. Then he finally realized why she kept stealing furtive glances across the table.

Icharus. And Isobel.

Everything suddenly became clear in his mind – her withdrawal when Icharus came in was because of Isobel. He studied her curiously, wondering if she even recognized her feelings for what they were.

She hadn't, he decided, and his frown deepened. It troubled him to think she might have been this way the entire time since the Van Kerstens had come to Sleepy Hollow. He cast a glance at Icharus, noting his equally dark mood, and guessed she likely had.

He sighed inwardly, suddenly feeling he had been quite negligent in his duties as the person Brom had charged to watch over when he was no longer able.

It was as clear as the sadness on Katherine's face that she had fallen in love with Crane. It was as plain as the quick, hungry glances Icharus swept in her direction when he thought no one could see that he wanted her as badly as she wanted him. And it didn't take a genius to figure out neither of them had told the other of their feelings.

"Icharus, have you taken Katherine out to see the progress we've made on the inn?" he asked in an attempt to draw the two of them into the low murmur of conversation.

Icharus only shook his head, keeping his attention squarely focused on the meal in front of him.

Katherine offered a wobbly smile in a feeble attempt at cordial conversation, but he could see the jumble of confused emotions in her eyes.

244

"There hasn't been time, Callum. We've all been so busy—"

That much was true, he supposed, but thought surely Icharus could have taken a few moments to show her how her idea was taking form. He slid another glance in Icharus's direction and forced back a commiserate chuckle.

The poor idiot has no idea ...

He pushed away his plate and leaned back in his chair, pretending to doze for the moment while the others finished their meal, but all the while he watched Katherine watch Icharus – and cast visual daggers at Isobel she thought no one else could see.

Soon, the meal came to an end, and Callum shot up from his chair, hurrying around Icharus to make a showy bow before Isobel. "Mistress Van Kersten, would you join me outside for a walk? The weather has turned somewhat agreeable, and it feels a bit stuffy in here."

She turned a pleading look toward Icharus, which he ignored under the guise of a yawn. Her disappointment clear in her gaze, she turned back to Callum. "I suppose it would be all right. Father?"

Nicolaas waved his assent. "Go on with the lad, girl. The fresh air will do you good."

Callum grinned.

"Excellent, sir. Thank you," he said, and then turned to Eleanor. "Mistress Eleanor, would you care to join us?"

The younger of the two by the stretch of a few minutes, Eleanor smiled, but shook her head. "Thank you, Master Mather, but I'm afraid I shall have to decline. The boys were feeling a bit rowdy today. As you've already pointed out, the weather is a good deal more enjoyable now, and young boys much prefer to be outside at such times, as I'm sure you can remember. I've promised Mother I would sit with them beneath the oak near the house for a bit before dark."

Callum glanced at Katherine again and almost shook his head. Only a blind fool could have missed the change in her. She had relaxed so quickly it was immediately noticeable.

"Crane, do be a gentleman and bring Katherine along. I'm sure she'd like to see the inn, and we've a bit more light left before evening."

Katherine's gaze flew to his, and Callum looked away, unable to bear seeing the utter gratefulness in her eyes.

Icharus slid his chair back, and stood. "Of course. Katherine, you may wish to bring a shawl. The air is still a bit chilly out."

She was already shaking her head.

"No, I'll be fine," she said, a smile curving her lips. Callum was greatly relieved to see that, unlike the one she had attempted earlier, this one actually reached her eyes.

* * * *

Outside, her hand resting lightly on Icharus's arm as they walked down the lane, Katherine said, "You didn't have to walk with me, Icharus. I can walk down on my own."

She turned to look at him, trying to fathom his mood wondering if he would have preferred to go with Isobel. She looked away, her mind refusing to dwell on the possibility.

"Actually, I've already seen the inn, several times. I've been riding out to the Bleeker place in the afternoon with Mary, and I must say I am quite impressed with the progress you've made."

"We've made," he said. "I could never have done so much this quickly on my own."

She nodded. "Yes, all of you have done well."

He didn't reply, and she fell silent, listening to the sound of their footfalls in the road.

"What is bothering you, Katherine?"

She cast him a questioning glance. "What do you mean?"

He stopped, right in the middle of the lane, and turned her to face him. He reached out and smoothed his finger along the upper curve of her cheek, just under her eye. "You've dark circles here, and I know you haven't been sleeping well."

She frowned and tried to look away, but he opened his palm against her cheek, forcing her to face him. His concern was real. She could see it in his eyes. She shrugged. "I've been restless."

He shook his head. "Do you take me for a fool? I see you climb those stairs every night, so tired your feet fairly drag, and yet, I hear you moving about in your chamber until just before the sun starts to rise."

She pulled away from his touch, turning to gaze toward the tall, two-story frame that would soon be the first inn in Sleepy Hollow. "I'd rather talk of other things, if you don't mind."

He hesitated, as if he wished to continue the conversation, but after a moment, he nodded reluctantly. "The fields are almost ready for turning. In another week, we should be able to plant crops. With a bit of luck, Sleepy Hollow will reap a bountiful harvest this fall."

She nodded, hearing all he said, but her mind did not supply a response. She should have felt ecstatic at his news, would have before the Van Kersten's arrival, but now all she could think of was that, come harvest time, Icharus would leave Sleepy Hollow.

His obligation to her, such as it were, would be fulfilled, and he would return to his home, his life, in

Wake Grove. Without her. And she would be miserable.

She'd walked a number of steps ahead of him before she realized he had stopped and she was practically pulling him forward.

Forcing a smile to her lips, she stopped and looked up at him. "Well? Are we going to see the inn, or no?"

He shook his head. "I'd rather not."

Her smile faltered. "Oh."

"Not if you aren't going to enjoy it."

She smiled again, but her thoughts remained troubled. "I *am* enjoying it."

He looked away, and after a moment he turned heading back toward the house, shaking his head once more. "No, you aren't."

She hurried round in front of him and caught hold of his coat. "Will you stop? Please. I want to see the inn with you."

He stared at her and his eyes turned dark. "I want to kiss you, Katherine. A real kiss. One that makes you forget where you are, who you are, and leaves you yearning for more."

Her physical response was immediate.

She felt hot all over, and her cheeks burned. Her eyes met his, and though she said nothing, he seemed to know exactly what she yearned for.

He reached out to her, one hand cupping her cheek as his fingers slid into her hair while the other slid around her waist just above her hips, and pulled her closer.

"Icharus …"

"I've wanted to kiss you for so long, Katherine. Wanted to feel the warm heat of your lips beneath mine, wanted to taste your sweetness, the heady thrill of your response …"

He continued to draw her ever near, until his lips were a mere whisper from hers. "I lay in my bed across the hall at night and I crave the taste of you, Katherine, but I dare not open the door for fear you will turn me away."

She pressed her palms against his chest, pushing him away even as she leaned closer, wanting everything he had just said and more.

"Every time I look at Van Ripper, I feel a fury rise up within me because he wants you too, and I don't want him to have you. My desire for you has become a madness inside me."

Katherine wanted nothing more than to press her lips against his, to feel the earth fall away while she lost herself in his kiss, but they were standing in the middle of the lane where anyone could see. She grabbed a handful of his coat and gave a little shake. "Icharus, please!"

"I want to please you, Katherine. In fact, doing so has become my one desire," he said.

His lips feathered softly against hers and she groaned, pulling away from his embrace.

"Icharus, no! We can be seen ..." she finally managed.

He pulled back and blinked, much like a man who had been snatched from slumber and plunged into a beam of bright sunlight. He released her immediately. Without a word, he laced her arm through his and headed toward the inn.

After a moment, she peered up at him from beneath her lashes. "You really want to kiss me?"

He closed his eyes. "So very badly I ache."

She shook her head from side to side, unable to believe what he had said. "But what about Isobel?"

He came to a halt so suddenly she almost tripped. "Isobel?"

She nodded. "She's obviously interested in ... in getting to know you better. She's so very lovely, I... I

249

thought you must feel the same."

"*Isobel*." He narrowed his eyes, thoughtful for a moment, and then he started to laugh.

Katherine looked away, feeling quite foolish. "It isn't funny. She's very beautiful. So is Eleanor, and …"

After a moment he quieted, and said, "Beautiful, is she?" He shook his head, a smile still lingering on his lips. "I honestly wouldn't know, Katherine, because for the past several weeks, my eyes have seen only you."

She bit her lip and turned her face aside, fighting back tears his words caused. "Please don't speak such nonsense, Icharus. I might believe you and … you're going to leave soon."

His expression turned dark once more. "And you're going to marry Van Ripper soon."

He started walking again, and she followed in silence, her mind full of questions but no ready answers.

Chapter 15

"You've fallen in love with him, haven't you?"

Katherine looked up at Callum, her eyes reflecting the uneasy curiosity his question wrought. "Whatever would make you say such a thing?"

He shrugged and sat beside her on the sofa. "The way you looked at him just now, when you thought no one else was watching, as if a mere smile from him would grant your greatest joy."

She rolled her eyes, but her cheeks burned with her mortification. "I did no such thing."

He snorted in disbelief, raising his brows high. "Or mayhap it's how the mere mention of his name earlier after your walk brought a rush of color to your cheeks and a silly, secretive smile to your lips."

Katherine thought immediately of Icharus's confession, and a feeling of warm joy swept through her. She couldn't meet Callum's gaze when she replied. "Or maybe it was the heat in this room that had my cheeks flushing hot."

He gestured toward Icharus, who was sitting in Callum's chair near the fire, discussing plans for the morrow with Nicolaas. "Or perhaps it is the way you're trying to watch him even now without appearing to do so."

He arched a brow, his eyes daring her to deny the truth of his words. "Thoughts of that man fill your every waking moment and many of your dreams, do they not?"

Katherine cast a furtive glance in Icharus's direction, a strange new awareness and a sense of wonderment filling her.

Love ...

She considered the word, comparing what she felt for Icharus at this moment with all she knew of its meaning.

Her father had loved her mother so deeply he had grieved himself to death when she was gone. She thought of the words she had spoken to Icharus just a few hours ago, that he'd soon be leaving Sleepy Hollow and of her feelings when she had said them. A trickle of fear slid through her.

Dear God, do I love Icharus Crane?

Katherine reflected on the matter, weighing the evidence. *Could* love *be the reason I want to spend every possible moment at his side?*

Is love *the reason I put off giving Brau an answer to his marriage proposal?*

Did love *leave me feeling envious of Icharus's attention when I wanted to send Isobel out of a room the moment Icharus entered it, or any other woman for that matter?*

Is it even possible to fall in love with someone without being aware of it?

She looked at Callum with every bit of the doubt and fear and uncertainty she now felt showing on her face. "I don't know."

* * * *

Callum's question plagued her for the next several days, preying on her thoughts morning and night, distracting her when she should be thinking of other things, like the new storehouse and stable that Icharus and the others were also working on, and the fields that soon would be planted.

She turned to Clara, handing her another garment from the basket at her feet.

"Clara, how did you know you loved John?"

Clara blanched, dropping the cloth Katherine held out to her.

Realizing too late she had brought up a subject best left alone, and feeling terrible for having done so, Katherine put a consoling hand on Clara's arm and said, "I'm so sorry, Clara. I should never have …"

Tears had filled the woman's eyes, but she shook her head. "No, it's all right, Katherine. I know John isn't coming back, but some days I miss him terribly."

Katherine nodded her understanding, and felt even more miserable for having brought the subject up.

Dash Callum and his pesky questions.

"Master Brau asked you to marry him?" Clara asked.

Katherine, distracted once again by her own thoughts, gave an affirmative shake of her head. "Yes, but …"

"I remember when John finally mustered the nerve to ask me," she said, a little smile curving her lips. "Poor man, he was so afraid I would say no."

Tears welled in her eyes again at the memories, and she squeezed them closed for a moment. She held out her hand for the next garment, and said, "It seems such a long time ago, yet I remember the look in his eyes as if it were only yesterday."

She grinned. "His palms were clammy, you know, if you can even imagine such a thing. John Tanner with sweaty palms? Heaven forbid!"

Katherine smiled. "He loved you very much."

Clara nodded. "Yes, I believe he did. At least as much as I loved him."

"So much he ached with it," Katherine whispered, unknowingly repeating the words Icharus had spoken to her the day they had walked to the inn. But he hadn't been speaking of love.

Clara studied her for a moment. "I hadn't realized things had become quite so serious between the two of you."

Katherine frowned. "Serious?"

She rather thought the time she had spent with Icharus was enjoyable. Pleasant. Exhilarating. Humorous. Katherine bit back a smile, remembering how Icharus had skillfully taken her away the day the Van Kerstens had arrived and she had been helping him move the stones.

Brau had been serious. Seriously frustrated with her for not being where he felt she belonged, but Icharus had been considerate of her wishes. He had been careful of her feelings. Spending the day working alongside Icharus had been fun, even, but not serious.

Clara nodded. "The last time I saw the two of you together you seemed a bit … distant toward each other. Mary told me you'd had an argument after the storehouse burned …"

Katherine's confusion cleared. "Oh, you mean Brau and I. Yes, we did have words, but we seem to have moved past it."

Clara cocked her head to the side, confusion in her gaze. "You weren't speaking of Brau when you asked how I knew I loved John, were you?"

She thought of Brau, of her feelings for him, and they were much like those she'd had for John, or Heinrick, or … well, maybe not Callum because she thought of him as she might a brother, but her feelings for Brau did not resemble those she had for Icharus Crane in the least.

Katherine's brows furrowed. "No."

Clara fastened another shirt over the line, and said, "I see."

Katherine handed over another garment, but Clara shook her head and Katherine let it fall back into the basket.

After a moment, the older woman shook her head again. "A woman's love for a man really isn't an emotion I can explain, Katherine. It is more something you just know, deep inside."

* * * *

Katherine was no closer to an answer when she returned to the house that afternoon than she had been when she'd left this morning. Having no wish to encounter Isobel or Eleanor just now, she headed to the kitchen. Perhaps Mrs. Porter needed help with the cooking, she hoped. But Edda had everything well in hand, as usual.

She handed Katherine a basket. "Take this, and spend some time in the sun, Miss Katherine. Nobody will fault you for taking a rest. Go find Master Callum or Master Icharus and share it with them if you want."

Surprised, Katherine's gaze widened. "A picnic?"

Tears pricked her eyes. "Oh, Edda. I haven't had a picnic since …"

Mrs. Porter wiped her hands on her apron and nodded.

"Since Miss Katrina were alive." She shook her head. "Lord knows that woman loved nothing better than a good meal taken outdoors with a strapping lad at her side … sometimes two. I used to think she lived for spring, 'til Master Brom caught her heart."

Katherine smiled, threw her arms around Edda, giving her a tight hug of gratitude. "Thank you, Edda."

Mrs. Porter chuckled. "You're most welcome, child. Now go enjoy your dinner. I got things to do in here."

Katherine took the basket and slipped out the back door with it before she peeled away the cloth to see what goodies Edda had smuggled inside.

A twinge of guilt pinched her when she saw the bounty packed inside. Crisp chicken, potato salad, a meat pie, berry cobbler – she hoped the others wouldn't mind when there was a bit less food to share come suppertime.

Hammering noises met her ears and she turned toward the source, considering Mrs. Porter's suggestion she seek out Callum or Icharus and invite them to share her dinner in the sun.

Should I go to the storehouse, where Callum is sure to be, or to the inn, where I know Icharus is working?

Her dilemma, she knew, was really no dilemma at all. With a smile, she took up the basket once more and headed round the house and down the hill – to the inn.

For the first time in many months, she allowed herself to simply relax and enjoy the moment while she walked, letting her gaze and her thoughts wander where they would.

The scenes and scents that met her senses were surprising. Ahead of her, the skeletal structure of the inn Icharus had helped her plan rose up from the ground like a monument. Both to her left and right, freshly turned earth basked in the warm spring sunlight, waiting patiently for the seed it would soon nurture.

Behind her, she could hear the workers even now toiling away at building a new storehouse and stable. She halted, and turned in a slow circle, surveying all that had been accomplished in the few short weeks since the snows had melted.

Her senses seemed to come alive, taking in the scent of sun-warmed grass, the smell of blossoms on the trees in the newly pruned orchard, the scent of freshly tilled ground. The hum of bees reached her ears, and for a moment, Katherine remembered.

She remembered running in the meadow across the way, laughing, while her mother and father followed more slowly behind her, their fingers entwined and smiles wreathing their faces.

She remembered playing seek and find with Anne, Dehann, Eustace and the others, darting between the trees and squealing with laughter when someone's hand caught her from behind.

She remembered laughter, and joy, and a happiness she had thought could not possibly ever go away ... and it had been good.

Looking around, she realized that everything she had hoped for, all the things that had whispered to her, called to her with longing from her past, was here before her now.

She looked up toward the framework where Icharus was working, and a feeling of happiness so great filled her she wanted to sing it to the world.

He's done it!

She knew it wasn't *exactly* the same – all things change over time, that was simply nature's way – but what it was at that moment was every bit as wonderful, if not more so, for knowing he had done it for her.

Somehow, without her being fully conscious of it until just that moment, Icarus Crane had managed to give her the greatest gift anyone ever could have given.

He'd done it.

He had brought back the home of her youth, the Sleepy Hollow she remembered from days gone by ... and she loved him for it.

With a bright smile gracing her face, filled with all the happiness she simply could not hold inside, she hurried toward the inn and Icharus.

She wanted to thank him. She wanted to kiss him. She wanted to dance about the meadow with him with their fingers clasped tightly together and their joyous laughter ringing out across the valley and beyond.

* * * *

Dirck was the first person she saw when she reached the inn. "I'm looking for Master Crane. Do you know where he is?"

Dirck pointed upward, and Katherine's gaze followed in the direction he'd gestured. The sun hit her full in the face, so she put up a hand to block the glare, and her breath caught in her throat.

Icharus was high in the rafters, balancing on his toes while he reached out to pull a large timber into place. He had taken off his coat, due to the heat she guessed, but he had also opened the laces of his shirt, and rolled his sleeves up past his elbows, showing off the tanned muscles of his chest and forearms as he strained to situate the heavy beam.

A shrill whistle pierced the air, and Katherine jerked her gaze to the young man at her side.

Dirck grinned. "He'd never hear you, with all this noise," he offered in explanation, and with a wave of his arm, gestured for Icharus to come down.

Icharus spied her immediately. He caught hold of one of the beams and swung himself out of the framework, hanging for a moment before he dropped to the floor beneath.

He walked over to where she stood with Dirck, and dusted his hands against his thighs.

"Dirck, go up and help your father with that beam,"

he said before turning his attention to Katherine. He smiled. "Behold your inn, Mistress Van Brunt."

She grinned. "Well, almost," she said, and he laughed.

Taking hold of her arm, he led her away from the worksite. "We'll be safer over here."

She followed him, but when he would have stopped, she gestured toward the tall tree near the brook.

"Actually, I thought we might sit over there," she said. "Are you hungry, Master Crane?"

His gaze practically devoured her on the spot. "Starving."

She held out the basket Edda had prepared. "Since today is such a beautiful day, I thought we might sit beneath the shade and share what I have in this basket."

Her voice was so playful, and yet so timid. Icharus arched a brow. "A picnic?"

She nodded, her smile teasing him, and he noticed the bright sparkle in her gaze. Almost regretfully, he looked back toward the inn where the others were still hard at work, and sighed.

Katherine stepped in front of him, peering up at him with those wonderful eyes of hers, and said, "Please. You've been working so hard. You deserve a rest."

Icharus started to protest, to remind her that he hadn't been the only one working, but the happy twinkle in her gaze stopped him. For the life of him, he couldn't allow himself to be the one who made that joyful shine disappear from her gaze.

"A picnic you say? Why, I remember as a child, Mum would pack a veritable bounty of pies and puddings and sweetmeats into a basket just like that one. We'd all go off to the meadow and spend the afternoon enjoying the warm sunshine and a meal made more delicious for having eaten it outdoors. Father especially enjoyed such times. He had rather peculiar fondness for eating."

Katherine smiled. "See? Your father knew that everyone must take time away from toiling to enjoy a good meal. Now, take this basket, if you please, and follow me."

His lips twitched, but he nodded and took the basket, hefting it onto his shoulder.

"Indeed, Mistress Van Brunt. It seems you are correct. Let us away, my dear." He gestured toward the brook. "After you."

Icharus found it a bit humorous that she chose a spot beneath the very tree his father had often spoken of … the very place Ichabod had wiled away many an hour spinning fantasies of himself and Katrina Van Tassel. He grinned.

"You know, my father used to come here of an evening," he told her.

Katherine had busied herself with spreading a colorful quilt over the ground and laying out the scrumptious smelling repast Mrs. Porter had packed into the basket for them. She sat down on a corner of the quilt now, and cast him a glance. "Indeed?"

Icharus nodded. "He told me so himself, many a time. He said he would come here to this exact spot and spend hours with his imagination, casting lurid images of himself and your Mother round in his mind. Many a time, he said, his mind would produce an image of the two of them sharing a kiss so vividly he almost thought the deed done in reality."

She chuckled. "And what of you, Master Crane? Will you spend this hour allowing some lovely female to enchant your thoughts? With whom shall you share a vivid but imaginary kiss?"

Icharus joined her on the blanket and leaned close. "I only indulge in real kisses, dear lady," he said, his voice husky.

She laughed, and he reached out, cradling her cheek in his palm. "Flights of imagination are for dreamers. I prefer to feel the warmth of real lips beneath mine, to watch as they part just the tiniest bit in breathless anticipation, to taste the sweetness offered... in broad daylight."

His thumb teased her lower lip, and her eyelids drifted downward.

"I prefer real lips, Katherine. Like yours. Now," he said, leaning ever closer as he spoke.

"Now?" she whispered.

He gave the barest of nods an instant before his lips brushed hers. He teased her lips with his own, brushing them against hers in a featherlike caress. Once. Again.

She sighed against his mouth, and he shifted on the quilt, pulling her against him, his fingers sifting through her soft curls.

"Katherine. I want to taste you." He breathed the words against her parted lips. He slid his tongue over her lower lip, and then his mouth closed over hers, his tongue sliding inside to taste the nectar of her kiss.

The feel of her own tongue timidly sliding against his near destroyed what bit of sanity he had left to claim.

Desire, hot and ready, slammed through him. He groaned and pulled her closer, deepening the kiss.

He devoured her mouth with his own, his tongue plunging again and again to taste of her sweetness, but he wanted more. His hand slid down, along the gentle curve of her side to her hip, and he cupped her bottom, pulling her as close as he dared.

A moan slid from her throat, and he broke away from her lips to kiss her there, and again at the tender area beneath her ear before he reached up to nibble at her earlobe.

Her hands seemed to have taken on a life of their own, one moment sliding through his hair while she held

261

him close, and then gliding across his shoulders and lower before coming back up again to tangle in his hair.

He delighted in the soft sounds coming from her in response to his kiss. How he wanted this woman, he thought, in every possible way. He shifted again. She wiggled closer ... and then froze.

"Icharus?" she whispered.

"Yes?"

She shifted away from him, and leaned up on an elbow. "I think we're lying in the potato salad."

* * * *

From his vantage point atop the roof of the inn, Brau glared down at the couple near the brook, fury filling him. He dropped to the floor and vaulted off the foundation, rage fueling his every step.

He didn't stop until he reached the pair, didn't realize they wouldn't know he had seen them, locked in a passionate embrace until he stood right over them, his cutting gaze slashing through them both.

"Brau, I didn't know you were here," Katherine said, her tongue flickering out to catch the berry juice that had spilled from her spoon onto her wrist.

She took the bit of pastry into her mouth, but all Brau could see was her, lying beneath the cad at her side, her arms twined about his neck.

"So I see. What are you doing, Katherine?"

"Picnicking. Remember when Mother and Father would bring us down in the spring, Brau? Mmm, this has to be the best cobbler Edda has made yet. Try it," she said, scooping up another bite and holding it out to Brau.

Icharus said nothing. He sat reclined against the quilt, sampling bits from the plate at his side.

They don't realize I saw them.

Though it made him all the more furious they

believed all was well – that they could simply say nothing of the kiss they had shared – he fought to rein in his temper. It would do no good to cause a scene…not at this moment.

He flicked a glance to Katherine again, and narrowed his eyes. "Katherine, what is that goo in your hair?"

Her gaze flew to meet Icharus's at the same time her hand reached up to her hair.

"I think it's potato salad," she said, and though she tried to muffle it, he heard the choked laughter in her voice, saw the look she sent Icharus and the answering laughter in his gaze.

His lips thinned. "Potato salad. In your hair. How?"

She laid her spoon aside, and folded her hands in her lap. "We had a slight mishap earlier."

Icharus wiped at his fingers with the napkin Edda had thoughtfully included in the basket. "Well, I seem to have lost my appetite," he said, and came to his feet before leaning down to help Katherine do the same.

"Must be the heat," he offered as an excuse. He turned to Katherine and gave a slight bow.

"My thanks, Mistress Katherine, for a most delicious feast," he said, and to hear his words, one would have thought he had been speaking of the food, but the look in his eyes spoke volumes of another subject entirely.

Brau squeezed his hands into fists. "I'll help you pack up this lot, Katherine, and you can go back to the house."

He shook his head. "You should have Edda bring up some water for your hair … and wherever else you need to wash away the potato salad … from your mishap, of course—"

"Was there a reason you decided to grace us with your presence today, Braughton?" Icharus interrupted.

He cast Icharus another scathing glance. "Yes, I finished my business in town early, and thought to come lend a hand at the inn."

Icharus rolled down his sleeves and nodded. "We've made quite a lot of progress there, and with the new storehouse as well. Why don't you come with me, and we'll have a look?"

He almost refused. Sweeping Icharus a telling glance filled with loathing, he didn't answer, but instead looked back to Katherine, who was repacking the basket at her feet in silence. She looked up, a radiant smile on her face.

"Yes, do go with Icharus, Brau. It's almost like home again. You'll see," she said, her delight obvious in the tone of her voice, in her gaze when she looked about, resting on each new accomplishment he knew she attributed the achievement of to Crane alone.

Finally, he gave a stiff nod.

"I'll speak with you later, Katherine, once you've had time to put yourself to rights. It seems the potato salad managed to find it's way onto more than your hair," he said, gesturing to the telling mushy handprint at her waist. He shook his head. "You can toss that dress into the fire. It's ruined."

Katherine nodded, and he turned to head back toward the inn.

Icharus waited until Brau had gone on ahead several steps before he tossed her a wink and whispered, "He's just jealous because he didn't get any."

He walked away, leaving her sputtering with laughter.

* * * *

Later that evening, Katherine waited in dread for Brau's request, knowing he would ask to speak to her privately before he left. At the same time, she almost made the request herself, wanting only to get the conversation behind her and done with.

Everyone had elected to sit on the porch when supper was finished, to enjoy the air and watch the sun go down behind the hills. It was a glorious sight to behold, one her mother and father had often shared.

But the tension in her would not let her take pleasure in the beauty of it this night, and she stood and went to Brau. "Walk with me? I'd like to speak with you before you go back to town."

Without a word, he laced her arm through his and led her down across the yard, out of hearing distance of the others. When she thought they'd gone far enough, she stopped and turned to face him.

"I cannot marry you, Braughton. I'm sorry."

He avoided her gaze. "Because of Crane?"

She flushed and looked away, giving a little nod of agreement. "Yes, because of Icharus. I love him, Brau."

He stared at her. "But you do not love me. Correct?"

Her brow furrowed. "Nay, that isn't it at all. I do love you, Brau, but my feelings for you are more ..." She shrugged, unable to find the word to describe how she felt.

After a moment, she said, "Friendly. You are my friend, Brau, and a very good one. I'd like us to remain just that."

He arched a brow. "Friends?"

She nodded. "Yes. Unless you find you cannot tolerate even that, and if you do I'll try to understand, but... I'll be hurt, Brau."

He scoffed. "Yet you think I am not hurt by your decision?"

She felt miserable. "I never wanted to hurt you. I never intended to fall in love, but Icharus—"

"Spare me your glowing diatribe for my adversary, please," he interrupted.

She looked at him, a silent plea in her gaze. "Brau? Time and again you've reminded me that your main concern has been for my happiness these past years. Do you remember?"

He nodded, but remained silent.

Katherine struggled for the words to tell him all that needed to be said. Finally she shrugged. "He makes me happy. Can't you see it within you to be glad for that and wish us well?"

He shook his head. "You are such an innocent, Katherine. You've declared your feelings for that man a number of times now, but my dear, has he made such a declaration of his own to you?" She frowned, and he nodded. "I thought as much. I saw you today, Katherine, down by the brook. I saw him kissing you, touching you, and I wanted to kill him."

Her eyes found his, and she gave a little shake of her head. "You shouldn't say such things, Brau ..."

He glared at her. "And he should not touch what is mine, Katherine. From the beginning I have said he did not belong here. Time and again, I have pointed out why – John's murder, the fire – but you simply turned a deaf ear to my words, and why? *Because he makes you happy.*"

She made to walk away, but he pulled her back. "Or is it because he makes you forget all that you've known to be proper behavior, allows you to ignore the dictates of your parents and society to engage in a temporary frolic with him? Is it because he allows you to speak when you should be silent, or because he sees nothing indecent in pawing your person in the full light of day, in full view of every man, woman, and child in Sleepy Hollow?"

He gave her a little shake. "Tell me, Katherine, do

you love him, or do you simply wish to crawl into his bed?"

She jerked her hands out of his grasp. "Take your hands off me, Brau, and don't ever utter such vulgar nonsense to me again."

Furious, she glared at him, her chest rising and falling in rapid rhythm. "I've tried to explain, tried to… ease your pain even, but I will not stand here and listen to your slander … of either Icharus or myself."

She stepped away, and then turned to look at him again, anger and pain mingling in her gaze. "I am no tramp to let anyone 'paw' me whenever and wherever they will, Braughton Van Ripper. I've told you I love Icharus, and I believe he loves me, too. But you will not have it. I am a good and decent woman, exactly as my mother and father raised me to be, and I am *ashamed*—"

"As you should be," he rejoined.

Katherine didn't think. She just raised her hand and slapped him. Hard.

He grabbed her hand. He said nothing, merely held her there, his eyes piercing her with a cold look. After a moment he closed them, releasing his tight grip on her arm. "I am sorry, Katherine. Put it down to jealousy, if you will, and regret that another man will have what I want and cannot have."

She cast him a doubtful, hurt-filled look, and he sighed. "Please. I apologize. I should never have said those things I said to you, about you. I was wrong."

She nodded. "You were."

He put his hands on her shoulders, and looked into her eyes. "Are you sure, Katherine? Very, very sure, because I truly do wish you to be happy, and I would hate to have to kill that man after all if he should hurt you later."

Her eyes filled with both pain and compassion for him, she gave a little nod. "I am sure, Brau. Very sure."

He sighed, and nodded. "So be it."

She reached out to put her fingers against his cheek. "Can we be friends still, Brau? You've been a part of my life for as long as I can remember, and I should hate to see you go…"

He looked upward, and then back at her, and offered a somewhat less than heartfelt smile. "Friends."

She waited.

After a moment, he nodded. "*Friends*. Of course."

She smiled up at him. "Thank you, Brau."

She laced her arm through his once more, giving it a little squeeze before turning back to the house where Icharus waited near the steps.

His only answer was a brief tilt of his head.

Chapter 16

Icarus watched the two of them from the long porch bordering her home. His eyes narrowed. He'd seen her strike Brau, and could only wonder at what he'd said to cause such a violent reaction in her. But then she'd looped her arm through his and smiled, was smiling even now as they headed back to the house.

He waited, his whole body taut with the need to go to her, to separate the two of them and soothe away whatever hurt Brau had caused. He refrained, but barely, instead waiting for her to come to him.

Brau halted a way from the piazza and leaned close to whisper something to Katherine. She studied him for a moment, and then nodded. Brau left her there, going round to the stables, Icarus assumed from his direction, and Katherine stood where she was until Brau rode the chestnut around the corner of the house. He reined in his mount beside her and leaned down to speak to her. She must have answered because he nodded, and then headed down the lane.

Icarus frowned.

What did he say to her?

He also wondered why Brau had decided to leave

while it was still light out rather than join them inside as was his usual custom. He vaulted across the railing and went to Katherine.

"Something amiss?" he asked when he reached her side.

She watched in silence until Brau disappeared beneath the cover of the bridge and then turned to Icharus, a melancholy sigh slipping from her lips. "I hurt him."

Icharus's brows arched high and he nodded. "I saw."

Katherine brought her hands up to cover her eyes. "Not that, Icharus. I mean I've hurt him inside, and I …"

Her voice broke, and she shook her head, letting him know she wasn't able to continue her explanation just yet. Hearing the sniffling sounds she made behind her hands, he sighed. Putting his hand against her lower back, he inclined his head to the right, although he knew she could not see him do so.

"We'll walk this way a bit," he said, guiding her away from the house.

She took a deep breath and wiped her tears away. "Thank you."

Icharus held his silence, giving her a moment to gain control of her emotions while they ambled along. When her sniffles finally subsided, he asked, "What happened?"

Katherine kept her gaze on the path in front of her. She sighed. "I told him I could not marry him." She leaned her head back and stared up at the evening sky. "I told him I couldn't marry him, and I think I may have broken his heart."

Her voice broke again, and she shook her head, fighting back the tears that threatened once more.

"Brau has always been the quiet sort, Icharus. Remember I told you he's never been a very demonstrative man …"

Icharus said nothing, choosing instead to let her speak what was on her mind without interrupting. If she were anything like his sisters, he knew she would feel better for having done so, and that was what he wanted, for her to cheer up so he could see the joyous sparkle come alive in her eyes again.

"I know at times he seems cold and unfeeling, but he is not. Not really. It's a mask he hides behind to cover his own feelings of insecurity." Icharus would have disagreed, but she insisted." You don't know him, Icharus, not the way I do."

She lapsed into silence. After a moment, she sighed. "All this time I believed Brau thought of me much like he would a younger sister, or favored niece if you will, but now… now I think perhaps I was wrong, that maybe he truly had begun to love me."

Icharus frowned.

This was definitely not the sort of conversation he desired to have with her. He did not know a man alive who would wish to walk with the lady of their heart and discuss her feelings for another man.

He bit back a sigh, knowing she needed to talk about what had happened, to get her own feelings out into the open where she could examine them. If it disturbed him overmuch to hear what she had to say … well, that didn't matter, couldn't matter.

"He did ask you to marry him, Katherine. A man usually does not pose such a question unless he cares for a woman."

Katherine shook her head. "No. Brau said he wanted me to be happy, and I believe that, but it was his reason for wanting it I had no faith in. He said he wanted to take me away from here, Icharus, but Sleepy Hollow is my home. I could never leave it."

She sighed. "In all the years I've known Brau, and

these past years since Father became ill, he's always been here, Icharus. He has always provided a shoulder to lean on during tough times and a friendly face to share an evening with when life was good. But he never acted like … like a man in love."

Her brow furrowed. "He was so concerned with proper behavior and so firm when it came to his beliefs regarding the correct roles for men and women. Maybe I've been wrong. His beliefs are much the same as any man … that the woman's place is to tend home and hearth while a man should see to other matters. Perhaps he believed by insisting I leave those other matters to him, he was proving his love for me, proving he was capable of taking care of all a man should, while I …"

She shook her head, confused.

"But he's been different these past weeks, since you came to Sleepy Hollow. Less gentle and pleasant and less …" She shook her head and raised her hands in a gesture of confusion. "Less 'Brau' I suppose. And that is why I can't help but wonder if love was responsible for that change."

Icharus cast her a confused glance. "Love made him less gentle and pleasant?" He shook his head, clearly not following the direction of her thoughts.

She nodded.

"I don't understand," he said.

Katherine shrugged. "Perhaps he felt threatened, first by your arrival, and then we both know the pressures we've all been under since … first John's death and then the fire …"

The depth of her confusion was reflected in her watery gaze when she looked at him. "I knew he cared for me, but he just never acted like I believed a man in love should act."

She lowered her head, and her next words were choked out through the coil of emotion in her throat.

"But now I wonder if perhaps he believed he was … in his own way, and I … I never wanted to hurt him, Icharus. He is my friend …"

Icharus stopped and pulled her into his arms, sheltering her in the warmth of his comforting embrace. He soothed her with gentle murmurs of understanding while his hands slid in a comforting pattern along her back.

A hoarse sob escaped her lips, and she gave herself over to his embrace, letting her head rest against him, unable to hold back her tears any longer.

His own heart aching for the pain in hers, Icharus simply held her in silence while she cried out her remorse against his shoulder.

Several minutes later, her tears spent, Katherine raised her head to look at him. A blush stained her cheeks and she pulled away to wipe the wetness from her cheeks.

"I'm sorry, Icharus," she said between sniffs and swipes of her fingers beneath her eyes. "I've drenched your shirt with half the water in the Hudson, it seems."

She gave a hoarse little laugh, and Icharus smiled.

"It was worth a bit of a soaking to hold you … are you sure you haven't a few more tears in there?" he teased, raising his brows up and down in a comical gesture that brought another little chuckle from her lips.

"I certainly hope not. Otherwise we'll have to swim back to the house."

"I wouldn't mind," he said, his voice a bit subdued now that the moment was passed. He sighed, thinking he must be the grandest of idiots to simply hold a woman close while she poured out her feelings to him for another man. He patted her shoulder lightly. "Better now?"

She offered a watery smile and a nod. "Yes, I think so. We can go back to the others now."

But the Van Kerstens, Icharus noticed when he looked toward the house, had already gone inside. He nodded, and with a gentle hand at her back, started forward.

They had almost reached the porch when he drew her to a halt once more. "Katherine, wait."

She looked up at him expectantly, but he couldn't quite force himself to meet her gaze. He chose to focus instead on the wide windows behind her. The words he intended to say tasted bitter in his mouth and though he hesitated for a long moment, he knew they had to be said. He sighed.

"You can change your mind, you know."

Her brows drew downward and she started to shake her head in refusal, but he stopped her. Looking down at her, his eyes searched her face while his thoughts centered only on how very beautiful she looked, standing there before him just now with her eyes misty pools of deep blue that reflected every bit of the confusion he himself felt at the moment.

For a second, he wondered if perhaps he should just let the matter lie, but knew he could not. If she believed Van Ripper truly loved her, that he would make her happy, he would do what was best for Katherine.

With a quiet, cheerless sigh, he said, "Brau will be back, once he's had a few days to salve his wounds. When he returns, go to him and simply tell him you've had a change of heart."

He shrugged, hating the advice he offered her now, but knowing it was the right thing to do. It was her happiness that mattered most to him, above all else. Even if it meant she would spend the rest of her life with another man.

"If his pain hurts you so ..."

Katherine put her hand on his chest, turning her gaze full upon him, trapping his own. She shook her head slowly. "I cannot."

The words were spoken so distinctly, so clearly, he knew she believed she had had no choice in the matter, not now, but he didn't understand why. If she cared so much for Brau, and his pain affected her so deeply, as it so obviously had, then it made no sense. Icharus's brow furrowed, and he looked away. "You said as much before, but you never said why …"

It was Katherine's turn to look away. But after a moment, she turned her crystal blue gaze his way once more, and said, "Because my feelings for Brau are nothing compared to what I've come to feel for…"

Remembering Brau's contention earlier that Icharus had not declared his own feelings for her, Katherine hesitated. But Icharus was staring at her now, his gaze anxious.

"For?"

She looked away.

"Someone else," she whispered finally, unable to speak the words she really longed to say. She walked away, leaving him standing there in the yard, alone with his thoughts.

She had almost reached the door when he called to her again.

"Katherine?"

She paused and looked back at him.

He motioned for her join him again. Uncertain as to the reason why, she cautiously descended the steps once more.

"Yes?" she asked when she stood before him again.

He seemed unable to meet her gaze for a moment, and when he did, he cleared his throat a bit nervously. She frowned and started to speak, but he looked at her finally, and what she saw in his gaze made her forget what she had intended to say.

"Just how do you believe a man in love should

act?" he asked, the look in his eyes one of tortured longing and intense desire – and something else.

Katherine stepped closer until she stood as close to him as she could without actually touching and raised her palm to his jaw in a lingering caress.

The start of a smile curved her lips the tiniest bit, and then widened into a grin. "I think you already know."

Icharus closed his eyes, releasing his breath ever so slowly. When he opened them again, she stood gazing into his eyes, her expression serious now.

"I love you, Icharus Crane," she whispered.

His gaze locked with hers, neither of them spoke for a long moment. Then Icharus lowered his head until his lips met hers in a tender kiss so gentle and so sweet it was almost reverent.

"And I love you, Katherine Van Brunt," he said, his husky voice barely above a whisper. "Forever."

He drew her into his embrace, resting his forehead against hers, and simply held her close, savoring the moment.

* * * *

A few weeks later, Katherine sat near the brook, gathering handfuls of the bright yellow flowers from along the banks, placing them in the basket at her side, a smile on her lips and her mind filled with cheerful thoughts of the future.

After her declaration the night she had sent Brau away, Icharus had asked her to marry him, and she had agreed. Although Icharus had preferred to rush into TarryTown right away to see the deed done, he had given in to her request to wait until the fall, after harvest, to be wed.

She picked another handful of jonquils and added

them to the basket, thinking how life often had a way of bringing things full circle. Ichabod Crane had once pursued her mother's hand. Twenty-five years later, his son had come to the Hollow, and would soon marry the daughter of the woman he had thought he loved all those years ago. She shook her head in wonder at the way of it all.

Soon her task was finished and she stood, letting her gaze wander once again over the village in awe. Everywhere she looked, Katherine saw signs – nay, proof – of the rebirth of Sleepy Hollow, and her heart was nigh filled to overflowing with the fullness of her joy.

Her smile widened. With the basket of jonquils she held swinging at her side, and a skip in her step, she started walking and some time later knelt, first beside her mother's and then her father's graves.

With great care, she gathered together a thick bouquet for each from the flowers she had picked and placed them near the headstones before moving further along to a tall stone marker near the back of the cemetery.

Kneeling on the mound of soft green grass before her, Katherine took the last of the bright yellow flowers, the first flowers of spring, and laid them tenderly against the marker.

She stood and sighed, a shaky smile turning up the corners of her lips while her fingers traced the carving in the stone: Baltus Van Tassel.

"Well, Grandfather, what do you think?" she asked, gesturing toward the village and beyond, her gaze traveling in the wake of her fingers.

Over the past several weeks, the desolate little village Sleepy Hollow had become during the past four years simply melted away, disappearing like a wreath of smoke in the sky, borne away on a warm, nurturing breeze of renewal and rejuvenation. In its place, new life unfurled.

Like the first flower of spring, row after row of lush vegetation unfurled delicate leaves, raising their faces to the sky in eager anticipation for morning's first kiss.

In the orchards, fruit trees buzzed with the hum of bees and sang with melodic birdsong while each limb, gracefully arrayed in blushing blossoms, shyly hinted at the gift of numerous fruit it soon would bear.

The newly constructed stables and storehouse rose majestically from the landscape and the inn, somehow a symbol to Katherine of renewed hope and the continuation of life in Sleepy Hollow, stood patiently waiting to welcome its first guests and the wooden sign Icharus had carved swung gently in the breeze from a wrought metal holder above the door, proudly proclaiming the name Tanners' Inn.

At home, the lawn was filled with laughter, happy laughter of the Van Kersten children and soon, a new babe would be born. Carter and Alaina were expecting the blessed event at any time, and Katherine found she too waited with glad anticipation for the newest Wesley to enter the world.

Come summer, Heinrick and Mary would welcome their firstborn. In the fall, she and Icharus would be wed, and finally, Katherine knew Sleepy Hollow would at last reap a glorious harvest, one the likes of which hadn't been seen since her grandfather's time.

She slid her gaze back to the high stone marking the final resting place of Baltus Van Tassel, and her thoughts were filled with memories – memories of spring and the merry twinkle that had always seemed to be in her grandfather's eye when she would sit with him on the porch, perched happily upon his knee, as the two of them looked down over the village.

She smiled and lost herself in memories of the past

to a time when Baltus would cup his bulbous pipe in one hand and gesture with it toward the rolling fields, all fat with newly sprouted crops and bursting with promise, and he'd say, "There's our hope for tomorrow, my girl. We've done the toiling and carefully laid in our prayers to the Father. We've entreated Mother Nature for her generous blessing, and see there how she's given it?"

Katherine would nod, and say, "Yes, Grandfather."

With a nod and a wink, he'd sigh, and then draw thoughtfully upon his pipe while gazing out over the fields once more. After a moment of silence, he'd say, "There's naught left for us to do but wait for it, girl. Wait, and wait, and wait. Then come fall, we'll enjoy a bountiful harvest."

Although she would already be grinning excitedly by that point, knowing exactly where the conversation was headed, she'd never once failed to ask the next question.

"But what shall we do now, while we wait, Grandfather?"

He'd look at her then, his brows arched high in pretended surprise at her question. His big hands would clutch at her sides, and always there would be a twinkle in his eye.

"Now? Why now we celebrate, my girl!" he would say and toss her high into the air. She would scream with a fit of high-pitched giggles as young girls are wont to utter, and then she would climb down from his lap and race off to spread the joyous news.

She looked back at the gravestone, curious at the vividness of her memories. It felt almost as though she had gone back in time and was sitting there on her grandfather's knee once more, waiting in breathless anticipation for him to make 'the announcement'.

After a moment, she smiled. "You are right, Grandfather," she whispered, and taking up the now empty basket, hurried down the lane to spread the news.

Finally, it was time to celebrate once more in Sleepy Hollow.

* * * *

Later that evening, Katherine sat with Icharus in the parlor, discussing the coming jubilee. The Van Kerstens had gone upstairs for the night, leaving the two of them alone. At that moment, Icharus sat a bit sidewise on the sofa, half leaning against both the arm and into the corner, his arm draped along the back of it while his fingers twined through long ringlets of her hair.

She lay against his left side, her chin propped on the hand she had splayed across his chest, while the other busied itself with drawing slow circles on his sleeve.

"I want you to invite your family," Katherine said. "With Callum already here and if we can convince Balt to come over along with the others ..."

Icharus grinned. "You won't feel the need to worry where Isobel casts her eye?"

She raised herself out of his relaxed embrace and turned to make a face at him.

"Precisely," she offered, her voice laced with sarcasm, before relaxing back into his embrace.

He sighed and let his head fall back, resting it against the arm of the sofa while his fingers continued their play in the silky fall of her hair. "I won't leave you here, Katherine. I know it has been quiet of late, since the fire, but someone is still out there somewhere. Someone dangerous."

She pursed her lips in a pout. "But I have yet to meet your mother and ..."

He sighed and shook his head.

"No. I won't leave Sleepy Hollow, Katherine." He dropped a quick kiss on her pouting lips and urged her head back against his chest. "Not without you at my side."

She lay against him in silence for a moment, and then she nodded. "I suppose we could ride over in the carriage. We could bring Eleanor with us." She sat up, gathering the unruly strands of hair he'd been toying with into a single thick, riotous fall of curls. With a flip of her fingers, she tossed it behind her shoulder. "We can go tomorrow."

He gazed questioningly at her from his reclined position. "Why must we bring Eleanor?"

She cast him a speaking glance. "We'll need a chaperone, of course."

Icharus laughed and reached out to tug playfully at her hair. "A chaperone? You amaze me, Katherine," he said, giving a rueful shake of his head.

"I've lived here with you all these many months, alone, with no one else in the house other than Mrs. Porter and Mr. Rawlins to act as chaperones and now you're concerned about being alone with me?"

Katherine let her gaze wander appreciatively over his lean form, stopping here and there to linger admiringly over some particularly fascinating part of his anatomy before she brought her gaze, having gone all soft and dreamy, back up to meet his. "Yes, actually I am."

His own eyes had darkened during her leisurely and somewhat lengthy perusal of his person. "I've never given you cause to worry over your virtue, Katherine, although I have wanted you almost from the moment I first saw you."

She turned and laid against him, looping her arms about his neck and leaned forward for a lingering kiss. After a moment, she pulled away, sitting up beside him once more. "But we didn't plan to be married before and it well may not be you I have concerns about posing a threat to my virtue," she said, arching a brow.

One look into her eyes, gone soft with yearning after their kiss, was all the convincing he needed to know she had been speaking of herself. He cleared his throat rather awkwardly, and nodded. "We'll bring Eleanor."

Katherine grinned at him. "I thought you might agree."

He chuckled and reached for her, bringing her back down for another kiss, and another. It seemed he could not get enough of the taste of her, or of the feel of her hair, for his fingers had found their way into the silken strands once more.

Katherine sighed against his lips, thoroughly enjoying the attention he lavished upon her. She lay silent for a time, simply taking pleasure in the moment and offering all she knew how to offer in return. But soon the heat of his body lying so close beneath her and the delicious scent of him teasing her senses made her yearn for something more than a few lingering kisses and soft caresses that set up an aching awareness, an urgent longing deep inside of her for some forbidden delight of which she knew nothing.

She raised herself up to peer questioningly at him. "What is it like, Icharus?"

"What is what like?" he asked, distracted by his careful study of how the lamplight and shadows played over her features, softening them.

When she said nothing more, he lifted his gaze to hers in silent inquiry. A flush spread across her cheeks and she ducked her head, burying her face against his neck.

Her lips brushed his ear, and he thought he might go mad for want of her. Her innocent movements wreaked havoc on his sensual appetite, and he stifled a groan. She had no idea what her being this close to him was doing to his sanity, but there was no way in heaven he would enlighten her. Not yet, in any case.

"Being intimate," she asked in a hushed whisper near his earlobe, and he almost came undone. She couldn't know the jeopardy in which she'd suddenly placed her virtue with her innocent question.

His fingers froze in her hair, ceasing their play due to the immediate torment he felt in reaction to the evocative images her question brought to mind. A sudden volatile need rose inside him to explain it to immediately, detail by delicious detail, showing rather than telling her the answer she sought.

"Nice," he croaked, and bit back a curse because his voice had come out sounding very much like a growl.

Her lips found a particularly sensitive spot on his neck, and he squeezed his eyes closed against the breathtaking agony her kisses were wreaking inside him. He sucked in a breath.

"Just nice?" she asked, her lips continuing their torturous exploration.

"Very nice," he amended when he could draw an even breath.

She sighed and relaxed against him, her soft lips ceasing their tormenting play. "You aren't going to tell me, are you?"

"I don't think I can," he said, almost choking on the words.

She leaned up again, her frown reflecting her uncertainty. "Why ever not? There is no one else here. It's just the two of us."

Regretfully, he disentangled her arms from round his neck, lifted her gently, and sat up, closing his eyes against the images her innocent words conjured in his thoughts. After a moment, he ran his hands across his eyes as if he could erase the all-too-vivid, all-too-sensual pictures his mind continued to supply.

"And that is precisely why I cannot, Katherine," he said, his voice gruff. He stood a bit awkwardly, thanks to her guilelessly sensual inquiry, and offered her his hand. "Come. I'll walk up with you, but I think it's time we said goodnight."

He walked with her to the door of her bedchamber and waited while she opened it to go inside.

She turned to him and opened her mouth as if she intended to say something, then reconsidered. She shook her head and offered a hesitant smile. "Goodnight, Icharus. Pleasant dreams."

His own smile was somewhat apologetic. He reached out to smooth a curl from her forehead and then tempting himself almost beyond endurance, he leaned down for just one more taste of her sweet lips before he left her to seek out the solitude of his own lonely bed.

"Sleep well, Katherine," he said and he started to turn away but he hesitated. After a moment, he whispered, "Dream of me."

Letting his fingers glide through her curls one last time, he turned and walked away.

In his room just across the hall, Icharus lay upon the bed fully dressed, staring at the ceiling, his body throbbing in agony of need. Although he had agreed when Katherine had asked to wait until the fall to be wed, at this moment he feared he would not make it through the night without claiming her for his own.

He glanced toward his door, and then back at the ceiling. With an oath he swung his legs over the side of the bed, went to the door, and slid the bolt home, locking himself inside. Giving a nod of satisfaction that he had done all he could to protect her from himself for the moment, he crossed back to the bed and dropped onto the covers, still fully dressed, still aching … and still afraid he would give in to the demands of his frenzied passions before the night was through – bar or no bar across the door.

* * * *

Mounted on a midnight steed, its flanks glowing with an eerie silver light, was a man dressed almost entirely in black. The long sable cloak he wore furled and billowed mystically behind him in the breeze.

In one hand, the spectral rider held high a lantern, illuminating his unnatural manifestation with a mysterious light that created a peculiar diffused glow around both horse and rider. In the other hand, his fingers clenched tight around the silvery reins of his demonic-looking mount.

Snowy white and closed with an equally bright cravat, the collar of his shirt stood out in stark relief against the midnight black of his cloak, infinitely more noticeable in the darkness because the man wearing it had no head.

The horseman yanked hard against the reins, and the beast beneath him let out a chilling scream of fury. Springing up on his hind legs, the maddened animal swung his head to and fro, pawing feverishly at the open air.

Before the beast's feet could return to the ground, the horseman spun the lantern in an arc above him, in the space where his head should have been. With an unnervingly evil roar of fury, he gave the lantern a mighty hurl.

The sound of breaking glass falling against itself as it fell through the air played almost musically in the silence as the lantern exploded into a brilliant ball of orange fire ...

Callum jerked upright in his bed, his bare chest heaving and bathed in sweat. "No!" he called in a furious, fearful whisper into the darkness of his room.

"No," he said again, but this time the word came out as a wishful plea. He was shaking his head, though there was no one in the room to see him.

"Not again. Not again."

He knew his words were in vain. The vision had come upon him while he slept, but it had been a revelation just the same.

Soon, the Headless Horseman of Sleepy Hollow would ride again.

... but when? And how will he make the fury of his wrath felt this time?

Chapter 17

Morning dawned warm and bright on the mid-spring day of the festival, a beautiful day for a celebration, Katherine thought. Stretching languorously beneath her quilts, she smiled and sighed.

A few days previous, Icharus had sent Jericho into Wake Grove with a message for his family rather than going himself, and today, Katherine looked eagerly forward to welcoming them to Sleepy Hollow, and to meeting the woman who had given birth to the man she loved.

She had to admit to feeling a bit nervous, however. It was entirely possible Icharus's mother might find some dreadful flaw in her, though Icharus heartily denied the likelihood. Although Katherine could not readily guess what such a flaw might possibly be, she didn't think she could bear it if Elizabeth Crane found some reason to not like her.

There was too much to be done for her to lie abed worrying over things that may or may not come to light. She and Icharus had decided, now that the weather was warmer, it would be good to hold the festivities out of doors. There were tables to set up, lanterns to hanged, and myriad other chores to see to before the evening's revelries could commence.

Tossing back the covers, Katherine swung her legs over the side of the bed and headed for her wardrobe, hoping she had something suitable inside to wear. It was a festive occasion, after all, and she wanted to look her best ... for both Icharus and his family.

She chose a buttery soft yellow gown trimmed in white and laid it across the bed, then hastened through her toilette, combing her hair and pulling it back as she did every day. But for today, she chose to wear the set of gold combs her father had given her mother on their last Christmas together.

Emerging from her room some time later, she saw Icharus waiting for her at the top of the stairs. He straightened abruptly and his gaze slid over her in slow appreciation, from head to feet. He whistled low and she smiled. "Good morning, Master Crane."

"And a pleasant morning to you as well, Mistress Van Brunt. You slept well, I hope?" He leaned close, placing a quick kiss on her lips. "Ready for a wonderful day?"

She pulled him back for a longer kiss, one that left her feeling warm and tingly inside.

"More than anything," she said a few moments later. "But I am still a bit worried about meeting your mother ..."

Icharus chuckled. Lacing her arm through his, the two of them descended the stairs together. "Without cause, I assure you. Mum will love you the moment she sees you."

She turned to him, a slight frown marring her brow. "How can you be sure?"

He bent to kiss her again. "Because I love you, Katherine. That will be more than enough to convince her. You'll see," he promised.

Choosing to take his word for it for the moment rather than spend the day with her stomach in knots, Katherine nodded and her worried frown disappeared.

"That's better," Icharus said and led her to the dining room.

After breakfast, there was little time for nerves, Katherine discovered. The entire household seemed to buzz in a whirl of activity. Tables were carted out to the lawn, situated beneath a stand of tall oaks, and covered with white cloths. Chairs were brought up from the church, and the men hung lanterns all about, to be lit later in the evening when the day drew to a close and darkness began its descent.

The Van Kersten children had been allowed to run about between the tables on the lawn and the banks of the brook, and their shouts of laughter could be heard all the way in the kitchen where Katherine spent a good portion of the morning and afternoon with Mrs. Porter, Gwendolyn, and Olivia, putting together a number of tasty dishes for the coming celebration.

When the Crane carriage was at last spotted rambling up the lane toward the house, Katherine had long since forgotten to be anxious about meeting Icharus's mother and by the time the elderly lady was handed down from the conveyance, she realized there had been no need to worry after all, just as Icharus had promised.

Elizabeth Crane was a lovely woman despite the fact that her once-blond hair had gone almost completely gray. Katherine had expected his mother, from the speculative tales she'd heard in her youth, to be short and a bit round, with jolly cheeks and a happy smile wreathing her face. But the lady Icharus introduced to Katherine a moment later was none of that.

Neither tall nor short, Katherine found Elizabeth Crane to be of rather average height. Her eyes, a vibrant green like her son's did sparkle happily, and her lips were curved into a genuinely joyful smile. Though her features were a bit careworn, as would any woman's be who had struggled as the Cranes had in her younger years, Katherine thought her quite lovely.

Icharus bounded across the lawn and hurried up the steps to Katherine's side. "Mum, did you try to bring every dish you've ever prepared? You must have because the wagon smells positively delicious!"

Elizabeth turned and raised her arms to hug her son. "I would suggest you have a bite, son, but that old wagon must taste like moss at this point," she teased.

Her gaze turned to Katherine, sparkling merrily. "When Icharus was small, before Eliza came, his father and I often carried him with us into the meadow for a picnic of sorts when the weather was nice. While Ichabod and I busied ourselves with laying out the meal, Icharus would play near the wagon. More times than not when I retrieved him to join us, he'd have a mouthful of dirt and grass …"

She laughed. "For some reason unknown to us until this very day, he would crawl over and lick the dirt from the wagon wheels!"

She shook her head. "We never understood why, but you can see that even at an early age, Icharus showed quite an unusual love for land … and grass."

Icharus flushed at the revealing tale, and Katherine laughed. "Had I known his stomach so easily appeased, I would have spent less time in the kitchen this afternoon, and more out here on the lawn!"

Elizabeth's smile grew.

"You must be Katherine. Balton spoke of you often after he returned to Wake Grove." With a questioning gaze at Icharus, she said, "He seemed to think there was something special going on between the two of you."

Icharus slid his arm around Katherine's waist,

drawing her close to his side. "We're going to be married, Mum. In the fall."

By the time Icharus made his announcement, the rest of the Crane family had joined them. Icharus made the introductions, and each of his siblings offered happy congratulations to Katherine and teased Icharus, asking how he'd managed to deceive her into thinking him a worthy spouse.

They also each had a different tale to tell of Icharus's youth, and Katherine's sides positively ached from laughing before they all were through.

Then Katherine was inspired to relate the tale of how Icharus had met the challenges and nigh impossible task of bringing heart and soul back to Sleepy Hollow since he'd arrived. When she finished, ending with how her trip to her grandfather's grave had inspired tonight's festivities, Elizabeth's eyes glistened with tears. "You must have loved your grandfather very much," she said to Katherine.

Katherine blushed. "I did. He was very much at the center of my young world. He taught me so many things … I don't know how I would have survived later without him."

Elizabeth wiped at her eyes and drew in a steadying breath.

"But you have, my dear, and that is what truly matters," she said. "You survived, and now you are poised on the brink of a wonderful future."

Katherine glanced at Icharus, and smiled. "A glorious future filled with love and happiness to be spent at the side of a most perfectly adorable man."

Icharus frowned. "And just where is this 'perfectly adorable man' of which you speak?" he teased.

Katherine nudged him playfully. "You know perfectly well I was speaking of you."

Icharus's eyes gleamed. "Ah. For a moment I feared

I should be forced to try and win your hand all over again."

She shot him a look. "And would you?"

His gaze met hers and held.

"Most definitely," he said, and lifted her hand to his lips to press a lingering kiss against her knuckles.

* * * *

A short time later, the others began to arrive from the village – Mary and Heinrick; Carter and Alaina; Clara; Dehann; Anne; and Callum, who had apparently decided to ride up with the Tanners rather than come alone.

Katherine spoke with Mary for a moment about the babe she carried, and placing a hand against her enlarged tummy, murmured in awe of how strong the child's movements were.

Carter helped Alaina from the wagon, and Katherine laughed when Alaina said, "Oh, praise heaven you've put tables about!"

She smoothed the material of her dress against her and lamented the lack of lap space her own expanded girth afforded.

Katherine walked with the two expectant mothers to the table where Elizabeth and her daughters sat. She introduced the ladies and left them to chat about birthing and teething while she went up to greet the Tanners.

Clara was driving the wagon with Anne at her side while Callum and Dehann sat on the back, their feet dangling.

The cart drew to a halt in front of the house. Dehann jumped to the ground and hurried to assist his mother while Callum went to help Anne.

Nothing surprising there.

Callum had spent so much time at the Tanners, he was practically considered one of the family.

Then she noticed how Callum's hand did not fall from Anne's person the moment her feet touched the ground, but rather, came round to rest possessively at the small of Anne's back. Her eyes widened.

Callum and Anne?

Anne was positively radiant, the bright smile she wore from the moment Callum's hand touched hers to help her from the wagon never left her face.

Icharus made his way to her side, grinning at the somewhat foolish expression Callum wore. He leaned to whisper to Katherine. "Don't be angry with him, Katherine. He couldn't tell you. Not before he managed to work up the nerve to tell her mother... and ask Dean's permission, of course."

Unable to stop staring at the couple in shock, she cast a quick, sideward glance at Icharus. "Tell Clara and Dehann what?"

"That the reason he'd had no alibi the night John was murdered was because he was with Anne at the time."

Katherine's eyes rounded, and she turned her shocked gaze on him. "You mean ...?"

Icharus nodded. "Aye. Anne was quite distraught over it. She suffered with a terrible guilt, knowing where she'd been, what she'd been doing when her father died."

Katherine shook her head, one hand coming up to cover her mouth.

"Oh, my," she said. "She must have felt positively horrible."

Icharus nodded. "For a while. Mather had a very difficult time of convincing her that had she been anywhere other than with him, it still would not change the fact that her father had been killed."

Katherine shook her head, remembering how worried she had been. She turned and pinned Icharus with a glare. "You knew?"

He nodded again, unashamed.

Her eyes narrowed. "Just how long have you known?"

He shrugged. "Since before we met at Vandercleefs to discuss John's murder. Callum rode with me that morning. He wasn't quite sure who to trust with his confession, but in the end, he chose me."

Dehann and Callum went back to the wagon to help Mr. Rawlins and Mrs. Porter bring the dishes Anne and Clara had brought to the tables.

After a time, Callum made his way to her, Anne at his side, and Katherine scowled at him. "So this is the reason you would say nothing of your whereabouts?"

He did not pretend to misunderstand what her question was in reference to, though his face did heat a bit. He nodded. "I am sorry, Katherine. I wanted to tell you … I wanted to tell everyone, but Anne would have none of it."

Katherine looked to the young woman with whom she had shared a good portion of her childhood and offered an understanding smile. "You were able to persuade her at last, I see. I am glad," she said, and wrapped her arms about Anne. "I'm very happy for the two of you. You couldn't ask for a better man."

"Well," she said, her smiling gaze going to Icharus, "other than Icharus, but he is unavailable at the moment."

Callum and Icharus laughed, and Anne grinned.

"I won't tell Callum you said that," she said in an overly loud whisper. "He'd never believe anyone would think him second-best."

Callum arched a brow and asked. "Could you?"

She leaned close and pressed a reassuring kiss against his lips. "Never."

After the four of them shared a few moments of

friendly chatter, Callum drew Icharus aside. "I need to speak with you for a moment ... if Katherine doesn't mind, of course?"

Icharus glanced at Katherine. She and Anne were busy discussing how long it would be before Alaina would finally give birth.

Women talk. Icharus shook his head. He heard the words "easy birthing" and his eyes widened.

"Since I have absolutely nothing meaningful to contribute to their current discussion, I'm sure she won't mind."

Katherine heard him and chuckled. She shooed him away with a smile, and he and Callum walked toward the stables. "Has something happened?"

Callum shook his head. "Nay, I ... I had another vision."

Icharus came to a halt, a chill of apprehension pouring over him like the icy water of the brook in winter. "And?"

Callum closed his eyes tight for a moment, and sighed. "I am not sure."

He opened his eyes to peer down across the lawn toward the village. "Last night I saw ... the Horseman."

Icharus started to relax, but then he remembered what Callum had said to him before about the visions he'd seen in the past, that never had the sights he'd witnessed in his visions not occurred.

"Do you know who ...?"

Callum shook his head. "The man I saw had no recognizable features, Icharus. I know it seems farfetched, but... there was no *head* by which the man might be identified."

Icharus scowled. "Not as farfetched as it might seem. The night the storehouse burned, I chased just such a fellow through the swamps before he disappeared almost right in front of my eyes."

Callum peered at him for a moment, and then nodded. "I am hoping there is nothing to be concerned about, especially tonight, but I thought you should know."

Icharus was gazing down across the village, taking in all they had accomplished these many weeks past, a worried frown pulling his brows downward, and he sighed.

"Icharus, stay close to Katherine tonight, won't you? I don't know when or where my latest vision might manifest itself, but it may not be safe."

Icharus nodded. "Most definitely."

* * * *

Nicolaas, it turned out, was mighty handy with a fiddle. There had been singing and dancing, delightful food and wonderful company – a full day frolic and laughter – something much needed to revive the spirits of everyone in Sleepy Hollow. Icharus was quite happy to see that apparently it had.

Icharus stretched, fighting back a yawn while he watched Mr. Rawlins and Jericho move about the lawn, lighting the lanterns they had hung earlier in the day to ward off the darkness that had descended over the village.

He had spent most of the day at Katherine's side, mingling with his family and the villagers which, with her own family gone, seemed to represent hers, but now he bent to whisper into her ear. "I'll be back before you can miss me, but I need a moment."

She blushed at his reference to attending a need of such a personal nature, but smiled and nodded. "Hurry please. I shall miss you."

He grinned and slipped away toward the stables.

He was on his way back to her when he heard a low

rumbling sound rippling across the Hollow from the distance, and felt the small hairs on the back of his neck rise up in protest.

He had heard that sound before, he recalled, the night John Tanner was murdered and left at the bridge. Icy cold fear swept through him, and his thoughts turned to Callum's warning earlier that he'd had another vision.

Katherine.

Turning, his gaze frantically swept the group of people gathered on the lawn until he spied her, sitting with his mother and Kathleen.

Icharus felt his heart stop for a moment, and then start again, racing at thrice its normal speed. Suddenly desperate to reach her, he broke out at a dead run, praying he could make it to her side before the danger he now felt in the very air around him could show itself.

"Katherine!" he yelled, running as fast as his feet would carry him, willing her to turn and see him, to rush to his side, to the protection and safety of the house, anywhere she would be out of harm's way.

He saw her when she came to her feet and then stood frozen in place, her gaze transfixed, an expression of horror on her face as she stared down toward some point below him in the village – and then she started to run. But she was moving *away* from him, toward whatever it was she had seen.

"No! Katherine, for the love of God, *no!*" he screamed, but she did not appear to hear him because she kept going, and she had almost reached the lane.

Icharus stumbled, righted himself, and kept running, but God help him, he knew he was never going to make it. Strange though it was, in just that instant, the space of time between one heartbeat and the next, everything seemed to freeze. It was as though time simply stood still, coming to a halt while the horrible scene before him unfolded, movement by terrifying, heart-stopping movement.

He could see Katherine, mesmerized by and running toward whatever she had seen in the village below them, completely unaware of what was about to happen.

Somehow, he felt as if he had stepped outside his body and could also see himself rushing across the lawn in a desperate effort to reach her before something terrible could occur but being unable to do so.

Icharus hit the ground, hard, knocking the wind from his lungs.

Get up! his mind demanded, but his body refused to heed its command, until finally, he was able to draw a breath, and time restored itself to its normal speed.

Sucking in one great lungful of air after another, his mind struggling to comprehend what was going on, Icharus shot to his feet.

One second ticked by, then two, and a second loud explosion shook the silence, barreling up like an ominous thunderclap from the village below. A bright orange ball of fire leapt high into the night – and then there was madness.

* * * *

Katherine had been listening to Icharus's sister Kathleen and his mother chat about home and how it was much the same here in Sleepy Hollow when she thought she saw something move in the village below from the corner of her eye.

She'd excused herself and stood, walking closer to get a better look, and her earlier suspicion was confirmed. There in the darkened shadows near the inn, she could just make out a form. Someone was there, she was sure of it.

What were they doing?

She had already started forward, intent on finding out for herself when she remembered everyone in the village was enjoying an evening of friendly conversation and celebration on her lawn. Whoever was down there now did not belong there, and was surely up to some mischief.

She had started to run, but then the night exploded in a huge orange ball of fire.

Dazed by the explosion, Katherine froze and turned, wide-eyed, to observe the panicked flight of her guests. Behind her, they had begun to scream and run for the protection of the house and she could hear them yelling, see them gesturing toward the village below in fear.

"It's the Hessian!" she heard someone call out. "God save us, it's the Headless Horseman!"

She frowned and turned her head to search the darkness for whatever frightful sight they had seen, and her eyes widened, rounding in shock, for below her in the village was a most chilling spectacle to behold.

Mounted on a midnight steed, its flanks glowing with an eerie silver light, was a man dressed almost entirely in black. The long sable cloak he wore furled and billowed mystically behind him in the breeze. But it was the stiff collar of his white shirt she could not force her gaze to ignore.

In one hand, Katherine noticed, the spectral rider held high a lantern, illuminating his unnatural manifestation with a mysterious light that created a peculiar diffused glow around both horse and rider. In the other hand, his fingers clenched tight around the silvery reins of his demonic-looking mount.

Katherine tried to focus on the rider, taking distracted note of the way he held himself atop his mount in a most formal bearing, but again her astonished gaze was drawn to the collar of his brilliant white shirt.

Snowy white and closed with an equally white

cravat, it stood out in stark relief against the midnight black of his cloak, but the thing that made it infinitely more noticeable in the darkness was the fact that the man wearing it had no head.

While Katherine watched in stunned, fascinated silence, the Horseman yanked hard against the horse's reins, and the beast beneath him let out a chilling scream of fury.

Springing up on his hind legs, the maddened animal swung his head to and fro, pawing feverishly at the open air.

Before the beast's feet could return to the ground, the Horseman spun the lantern in an arc above him, in the space where his head should have been. With an evil roar of fury, he gave the lantern a mighty hurl.

The sound of breaking glass falling against itself as it fell through the air played almost musically in the silence as the lantern exploded through the side window of the inn, and within seconds Katherine could see tall orange flames leap high in the darkened interior, already beginning to spread.

A moment later, a blast so loud it deafened her for a moment rolled across the air, shaking the very ground beneath her with the force of its impact. Katherine clapped her hands over her ears to block out the sound.

The inn appeared to both crumble and erupt at the same time, hurtling fiery timbers, chunks of stone, and shards of glass in every direction.

Distracted by the horror of seeing the inn she had wanted so badly to see built, the first in Sleepy Hollow and somehow a symbol of a hopeful new beginning for her and the people of the Hollow, Katherine forgot momentarily about the ghastly Horseman with no head.

When she recalled the reason her inn was now nothing more than a blazing pile of wood, glass, and stone she looked back to stare, confused, at the place he had been a mere moment before, but the Horseman had disappeared. She shook her head in disbelief at the mind-numbing scene she had just witnessed.

"He's real …" she breathed the words in a terrified whisper. She gasped and lifted shaking fingers to her lips, horrified to realize what she had said.

But she was unable to deny with her lips all that her eyes had witnessed this night, even if it were completely implausible.

The Headless Horseman is real.

The refrain played over and over in her thoughts.

Real … exactly as Brau had said.

"Katherine?"

She heard Icharus call her name from somewhere nearby and turned her head in the direction of his voice, but she couldn't seem to find her own in order to answer him – not while the voice in her head continued to speak so loudly.

The Headless Horseman of Sleepy Hollow was real!

It was the last thought she remembered thinking before her knees buckled and she collapsed slowly to the ground.

* * * *

Katherine came awake slowly. Someone had carried her inside and placed her on the sofa in the parlor, she realized. She sat up.

Icharus came immediately to her side.

"You're safe, Katherine. I'm here," he said, his voice reassuring.

"The Horseman," she whispered. "I saw him, Icharus. In the village."

Icharus nodded. "You saw a man, yes, Katherine, but I promise you, there is no 'Headless Horseman'. It was a deception, nothing more … a very elaborate ruse conducted by a master of illusion it seems."

She shook her head, her thoughts still reeling. "Nay, I saw his horse, Icharus, and it was glowing…"

"Phosphorus," he explained. "Whoever the madman is, he must have coated the horse's flanks with it. In the darkness as he was, the chemicals would have made the stallion appear to glow."

She frowned. "But he just … disappeared. One moment he was there, swinging a lantern, and the next, he was gone. A sentient man could not have simply disappeared …"

Icharus shook his head. "He used the explosion as a distraction, Katherine. While everyone's attention was drawn to the inn, he fled into the swamp. Jericho, Nicolaas, Dehann and Balt are out there, trying to track him down even now."

She frowned, trying to assimilate all he had said in the whirl of confusion in her mind. Finally, she tipped her head in a hesitant nod, accepting his explanation for the moment. After a time, she noticed the awkward silence, and asked, "Where are the others?"

Icharus sat beside her on the sofa, his hand going out to smooth back her hair. "I sent everyone home. Gwen, Olivia, and the children are already upstairs."

He sighed. "I am sorry your celebration was interrupted, Katherine, and about the inn. I know how much it meant to you …" He shook his head.

Her gaze came up to meet his. "The inn …"

"It is gone, but at least no one was killed this time. We can be grateful for that much."

She nodded, but bent her head low, and though she made not a sound, he must have seen the tears that coursed down her cheeks because he stood and held out his hand to her. "Come on, I will walk you to your chamber."

She rose and let him assist her up the stairs. By the

time they had reached the top, her shoulders were shaking with deep sobs that wracked her body.

He opened the door to her bedchamber, and led her inside. When he would have left her there, she raised her stricken, tear-filled gaze to his, a choked sob escaping her lips.

"It's gone, Icharus. I stood there and saw it crumble into nothing, and you worked so hard … you worked so hard!"

Another sob tore from her lips. "It's my fault, I suppose, for wanting to make something new here, a memorial to the past and yet … and yet a sign of hope for the future."

He frowned. "Katherine, it could never be your fault …"

"But it must be!" she choked out. "I wanted to rebuild, and … and someone killed John for taking the trees from the Western Wood. I wanted nothing more desperately than to survive the winter, and the storehouse burned, taking away all that we had laid aside. And the inn … I wanted it so badly, Icharus … and it's gone! It's gone …"

She fell against him, pouring out her grief against his chest.

Seeing her pain, hearing the sounds of her grief, was destroying Icharus inside. He closed his eyes, weighing his need to stay with her now, to comfort her through her grief and his ability to control his passions if he stayed, as he yearned to do.

How can I leave her when she is so clearly suffering?

"Ah, God." He sighed, and pulled her close.

One hand tangled in the hair at her nape, the other holding her close, he lowered his head.

The instant their lips touched, it was as if a molten fire had been unleashed inside him. His mouth covered hers, and the voracious hunger that seemed to always rage within him for her spilled over into the kiss.

Again and again, his tongue delved into the heat of her mouth, plundering the soft sweetness he found. She moaned and he drew her nearer still, unable to get close enough to her softness, her warmth. If he could somehow draw her inside himself, he thought, it still would not be close enough.

Several kisses later, he realized her sobs had ceased and she no longer shook with the force of the anguish that had been tearing through her.

Icharus squeezed his eyes closed, and broke off the kiss.

"Katherine …" he breathed the words in a whisper against her mouth. "Katherine, we must stop…"

He pulled away and she looked at him with such anguish still haunting her gaze, he almost kissed her again, but he knew to do so was to invite madness.

"Why?" she asked, her voice thick with unshed tears. "Why must we stop, Icharus? I want you to kiss me… again and again."

His conscience played havoc with his desire.

Icharus considered her question and the declaration of her desire for his kisses for a moment, and then two. He reached up to brush a curl from her forehead, and sighed regretfully. "Katherine, my dearest love. You are so very beautiful, so desirable … and so very vulnerable right now. You are hurting, and I know you wish for me to stay, but I fear that if I touch you again, kiss you again, there will be no turning back for us."

Her gaze steady, she said, "I have no wish to turn back." Raising herself onto her toes, she pressed a soft, inviting kiss against his lips.

He felt her arms come round him, felt her fingers twine into his hair. He felt her sigh in sweet surrender, her body melting against him, and he groaned low in his throat.

Resting his forehead against hers, he gave her one last chance to change her mind. "You're absolutely sure?"

She nodded, and he closed his eyes, suffering in agony of the sweetest torture ever known. She wanted him. She had given her consent, and he was free to love her as he so longed to do, to taste her, to touch her, to feel her body next to him, over him, beneath him.

Very carefully lest he lose what fragile hold he had over his rampant need, he squeezed his eyelids shut and pressed a tender kiss against her forehead, while he fought back the rush of hunger that filled him, the near overwhelming urge he felt to crush her against him, to rip the gown and chemise she wore from her and take her there on the cold, bare floor like some depraved, savage beast.

He turned her away from him, his hands going to the row of buttons along the back of the lovely yellow dress. With great care, he unfastened each one, pressing a row of kisses along her spine in wake of his hands as he did so.

Finally, the last button was freed, and he eased the gown from her shoulders. It fell, pooling at her feet, and he bent low. Lifting first one foot and then the other, he removed her shoes.

He bent and lifted her into his arms. Without a word, he carried her to the bed and laid her there, nestled among the pillows, her eyes luminous with the remnants of her tears and soft with a curious, tender yearning.

Chapter 18

Taking every care not to frighten her, he sat carefully on the side of the bed and removed first his boots, and then doffed his shirt before coming to rest beside her. He lifted a strand of her hair and brought the silken tress to his face. Breathing deeply, inhaling the unique fragrance that was all Katherine, he said, "I have wanted to do this, to make love with you, since the day I first saw you watching me ride across the bridge."

Katherine lifted her hands to his shoulders, letting her fingers caress him there for a moment before coming up to thread through his hair. "I thought you were the most beautiful man alive."

He bent his head to kiss her again, and she sighed against his lips. This was what she had yearned for, to be held in his arms just as he was holding her now, to be kissed, tenderly, gently, as though she might at any moment disappear from his grasp.

His lips brushed hers so softly it seemed their mouths barely met before they were separated once more, but he came to her yet again, and each time he did so, he deepened the kiss more.

Katherine kissed him back, parting her lips for his

tongue, letting her own sweep against his and then dart out to savor the taste of where his lips had been when they left hers.

For a time, he merely played with her mouth, letting her get used to the feel of him beside her. She fully enjoyed every moment, letting her hands wander where they would – across his broad shoulders and down along his sides to the top of his thickly muscled hips and back again.

His own hands were busy with an exploration of their own, gliding down along her flat stomach and across her thighs and downward still until he reached the hem of her chemise. Catching it across his fingers, he swept his hand slowly upward once more, caressing the creamy smoothness of her thighs, taking the soft fabric up to reveal the wonders of her body to his questing hands.

His mouth left hers to nuzzle against her neck at the sensitive spot just below her ear. He heard her draw in a swift breath and smiled against the delicate skin of her throat. He repeated the caress, while his hands discovered yet another bounty.

Gliding, ever slowly so as not to steal her from the hazy web of passion he had woven around her, his hand moved upward to caress her breasts.

Icharus bit back a groan.

Sweet God, what divine torture. Much more of this and he knew he would not be able to control himself.

His hands slid down the length of her legs once more and then back up her thighs to the top of her stockings and the garters there. With a sweep of his hands, he removed first one, and then the other, his eyes devouring the bare, silken flesh he uncovered as he did so.

His hands went to her breasts, dipping beneath the fabric of her chemise to caress them at his leisure. From valley to peak to valley again, he drew his palm across her soft flesh, enjoying the feel of her in his hands, against his skin. Hot. Flushed. Aching.

He trailed kisses along her neck down into the vale between her breasts, pulling the material of her chemise aside, giving him greater access, and then when he could wait no longer, he took the rigid peak of one breast into his mouth, his tongue swirling round it for a moment before he suckled deep.

She gasped, and called out his name.

He lifted his head the tiniest bit. "Do you want me to stop?"

She shook her head frantically. "Nay, oh, nay!"

Silently thanking the heavens for her answer, he repeated the caress on her other breast, only this time, he let his hand trail down to the nest of curls at the juncture of her thighs.

He brushed his hand against her there, up and down, up and down, exerting the slightest pressure while he continued to suckle at her breasts. Again and again he repeated the caress – until he felt her body surge against his hand in soundless supplication.

He shifted and his mouth found hers once more. She met his kiss almost wildly, her tongue sweeping out to duel with his while her hands grabbed at his shoulders, his waist, his buttocks in a vain attempt to bring him closer.

Icharus thought no man could ever have had his sanity tested such as his was at this moment. The innocent wildness of her passionate response to his loving was all but driving him mad, yet he knew he must wait, must go slowly with her. He wanted this time with him – her first time with a man – to be perfect, a passionate voyage into ecstasy she would never forget.

He shifted against her yet again, bringing one leg up between her thighs to nudge them apart the tiniest bit.

His hands slid along the length of her until he found the hem of her chemise. He pulled it up, and over her head before his hands slide back down to that most intimate part of her body.

Drawing his fingers slowly against her moist cleft, he slid the tip of one inside her heat, letting it glide slowly upward until it pressed against her most sensitive spot. He thought she might pull away from the caress, but she did not. Instead, she moaned low, and shifted, opening for him.

Lifting himself onto one elbow so he might see her better, he let his fingers brush against her again, sliding across the tight nub of her passion and lower. Finally, he dipped just the tip of his middle finger into her tightness, and it was all he could do to refrain from snatching her close with a vicious growl, from ripping away his breeches and plunging his hard, aching shaft into her right then and there.

She was so wet. So hot. So ready for him.

Icharus squeezed his eyes shut, not daring to imagine himself thrusting into her, and yet, the very image would not leave his mind. He ground his teeth tightly together to keep from groaning aloud in anguished ecstasy.

Her breathing had become quite ragged, and she thrashed against the sheets, moving her head frantically from side to side. He knew the moment was nigh upon her, that instant of bliss wherein she would come undone, and almost shouted with relief.

His wait was over.

He pulled away from her, anxious to remove the rest of his clothing, but she whimpered in protest, her arms closing around him to prevent his leaving her side.

"Nay, do not leave me!" she breathed, her voice an urgent whisper of panic.

He shushed her, calmed her with a brush of his

hand across her brow that ended with his fingers caressing the length of hair he'd buried them in. "Only for a moment, love."

Reluctantly, she released him, and he hurriedly shed his breeches, eager to join her once more.

Katherine's breath came rapidly, and her body was heated with a warm tingling she had never known before. Opening her eyes, she watched him pull away the last of his clothing and then settle on the bed beside her once more, and she reached for him.

He leaned forward and kissed her tenderly, his beautiful green eyes watching her all the while. She twined her arms about his neck and pulled him close. She wanted to feel him, but he pulled away.

His gaze traveled the length of her and came back to linger on her breasts. The tips puckered, and Katherine moaned. She wanted to feel his mouth on her again, but was too timid to voice her desire. Instead, she pressed her arms together, forcing the aching peaks upward.

He seemed to understand her need because he dipped his head to nuzzle her there for a moment before laving each aching bud with his tongue. Finally, he took one rosy tip deep into his mouth and suckled. She almost cried out from the pleasure of it.

Instead she reached for him and pulled him closer, and then closer still. He continued the sweet torture, loving one and then the other taut peak until she thought she might scream from the pleasure his caress evoked.

Her hands clutched at his shoulders and she wished he might never move from just that spot ... until his hand touched her there again, his fingers gliding against the moistness at the apex of her thighs.

She whimpered from her body's almost violent reaction to the shock of his touch. Like lightning, heat flashed through her, searing her to her core, and she wanted only to be struck again.

Without taking his hands from her, he moved, settling his legs between hers, and she stiffened the slightest bit. When he only lay slightly against her, keeping his upper body raised while he dipped his head and kissed her again, she began to relax once more.

He was so hot, so smooth, so big.

His presence enveloped her, the feel of his body against hers consumed her in flames of reckless heat that spread outward from the juncture at her thighs, and she wriggled against him, wanting something, needing more, seeking relief from the intense pleasure building inside her.

He sucked in a harsh breath at her movement, the sound of it hissing through his teeth, and he closed his eyes. "God."

The single word, uttered in such a guttural tone, went through her, filling her with a sense of elation and delighted surprise. She'd affected him. Very much.

She moved against him again, and he choked out a groan.

"Katherine, for the love of God ..."

Sliding his hand between them, he touched her, opening her. And then she could feel that part of him, there. The heat of it sent her senses reeling, and her head fell back against the pillows.

He moved, just a bit toward her, and then back. The motion pressed the two of them closer, that most intimate part of him against her core, and Katherine thought she might well fly apart into tiny pieces at any moment.

She cried out.

He covered her mouth with his own, ravaging her lips now with a deep, intense kiss. He continued to move against her as he had before, closer and then away, again and again until Katherine thought she would die from the sheer pleasure of it.

Her body sprung taut, she thrashed beneath him, whimpering her need. Begging for something, anything that would end this exquisite torture she suffered.

Icharus's mouth left hers and he watched her, torn between ecstasy and angst, her lovely body arching beneath his own, and each breath blew from him in harsh gasps. She writhed and swayed, and he thought he might burst from the intensity of the pleasure she was giving him, simply by enjoying the moment.

He pulled away from her, held himself back, and a low, keening moan of protest spilled from her lips until, with a little nudge, Icharus positioned himself at her entrance and rocked forward.

Her moan became a gasp, and then a groan. He continued to rock against her, pressing himself a bit deeper inside of her with every thrust of his hips until finally, he could take no more. The sweet torture of her slick heat gliding against his hardness was more than he could stand.

"Ah, God," he groaned. He slid his hands beneath her, pulled her close, and kissed her. Hard. With a single thrust, he entered her, and a fierce growl rose up from his throat.

He heard her cried out, and he did not know if her cry was one of pleasure or pain, but he was too far gone to know the difference.

Holding himself still, fighting his own need to move inside her, feel the heat of her surrounding him, he raised his head so that he could see her expression. He did not wish to hurt her.

She caught him back, pulled him down to nip at his earlobe with her teeth. "Icharus, please! Oh, God, please!"

His jaw tightly clenched, he started to move inside her, slowly at first, but she would have none of it.

Lifting her legs, she clamped them tightly about his waist, and thrust upward, frantically seeking release. He could feel her sleek, inner muscles squeezing against him, sucking him deeper and deeper inside her with each thrust.

Madness. Insanity.

Never had he felt with such intense feeling when he was with a woman. Never.

Katherine froze, her eyes going wide an instant before he plunged into her again. Hard. Her body seemed to explode into a million particles of particles of light, airy substance without form while hot rivers of ecstasy pulsed through her, over her, around her.

Such was the force of the pure bliss flowing through her, at the pinnacle of her release, her body quivered and shivered anew with every beat of her heart, which seemed to correlate with each new spasm of her nether region.

It seemed a vacuum had formed somewhere deep inside her body, and was even now drawing her into her own self while flinging her very essence forth into a vast void – both at one and the same instant.

A scream ripped from her throat, and Icharus caught the sound with his kiss an instant before his own climax thundered through him.

A harsh groan forced its way from his lips as his body shook with the intensity of his release. He thrust hard once, again, and again. And then no more.

He collapsed against her softness, but after a moment he withdrew himself from her fierce embrace to lie beside her before his body relaxed in sleep.

He had dozed but a moment before a soft sound reached him in his slumber, and his eyes flew open. He raised his head from the pillow, instantly alert, listening carefully, and then chuckled low.

Beside him, Katherine lay with her arms partially

around him still. Her dark lashes rested against her cheeks, and her sable curls were wound about them both. Her lips were slightly parted, and a soft snore slipped past.

A smile curved his lips, and he raised himself up on an elbow, partly to disentangle himself from her curls, but mostly so he could watch her while she slept.

* * * *

Katherine woke with a sharp pinch in her side a short time later. Rising up on an elbow, she swept her hand along the sheets beneath her side, searching for whatever had been causing her pain. Her fingers closed around the object, one of her mother's gold combs.

She glanced at the other side of the bed where Icharus lay sleeping and smiled. She had been so eager for Icharus's loving she had forgotten to take the combs from her hair.

Carefully, she searched beneath the covers for the second of the pair, and finding it, she quietly placed them both on the table beside her bed before turning onto her side so she could watch Icharus sleep, but her thoughts turned instead to the troubling events that had occurred earlier this night.

As much as she wanted to believe Icharus's explanation of all that had happened, did believe it really for the most part, she knew there was something more, something she should remember, but the memory of which lay just beyond her grasp.

Her thoughts troubled once more, she turned onto her other side and stared out into the darkness of the room while she tried to force the memory she knew she should have to the surface.

No matter how hard she tried, her thoughts seemed wont to return to the combs, her mother's combs. Gold combs. Her eyes widened, and she covered her mouth with her hand to silence the gasp that burst from her lips.

Remembering now, she eased carefully from the bed so as not to wake Icharus. She went to the wardrobe and pulled out a gown. After dressing as quietly as she could, she took the combs from her table and crept from the room, closing the door softly behind her.

Downstairs in her father's study, she sat at the desk, thinking back over the past months, back to the time before her father had fallen ill when that first murder had occurred in Sleepy Hollow, her mind desperately searching for answers.

Lifting the combs, she tried to remember. Her father had given them to her mother, but he had not purchased them for her. Nay, they had belonged to someone else ... but that someone would never wear them again.

The combs had belonged to Minerva.

Gold combs.

Gold.

That was why Minerva refused to leave the Western Woods, she remembered now. William had discovered a bit of gold in the forest and had taken it to a jeweler in the city where he'd had the combs made.

William had told her father of his find, had asked if they should look for more, but her father had said no. He had everything he needed in life and did not wish to complicate matters with news of a gold strike in the Hollow.

William, however, had promised Minerva a life of ease, and he had attempted to extract the ore from the forest – and he had died in the process. She did not remember how, only that he had fallen to his death somehow.

Minerva had been unable to accept the fact, and refused to leave their little cottage in the Western Woods, insisting her William would return soon and take her away to the city, as he had promised.

There was certainly more, but she had been too young at the time to comprehend the importance of it all. She did remember that her father and John had argued about it later, after Brau found Minerva murdered in the woods.

Why had they argued?

The memories fought her, refusing to come to the fore of her thoughts, and Katherine frowned. Whatever it had been, no one had spoken of it after that afternoon, and she hadn't thought of Minerva until John was murdered – just days after he had begun to harvest the timber from the Western Woods.

Was it possible someone outside *the Hollow had somehow learned of the gold?*

Yes, that was it, she was sure of it now. Someone had found out about the gold William found in the Western Woods and thought to have it for themselves. When John and Dehann began harvesting the trees, they must have gotten scared, become afraid they would be discovered. Perhaps John *had* discovered whoever it was. That would certainly be motive enough for someone to kill him, she thought.

The longer she considered it, the more her idea of what had happened seemed to make sense. The question then was how had someone outside of the Hollow learned of the gold? Her father was gone, but he would have spoken of it to no one. Neither would John have done so. The only others who might even possibly know of it, other than herself, were Heinrick and Brau …

Frustrated, she sighed. It seemed she had come full circle, back to the day she had joined the others in Heinrick's office, back to knowing what she had known then – neither Heins nor Brau would have murdered John.

But someone had.

Someone had also broken into her father's study and searched it the very same night.

She believed they had been searching for the papers she had given to Icharus. Obviously no one had thought to search there for them before because, like Brau, they hadn't believed any such papers existed … until Icharus came back to Sleepy Hollow.

She sighed. Brau again.

Brau had questioned her more than once regarding Icharus's motive for coming into the Hollow to help her, and just then, she realized he must have thought she had used the documents as some sort of bribe, to keep him in the Hollow until he had accomplished all she wished.

She flushed with shame, knowing that had been exactly her plan when she'd sent Callum to fetch Icharus back after Heins had given her the letter from her father. But her conscience had prodded her and she hadn't been able to withhold the certificates that truly belonged to him.

But why would Brau care whether or not I had those papers? Why would he want them badly enough that he'd send a thief into my home to search for and then steal them?

She shook her head. No, Brau would not have done so, and yet it had happened.

Had he mentioned to someone that Icharus had come to the Hollow, and the reason he believed he had come?

Her father had warned her that there were others who wished to have the documents, and he'd cautioned her to say nothing of them to Brau. She had not done so, but she believed Brau had drawn his own conclusions on the matter. Still, she could not believe him guilty of an attempt to steal the documents.

In any case, she had given them to Icharus, and he had stayed in Sleepy Hollow to help her without any inducement other than his gratitude to her father – at first – as he had said.

And then later the storehouse had burned.

Why?

After long moments spent searching her thoughts, Katherine could only assume whoever had set fire to the barn had wanted one of two things: they had wanted both herself and Icharus dead, or they assumed with the storehouse gone, she would believe she had no other recourse but to leave Sleepy Hollow.

But why would they want Icharus dead? If it's the gold they wanted, why kill him?

All they needed was for her to relinquish all rights to Sleepy Hollow, either by deed or desertion.

Icharus's words came back to her now, about how Brau had done nothing during those years while her father lay ill to stop the village from falling into ruin. She remembered he had said that it almost seemed he had wanted it to fall into disrepair, and at this moment, she realized it was true.

Brau wanted to take her away from Sleepy Hollow, to the city. She wondered if this might be the reason behind his wanting to take her away.

Tears pricked her eyelids. Everything seemed to come back to Brau, and it almost broke her heart to think he might be the one responsible for so much heartache, for death, for cruel destruction in her beloved village, but she could think of nothing else, no one else. If her guess were right, he would return to Sleepy Hollow at some point today.

Although she still did not have the solution she sought, one thing was certainly clear. Whoever was responsible for the things that had happened in Sleepy Hollow after her father's death meant to continue wreaking havoc in her village until whatever goal they had in mind was met.

Although it would likely break her heart, she knew what she had to do. A sob rose up in her breast. She pulled a pillow up to her mouth to cover the sound of her weeping and let the tears fall until there simply were no more, and exhausted from the emotional turmoil of the night, she slept.

It seemed only minutes had passed when next she opened her eyes. She raised her head and glanced toward the windows. The sun had started to rise while she had been lost in her sorrow. She could hear Mrs. Porter coming up the back stairs, headed for the kitchen to start breakfast.

"Edda?" she called softly. "Could you join me for a moment, please? I would like to you to help me with something upstairs before the others start to rise."

* * * *

Some time later, Icharus descended the stairs, humming a lively tune. It was one he had often heard his father hum when he'd been particularly happy, Icharus remembered and he smiled, thinking now he knew precisely the reason why.

He had awakened alone in Katherine's room, and at first he'd waited for her, thinking she was but answering a call of nature and would return soon, but after almost half an hour passed, he decided she had already gone downstairs to start her day.

Hurrying through getting dressed, his thoughts on how they had spent the wee hours of the night just passed, Icharus smiled and rushed downstairs, hoping to at least meet her in the dining room before she finished her morning meal.

At the bottom of the stairs, he turned to go into the dining room, but just before he stepped through the doorway, he noticed two large bags sitting in the foyer

… his bags.

His steps faltered, halted, and a sudden, queer feeling of premonition chased its way along his spine. Slowly he turned, his gaze wary, to see Katherine sitting stiffly on the sofa in the parlor.

Her face was pale, her back ramrod straight. She offered neither smile nor even a friendly morning greeting, like she usually did. She did not bother to acknowledge his presence at all, but rather held to that strange, unnatural silence. He frowned.

Something is not right.

Watching her curiously, cautiously, he stepped into the parlor. "Katherine?"

She turned then and raised her gaze ever so slowly to meet his. He did not like what he saw. Her eyes were cold. Dim. Lifeless.

"I want you to leave, Icharus."

He stiffened, feeling as if he'd had the wind knocked out of him.

Leave? Surely she did not mean what he thought she meant? Nay. His mind refused to accept it. She'd simply had a bad scare last night, and this morning, thoughts of it had come back to plague her. She just wasn't quite thinking clearly.

With a hesitant smile, he crossed the room to kneel in front of her, taking her hand – *her cold hand* – in his. He chafed it lightly with his own, hoping to bring some warmth to her chilled fingers.

"Katherine, I know last night was … was frightening for you. Seeing what you saw, and then feeling the frustration you must have felt, losing the inn you wanted to build so badly, but …" he started, but she was shaking her head.

"No," she said, and his smile disappeared. Her voice, like her eyes, was cold.

"Do not try to rationalize it for me, Icharus. I was

there. I know how I felt, and I know what I saw." Something flickered deep within her gaze, and she turned away. "I want you to go away."

Stunned by the cruelty of her words, he came to his feet and stood staring down at her in disbelief. "Go away?"

She nodded. "Yes. I want you to leave Sleepy Hollow. Now. Today."

He shook his head, a short bark of incredulous, disbelieving laughter escaping his lips. "Katherine, please! You cannot possibly mean what you are saying …"

She stood then, coming to her full height in front of him. Her eyes hadn't changed. She continued to stare at him with ice in her gaze.

"I can and I do," she said quietly. "I … I've had a change of heart, Icharus. I am going to marry Braughton … if he will still have me."

She walked to the wide windows overlooking the village, and stood staring down in silence at the place where the inn had been only the night before. After a moment, she turned back to him. "Go home, Icharus Crane. I should never have asked you to come back to Sleepy Hollow."

Without another word, she turned and left him there where he stood in the parlor, his body frozen in shock, his heart breaking, his mind numb.

Distantly, he heard her footfalls on the stairs, heard her walk along the second story hallway until she reached her chamber, and then he heard the low click of the door when she closed it, shutting him out of her thoughts, and possibly her life.

He started to go after her, to demand an explanation, to beg her to reconsider her sudden change of heart but a loud commotion, someone was pounding with their fists at the door, halted him.

Mr. Rawlins hurried forward, but Icharus was there ahead of him, pulling the door wide to find Balt and Jericho on the other side, their expressions grim. "We've found something."

His gaze went to the stairs. He wanted to talk to her, needed to know what had upset her so, but he must also keep her safe. He turned back to the men waiting for him on the porch. "I'll be right out."

Calling for Mrs. Porter, he said, "Edda, when Katherine comes back down, please ask her to stay inside and wait for me. We will talk when I return."

He hurried to the stables, and moments later rode out on Defiance, with Balt and Jericho leading the way.

Chapter 19

Icharus didn't know how long they had been riding, deep into the heart of the Western Woods, before Jericho finally reined in his mount.

Balt drew his own steed to a halt next, and slowing Defiance, Icharus looked around at his surroundings and frowned. "Well? What have you found?"

He could see nothing but a dense growth of trees, and a good distance ahead, a small clearing in the middle of the woods. He peered into the clearing, his gaze catching on something. Edging Defiance away from the others, he sought a better look. What he found at the farthest edge of the natural opening in the woods was the ruins of a small cottage, broken down, weather-worn, and quite overgrown with vines and moss.

Minerva.

Jericho and Balt had discovered the home of the Witch, he thought. He could have saved them the trouble. Katherine could have easily pointed them here if only they had asked. His frown became a scowl. He'd ridden all this way just to see the remains of a cottage.

He turned to Jericho and Balt. "Minerva's cottage. What of it?"

With a quick tilt of his head, Jericho gestured toward the woods ahead. "Listen."

Icharus strained to hear whatever it was Jericho seemed to think important for him to hear, so important he'd brought him all the way out here into the middle of the forest when all he'd wanted to do was follow Katherine upstairs and demand she explain what had happened after they had made love, after he had held her close, so close he could no longer define where his own existence ended and hers began ….

Water.

The faint rushing sound that met his ears could be nothing else, yet he had seen no sign of either spring or brook while riding here.

Giving Defiance a nudge with his heels, he started forward. That's when he noticed the tracks on the ground. A wagon had come this way recently, as recently as last night. He frowned and followed the tracks until they stopped. He raised his head and peered upward to … the waterfall.

Spilling from a thick outcropping of rock, high up on the face of the tall peak, it rushed downward, forming a small, round pool at the base of the rise. Icharus shook his head, thinking it odd how the pool must run back into the side of the mountain from someplace near the bottom of the pool because there was no stream anywhere in sight for it to flow into.

He remembered Katherine saying something about a waterfall, but he could not clearly recall their conversation at the moment. His mind was too clouded with the confusion and pain of her desertion.

Katherine.

He sighed. He needed to get back to her.

He turned to Jericho again.

"I've seen the cottage, and the waterfall, and I am sure there is something significant about it all, but just now ..." He closed his eyes. "Just now I cannot think what it might be. I need to get back to Katherine ..."

Jericho hastened to explain. "Someone's been coming into Sleepy Hollow, through the haunted Western Woods in a wagon ... why would they do that, Master Crane?"

He peered at Icharus for a moment before he looked away and shook his head. "Everyone in Sleepy Hollow avoids this forest as if the Devil himself had made it his abode. Other than myself and young Tanner ..."

With a gesture toward the deep ruts in the forest floor made by the recent passing of a heavy-laden cart, he said, "These tracks prove someone has no fear of the Devil, someone who is clearly trespassing where they have no right to be, but who could it be, Master Crane? What are they doing so far back here in the forest, and why would they need to bring in a wagon?"

"Possibly to cart out the gold," Dehann said.

Icharus's gaze flew to a spot behind the small pool at the base of the waterfall, to where Dehann now stood although he'd been nowhere to be seen but a moment before. "Gold?"

He nodded, and came forward, holding his open palm up so the three of them could see what he held in his hand. "One of these I found the night my father was murdered, Icharus. Da had it clutched in his hand."

He handed up a small gold nugget about the size of an acorn.

"This morning I discovered a similar one near the hull of the inn." He shrugged. "I knew there must be some connection, so I came out here ... to the place Father had ridden to before he was killed."

Dehann shook his head. "I would have ridden out with him that afternoon, but he sent me into the village with Mum and Anne. Said he'd be along soon... he only needed to check something he'd seen earlier that morning."

Icharus scowled. "Why did you say nothing of this before, Dehann? Did your father mention what he had seen?"

Dehann looked up at him. "Tracks, Master Crane. Father said he'd seen tracks in the forest, and wanted to see where they led, but I—"

Dehann made a sound of self-deprecation. "I thought he'd meant animal tracks. That's why I came ahead with Mum and Anne. I never thought there was reason to fear …"

Icharus nodded. "The waterfall … there is a cave behind it, is there not?"

Dehann tipped his head. "And enough explosives inside to blow half the side of this mountain away if one were so inclined."

Icharus straightened. "Explosives."

Everything was becoming clearer by the moment. Someone had discovered the waterfall, the caves behind it, and was blasting into the side of the mountain. That explained the rumbling explosions he had heard the night John was murdered, and last night before the inn had crumbled to the ground.

Dehann nodded. "Find out who has been mining the gold from the cave behind the waterfall, and you shall have your 'Headless Horseman.' "

Icharus nodded, knowing it was true.

But who would know about this place? he wondered. *Who could have known about the gold?*

He searched his thoughts, and could think of only one.

Brau.

Suddenly, everything made perfect sense. It was the gold Brau wanted, not Katherine. Gold was the reason he'd asked Katherine to marry him, and to leave the Hollow.

He tugged at Defiance's reins, wheeling the horse around. "I have to get back to Katherine. Say nothing of what we have discovered to anyone ... especially Braughton. If he should find out what we know ..." he cautioned.

He felt a chill just thinking of all the man had shown himself capable of doing.

Brau had already killed a man he called friend. He had cold-heartedly destroyed what he knew to be their last hope of surviving the winter when he set fire to the barn, and last night ... last night he had rigged the inn, Katherine's inn, with explosives and burned it to the ground, breaking her heart and possibly her spirit in the process.

This morning Katherine had told him she'd had a change of heart, that she intended to accept Brau's proposal.

But why? Why?

Suddenly, his head came up.

She knows.

Katherine knew Braughton was after the gold, and she was going to give it to him. She was planning to marry Brau, not because she had discovered she loved him after all, but because she *did* love her home, the people. She would sacrifice herself by marrying a man she did not love because she believed it was the only way to stop the attacks on Sleepy Hollow.

"I have to get back to her."

With a swift nudge of his heels, he sent Defiance flying through the forest, pushing the stallion as far as he dared. He had to reach Katherine before Braughton did.

* * * *

Katherine saw him arrive from her chamber window and hurried immediately down the stairs to meet him at the door. "Good morning, Brau."

Brau's cautious gaze met hers, his expression unreadable. "Katherine… I saw the inn on my way up. Is everyone unhurt?"

She nodded. "No one was harmed, either by the explosion or the fire, Brau. Thank heavens."

He nodded, but the look in his eyes was certainly a bit wary.

He offered a hesitant smile. "That is quite a relief to hear."

Katherine's smile was bland. "I am glad you came back, Brau. Icharus said you would, once your hurt had time to subside, but I wasn't sure."

Brau peered at her, suddenly becoming much more the Braughton he had seemed of late. "Of course I came back. I will always come back for you Katherine. But are you quite sure you're all right? You sound … odd."

Her laugh was brittle. "I am fine … just a little out of sorts from the upheaval last night."

Brau studied her carefully for long moments. Finally, he closed his eyes and sighed. When he opened them again, he said, "You know, don't you?"

He had kept his voice low, so none other than she would hear him, Katherine guessed. She stared at him, hoping her gaze did not reflect the intensity of the pain she felt, the anguish that had rolled over her in waves since she'd heard Icharus ride away on Defiance hours ago. She nodded. "I know enough to have guessed you would come to Sleepy Hollow this morning. And I am glad you did because …"

Brau studied her, watchful. "Because?"

She hesitated, but after a moment, she spoke again, quietly. "Because I've had a change of heart, Brau. I will marry you, if you still desire to have me."

Something flickered in Brau's gaze, but after only a momentary hesitation, he nodded. "Of course." Seconds later, he asked, "What of Crane?"

Katherine's gaze held his. "I asked him to leave. He should be out of Sleepy Hollow by sunset."

Sounds from overhead alerted them the others were about to descend. Brau's gaze flitted to the top of the stairs, and then back to her. He drew a deep breath. "Katherine, there is something I must tell you ..."

Katherine arched a brow. "There is much you should tell me, Braughton," she started, but the sound of footsteps near the top of the stairs gave her pause, and she nodded toward the back.

"Come. We'll speak in Father's study," she said and hurried along the hall.

Inside the room she crossed to stand at the front of the desk, her bearing unusually tense. Her shoulders did not droop, but Brau could feel the depth of her dejection like a live entity between them.

He hurried around her and after a quick glance toward the window, sat at the desk. Taking up her father's quill, he rapidly scratched something onto a sheet of paper. Dusting it quickly, he folded the sheaf and slid it into his pocket and returned the quill to its stand. Finally he looked up at Katherine. "You have truly had a change of heart, Katherine? You are certain you now wish to marry me?"

She stared at him, her gaze cold, devoid of emotion. "Is there any other way?"

Brau leaned back in the chair, not even pretending to misunderstand her question. His brow furrowed while he considered her inquiry. "You could both simply disappear ..."

She gave a short, negative shake of her head. "Or you could simply tell me why we should. I know you did not kill John, Brau. The same as I know it was not you who burned the storehouse or ..." She drew in a breath. "Or destroyed the inn last night. But I also realize you

331

know who did."

"You know who is responsible for everything that has happened in Sleepy Hollow these past months." She looked at him, no longer attempting to hide the pain and anguish she felt.

Her gaze pleading, she said, "You said you cared about me Brau, and I believed you, but now I am not quite sure. For the love of God, please! Whoever is behind these attacks in Sleepy Hollow wants something, Brau, and you alone know what. You must tell me what that something is ..."

"He could do that, I suppose."

Katherine's gaze flew toward the now open windows where a tall, rather thin man bowed low to step across the sill to push away the curtains. Gaining his footing inside the room, he straightened and looked directly at her. "Surprised, little cat?"

His dark gaze sparkled with cold laughter. He crossed the room, nodding once to Brau before making his way to the front of her father's desk where he propped one hip and lounged indolently, his gaze raking over her from head to toe.

"I think you are," he said. "But not half as shocked as you were when you saw me last night, eh?"

A little trill of laughter followed his words.

"*Lars.*" Katherine spat the name from her lips as if it were poison.

His brows arched in surprise, and he nodded. "So you do recall my name. Braughton did not think you would remember his dearest Uncle, but I see that he was wrong."

She glared at him. "I remember you. My grandfather forbade you to ever come back to Sleepy Hollow, Lars Devissier."

He smiled. "Yes. Yes, that is true."

He stood up and sighed. "Alas, little cat, your

grandfather is no longer here … nor is your father."

Her stare remained cold. "What do you want?"

The iciness of her tone seemed to surprise him, but he recovered quickly, and smiled. He twisted a bit to the side and took up the little statue her father kept on his desk.

"Freedom."

He studied the figurine for a moment before continuing. "Prosperity."

He turned and replaced the knickknack. "I want *the gold*, my dear. The same thing I desired when your grandfather had the authorities take me away … only this time, I shall have it."

Gold.

The waterfall.

Minerva.

Memories filled her thoughts in rapid succession. "My father had you banished from Sleepy Hollow forever, Lars. When the authorities discover you have returned …"

Lars arched a brow and spread his hands wide. "Who is there to tell them?"

A deep frown furrowing his brow, Brau stood and shook his head in a silent gesture for Katherine to say no more. "No one, Uncle. Even if someone did, it would not matter. Not anymore, because Katherine has agreed to marry me after all." He turned to Lars with a smile. "Congratulate me, Uncle."

Another trill of laughter spilled from the tiny man, and he winked at Katherine. "But only as a last resort, eh, my little cat?"

Katherine turned away, refusing to look at him. He stood, and came round to stand in front of her. "Where are the certificates, Katherine?"

She still would not look at him, but neither did she pretend to misunderstand. Her gaze flickered to the section of shelving where her father had kept the documents that named Ichabod Crane or his heirs' sole owner of Wake Grove.

"Safe."

He chuckled at her vague reply.

"Safe." He nodded, and continued to smile. "Yes, safe."

He grabbed her by the arm, and forced her to turn, to meet his dark gaze. "But not *here*."

Her eyes came up slowly to meet his, questioning.

He shook his head. "You forget so swiftly, kitten? I've already searched your father's study ... the night I murdered your woodsman."

A cold smile lifted her lips. "John Tanner was not so easy to kill, was he?" She shook her head. "Nay, nothing as simple as Minerva."

She could tell she had surprised him with her knowledge, but he covered his shock swiftly. "Minerva was more in touch with her sanity than I realized. She thought to go to your father, as her fool of a husband William had, to tell him about ... but you are right. Killing Minerva was easy."

She felt her stomach churn.

Lars laughed. "Does it frighten you, little cat?"

Katherine glared at him. "It sickens me."

He turned away from her with a shrug. "No matter. Nor will it matter should you wed my nephew if I do not have the papers. Where are they, Katherine?"

She held silent, and he shook his head, his expression regretful. "So sad, really. I had thought to spare you, but if you insist..."

"They are upstairs, hidden in a trunk inside my chamber," she whispered.

Lars's brows rose. His dark gaze bore into hers for a long moment. Finally, he seemed to be satisfied she spoke the truth, and he turned, nodding to Brau. "Go with her. I will wait for you in the usual place. And Braughton?"

Brau gave his uncle his full attention.

"If you ruin this for me again, I will kill you."

Katherine noticed something flicker within his gaze, a spark akin to fear mixed with hatred she thought, but Brau nodded and came to her side, his hand slipping automatically to her waist.

"Say nothing," he whispered as he led her from the study.

Brau climbed the stairs with her and then followed her to her chamber. The minute they entered the room, he turned her to face him, fear evident in his eyes. "Katherine, do not think to outmaneuver him with a clever ploy. He will not simply take your word that the documents you give him are what you say they are. He will verify ..."

"And he shall not be disappointed," she said, and turned away. She went to kneel before a small trunk resting on a three-legged table in the corner of her chamber.

With shaking hands, she lifted the lid of the trunk where she had placed the parchments, and took them out, her fingertip reverently tracing the name on the front – Crane.

She stood and turned, holding the documents close to her breast. Brau made to take them from her but she snatched away, tucking them carefully into her bodice. "Nay. If Lars wants them so badly, he will have to take them from me himself ... but he will have to kill me first."

She meant it. He might have to spend the rest of his life nursing a broken heart, a heart she'd broken, but Katherine was determined that Icharus would not be denied the land he and his father had worked so hard to obtain.

"Katherine …"

"Now is not the time, Brau. We should go."

Nicolaas turned when they reached the bottom of the stairs with a smile of greeting on his lips. Realizing it was Brau, rather than Icharus at Katherine's side, the smile faded. Offering a hesitant nod in their direction, he said, "Braughton. I hadn't realized you were here."

Brau gestured for Katherine to continue on to the door, and turned to Nicolaas. "It is such a lovely day, I thought I'd bring Katherine for a ride through the countryside," he offered by way of explanation.

He held out his hand to Nicolaas.

Nicolaas took it, and arched a brow, but Brau shook his head and smiled a bit ruefully. "Follow my words, Van Kersten. She will be safe. Crane will have her for a lifetime. I believe it only fair that I have today."

He gave Nicolaas a hearty clap on the shoulder, and then turned to Katherine. "We'd best be off, if we've a hope of returning before sundown."

Katherine stepped out into the sunshine, and Brau followed, closing the door behind them. Katherine cast him a look. "He's never going to believe you came to bring me riding, Braughton. He knows about before, that I turned down your offer of marriage."

Brau led her down the steps, and swung up onto the back of his mount before reaching down for her. "I never thought he would. Hurry, Katherine. We haven't much time."

Katherine frowned at his somewhat cryptic reply, but raised her hands to his, let him lift her up before him. A moment later, the two of them rode down the lane into the village and across the covered bridge leading out of Sleepy Hollow.

Katherine turned her head to cast one last look back at the village, fear churning inside her like some wild thing bent upon destroying her from within, and she wondered if she would ever return.

* * * *

Icharus thundered up to the house, Defiance's hooves plowing up the dirt beneath them, and slid to the ground before the huge stallions churning feet could even come to a halt.

"Katherine!" he yelled, tearing up the steps to swing open the door.

"Katherine!" he bellowed again, racing toward the steps.

Nicolaas's voice stopped him. "She's not here, boy."

Icharus felt his blood turn to ice in his veins. "Where is she?"

Nicolaas crossed his arms over his chest and nodded toward the door. "Seeing the countryside with that Van Ripper fellow."

Icharus let his head drop back and squeezed his eyes closed. *Brau*. He'd arrived too late, and she was already gone. Gone to marry Brau. No. He could stop them, had to stop them before … He brought his head back up and asked, "When did they leave?"

Nicolaas shrugged. "Nigh onto an hour ago, maybe more."

Icharus nodded.

Too long. Too bloody long.

"Can you tell me where they went … where he took her?"

Nicolaas eyed him carefully. "He didn't exactly say."

Icharus ran a hand over his eyes.

How many places were there in the towns and villages neighboring Sleepy Hollow where one could be married? Too many.

In the time it would take him to ride to each one, it would be too late. After a moment, he went back to the door, calling back over his shoulder to Nicolaas. "When Callum and Dehann arrive, send them into TarryTown to fetch the constable, and bring him back here where they should wait until I return. Balt and Jericho will be here soon as well. Let them know I plan to seek out every parish within a day's ride of Sleepy Hollow. I have to find her before she ..."

Nicolaas frowned. "Shouldn't I send them to the tavern in TarryTown?"

Confused, Icharus halted and turned to peer at him. "The tavern?"

"Aye. At least I believe that is what he intended. 'Follow my words,' his note said. I didn't understand until they were already long gone, but," Nicholaas shook his head. "Strange one, that."

Icharus wanted to shake the man. "What note, Nicolaas?"

A somewhat quizzical smile playing across his lips, Nicolaas held up a piece of parchment with a few tiny words scrawled across its face. "The one Van Ripper pressed into my hand just before he led Mistress Katherine out the door."

Icharus snatched the parchment from his hand, and read the four simple words Brau had written there.

St. Julien's Temple.

Icharus frowned. *Why would Brau take Katherine to a deserted hovel in the woods in back of the Cock and Crow tavern?* It was nothing more than a broken down, abandoned old woodcutters hut Davrel St. Julien had jokingly dubbed 'St. Julien's Temple' after being snowed inside it for nigh onto a fortnight with naught but a traveling priest for company.

Still, their apparent destination did not bother Icharus half as much as the last word Brau had written on the page.

Hurry, it said, and Brau had underscored it with thick double lines.

It made no sense.

If Katherine had told him of her decision, and surely she had, why then would Brau reveal their destination?

He had to have known Icharus would follow them, to have known he would never let Katherine marry him, so again Icharus wondered, w*hy?*

It could mean only one thing: Van Ripper sought to lead him into a trap. At least, that had been his first thought. It was Brau's final word, the last word he had written, that disturbed Icharus most, leaving an uneasy feeling of anxious urgency in his gut.

Hurry.

Something about that word, something about the way Brau had clearly emphasized it, did not sit right with Icharus. The very thought of it permeated him with a sense of dread.

It was almost as if Braughton wanted him to follow because … *something wasn't right.*

If Katherine had told Brau of her decision, he would simply have ridden into TarryTown with her and the two of them would have been married.

Or he would have taken her to his home.

But one thing was certain, Icharus realized, remembering what Katherine had protested most in her relationship, such as it were, with Brau: the man would *never* drag Katherine, his bride-to-be and a female whose place was either in the home or to stand quietly at her man's side, about the countryside to steal into an abandoned old cottage in the woods. That could only mean Brau had *wanted* him to know he should not be the focus of Icharus's concern.

But who should? Icharus wondered, his mind

339

desperately trying to put the pieces together.

His blood ran cold. "Nicolaas, have Callum and Dehann fetch the constable to the Cock and Crow. Tell them to ask for Davrel, tell him Icharus sent them, and have him bring them immediately to St. Julien's Temple. Davrel will know where to go," he said, and hastened out the door.

* * * *

It seemed to Katherine they had been riding through the forest for hours before Brau finally bent his head and said, "We are almost there."

She nodded, and a few moments later, he pulled Thunder to a halt near the front of a dilapidated old building that could only be called a hut or shack from the look of it. He held her while she slid to her feet, and then swung himself down from the horse's back.

He led her toward the building, speaking low next to her ear as they walked. "There was an old priest who stayed here once. We will wait inside until dark before we travel on to …"

Lars opened the door, and his gaze narrowed on Brau. "That is enough, Braughton. She doesn't need to know where we shall be going from here."

Brau nodded, and Lars peered at him. "Were you followed?"

Brau shook his head. "Nay. They think we have merely gone for a frolic through the countryside."

The thin man nodded. "What of Crane?"

"Gone," Brau said, ushering Katherine through the door. "Back to Wake Grove. Katherine sent him away."

Lars grunted. "And the certificates? You do have them, do you not?"

Brau cast a worried glance at Katherine before dipping his head in a hesitant nod. "We do."

Lars grinned. "Excellent. I had begun to believe you untrainable, but there may be hope for you yet, my boy. I'll have them now, if you please."

Brau led Katherine up the two steps and opened the door for her. Lars followed them inside.

"Well? Where are they?"

Once again, Brau dipped his head toward Katherine. "Katherine has them."

Lars turned to look at her. "Well, girl?"

She smiled and reached into her bodice. But it was not the documents Lars wanted she retrieved from the valley between her breasts.

Rather, she slid a silver-handled dagger slowly upward and held it in front of her. "You can retrieve the certificates the instant my dead body touches the floor, Lars Devissier, but not a moment before."

Brau's eyes flickered, and Katherine thought she saw a moment's admiration in his gaze, but then he started forward. "Katherine, have a care …"

She turned an almost feral gaze in his direction. "Stay back!"

Lars laughed.

"Very nice, my dear," he said. His eyes ran over her for a moment before coming back to peer into hers with deadly warning. "Yes, a clever diversion. But a waste of time."

With a movement so swift it barely registered on her thoughts before his fist slammed into her wrist, he knocked the weapon from her grasp and almost snapped the slender bones in her arm.

Katherine cried out, and the dagger clattered to the rough wooden floor.

He grabbed her arm and pain seared through her, but he ignored it, and snatched her close. "Where are the documents, Mistress Van Brunt?"

Katherine blinked back tears caused by the pain in

341

her arm he held in a vice-like grip and turned her face away from him, refusing to answer.

He turned his dark gaze on Brau.

"Inside her bodice," she heard him say a moment before Lars plunged his other hand deep into the neckline of her dress. The material tore, but he didn't seem to notice.

Having snatched the packet from her gown, he immediately released her and unfolded the document, his greedy eyes scanning the words penned onto the certificate he had withdrawn.

After ensuring everything was as it should be, he turned back to Brau. "Tie her into the chair."

Brau frowned. "Should we not fetch the reverend?"

Lars shook his head. "We've no need for him yet … although she most certainly may desire his services later."

Brau nodded and reached out to take her by the arm, the same arm Lars had nearly broken only a few moments before. Katherine cried out and dropped to the floor, cradling the injured limb to her chest.

Brau released her immediately. "My apologies, Katherine. I did not mean to cause you pain."

She bit at her lower lip and shook her head, and he could see the fine sheen of tears glazing her eyes. He bent to assist her to her feet, but doing so apparently unbalanced him for a moment, and his hands grabbed at the floor beneath him for purchase.

He righted himself quickly, but not before Lars turned to stare at him in disgust. "Clumsy fool."

Brau said not a word, merely led Katherine to the chair his Uncle had mentioned, half-broken and covered with a thick layer of cobwebs, and began to tie her into it as he had been instructed. When he was sure she was secured, he turned to Lars.

"Why are we here, Uncle?"

"Crane."

Katherine's gaze flew to his. "Icharus will not come. I sent him away…"

Lars shook his head. "He will come. He will come … for you," he said, pointing at Brau.

Brau stiffened. "And when he does?"

Lars shrugged. "We will kill him."

Brau's gaze shifted to Katherine. "She will not be pleased should you do so, Uncle. She loves him."

Lars snorted derisively.

"Love. A ridiculous notion, that." He shrugged. "It is of no matter, for she will join him soon enough."

Brau's gaze fell, and he went to sit with his back against the wall near the chair he'd tied Katherine into.

Lars tilted his head to one side, listening intently for a moment, and then walked to the door. "Stay with her."

The instant the door closed, Brau scrambled across the floor, his hands going immediately to the knotted ropes he had used to bind her.

"He means to kill us all, Katherine," he said, his voice low. "We have to get out of here."

He shook his head and sighed repentantly. "I'm sorry, I… I never thought it would go this far …"

Katherine was shaking her head. "No, he won't kill us, Brau. Icharus will not come because I sent him away and Lars … he needs me to gain control of the mine in Sleepy Hollow."

Brau's fingers were working furiously against the knots he'd tied only a moment before. "Not anymore."

His fingers slipped and collided with the rough frame of the chair. He muttered a curse and shook his head. He caught hold of the chair and looked at Katherine, something akin to panic in his gaze. "It was the papers, don't you see?"

She frowned. "What do you mean?"

Brau ducked his head, concentrating on a

343

particularly difficult knot. "Now that he has those, Lars has no need of either of us ... not you, Icharus, or me. He will have the priest wed you and I, and then..." He grabbed hold of her shoulders and gave her a shake. "He plans to *kill* you, Katherine, do you understand?"

He released her almost as quickly, his attention on the rope once more. "He will kill you, and with you gone, there will be no one standing in the way of the gold he desires ... either in the caves behind the waterfall in Sleepy Hollow or the vein that runs across into Wake Grove."

Katherine lowered her head. "Icharus will," she whispered.

His fingers froze. He put a hand beneath her chin and lifted it until her gaze met his. "What do you mean, 'Icharus will'?"

Chapter 20

"The certificates Lars has …"

Brau frowned for a moment and then his eyes widened. "Forgery."

Katherine nodded and whispered, "I copied them …"

Brau grinned at the ingeniousness of her ploy. "Word for word," he said.

Katherine blushed. She hadn't known Brau had overheard her conversation with Icharus that first night he came to Sleepy Hollow, but apparently he had.

Footsteps sounded near the door.

"Hurry, Brau," she whispered urgently.

After a moment, the sound of footfalls faded and Brau quickly released the last of the knots he'd tied earlier, and then leaned down to whisper near her ear. "Listen to me, Katherine. Crane will come. He loves you."

"He will never find us out here …"

Brau shook his head. "I gave our direction to Nicolaas before we left. When Lars comes through that door, you must flee. There is another door just there, to your right," he said, nodding into the darkest side of the room. "Find the path at the back of the building and follow it to the Cock and Crow. When you get there, ask for Davrel St. Julien ..."

"Davrel? Your friend who ..."

"Davrel has land in the north, but prefers to make his abode here. He owns the Cock and Crow... but the important thing is that he can be trusted. Tell him to fetch the constable and come here as swiftly as he can... and you wait there until Icharus comes to fetch you to safety. Do you understand?"

She nodded. "Brau?"

"Yes?" he asked, and looked up into her misty gaze.

"Why are you helping me ... helping us?"

He lifted his fingers to her cheek in a gentle caress. "We are friends, are we not?" She nodded, and he shrugged. "It is the sort of thing friends do."

Her lips curved upward in a wobbly smile.

He dropped his hand from her cheek and made his way to the darkened corner behind the door – to wait for Icharus.

Just imagining what he must think of her now ... Katherine bit her lip to hold back the sob that rose in her throat. She had hated being so cold, so cruel, but she'd known there was no other way. If he had been there when Brau arrived, as she had known he would, Icharus would never have let her go with him.

It had been the only way she knew to flush out whoever was behind the treachery in Sleepy Hollow, and it had worked. Not only had she brought Lars out, she had managed to get herself spirited away to some forsaken woodcutter's cottage where even now she sat facing a possibly gruesome death.

Lars was not squeamish when it came to getting rid of those he no longer needed. He had proved that more than once.

She shivered, casting a quick glance at Brau, a

twinge of sadness welling up inside for him. Lars had used him, his own nephew, as a pawn in a vicious game, a chancy play for wealth that may very well cost Brau his life.

While it gave her a great sense of relief to know Brau had not been the one to murder either Minerva or John, and that his only crime had been one of neglect when he could have prevented the decline in Sleepy Hollow, it also saddened her that his own desire for whatever his Uncle had promised him had brought him to such an end.

She lowered her gaze, unable to bear the look of intense regret and anxiety in his expression. Tears came to her eyes and she forced them back.

Sounds of a horse and rider leisurely passing through the area reached her ears. Katherine tensed, waiting anxiously for whoever was coming up the lane, unaware of their presence in the little cottage, to either stop or pass them by.

Where is Lars? He should have returned by now. Straining her ears, she tried to hear what was going on outside.

* * * *

Icharus sat atop Defiance, looking for all the world as though he were merely idly surveying the scenery while he rode up to the front of the woodcutter's hut. At least he hoped anyone who saw him would think he was merely passing through, idling the day away.

Drawing Defiance to a halt a moment later, he slid carefully to the ground, his eyes searching the surroundings for any sign of mischief before he looped the reins over a low branch and quietly climbed the steps into St. Julien's Temple, which was truly nothing more than a tiny, one room cottage.

Giving the door a slight, cautious nudge, Icharus waited to see if anyone would meet him there. No one did, and he frowned. He wondered for a moment if Brau had mislead him after all, sending him here as a distraction, rather than reveal his true destination. It was so very silent inside, he was almost afraid to slip into the darkened interior for fear of what he might find when he did so.

He pushed again, took a step inside, and quickly closed the door behind him. There were no windows, so it took a moment for his eyes to adjust to the darkness of the interior.

"Katherine?" he called in a hushed whisper.

A voice came from the darkness at the back of the room. "Light the lamp, Braughton, so Master Crane can see me at least once before I kill him. I shouldn't like to deny him that pleasure."

Icharus stiffened. A light flared beside him, and he turned toward it. Brau held the lantern high, illuminating the tiny room, bathing it in light.

Brau stood near the corner, but he was alone.

Where was Katherine?

His brow furrowing in confusion, Icharus turned in the direction of the voice he had heard, and the breath stilled in his lungs, suffocating him with fear.

Having leapt from the chair when the door swung slowly open, expecting Lars to be there in the entrance, Katherine had turned and raced for the exit in the back Brau had told her about, and had run right into Lars's chest.

He'd caught her to him, pressed a cold metal blade against her throat with one hand. In the other he held a pistol, the hammer already drawn.

Katherine.

Icharus's gaze ran slowly over her, taking note of the fright in her eyes, the jagged tear in her bodice, and

348

the way she held her arm protectively against her body. She was hurt.

He turned his gaze on Lars, fury rushing up inside him. He was going to kill the man. "Release her."

Lars laughed. "I think not. Make the introductions, Braughton. I don't believe Master Crane knows who I am," Lars said, his tone mocking.

Brau's gaze flickered to his uncle and then to Icharus before he nodded in deference to his uncle. "Icharus Crane, my uncle, Lars Devissier." He arched a brow and turned back to his uncle. "Or you may recognize him as the fiend who killed both Minerva and John Tanner, burned your storehouse and set off explosives to destroy the inn in Sleepy Hollow last night."

He made a small bow toward Lars. "Uncle Lars, meet Icharus Crane... the man who is going to kill you for hurting the woman he loves."

Lars glared at him. "Your insolence is intolerable, nephew. You should have learned better than to cross me by now."

Brau shrugged. "What I say or do matters little now, Uncle. You plan to kill us anyway, do you not?"

He turned his attention back to Icharus. "You should know that Lars has the certificates Katherine had been holding, the documents she promised you in return for aiding her in Sleepy Hollow."

Icharus shook his head. "That is impossible."

Both Brau and Lars peered at him. Lars laughed. "Impossible? Not so. I have them here. Would you like to see?"

Icharus met his gaze unflinching. "I have no need to do so. Katherine gave me the papers the day I came back to Sleepy Hollow."

Brau's lips turned upward in a grin, his eyes cold. "The documents you hold are forgeries, Uncle."

Lars grabbed a handful of Katherine's hair and snatched her head back so she was forced to meet his gaze. "You treacherous little—"

Icharus stopped him with a look. "I said release her, Devissier. Now."

His command was met with a trill of laughter. Lars made a tsking sound, and pressed the blade he held at her throat closer to her skin, drawing a thin red trickle of blood from the flesh there. "So foolish. Will you force me to do so, Crane? I think not, but come ahead then and try if you must. She will be dead before you take a single step."

Brau, his attitude one of unconcern for the dire circumstances in which they found themselves at this moment, sighed and sat in the chair he'd tied Katherine in earlier.

His expression had gone cold. Unreadable. "Enough of this, Uncle. If you intend to kill her, do so." Icharus made a protest, but Brau said, "Relax, Crane. 'Tis a bluff. He will not kill her because he knows should he do so, he will not leave here alive."

He pinned his uncle with a glare and shook his head. "Nay, he will not harm Katherine. She is his only assurance that he will live long enough to leave this place, and he knows it."

Something flickered in Lars's gaze, and he offered a nod of admiration to his nephew. "Astute of you, Braughton. You are right, of course."

Brau stretched his booted feet indolently before him and crossed his arms over his chest. "Come ahead then, Uncle. I volunteer to be first."

Lars considered his nephew for a moment, hesitant. Finally, he said, "Very well," and shoved Katherine aside, drawing careful aim on the center of Brau's chest.

Katherine stumbled and fell against the rickety wall, striking her temple as she did so. Slowly, she crumbled to the floor.

In the same instant Icharus made a dive at Lars, Brau tossed the silver-handled dagger the man had knocked from Katherine's grasp earlier. It flew through the air, flipping end over end before coming to rest, buried deep into Lars's chest.

The pistol fired as Lars sank to his knees in the floor, striking Brau in the shoulder. He fell from the chair he had been sitting in and clutched at his arm, moaning in pain.

Icharus rushed to Katherine where she lay, unconscious, on the floor. "Braughton are you able to stand?"

Brau shifted on the floor, holding his injured arm. He coughed, struggling to gain control of the fiery pain. "Give me a moment."

Icharus bent and gently lifted Katherine into his arms.

"The others should be here soon. I'll take Katherine outside, and then come back for him," he said, motioning over his shoulder to the man who now lay sprawled in the floor, unmoving.

* * * *

Callum and Dehann stayed outside with Katherine while Icharus and Brau explained all that had happened to the constable.

Lars was not dead, but had lost a great deal of blood. He was taken into custody, and would soon face the judge for his crimes in Sleepy Hollow. He had survived this day only to spend those left to him knowing he would soon face the hangman's noose.

Icharus exited the woodsman's hut first, with Brau and the constable following him, leading a now subdued Lars.

Katherine turned her head to the side, unable to bear even to look at him, for to do so made her heart break all over again.

Icharus went to her side. "Katherine?"

Hesitantly, she raised her eyes to meet his gaze, tears spiking her lashes. He lifted his hand to the small cut on her throat, and made a noise deep in his throat.

He sighed. "I know why you did what you did, Katherine. At least … I believe I do …" he said, his voice hesitant, seeking assurance.

"You would not have let me go with him otherwise …"

Icharus nodded. "Aye, you are right. I would never willingly let you put yourself in danger, Katherine. Even for me. The moment I realized what you had done, and why …"

He closed his eyes, fighting the nigh overwhelming emotion rising inside him.

Katherine put out her hand, touching him, and Icharus drew her carefully into his embrace.

"When I saw Lars holding you …"

She shook her head, tears spilling down across her cheeks. "It is over, Icharus. Take me home. Please."

Icharus nodded. He turned to Brau. "Van Ripper?"

Brau raised his head, and Icharus put out his hand in a gesture of friendship. "Thank you … for all that you did today. I know it was not easy for you."

Brau looked at him for a moment and then at the hand Icharus had extended. Finally, a smile turned his lips upward, and reaching out with his good hand, he took it, giving it a shake.

"Thank Katherine. She is the one who reminded me what true friendship really means. I had quite forgotten."

Icharus smiled. "You'll visit? And you will be there for the wedding, of course?"

Brau's gaze flickered to Katherine's, and he

grinned. "I wouldn't miss it for all the gold in Sleepy Hollow."

* * * *

Home once more, Katherine and Icharus explained all that had happened to the Van Kerstens while Mrs. Porter fussed over the tiny cut on Katherine's neck and then gently wrapped her wrist.

Everything had finally quieted, and with evening swiftly approaching, Katherine stood with Icharus on the porch of the Van Brunt mansion, resting her head against his chest, his arms holding her close while they looked down over the small village of Sleepy Hollow.

The land was full of promise, and her heart was filled with love. In time, she knew, everything would return to the way it had been before, when her grandfather was alive: ripe with beauty; spilling over with abundance; full of love and ringing with the joyous laughter of happy times.

Katherine turned in his embrace, nuzzled her cheek against the warmth of his chest and sighed.

I am home again. Home. At last.

She smiled.

The legacy of Baltus Van Tassel would certainly live on in Sleepy Hollow … thanks to Icharus Crane.

About the Author:

Leshay, a Georgia native, resides in the North Georgia mountains - with her husband, six kids, and a chihuahua named 'Pocket.' When not otherwise engaged in generating new and exciting romance novel concepts, she spends her time catching up on mountains of housework neglected while writing! You can reach her on the web at:

www.MorganLeshay.com